The Jade Cross
Book 3
JADE CROSS TRILOGY

HAROLD W. WEIST

ISBN: 978-1-64314-888-5 (Paperback)
        978-1-64314-889-2 (Hardback)
        978-1-64314-890-8 (E-book)

Library of Congress Control Number: 2023919433

AuthorsPress
California, USA
www.authorspress.com

PROLOGUE

I Corps
Hoi An Area, Viet Nam, August 1966

THE GODDAMN SLUGS WERE hitting the trees with horrendous thuds. The sound of the leaves being torn and smoldering from the tracer rounds made the Gunny Sgt's spine cringe. That funny feeling you get in your back when you're about scared shitless. "What the hell's going on?" was all he could wonder out loud. Whoever was laying fire on them was firing pretty high which could change in a second. The Gunny had a habit of speaking his thoughts out loud, to no one in particular, at times when things were tense, dangerous, or even funny. Then suddenly, he felt a kind of calm take over his whole being. It's typically that way with him whenever the shit hits the proverbial fan or something screws up. Now the Gunny just casually wonders that, if it is his turn and, "How bad is it going to be?"

The day before the slugs started flying, Travis Tolbane, Gunnery Sergeant, United States Marine Corps, woke up stretching his six-foot four inch, brown-headed, 225 lb. frame, with the usual slight hangover from Jim Beam or a few Papst Blue ribbons, and already sweating from the heat of August in Viet Nam. He reached his hand above his slightly crooked nose and wiped his brow. He could hardly wait to get to the piss tube, a urinal made from a 155 mm artillery ammo tube and inserted into the ground.

The Gunny became more fully awake when the deafening roar of a couple of United States Marine F-4s screamed down the Da Nang runway a couple of miles away. Speaking to no one in particular, the Gunny mumbled, "Stick your F-4s up your Fly-boy asses! Those must be the noisiest bastards in this world." He never expected to be in this kind of crap when he enlisted over nine years before. Most of the time no one really knew who the enemy was. It was like the cluster fuck his drill Instructor had pounded into the recruits' head. The People in the country-side had to serve their masters, Free World Forces, The Viet Cong and the North Vietnamese Army.

He thought about when his team was on TAD (temporary assigned duty) to the 7th Marines at the Combat Base, Chu Lai. Their Captive Collection Point and Interrogation Center sitting at the end of the runway on a sandy rise and was also quite noisy with various types of aircraft soaring overhead, but not quite as loud. "I can't believe we're two miles from this damnable runway and those F4s can still wake the dead." Little did the Gunny know that one day the Da Nang air strip would be an international air terminal and he would be flying into this air strip as a civilian on a personal quest.

After completing his personal morning duty of teeth brushing, brown hair combing, and his daily constitutional duties, Tolbane looked around at the hard-back units, wooden frameworks with GP (General Purpose) tents draped over the frames, the interrogation huts, 8X8's made of plywood, and the Captive Compound, located on the south side of the Da Nang air strip gate and south of Dog Patch, a small Vietnamese sub-hamlet, South and below of Hill 327, also called Freedom Hill, where the Third Marine Division Headquarters was located near the top. The 3rd ITT[1] was just a little part of the war stuck in the midst of a huge Force Logistics (FLSG) supply area for the Third Marine Division. At least there was a small Staff NCO Club nearby at the Force Logistics Supply Group (FLSG), where he could relax and wind down after a long day of interrogations.

Last night, Gunny Tolbane did more than wind down. He had interrogated a Viet Cong Suspect for several hours, getting the usual, "Khong Biet!"[2] from Nguyen Van Hai. Hai had been caught after a short firefight at Tra Ke Ba, a sub-hamlet east by northeast of Hoi An City, by a squad from the First Battalion, First Marine Regiment, First Marine Division[3]. Nguyen was found riding his buffalo in a small field, muddy, wearing only black shorts, no shoes, and armed with a K44.

Nguyen Van Hai insisted that he was not involved in the firefight that had just gone down, that he did not have a rifle or grenade, that he is only a member of the Tra Ke Ba Farmers Association, and that he only supports the Government of South Viet Nam and the Americans. All of the people in the hamlets and sub-hamlets were organized into various associations by the Viet Cong, such as Farmers, Old Men, Old Women, Young Women, Young Men, Hamlet Security, etc., including Hamlet Guerrillas. The phrase Viet Cong was actually coined by the Diem Presidency and meant "Red Viet." The correct phrase was Cong San, which means "Viet Communist."

Finally, demonstrating understanding and empathy as only a Gunnery Sergeant in the United States Marine

---

[1] 3rd Interrogation Translator Team.
[2] Vietnamese for "I don't know.
[3] to be referred to as 1/1/1

Corps is able to, the Gunny convinced the Viet Cong Suspect to come clean. Nguyen told the same story that most suspects do, about being forced into duty by Viet Cong Cadre. What made Nguyen Van Hai's story different was information about booby traps in the area where 1/1/1 conducts its operations. This information is why the Gunny did more than wind down that night.

Using the land Line phone system, he knew he had to notify Lt. Col. Van D. Bell's 1/1/1 as quickly as possible of the information relevant to the Battalion's safe operations and keeping down the WIA/KIA count of his unit. He also needed to arrange for the 1/1/1 Scouts to pick up his interpreter, an MP Guard, himself and the captive at 0-dark-0630 hours in front of his Teams' CP.[4] Gunnery Sergeant Travis Tolbane, USMC had been up and down this street before. He had taken captives to this Battalion on three other occasions, all were successful. He always believed these patrols had actually helped the unit's safety.

After Tolbane completed his morning toiletries, he crossed through the fence adjoining the MP/Captive Collection Point compound, where his team operated, to the Marine Air Group Mess Hall for some chow. After chow (green scrambled eggs, limp bacon, toast, and coffee) the Gunny strapped on his TO[5] weapon, one Colt model 1911A, 45 caliber ACP pistol with belt, holster, and several 45 and M14 magazines in pouches. He slung on his pack, grabbed his M-14 rifle[6] then took off to the interpreters hard back area, where he linked up with his interpreter and friend, Staff Sergeant Nguyen Van Ba, ARVN[7]. The Gunny and Ba went to the captive area to retrieve the now

---

4   Command Post.
5   Table of Organization
6   Not standard issue for an interrogator.
7   Army Republic of Viet Nam

confirmed Viet Cong. An MP, Private Slater, had seen that the prisoner had been fed, did his morning constitutional, and made ready for the trip. Gunny Tolbane signed for the captive, took him into custody, then the small party moved to the compound gate to await the 1/1/1 scouts.

Four 1/1/1 scouts arrived a little after 0630 hours, loaded them into one of the two Mighty Mites[8] and started the twenty-five-mile trip from the FLSG area to the Hoi An Enclave. Hoi An City had been an ancient Chinese trading port originally named Fai Fo. It was a quaint city in the southeast area of Quảng Nam Province, and 1/1/1's enclave was just north of it. The trip to the battalion enclave would be down highway 1, a narrow, not well-kept, paved road, and considered to be in "Indian Country." It was a wild ride. It scared the hell out of the captive, Nguyen Van Hai, and most likely everyone else. The drivers pressed the vehicles to their utmost speed. This was necessary in case they were ambushed or passed over a command detonated mine. The Gunny thought it was like a little girl who stole her brother's bicycle and rode it over a bumpy road: "I'll never come that way again." She said.

The group arrived at the 1/1/1 enclave in one piece. They let out a collective sigh, thankful that "Victor Charley or just Charley"[9] wasn't up and about on the road they had just driven down. The enclave had a sandbagged perimeter about three-and-one-half-feet high with fighting holes or bunkers sandbagged into it every so many yards. Except for the Battalion Command and Operations Center (COC) bunker, which was heavily sandbagged and timbered top to bottom, the encampment was composed of hard-backed tents. It had a sick bay, a mess hall, a supply tent, an Enlisted Club, and a SNCO/Officer club; both clubs were just plain

---

[8]   a small jeep-type vehicle, a maintenance headache for the USMC
[9]   a slang term used to refer to the Viet Cong.

hard-backs, and hard-backs for supporting elements, etc. The bulk of the hard-backs were used for the headquarters marines and whichever infantry company was in garrison being rested or resupplied or was in reserve.

Gunny Tolbane, upon arrival, went straight to the COC bunker. The bunker was the heart and soul of the battalion operations. It housed the S-2 (Intelligence and Scout Section), the S-3 (Operations Section), the Comm. Section (Communications), the Battalion Commander, and any other personnel needed for every day/combat operations and control.

Tolbane reported straight to the S-2 Officer, 2nd Lt. Jerome Bickel. In the Two Shop, where the S-2 officers are found, in a little corner of the COC. The S-2 officer was reviewing some patrol routes with the S-3 officer, Major Tim Springdale, and the Chief Scout, S.Sgt. Bob Wise. The Gunny reported in the manner required of Marines: "Sir! Gunnery Sergeant Tolbane reporting for duty as ordered. I have with me one interpreter, one MP, and one Viet Cong Confirmed, Sir!"

"Stand at ease, Gunny," replied the Major. "Glad to have you aboard. Be with you in a minute."

The four, having worked together before, shook hands and got down to business. The Gunny handed the Lt. a copy of his interrogation report and explained the information he had obtained from the captive. Plans were made to recover or blow in place a couple of booby traps. The Major and the Lt., with recommendations from the two Sgts., established the radio frequency, radio call signs, amount of ammo, amount of "C"s[10], medical support, egress and ingress points to the enclave, desired patrol routes, issued maps, and size of the patrol. In other words, they determined the "Beans, Bullets, and Bandages," the daily staples for Marines in hostel situations.

---

[10]   C Rations, an Individual Meal.

The patrol would consist of the gunny's group of four, Ba included, one Kit Carson Scout, a Viet Cong who has rallied to the Government of Viet Nam (GVN), side, an ARVN Sgt., a full 14-man Marine squad including a grenadier with an M79 launcher, one M60 machine gunner with assistant gunner, one engineer, one medic, and one scout, for a total of 25. Gunny Tolbane felt something was wrong with the line-up and mentioned to the Lt. that he, the Lt., had forgotten to count the Chief Scout, S.Sgt. Wise, as the patrol leader. In response, 2nd Lt. Bickel gave the Gunny the "Good Scoop." SSgt. Wise had other duties to look to; therefore, he told the gunny, "You get to be the big kid on the block today. A Sgt. named Parnell will be in charge of the squad and you, the patrol."

"You got to be having the Hershey Squirts (dysentery), on me, Lt. I'm not a ground pounding grunt patrol leader."

"Gunny," chided the Lt., "I just don't have anyone else to send as a patrol leader. You've worked in support of us a few times and your talents in the field are respected by members of this Battalion. I have every bit of confidence in you to have a successful patrol and make one our patrol areas safer for the troops to patrol."

2nd Lt. Bickel went on to build up the Gunny's confidence as a leader, and some of the confidence required a good set of hip boots. Gunnery Sergeant Tolbane finally gave in and told the 2nd Lt., "I'll make you proud, Sir. We'll plant a flag on every hedge row for you, Iwo Jima fashion." The Gunny snapped to attention, and with his best Marine Corps attitude barked, "By your leave, Sir!" 2nd Lt. Bickel smiled at the Gunny and bade him, "Cary on Marine!" The Gunny performed the appropriate about-face movement and stormed from the bunker feeling like he had just been dipped in the Hersey Squirts.

The patrol was mustered and briefed by Gunny Tolbane and Sgt. Parnell, then supplies were issued at the supply tent. C Rations, flak jackets, ammo, radio, and C4[11] were distributed, and the Gunny even managed to commandeer an LVT P5[12] for a short ride towards their' patrols destination. The LVT P-5 was on its way to resupply Bravo Company and could only take them about a klick (kilometer) from the enclave. But that's one less klick to hump in the miserable heat of the Viet Nam day with the combat load on your' back.

After a bumpy and dusty ride, the LVT P5 dropped the patrol off and headed the tractor in a different direction. The Gunny and the Squad Leader got their heads together. Sgt. Parnell would set the order of march. Light Foot, PFC Bill Williams, one of the battalion scouts, would take the point followed by the 3rd Fire Team, then the M60 and assistant gunner, then Sgt. Parnell, the radio and, Gunny Tolbane and his interpreter Ba, the Kit Carson scout, the ARVN Sgt., the MP and the captive, and then the engineer. The 1st Fire Team[13] covered the rear while the 2nd Fire Team split up and took the left and right flanks, and the 3rd Fire Team provided security for the patrol's center.

The patrol started toward Tra Ke Ba (Ba being the third). The trail alternated with paths going through wooded areas, over rice paddy dikes, and along mangrove swamps. Each patrol member alternated covering to the left or right with their weapons. In some spots, the captive was placed on point in case the path was mined or had some other type of trap waiting, especially when crossing the paddy dikes. It was better to lose a captive than a Marine. A couple of times, the patrol utilized cover and/ or fire team tactics when moving through areas where an ambush could be waiting.

---

[11]   An explosive.

[12]   A tracked amphibious vehicle that can carry cargo or troops.

[13]   Each Marine Squad has three fire teams.

The Patrol finally reached Tra Ke Ba (#3) without incidence. The Gunny and Sgt. Parnell looked over the situation and decided to approach the sub-hamlet with extreme caution. Sgt. Parnell called in the 2nd Fire Team, briefed them and then dispatched the team to enter the Ville[14] on command while the 1st Fire Team and the M60 Team positioned themselves to lay down supporting, suppressing, and/or covering fire. The 3rd Fire Team assumed the security for the rest of the group.

Tra Ke Ba was the typical sub-hamlet out in the Bush. There were seven grass huts set at the eastern edge of a little glade, a little stream running to the southeast side, six huts on the west side, and a few paddies about a hundred meters northwest of the little cluster. Children were playing with sticks. Pigs and chickens were wandering around, and a few betel nut chewing Vietnamese women were chattering endlessly at one another and spitting the horrible red spittle like they were baseball pitchers.

Even though the sub-hamlet looked like life was going on as usual, the 2nd Fire Team moved by maneuver into the Ville with ease. The rest of the patrol moved in, and the 1st and 2nd Fire Teams set up a perimeter while the Gunny, the Sgt. and the 3rd Team checked out the hooches[15] for guns, ammo, documents, rice stashes, etc. The Kit Carson Scout and the ARVN Sgt. wondered around and did their own search and questioned the inhabitants extensively. Finding nothing in or around the hooches, the Gunny got down to the business at hand.

Gunny Tolbane, his interpreter Ba, the MP, and the captive moved in to one of the hooches and sat on the dirt floor. The Gunny reviewed with the captive his story about the booby traps in the area then made plans with the squad

---

[14]   GI slang for a Vietnamese sub-hamlet, hamlet or village.
[15]   GI slang for the huts.

leader, the scout, the engineer, and the attached Vietnamese, the Kit Carson Scout and the ARVN Sgt. to move alertly into the wooded area, and then find and blow the traps.

Leaving the three fire teams and bringing the Machine Gun team, the group moved into the woods. The captive led them to two punji pits. The engineer blew them in place. No secondary explosions, thank goodness. The Viet Cong sometimes booby-trap their punji pits with grenades or artillery shells. The captive then showed them an old hand grenade tied to a stake with an old, rusty trip wire dangling from it. The pin, even though the crimp was straightened, probably could not be removed. It was rusted in place and the engineer did something to make it go "poof." The last item was a five-pound Chi Com shaped charge in a little spider hole. It was not set up as a trap yet. The engineer blew it in place, and the group moved back to the hooches to make plans for their return to the enclave.

The Patrol took time out to eat some "C"s and relieve their bladders. Any of the "C"s that were left were given to the villagers for their inconvenience, and the, Corpsman Dick Kruse held a short sick call, treating small cuts and bruises, and handing out aspirins, and winning the peoples-hearts and minds, at least while they were there. The patrol then began to hoof it back to battalion, using the same order of march. This time, they went a little north, then turned generally in a westerly direction and began moving along the opposite side of the paddies they had approached on. Using the same paths to return could be hazardous to one's health and welfare.

The patrol moved at a steady pace, but alertly. So far "Charlie" had stayed home and the trek had been uneventful. Arriving about a half klick from where the LVTP-5 had dropped them earlier in the day, the shit hit the fan. The patrol had moved toward a tree line along an old worn path.

The wooded area had been a welcome relief as it was darker and cooler than being in the sun, which was beating down on the patrol and was starting to take its toll. The patrol's thirst was also mounting and their uniforms were soaked white with salty perspiration. Their legs were feeling like a hundred pounds each from walking through rice paddies with muck trying to pull their boots off each time they lifted their leg.

They were passing an old deserted hooch, which was about twenty meters off the trail and had what looked like some fighting holes around it, when they heard two thunks that sounded like two M79 grenade launchers. By the time the rounds hit close on either side of the point scout, all hands had hit the deck and they pulled their collective asses as low to the ground as possible. With the explosions came intensive small arms and automatic fire. "Thank God," Gunny Tolbane thought, that whoever was cutting loose on them didn't know about an old Marine Corps adage that simply states, "Lights up, sights up, lights down, sights down." All of the rounds were hitting high. Meanwhile, Sgt. Parnell was hollering to the troops, "Keep your heads down and hold your fire." In moments like these, fire discipline and ammo conservation can mean the success or failure of the mission or the return to base.

The volume of fire was very heavy and the noise was deafening. Gunny Tolbane, wondered aloud, "Where in the hell did the Viet Cong get M79 Grenade Launchers?" He hollered above the din to instruct Sgt. Parnell to call Battalion S-3 and get Arty (artillery) to put their 105s on that zone. The radio man crawled up to Sgt. Parnell so he could radio the S-3 shop. Parnell checked his map for their coordinates then got on the horn to Red Dog, 1/1/1's call sign, and gave a Sit Rep[16] and requested a Willy Peter[17]

---

[16] Situation Report.
[17] White Phosphorus.

spotter round to be followed by Hotel Echo[18] rounds after adjustment.

"***Request Denied!***" was the S-3's answer. "Can't do it; there's friendly troops in the area." Parnell looked like he would explode as he yelled in to the mike, "I don't give a flying fuck who's there. We need Arty. No, damn it. The Gunny can't get to the radio. He's got his ass pinned to the ground." The Sgt. listened a moment then shook his head and handed the mike to the radio operator. By now the firing slowed and the Gunny had inched his way to Sgt. Parnell.

"Hey Sarge! What the hell's going on! We getting Arty or what?" the Gunny bitched.

"There's an ARVN Commando Company or some such shit back in there. The Three won't give us any support. They want us to make contact with them and smooth over our fuck up." "Well, BOHICA![19] Our fuck up?" Tolbane was about to blow his top. The Gunny grabbed the mike and hollered into it, "Who the hell's the mental midget that figures this is our fuck up?"

"This is 2nd Lt. Wosterman, the Duty Operations Officer. How dare you speak to me in this manner, Gunnery Sergeant! From this point on *you will* follow standard radio procedures and *you will* utilize proper military courtesy and respect when addressing an officer. Additionally, if you knew what you were doing, you wouldn't have gotten your patrol into this mess."

"Well, 2nd Lt. Sir, the Gunnery Sergeant respectfully requests that you get your ass out here and operate on these zipper heads yourself, Sir!" Tolbane bitched back. "On second thought, put Ops. 6 (Major Springdale) on the horn and then go find your pacifier and become fornicated by yourself!"

---

[18] High Explosive.
[19] Bend Over, Here It Comes Again!

As luck would have it, Major Springdale had just walked into the COC and was listening to the exchange on the radio and chuckling out loud. The major calmly walked over to 2nd Lt. Wosterman and took the radio handset from him and spoke slowly and evenly. "Red Dog Charley (The patrol's call sign), cool down son. I'll have a word or two with the 2nd Lt. about using the proper military respect and courtesy when he speaks to a Gunnery Sergeant in the United States Marine Corps."

More seriously, the major asked, "Just tell me what all that shooting I hear is about and maybe we can get some kind of solution short of the Enola Gay & her pay load for you."

After a short discussion between them, Tolbane and Major Springdale decided the best course of action was for the patrol to make physical contact with the ARVN unit. By now, all small arms and automatic weapons had ceased firing. There was a deadly silence.

Sgt. Parnell repositioned his troops into defensive positions, and he and the Gunny put their heads together to formulate a plan. Once a course of action was agreed upon, the Kit Carson scout and the ARVN Sgt. were called up to the Gunny and Sgt.'s position, and Sgt. Parnell passed the word that his troops were now under the Gunny's command.

Sgt. Parnell, the Scout, and the ARVN Sgt. cautiously crept to the rear of their position and crawled north, moving much deeper into the tree line, and then angled back towards their immediate foe's position. The Gunny watched them crawl off with a lot of apprehension. Tolbane had no idea what kind of a reception was in store for the small team by the supposed "Friendly Troops."

About half an hour later, Sgt. Parnell, his two-man team, and two ARVN soldiers from the ambushers, one of them a Lieutenant, emerged from the heavy tree line in front of the Marine's defensive position. The Gunny had the sights of his M14 on the ARVN Lieutenant and had to fight his emotions with all his self-discipline. Initially he just wanted to blow these two little creeps away.

As the group approached Tolbane, who was red with anger, he exclaimed "What the hell's fire is going on here asshole?" The Gunny then literally screamed at the officer, "I'd like to take those gold pips off your damn collar and stick them right up your collective Ho Chi Minh asses!"

Tolbane's face was getting redder and redder, and his neck muscles seemed to bulge as if to explode. "This would not be a good time for any "Xin Loi's[20]," he stated. The thing that had really pissed off the Gunny was the smile on the officer's face and all of the teeth he was showing to the world.

After the Gunny informed the ARVN Lieutenant that he was about to call the CP and inform them that NVA (North Vietnamese Army) troops had overrun the ARVN position and instruct them to lay down an artillery barrage. Then two sides calmed down enough and began talking sincerely. The Gunny thought that they should move to the area by the hut. Soon the small group began to grow. The ARVNs wanted to talk to the prisoner, Tolbane said "It will be an Icy day in hell before you talk to this man.," even though by agreement with the powers to be, he must let the ARVN question the prisoner.

The engineer, the Kit Carson scout and the ARVN Sgt. the MP, the M60 Marine, the Point Scout, and the Interpreter were also with the group. The rest of the patrol were brushing off their weapons, drinking water, or doing other little tasks. None of the patrol were paying any attention to the group by the hut. The Marine carrying the M-60 machinegun spotted a small mound of loose dirt, about a two-foot square, a few feet from the far corner of

---

[20] Very Sorry!

the old weather-beaten hovel, that looked like something could be buried there. He called the Gunny over to look at the spot. The Gunny looked at it and called the engineer over to check it out. While the engineer probed the mound of dirt, the group moved back to a safe spot away from the mound in case of an explosion.

Tolbane watched the man work with an intense interest. He could see the engineer digging a hole into the ground and wondered what might happen if there was an explosive device in it. The engineer suddenly called to the Gunny. "Hey, Gunny, bring your lifer ass over here and take a look at this crap."

The Gunny walked over, looked into the hole and said, "Well, I'll be damned!"

While the engineer was taking out a weatherworn, black enameled box wrapped in cloth, with a clear plastic wrap of some type around it, the Gunny's exclamation had caught the attention of the rest of the group, and they came up and surrounded Tolbane and the engineer. The box was handed to the Gunny, and he squatted, set the package down on the ground and pulled the plastic wrap and cloth off of it; while everybody was looking at it with curiosity, he opened the hinged lid.

The group was stunned to silence to say the least. No not stunned, but was awed to the last man standing! Not a one in the group could believe what their eyes were seeing. It was several quiet moments before anyone composed himself to speak. Gunny Tolbane looked at the bunch of raggedy assed Marines and ARVNs finally said to all, "What the fuck, over! This takes the friggen cake!" It was a magnificent jeweled Jade Cross. The color was a deep lustrous green and the large ruby in the center seemed to radiate an awe-inspiring glow. After being awed for a period of time it was decided to rebury it. They did!

CHAPTER 1

Year 1999, Nashville, TN.

Thank God Tolbane had knelt down during this mild, partial moon, and dark night. Clouds were hiding the partial moon at the time. He had bent down to pick up a quarter that lie on the deck in an alleyway between the two wings created by the H style of the building at the south end of Perkins Mall, even though he didn't need the money. He heard what sounded like an AK-47 firing and slugs thumping and ricocheting from the mall walls and a compactor, just missing his head and body by what he felt was only inches.

At 2230 hours, six foot four, now 237 pounds, brown-headed Travis R. Tolbane, Master Gunnery Sergeant, United States Marine Corps, Retired, and the current mall security manager, had just exited the mall, loosened his tie, and unbuttoned his suit coat when the first shots were fired and began ricocheting between the walls.

Tolbane had just completed a long, tiresome day at Perkins Mall, which is located at the intersection of Nolensville Road on the west side, Harding Place to the south, and is adjacent to Seven Mile Creek in the east and

Welch Road to the north. About 100,000 cars pass through the intersection of Nolensville Road and Harding Place each and every day, many of them stopping at the mall. Most of the shoppers are honest, hard-working people spending their hard-earned money. But not all of shoppers could be called society's best citizens. Some were down right useless crooks.

Throughout the day, Tolbane and his security team had assisted two of the anchor stores, Dillard's and Marshalls, in chasing and apprehending a grand total of seven shoplifters, gave criminal trespass warnings to five vagrants, and busted, with a slight struggle, two homosexuals going at it in the men's rest room. The action was the fun part of the job. The not-so-fun part was filling out all of the paperwork the mall manager demanded to cover his butt and going to the Magistrate's night court at the Criminal Justice Building in downtown Nashville to testify against any violator he was personally involved with. Whenever Tolbane makes a citizen's arrest, the Nashville Metro Police Department is notified immediately and sends a unit to the mall to make the arrest, read the individual his rights, transport the individual to the Criminal Justice Building, and checks them into the lockup, then they are brought before the Magistrate to establish probable cause for the arrest and to set a bail, or remand to custody. Although all the action makes the day go faster, it also makes it very stressful, but not nearly as dangerous and stressful as tip toeing through the rice paddies in Viet Nam, unlike tip toeing through the tulips like Tinney Tim.

As Travis exited the portal, he looked up to check the sky. Though the sky was kind of clear and the moon was partially full, there were so many dark clouds drifting across the sky in places that they sometimes blocked the moon over large areas. He tried to remember a literary work he once read and dreamed about as a kid. Something in reference to the moon being a ghostly galleon tossed about a cloudy sky by a torrent of darkness, or something similar. Travis guessed it must have been the literary work, "The Highway Man," or not!

He had started to turn left on to the sidewalk to head to his becoming legend Marine Corps Green pickup truck with a yellow Eagle globe and Anchor painted on each door, but then he spotted a quarter lying on the deck near the alley entrance and stooped to retrieve it when all "Billy Hell" broke loose.

Tolbane scooted back into the alleyway and drew his hand carry, a Charter 38 Special with a two-inch barrel and loaded with five Hydra-Shock rounds. Once again, Tolbane gave thanks that some "friggen idiot" didn't know diddly squat about "lights down, sights down" and vice versa. The old Master Gunny was wondering aloud as was his habit, "Hey God, why the hell me again?" The only excuse he could come up with was, "Yo, Bro, why not me?"

About thirty to forty meters ahead, a Vietnamese came out from behind a car and was running toward Tolbane and bringing an AK-47 to his shoulder, preparing to fire at him. Tolbane squeezed off one round toward him, and it ricocheted off of a pickup truck's grill and struck the Viet in the upper groin and penetrated into his spine. The Viet fell flat on his face, paralyzed for life, and just laid there.

Tolbane thought, "Just the way I aimed it. I got a Six o'clock sight picture, took a deep breath and let it halfway out, and slowly squeezed the trigger. All that Boot Camp training stuff finally paying off. Talk about your' blind luck. Not so lucky for the dude." Tolbane could compliment himself easily.

Just then, another stream of rounds from the southwest part of the parking area hit the wall above his head. Tolbane rolled to the other side of the alleyway, stuck his pistol around the corner, and fired two quick shots in the general direction he thought the shots were fired from. Tolbane then emptied the five chambers in a dumping motion and reloaded them from the loose rounds he carried in his pocket. He picked up the two unfired rounds and placed them into his pocket. Tolbane's pistol had only a five-round capacity, and he didn't want whoever was out there to know it. Tolbane moved farther back into the alley, and with the benefit of his six-foot four-inch frame, he crawled upon an enclosed garbage compactor that was about seven or eight foot high. From his spot on top, he could see anyone coming into the alley way before they could see him, which could mean that split second difference between life and death.

Tolbane lay as quiet as he could, not letting himself get antsey and make a mistake. He could hear someone out in the parking area hollering what sounded like Vietnamese commands, in the Southern Vietnamese dialect. Part of what he heard sounded like, "Tolbane! You die tonight." He thought out loud to the whole world, "Think again, you ass wipe. Not tonight or any other night." Then there was another string of fire from off to the right side of the alleyway that struck the lower wall of the building's side and ricocheted throughout the alleyway, striking the garbage compactor he was standing on with weird pinging and zinging sounds.

"Shit, they wised up and started shooting lower," opined Tolbane, to himself.

The Nashville Metropolitan Police Department's South Precinct Patrol Units use the far northwest corner of the mall parking area to meet with their duty sergeant on a nightly basis. Sometimes there may be as many as five or six patrol units there at one time. Tolbane was getting worried that the patrol units couldn't hear the gun shots. Suddenly, he heard the sound of sirens and saw the flashing strobe lights reflecting off of cars in the lot. The police were responding from the east and west sides of Perkins Mall. He looked up and muttered to himself, "Thank you God."

Tolbane heard the Vietnamese voice again, only this time it sounded like a higher pitch, and maybe even more stressed. Tolbane thought some of the words had something to do with getting the hell out of Dodge, like di mau di.[21] and he also heard, "Tolbane, you're going to die sometime." Then there was a single shot, which sounded like a hand gun, a couple of car doors being slammed shut, and the sound of tires squealing. The parking lot was left with a cloud of smoke and the smell of burning rubber in the air. The speeding vehicle turned right on Harding Place, flew through a red light, and just missed being T-boned.

Tolbane took the chance of looking up very slowly at the South parking area and saw two Metro cars speeding from the mall's west side, turning south on to Harding Place, then heading west. The cars were lucky because the west-bound traffic on the street was almost non-existent at the moment. A couple of other Metro cars came from the back side of the mall with their blue lights flashing and sirens wailing and tried to pull west onto Harding Place too, but they had to slow to a stop and wait for the traffic to clear because the traffic had just been released from a stop light on Harding Place, east of the mall.

One Metro unit came from the west side and pulled in front of the alleyway and stopped. The dazzling, blinding, blue and white lights of the car lit up the area and reflected swatches of blue and white every which way, lighting everything in their path. Tolbane wondered if this was a strobe light special at a Disco joint. Maybe a disco inferno.

Metro officer Cpl. Karen Watson, all five foot seven inches, 135 pounds of her, opened the door, shaking her

---

[21] Hurry up, Vietnamese imperative.

head and causing her short, dark brown hair to muss up. She stared at Tolbane and commented, "Damn it! Tolbane, I should have known it would be you waking the whole city of Nashville and the dead with all that shoot 'em up crap. Get down off that, that, whatever that damn thing is, and tell me just what the hell is going on here! Oh, by the way, in case I forgot that you're here, are you okay?" Then she quipped, "Please Tolbane, tell me that you got yourself killed and gone to your destiny in hell where you belong, kissing the Devil's butt, and I'll be one happy cop."

MNPD Cpl. Karen Watson was an 11-year veteran police officer with Metro Nashville. From the time she was a rookie, she had responded to and assisted the Perkins Mall Security in many fights, shoplifting apprehensions, armed robberies, various domestic squabbles at the mall, and whatever else popped up. She and Tolbane had seen a lot of rough times and good together after he became the security manager. Cpl. Watson was now a seasoned training officer. Presently, she did not have a trainee to train and was subbing for the South District Night Sergeant and had been giving the nightly briefing to the South District patrol officers coming off, the others on duty when the shots were fired.

Tolbane let himself down from the compactor really slow and easy. Even then, he slid and nearly fell on his, precious to him, behind. When he was back on earth, he said to Karen, "Remind me to ask the mall management to put a ladder on that compactor so people won't break their dumb ass necks getting down from it after getting shot at from time to time."

"By the way Cpl. Watson, I guess you forgot that we Marines are an indestructible breed, huh?" chuckled the Master Gunny. "Looking around here, you might say that someone needs more marksmanship training. Maybe, like two months on the Able Range[22] snapping in, studying elevation, estimating windage, and learning to get a good six o'clock sight picture, and developing their rifle marksmanship and all the crazy horse manure that goes with it."

"Don't give me any of that Gung Ho Leatherneck clap trap, crap of yours' Travis," Watson replied. "You're not back in the magnificent Corps any more. You're not hitting the beach here! You're in the, and I quote, 'Music City, USA,' unquote, and I think a long night in the dumb ass drunk tank would serve its intended purpose for you. I could oblige you in an instance, in fact less than a heartbeat."

Tolbane replied, "Don't get your little pink panties get all pulled up in your crotch and get you into a snit or have a giant hissy fit. Let's go check on that dude I just spotted lying out there while I try to get the happenings straight in my mind. All I can think of right now is how that quarter lying there on the deck more or less saved my scalp." Cpl. Watson wondered about what quarter his feeble mind was referring to. "I need to pick that thing up right now." He did. He kissed the quarter and dropped it into his pocket. Once again, she just shook her head at him.

Tolbane and Watson both had their handguns in a ready position as they neared the Vietnamese shooter. As they closed in, they could see a large pool of blood that had flowed from Tolbane's shot. What surprised the Master Gunny was that the shooter also had a head wound, which had strewn brain gore and bone matter all over the paved lot and created another pool of blood. It looked like his leader had left nothing to chance. Tolbane quipped, "I guess he won't confess anything tonight, so I dub him a Viet Cong Guerilla Confirmed."

They both holstered their weapons. Tolbane contemplated a moment "This dude looks like he could be

---

22 The old 'A' rifle range course in Marine Terminology.

Vietnamese as well as the others that hollered at me. Why would any blessed Vietnamese want to blast me?"

"I can think of about a few thousand reasons why," was Watson's reply.

Then Tolbane told Cpl. Watson what had transpired when he was exiting the mall; how he had heard Vietnamese being spoken from a couple of directions, how some of the words were clear and some words were not loud enough to understand, and how he had heard the last shot. He included in addition as to how he had carefully sighted in on a car grill, using elevation, windage and a six o'clock sight picture.

Tolbane then surmised speaking aloud, "I guess that by systematic deduction, someone didn't want to take a chance that this dude would live and talk to us." Watson thought aloud, "No shit Sherlock." He then walked over to the pickup truck his errant round had hit and took a good look at the gouge in the grill. "Hope this guy has some good auto insurance," he mumbled aloud to no one in particular.

Every night, a night watchman is on duty inside the mall. His job is to respond to any store alarm, check all lighting inside and out for burned out bulbs, notify police or fire in case of any emergency, check on abandoned cars in the parking area left over night to see if they were stolen, or etc. Tonight, the watchman just happened to be a very outspoken George Pickway. George came out of the alleyway door, walking in a kind of a wobble. He had bad legs from an auto accident a few years before and was lucky enough not to need a cane. As he approached Tolbane, Cpl. Watson walked over to her squad car to call in the information, to a detective, that Tolbane had given to her.

"Hey Tolbane!" he was shouting. "You sure make the nights interesting here. I called 911; however, the fuzz had already called in the "shots fired!" By the way, I've got a couple of phone messages for you."

"Oh crap," he mused. "I left my cell phone on my desk, and it's turned off."

"Oh, shit is the word alright. What the heck's going on here anyway?" exclaimed Pickway looking at the remains of the dead Vietnamese. "Can't you stay out of trouble for at least one minute? You're more friggen bother than you're worth sometimes, you know that?"

"Yeah, yeah, I know all about it George! I've heard your crap before. What've you got for me tonight?"

"Mai called and said she got a ride home from the ice rink so you don't need to pick her up tonight. She and a couple of girls she knows are stopping at the Waffle House in Hermitage on the way. The girls are going to Lebanon from there and will drop Mai home on the way." Pickway also informed him, "Your buddy, the one and only, Detective Sgt. Parnell wants you to get to Nguyen Van Ba's house ASAP. He wouldn't say why, only that you're a worthless ingrate, and I won't repeat the rest of the superfluous verbiage he enunciated very clearly about your very nature."

Nguyen Van Ba had been Tolbane's primary interpreter when he served his first hitch in Viet Nam, and Tolbane ran across Ba during his other two assignments there as well. They were on many operations, sweeps, and county fairs together and had several close calls over there. Travis had visited Ba's home in Saigon, now Ho Chi Minh City, where he first met Ba's half-sister, Nguyen Thi Mai. Tolbane had saved her being raped by a Vietnamese Soldier when she was 10 years old. Mai is part French, part Vietnamese, and presently Tolbane's beautiful and stacked live-in paramour. Ba and Mai were able to leave Viet Nam just before the North Viet Nam's invading forces reached Saigon in 1975, and they had a horrific life while trying to reach the United States for a new life.

Detective Sgt. Parnell, MNPD, had been a Marine Sgt. He still considered himself a Marine, as all Marines do,

Semper Fi for life, and had been with Tolbane and Ba on a couple of patrols in the Nam with the first Battalion, First Marine Regiment, First Marine Division. A twist of fate had brought them together here in Nashville, along with Ba and Mai. They had become a very tight-knit group and enjoyed a lot of activities together. A good part of the time, to see one was to see all four, and later a fifth Lady friend named Carly joined the group.

When Pickway had finished giving Tolbane his messages, Cpl. Karen Watson came back over to Tolbane and informed him that crime scene folks and some suits were on their way. She had scoured the crime scene as well as she could on her own and asked him, "Do you want to give me a hand blocking off this crime scene since you messed it up? It sure would help a lot to get it done before they arrive."

"Give me a couple of minutes, Karen. I've got go into my office, get my cell phone, and return an ASAP phone call from the Grand Poohbah of MNPD, Detective Sergeant Parnell. It has something to do about Ba. I'll give you a hand taping the area off after that." He and Pickway slowly walked back into the mall, chattering at each other.

Reentering the mall, Tolbane went to his office to retrieve his phone. Upon entering, he picked up his cell phone and turned it on. Then he sat down in his comfortable desk chair, spun around one complete turn and began pondering what had just occurred. As he lifted his right leg to the top of the desk, he mumbled aloud, wondering, "What the hell just happened here? Why did I suddenly become a target?"

Suddenly Tolbane lay with his hands and feet handcuffed to the posts of the huge, decorative, four-poster bed. He looked up and saw the most magnificent sight he had ever seen. She, whoever she was, was balanced on the head board, her legs spread slightly and toes griping the edge like a diver on a springboard preparing to do a back dive. She was as naked as a jay bird! God, what a beauty! What a sight! Without looking down, Tolbane knew he had the largest and hardest erection ever through-out mankind. Suddenly, she bent from the knees, arms hanging down, then she sprang into a back summersault in the tuck position, and she was going to land on his… Suddenly the sharp rings of Tolbane's cell phone startled him. He awoke with a start and grabbed his cell phone.

"City Morgue here. You stab 'em, we slab 'em! Tolbane here, speak your piece whomever you may be."

"What the hell are you up to? Are you daydreaming again or pulling your friggen diminutive pudd?" Sgt. Parnell was pissed off, stressed, and his tone of voice indicated the same by his sound of emergency. "I've been trying to reach you for nearly an hour now. Don't you answer your damn cell phone anymore? I know! You were daydreaming again or fast asleep and didn't have it turned on, or some such shit."

"Me, daydreaming? I don't daydream. I'll have you know I was in a cognitive state in deep cogitation over some serious crap that went on here at the mall a while ago," Tolbane muttered. He then wondered if Mai could do back flips for him.

Sgt. Parnell just shook his head. "I know you shot up the place. Look here, we've got a gruesome and hideous crime scene here at Ba's house. You're not going to like it one it one damn bit. So, get your not-so-slim-nor your' ever-loving anymore butt over here ASAP. I already talked with Corporeal Watson on the horn and she won't be expecting you to help tape off the area. You got that!? Good, just do it!"

"I'm out of here and on the way," Tolbane all but screamed into his cell phone transmitter. As he dashed out of his office, he stopped to turn off the light and lock the door and was trying to think of Sgt. Parnell's statement about a gruesome crime scene at Ba's. What the hell kind of crime could have taken place there? Was it a break-in, a car theft, or what else could have happened at Ba's home?

He raced out to the mall parking lot and jumped into his Marine Corps green 1999 Dodge Dakota 5.9 RT extended cab pickup with an automatic transmission, which of course, had a large Eagle, Globe and Anchor painted in yellow on each of the two doors. When he inserted the key and started the Dakota, the strains of Andrew Lloyd Webber's "Music of the Night" from the *Phantom of the Opera* sung by baritone Justin White emanated from the CD player. Normally, Tolbane would take his time driving and sing with the music, but not tonight.

He pulled into traffic on Nolensville Road going north to I-40 as fast as the traffic would let him. As Murphy would have it, he caught every red stop light between Harding Place and I-40. Just goes to show that Irishmen named Murphy shouldn't make traffic laws. He kept telling himself that he should have driven east up Harding Place and hit I-24 west to I-40. It could have been faster. When he reached I-40, he drove it west to the Charlotte Avenue exit about twenty miles an hour over the legal speed limit of '55. When he got off the exit, he drove towards town, turned at the second left, and zoomed about five blocks to Ba's house.

Tolbane never gave it a thought that someone else could be lurking in the area as he was driving out of the mall lot. A figure, an Oriental, short in stature and dressed in dark clothes and wearing a black mask, stood on the mall roof and watched Tolbane drive recklessly out of the mall entrance. He climbed down the back side, climbed into his car, and drove out of the north parking area, taking his time. He knew where Tolbane was going. He felt fine. His plans were right on schedule. He pulled out has cell phone and called one of his geese and told him, "He's on his way, report his activities as they happen."

As Tolbane sped up the street and got closer to Ba's place, he could see the flashing blue and white strobes of a few Metro Police cars forming a blockade on the street and a few Metro officers milling around in front of the house, which had the standard yellow crime scene tape around a large portion of it. He mumbled aloud to himself, "What in the hell is going on here anyway? This is a most fucked up night. What kind of hell night is this, a night of infamy to go down in my history?" With this many cops on the scene, he decided it must really be a serious incident, and he hoped Ba was all right.

He had to park about three houses down from Ba's because of the police blockade and had to walk to the house. Ba's place was a small but really quaint house. It had a full bath with shower, one bedroom, a kitchen, a living room, and a small room that Ba used as a kind of office/study/loafing room. There is a cement slab in the back, about 18x18 feet, with one of those rollup awnings that Ba uses for a patio, and of course it's his barbecue area. He keeps his large propane barbecue/smoker & grill on it, along with a table and a few chairs. He has a few religious paintings and a couple of crosses on his walls. Ba had become a Catholic shortly after fleeing with Mai from Viet Nam to America in April 1975 and seldom ever missed a morning mass.

Walking up the sidewalk and approaching the house gingerly, Tolbane spotted an officer he was familiar with, although he didn't remember the guy's name, and waved to him. The officer, after greeting him, told Tolbane, "Better get your butt inside quick because Sgt. Parnell is hopping mad and chewing on ten penny nails. He is pissed off to high heaven too!" Tolbane got his butt in gear and hurried on into the house quickly.

When Tolbane opened and entered the door, Detective Sgt. Parnell was standing there. he raised a hand to him, stopping him from entering into the room any farther. Rubbing his left hand over his thinning hair and then holding up his right hand to a stop position more forcibly, Parnell stated to Tolbane.

"Look my friend! Before you go any farther in here, I need to warn you again before you go any farther, that it's not a pretty scene back there in the kitchen. I know you've seen blood and guts many times, but this one takes the damn cake. It's really gross. This is now an official MNPD homicide investigation. There's a body there that hasn't been identified officially yet, but between you and me, I believe its Ba. Now listen up and listen tight!"

"Travis, you are not going to like this one bit. I know I don't. You'll be shocked and pissed off at the same time, and I want you to put your thinking cap on and stay as calm and cool as possible. I'll need some input from you as to the body's identification. I know you'll want to rant and rave, jump up and down, curse and kill everyone and everything, just like Mike Hammer would, in sight, but just stay cool for a while."

"You've got my word on it," Tolbane answered. He couldn't conceive any thoughts as to what he may have to witness. For his friend Parnell's demeanor and stance, it must really be a very nasty scene.

Parnell answered, "I'll hold you to it my friend. Right now, I need you to take a couple of deep breaths and gather your composure. Here, pull on these throw away booties. When I arrived here late this afternoon after an anonymous 911 call, I nearly went to pieces myself. You're going to be shocked to your limit, so be prepared and follow me."

Tolbane got this gut feeling like his stomach was in his mouth at the thought of something having happened to

Ba. What about Mai? Is this going to be something that will hurt her? He followed the detective into the kitchen area. Approaching the unknown horror that waited for him and Mai was like tiptoeing over a hot cement sidewalk in bare feet. He actually gagged a couple of times before entering due to the smell of death and the beginning of the disgusting stench of the decomposition of body tissue.

CHAPTER 2

TOLBANE COULDN'T BELIEVE WHAT his eyes were seeing. He had seen enough blood, guts and gore in his lifetime that he thought he was immune to it. But this sight and smell was horrendous. There was a nude body that absolutely had to be Ba. The body was posed like Jesus Christ on the cross with cement nails driven through his wrists and his crossed ankles pinning the body to the hardwood floor. Tolbane thought he might puke and he turned away from the sight for a moment, gaged a little, took a couple of deep breaths, and regained his composure. The body had hundreds of cuts and slashes, pieces of skin peeled from the face, and what seemed to be the cause of death was a long slash from below the right ear to the left ear that severed the carotid arteries. The head looked like it was almost decapitated from the body, as the cut was all the way into the spinal column and the vertebrae could be seen. Tolbane then noticed that the genitals had been cut off and shoved into the mouth. This was almost too much to bear, even for a retired Marine and combat veteran, who had seen it all, to bear, or anyone else for that matter.

"Can this savaged body really be Ba?" he uttered to Parnell. Tolbane steeled his feelings as much as possible and looked closer at the soulless body. Looking at the right bicep, he noticed a large portion of skin had been sliced away. "Parnell, look at this. It looks like someone sliced off his tattoo."

"I'd say you're right about that. That was one crazy tattoo he had," opined Parnell. "I remember when he first showed it to me."

Tolbane replied, "I remember when Ba got that tattoo in Saigon. We had been looking around in a small shop right up the street from the capitol building when Ba saw a bunch of shoulder patches. He really liked the one of Snoopy. It was round, red and white, and had a white Snoopy dog saying 'Happiness is a Warm Pussy.' Before you could blink an eye, he bought it. Then he got this crazy idea of getting it tattooed on his arm. He dragged me along till we found a tattoo parlor, and sure enough, he got the Snoopy tattoo. He was as happy as a kid opening his/her Christmas presents. Why would someone cut that off as well as part of his face? It's like somebody doesn't want him to be identified for some ungodly reason."

Tolbane shivered a little and said, "What kind of bloodthirsty bastard would do something like this? It reminds me of how some of our missing Marines were found in VC[23] controlled areas. They had died from torture and genital mutilations, the genitals stuffed in the mouth like this. This is an inhuman animal that's done this, and I'm going to get the son of a bitch that did it. As of now, he's one dead bastard. That goes double for any of his asshole pals that might be around him, too."

Sgt. Parnell nodded his head in agreement and said, "It looks like the dirty work was done in the bath tub over a long period of time, a couple of days maybe, and he bled out there. I don't think you noticed, but his finger prints have

---

[23] Viet Cong; Red Viet.

been sliced off also. We're waiting on the county coroner to get here and check things over before the forensics team can really get to work. Let's go to the living room and sit. You look kind of green around the gills and it might help."

After the two friends found a seat and sat down, Parnell looked over at Travis, made eye contact with him and was deeply concerned for his friends wellbeing. Travis looked not only worn and drawn, but he seemed to have what the Corps calls, "The thousand-yard stare." Parnell needed to distract Travis so he could get himself together.

"Tolbane, why don't you relax and tell me what happened at the mall? Cpl. Watson said that there were some Vietnamese involved in that mall melee. Maybe there's some connection to your incident at the mall and Ba's death."

Tolbane's brain felt numb, and he was kind of startled by Parnell's statement and said, "Huh! Parnell, can you repeat that? I didn't quite hear you. My ears are still ringing to high Heaven a bit from the mall shooting. I think I got that tinnitus or whatever it is you get from loud noises like bombs, mines or shooting or somethings like that which drive your' mind crazy. Hell, I don't really know what to think about all that junk anymore."

Sgt. Parnell patiently repeated himself to his now hearing impaired and mentally challenged dumb ass partner who probably had been day dreaming in la la land again.

Travis thought for a minute about what had happened. He was not really sure where to start, so he began with the kind of day he had, how he was leaving for the day, found the quarter, and then the shooting began.

He made sure that he told Parnell about the Vietnamese voice he heard and what he thought was being said. When he got to the part about Mai's phone call he nearly callapsed.

"Oh my God!" Travis, his eyes watery, suddenly shouted at Parnell. "How will I be able I to tell her about her half-brother's murder. She'll be devastated. What the hell am I going to do? She'll hate me, she'll curse me, and she'll probably be utterly devastated physically as well as mentally. She'll be a broken woman. How will she ever come to grip with this? I can't even get a handle on this myself, so how in the hell will I ever be able to comfort her?"

Sensing Tolbane's anguish, Parnell walked over to Travis and put his hand on Travis's shoulder. He had never seen his ever-so-strong friend this broken up. Usually, Travis's face looked taught and serious, deeply tanned, with eyes that could burn into your sole. Now his face looked sagging and sad, the corners of his mouth turned down, and his blue eyes seemed teary. Parnell really felt sorry for Mai and for his friend.

"If it's any consolation for you, I'll go with you and you can comfort her while I explain what I can to her about the murder."

Travis sighed and replied, "Yeah! That just might be the best thing to do. Thanks for being here for us Parnell!"

What the two didn't know was that while they were looking at the mutilated body, a small, dark-colored car pulled to the curb on the next street over. An Oriental figure, masked, dressed in dark clothing, similar to a ninja's garb, got out of the car and walked quietly between the houses, stopping beside the one across from the crime scene. The figure looked across the way to see if any of the police officers were looking his way. They weren't. The figure got down into the prone position, slithered to a tree, and climbed up to a solid limb. He took out a pair of opera glasses and began watching the crime scene house in ernst.

While sitting and waiting, Tolbane began thinking about all of the bad luck he had with people close to him dying in so many different ways. He first thought was of his brother Jim. Jim died when he was only nine years old and Tolbane was nearly seven. They lived with their parents in a very nice and quiet part of town. The home had two stories: three bedrooms and a full bath upstairs and a master bedroom, full bath, kitchen, living room and entrance hall below. The one side of the house had a large lawn where the boys played. One fateful day, Tolbane and his brother were kicking a ball around in that yard when they heard a police siren screaming. The two boys ran to the front to see what was happening. Jim, being older and faster, got to the front of the house first. As Jim reached the front, a car being chased by the police and driven by a teenager, lost control, jumped the curb, tore through the front yard, and hit Jim, killing him instantly before ramming into the house next door. Needless to say, Travis and his parents were devastated over the incident. He never found out the sentence the ass received. His parents would never talk about it.

Tolbane's reverie was interrupted by Sgt. Parnell. "Travis, I just got a delayed call from the Coroner's office saying he is on his way, but he just pulled up and he definitely won't like your being at this crime scene. How about you get into your truck, take a couple of deep breaths, and go to Hermitage. There's that Waffle House we always go to that Mai's friend Carly works at. Get some coffee and an omelet or something. Damn, I forgot! It's always waffles and gobs of bacon and syrup for you. Try to relax and fill your always-growling stomach. As soon as the Coroner is done here, I'll give the crime scene guys some directions on what I need done. Then I'll join you and we'll figure out how to tell Mai about this. You should have your head a little straighter then."

"Parnell, I'll be very honest with you. I've never been so shocked, so befuddled and so shaken like this in my whole damn life. This crap just doesn't make a lick of sense to me. How in the hell could this have happened to us? How Ba must have suffered through-out the torture and debasement of his body. I can't believe he would have done something in his life that deserved this kind of death. I'm glad you thought of my going to the Waffle House in Hermitage. I'm completely at sea right now. Maybe the ride there and getting some chow and talking to Carly will help me with my sanity."

"Travis, again, I'm really sorry for Ba's death," Parnell said sincerely, then as Tolbane was going out the door, Parnell quipped, "Now drive carefully and don't forget to pick up your road kill, you know, that flat little animal that lives on the yellow line, after you smash it. It's legal here in TN now. You could make a great stew with it."

"Yeah, yeah, I hear you," Tolbane muttered on the way to his truck. He unlocked the door and lay across the seat on his back and reached up under the dash panel and grabbed his hideaway. Tolbane took the wrapping from the weapon and its magazine. He inserted the 8-round magazine, released the slide, and injected a round into the U.S. Colt Model 1911A1 .45 ACP pistol he possessed; it was by compliments of the United States Marine Corps. This semi-automatic hand gun had been his TO[24] issue weapon in Viet Nam. He had acquired two extra government issue M1911 45 cal. Pistols giving him three, one which he turned in to the armory, keeping two of them. When Tolbane rotated back to the States he shipped them back in his footlocker. Tolbane liked these weapons. They had drawn blood before.

Leaving the safety off, he shoved the weapon between the driver's seat and the center console. He took out his cell phone and called Mai. When she answered he swallowed and said, "I can't talk about what's happening right now. Let Rant and Rave outside and give them our 'Guard'

---

[24]   Table of Organization.

Command, and lock the door and put on the alarm. A little Later Parnell and I will be there and explain what's going on to you. Make sure you get out your 9mil. semi-automatic, put a round in the chamber and have it handy. Love you and be alert!" Then he hung up.

Rant and Rave are male German Shepherds that came from the same litter. They both have a high pedigree and cost Tolbane an arm and a leg for each. He didn't regret one second from the time he picked them up and had a professed dog whisperer help him train them. They were trained to guard their home and could be vicious when attacking. The two-acre property was fenced in with a four-foot-high brick fence. Whenever the dogs were put on alert, one would go to the north side of the house and the other to the south. Each dog had its own dog house at its station. The dogs would lie in the house and remain alert until they were given the command to stand down.

Tolbane left the house where Ba's body no longer lived and climbed into his green machine, and when he started the Dakota, the music from *Phantom of the Opera* mirrored his mood. "Wishing you were somehow here again!" was playing, and it tore into his mind and soul. He turned off the disc player before he would go nuts.

After driving onto I-40, Tolbane drove slower than usual with the driver's window down. He set his cruise control at 50 mph, five miles an hour less than the speed limit. He was trying to put the night's events into a proper perspective. Two separate events and at two separate areas. It seemed unlikely that the two could be related, yet they both involved him and Vietnamese. It was really gut-wrenching and seemed to be a losing battle. His thoughts kept jumping to the loss of his long-time friend. So many memories were clouding his thoughts, of the sadness of war and the wonderment of peace.

He thought of the events that bond men together and can never, ever be forgotten or torn asunder. Sometimes there was be laughter, sometimes there were hugs, sometimes there were tears, and in their line of work they could not but have blood and pain as part of their lives. The memories lingered on and on. What of his beautiful, wonderful Mai? How devastated will she be? How will he tell her that her beloved step-brother was gone? And should they tell her how badly he was chopped up, and being nailed down in a cross position? Tolbane couldn't get these thoughts out of his rabbit assed mind, and a couple of times he became distracted by the thought and nearly ran off the road, just barely catching himself in time to avoid it.

Each time he saw a vehicle approach in his rearview mirror, Tolbane would slow a little, take a breath, and grasp the .45's hand grip, depressing the hand grip safety. When the vehicle would pull into the next lane to pass, he tensed up until the vehicle passed him, then he would let out the breath he held and relax as he re-engaged the cruise control. Tolbane repeated this sequence several times until he reached the off-ramp at Hermitage.

Tolbane pulled into the Speedway station he always used that was close to the interstate on Old Hickory Blvd. in Hermitage and topped of his fuel tank, checking all directions to make sure no one was after him. He filled his gas tank, went inside, grabbed a twelve pack of Bud, and paid the clerk. He then drove to Waffle House, which was a half block farther down on the same side of the road. He pulled in, set the emergency brake, turned the key to shut off the engine, slipped the .45 back to its hiding place, and just sat there his hand on his hand gun in his coat pocket.

Travis didn't roll up the window, didn't open the door, didn't look up; therefore he didn't notice that the dark clouds had drifted away and the moon no longer tossed in the sky like a ghostly galleon while that mythical Highwayman came riding up to the old Inn door. He pulled the headrest up a little higher, tilted the seat back, and laid his head on it and closed his eyes. Usually in this position he would probably nod off. This time he tried to concentrate on the evening's events letting his mind go blank, letting his sub-conscience try to evaluate all that happened and make some sense of it all. Why was he ambushed? Why was Ba mutilated? What other shit awaited him? No solution coming, he fell into a deep somnambulistic state.

CHAPTER 3

Travis tried to make sense of what had happened. Who could want Ba dead enough to kill him in such a way? To be tortured like that must mean that Ba must have had some knowledge or had something that his killer or killers needed. God! He must have really suffered.

He thought of himself then. What about me? Where and how do I fit into this scenario? He's Vietnamese. Why was I ambushed at the mall like that by Vietnamese? If this wasn't so tragic, it would sound stupid. Why does shit hitting the fan like this always happens to me? Ba's death reminded him of the death of a wonderful lover of his a few years ago, the gorgeous and wonderful, Kaila.

Travis had sunken in to a somnambulistic state that was neither a trance, nor asleep, nor fully awake. His mind was telling him that Ba is dead. The guy is dead. What guy? The guy was dead as hell. Where had he heard or read that before? As his thoughts wondered, a memory from his teenage years came to.

He was about 15 or 16 years old at the time. One Saturday afternoon, $00.10 for admission, $00.25 for popcorn and milk duds in his pocket, he went to see a movie at the Lyceum movie house, and upon entering the theater he found one of his school buddies behind the candy counter making popcorn. While they were talking, his buddy told him about this line of mystery novels that he liked. His buddy was really thrilled how one of the books started with something about some guy being dead as hell, or something similar to that. Someone was always dead as hell in in all mystery novels. Try as he might, Tolbane's subconscious could not bring up the book title even though he had read it five or six times. This time, however, he wasn't just reading a book, and the guy was really as dead as hell, no fiction, that was for sure.

Suddenly Tolbane was brought back to reality. A hard rapping on his front wind screen shocked him to life and caused him to pull his hand gun from his pocket and point it at the window. His years of training and experience kept him from shooting instantly. Red headed Carly Weems, a part of their group, and a waitress at the Waffle House, jumped back, grasping on her throat with her right hand, her beautiful green eyes wide with surprise, and gulped down a shriek. Tolbane put down his weapon, and before he could apologize to her, Carly raised her voice and uttered, "My God Travis you dumb ass! You scared the living daylights out of me. I swan! I thought you were going to shoot me. Are you some dumb ass dim wit or what?"

"I'm sorry as hell, Carly! I guess I'm the 'or what' tonight." Travis could not apologize enough to her. While looking around and checking the area, he briefly told her a very short version of what had transpired at the mall, but not yet about Ba. He told her that he would explain more to her on her next break. She nodded her understanding, told him he was forgiven this time but warned him not to let it happen again or she'd brain him, and bade him to follow her into the diner.

Travis followed her; indeed, he followed her, never taking his eyes of her undulating derriere. Carly was red headed, about five foot eight, 135 pounds, and well proportioned. She had a great pair of legs that came all the way up to her tush and she was very buxom, with a pretty face and long, curly red hair. A real live, American-made, home-grown beauty if there ever was one. If it weren't for his Mai, she would be first on his list for courting and hanky panty. He still couldn't decide which one had the best legs. He guessed he would have to call it a tie. What a tie it was at that. On second thought, it had to be Mai's. She would kill him if hers weren't the best he'd ever had the pleasure of squeezing his face.

Travis first met Carly when his group of four—Himself, Ba, Mai and Parnell—started going to the Waffle House in Hermitage after a night out on the town. She had just started as a waitress, and she catered the group well. She was very friendly and outgoing, not to mention drop dead gorgeous. About six months later, she became a part time member of the group, then a full-time member.

The group was at the Nashville Flea Market one time when they came across Carly and her seven-year-old son. Her son lived with his father in Arizona and visited Carly a week at a time every couple of months. Travis remembers it well, for it was the first time he had seen her without her work uniform. Three-inch heels, hot pink short shorts, and a teal top with a V-neck that really fit her proportions and complimented her green eyes and red hair. Mai thought she might have to put blinders on Travis, or maybe even blind him. She did put her hand in front of his eyes for a moment and reminded him where his eyes belonged, or else he might end up holding them in his hands. She also chastised her brother Ba for his sheepish grin and wandering eyes. She could tell what Ba was thinking. Parnell was smart and hid behind Travis in order to avoid Mai's wrath.

Carly became the fifth member of the group then and whenever her schedule would allow. It didn't take long for Carly and Mai to strike up a sister-like relationship. Whatever fact, fiction, or gossip one of them knew, it was a safe bet that the other also knew all the details. Both were shopaholics and Travis could always feel a tug at his wallet whenever the two went shopping together. Somehow if he was along, Tolbane always ended up having to carry Mai's packages to the pickup and into the house.

Upon entering the Waffle House, the night crew hollered out their usual greeting to all of their customers when entering. Travis waved to them and went to his usual seat in the far booth by the side window where he could watch the side and front and where he could see everybody who entered; not that he was paranoid, just curious. Tonight, however, he felt it was warranted. While he was seating himself, Carly was calling out his usual order, a whole wheat waffle and a double order of medium crisp bacon, followed by a double order of grits with lots of butter and a bottle of syrup for the waffle. Sometimes she thought he needed a gallon bottle of syrup as he needed his waffles to swim in it like synchronized swimmers.

Then Carly brought over a cup and a pitcher of coffee and poured the first cup for him. Travis looked at the steam rising from the freshly brewed staff of life and decided he needed to let it cool a little. He also wondered if one pot would be enough. Carly was watching his demeanor and decided that he seemed so different this night, just a sad, forlorn, and lonely man. When his order was up, she brought it to his booth. She said softly, "I should be starting my break about the time you finish your chow. Don't forget, I'm a good listener."

Travis had just finished his meal and was thinking about ordering another round of bacon when Carly went on her break and sat opposite him in the booth with her own cup of coffee. He was just about to tell her the sad news when Sgt. Jim Parnell came in, slid into the booth, and sat beside Carly. He looked tired, like the last, and wilted rose of summer, and Travis looked like warmed over oysters without the stew. Carly looked back and forth between them and feared the worst. She knew it must be bad news.

Parnell said, "You didn't tell her, did you Tolbane?"

"Tell me what?" she questioned. "Come on guys, give."

"I told her a little about the mall shooting, and I was waiting for her to start her break to tell her the rest. She had just sat down when you came in. Should you or I be the bearer of bad news tonight?"

Parnell sighed, looked at Carly, not really wanting to tell her, but he broke the miserable news to her. Carly, "Ba was horribly murdered earlier today or late yesterday afternoon in a very mutilating and vicious manner, I'll spare you the graphic details. Travis was attacked at the Mall. Both of these attacks were most likely were done by Vietnamese. We don't know at this time why these things have happened tonight."

Carly's tears began flowing as she sucked in her breath, gave out a moan, and laid her head on her forearms on the table top. Her loud moan and sobs caused fellow workers and customers to look their way. Tolbane stood and stated to the crowd that she just received bad news from the police about a good friend's tragedy. Everyone then went back to work or to their food and conversations.

Parnell and Tolbane took turns, each relating his part of the earlier events to Carly. Neither of the two spoke of how badly Ba was cut up or how he was staked out on the kitchen floor. Her tears and sobbing had slowed, and she dabbed her eyes with a napkin as she listened and digested the details. She reached across the table and placed a hand on Travis's hand. "Good God Travis!" She asked with her voice cracking some, "What about Mai? Is she all right? How is she taking Ba's death?"

"She hasn't been told yet. When I called her, I only warned her to put the dogs on alert, put a round in the chamber of her hand gun, because something strange had happened. I don't know how, but Parnell and I will break the news to her when we get to my place. This is something that needs to be done in person; informing her on the phone just wasn't the way to go," Travis answered. "It would be the cruelest and way beyond belief. I could never do that to her. It'll be bad enough as it is."

Tolbane was interrupted then, a customer raised his voice and started to get lippy to a waitress behind the counter, demanding something about how his food had been prepared. Parnell got up from the booth, walked over to him, showed the customer his gold badge, and told him to either calm him down or leave immediately. When the guy calmed down, the waitress made things right for him, and he busied himself in his food. Tolbane felt like putting the man's face in the food so he really could really enjoy it.

"What an ass that guy is. There's always somebody, just like that one, that can't be respectful to us here. Commenting on how you like your food and asking a waitress to have it re-cooked is one thing, but this disrespect has no place here or any other place." Tolbane nodded to Carly when she finished her statement, and she nodded a yes. She had seen, and served her share of assholes during her life.

Carly told Travis as she got up from the booth, "I have to go back to work now. My break's over. I'm so sorry about what has happened to you and Mai, and my heart goes out to you two. Ba was really a nice guy. I liked him. He was a good friend of mine too. If you or Mai need me to help with anything, don't hesitate to ask. Anything at all that I can do. Just ask!"

Of course, the last part of this statement got Travis's juices flowing. He wanted to ask about back flips, but he held back what he'd like to say to her and instead said, "You've got it Carly. If we need someone to talk with or help out, I can't think of a finer person to ask than you. I'm sure Mai will need your support in the next few days. She'll be devastated and, except for me and Parnell, will need a good friend to lean on. I might need a kind soul too."

Then Tolbane's juices had cooled off and he reminded himself that as long as he was with Mai, he'd turn Carly down even if she were to ask. Semper Fi, Do and Die, and all that good stuff. Carly got up from the booth, went behind the counter, grabbed a pot of coffee, and, with watery eyes, started checking if customers needed more coffee or wanting to order anything else. Out of habit, knowing Tolbane she even placed another order for medium crisp bacon and another waffle to go along with the syrup. She knew he'd devour it like a vacuum cleaner sucks the dirt the minute she set it on the table.

As Parnell started back to the booth, satisfied the guy wouldn't cause any more trouble, his cell phone rang and he stopped to answer it. He listened for a minute or two, spoke a few words, then continued on to sit again opposite of Travis.

"That phone call was from one of our crime scene techs at the mall. He is wondering why all of the incoming round scars were high on the building's walls except for very few dents on the trash compactor. He is of the opinion that maybe the attack was a warning of some kind to you rather than an attempt to kill. He'll go back during the daytime to have a better look at the scene. Also, the coroner just arrived to check the body of your confirmed kill that you had carefully sighted in on, according to Watson. Yes, the Corporal told me about your expertise with that water gun you carry. And no, the Coroner didn't tell the tech anything about Ba's crime scene except that the day shift will inform me of when the autopsy will be done, then later the results." Parnell related to Travis. "The getaway car was found, and so far, it looks like it's been wiped clean. It'll be hauled downtown to get a good going over by the techs."

"Damn it! They sure didn't seem to be shooting high at the time, I felt those projectiles breeze past my face. I really felt that those dirty little bastards were trying to do me in. It really scared the shit out of me big time. Did he check the dumpster/compactor really well? I know I heard the rounds clanging and ricocheting from it when I was on its top. Maybe he'll see better during daylight." Travis stated further, "I'm just at a loss of words over this dumb ass crap. It just doesn't make any sense to me. Who, besides a few hundred jerks more or less would like to off me, and as for murdering Ba, you got to be kidding, don't you?"

Parnell giggled, which he seldom did, and chided Tolbane, "You! At a loss for words? That damn sure would be a historical first." He added, "Let us get the hell out of here. We need to go see Mai, then you need to get some sleep. You have to be downtown in the AM to give your statement. Someone from the day shift will take it. I think they want you about 0730 hours. I know. You don't get up until the Lord only knows when. You, between the mattress and the blanket, make the perfect sandwich."

"Wait a few more minutes," Tolbane said. "I need another cup of coffee at least to get me through the night." He tried the pot, but it was empty. With that said and the pot empty, he waved his cup at Carly. Of course, she hurried to him with fresh pot of coffee and as usual did the pouring. He motioned her head down and whispered in her ear. "Don't tell anyone, but I need another order of bacon and a toothpick too.

Finishing a couple more cups of coffee and the additional order of bacon Carly had already ordered, Tolbane left a big tip on the table, and he and Parnell got up and told the night crew so long. He was apprehensive as to what the rest of the night would be like. It seemed to him it was like a horror movie he definitely did not want to see, ever. Not in the least. He was really afraid of what this would do to Mai.

Tolbane really wanted to kill someone!

CHAPTER 4

AFTER TELLING CARLY THEY were leaving, the pair left and headed to their vehicles, Parnell went to his unmarked unit and Travis to his one and only beloved Marine Corps Green pickup. Travis made sure to look carefully in all directions making sure everything in the area looked clear, and then got in the driver seat, retrieved his .45 cal. APC, and followed Parnell out of the Waffle House lot.

On entering the on-ramp to I-40 with Parnell leading the duo floored their vehicles and headed towards Mount Juliet. Parnell had his blue and white strobe lights, mounted in the front end of his vehicle, on, and Tolbane followed at a close rate of speed. The duo left I-40 at the off-ramp to South Mount Juliet Road., They turned left onto the first road, Belinda Parkway, a mile and a half later turned right onto Sunny Meade Drive. At the drive's end, they turned left where the paved Rutland Road ended and continued on the dirt track. They slowed and turned right onto a dirt road that looked to be nothing more than a lane a farmer used for access to his cornfield or whatever he was planting at the time. About quarter of a mile later, they came to the gates of Tolbane's home.

The two-acre property was completely encased by a four-foot high brick wall, with a decorative cast iron eight-foot-high double door gate at the front. In the center of each gate door was a gilded plaque with an Eagle, globe, and Anchor—the official emblem of the United States Marine Corps—about two-and-a-half-foot square. On the left side of the left gate was a keyed metal box which held a key pad to electrically open the gates and an intercom to the house.

Unseen to Tolbane and Parnell, a dark-clothed Vietnamese was watching through binoculars from a slight rise in a wooded area close to Beckwith Road. He had been watching the house several hours a day for three days as he had been ordered. He retrieved his cellular phone and hit a quick dial number and waited for six rings before it was answered by the Masked Man who had hired him.

"Yes, what is it goose!"

The dark-clothed one stated, "Exalted Tran Hung Dao, the two men just arrived at the Tolbane place driving in separate vehicles. He's calling off the dogs now and opening the gates and driving in."

"That's very good! You can go home now. You'll be called when needed tomorrow."

"Thank you Exalted One!" He ended the call and then crept off to find his car parked along Beckwith road, then drove home to his wife and a nice warm bed as the fall evening had chilled. He was content knowing that tomorrow his wife would find a large, fat envelope filled with a lot of Dong, Vietnamese money, in their mail box. That would make her happy as usual.

Tolbane picked up his .45, got out of the pickup, looked around, then walked to the gate and called to the dogs, Rant and Rave, that had come out from their dog houses and approached the gate, "Stand Down!" He then entered a code into the keypad on the gate post panel, and as he stepped aside, the gates slowly opened outward. While the gates were opening, he punched the intercom button and let Mai know that they had arrived.

The two then drove through the gates and stopped close to the house. They left their vehicles, and Travis entered a code into a keypad by the door and the gates closed and the door unlocked. Travis then went to his pickup and placed his .45 in its slot and moved back to the house. The dogs sat quietly by the door as they had been trained until Travis reached out and began to ruffle their ears. The dogs then responded by putting their front paws on his shoulders, nearly knocking him off his feet, and licking his face and giving happy barks to him. Parnell also patted their flanks, and the dogs bounced around and howled with glee at the attention they were getting.

After a couple minutes, Tolbane put the dogs back on alert once more and they retreated to their stations. Mai, in her teddy, her ample bosom, her long black hair halfway down her backside, and those sleek legs with the gorgeous thighs, already had the door opened when Travis put the dogs on guard, so Tolbane just grabbed her into a big hug and lifted her in the air and carried her inside. She smiled and waved and said hi to Parnell while enjoying the ride. Parnell waved back. Travis carried her through the hallway into the living room, gently lowered her to her feet, and hugged her tighter and they locked lips. Then he took her by the hand and led her to the couch where they sat, an arm around each other's shoulders. Parnell sat in a recliner across from them. Mai looked at Travis' face and eyes then at Parnell's and saw the same image of grief in each. She now knew something really bad had happened and felt concerned for them, not knowing what in truth the situation was.

Parnell looked at the two of them clutched close together and felt an immediate sorrow for them. He had never known another couple that was as dedicated to each other as these two were. He felt that he would never have a true love like these two had for one another. Before Tolbane could speak up to Mai, he said, "Travis, don't you say a damn word, not even one. I'll explain all of tonight's events to her as I know them. You just hold her tight!" At this Mai grabbed Travis Shoulder even harder. Travis responded in kind, thankful that Parnell chose to tell her the heartbreaking news.

"There were two events tonight. The first I'll explain after telling you the second one. Travis was attacked at the Mall tonight." Mai took in a sharp breath and held it. "Three or four Vietnamese ambushed him with, we think, semi-automatic weapons, probably AK-47s, as he left out the ally door at his usual time. We know they were Vietnamese and/or other Asians because Travis heard them shouting in Vietnamese, something about killing him. Thankfully, due to the poor lighting, they were firing high and missed him, but not by much. The only damages done were chipped walls and a bullet-dented trash compactor. Travis lucked out again." Mai let out her breath and moved her lips to Travis's cheek and lightly kissed him.

Mai quipped, "Maybe they didn't know about my big lug's favorite sayings, "Lights up, sights up. Lights down, sights down. And a Marine is indestructible too." Tolbane couldn't help but to grin a little.

"Mai, fortunately the MNPD mobile units were having their shift change briefing at the northwest corner of the mall and responded quickly. Two shooters disappeared. One was wounded by your guy, who claims it was a good mile long shot with a little pea shooter, and later killed by the remaining perp. That guy jumped in a car and took off. A patrol unit took after him and chased him up and down streets until the perp lost the unit. The car was later found, completely wiped of any evidence"

"Cpl. Watson was there at the mall and took charge of and secured the crime scene. I later got Travis on his cell phone and had him respond to another crime scene in Nashville." Parnell noticed that Mai relaxed some and was looking at Travis with a slight smile, seeming a little relieved he was alright.

Parnell said, "Yes, he's one lucky guy, and lucky for you too. It pays to be a pea brain. Him I mean, not you Mai. Right now, we have no idea as to who did this, or why this happened to him, or why it happened tonight. We think it was connected to the crime we discovered earlier in the evening from an anonymous phone call. Travis can give you the complete details about the mall shooting later on. Our main concern right now is the other crime scene, one I hate to talk about."

Mai smiled at her big lug and told him, "God, I'm so happy you're all right Travis. I don't know what I'd do without your shoulder to lean on. You've been my go-to guy since I was ten, when you saved my virginity from that ARVN soldier. I'd be so lost without you, for you are my strength and my rock."

"Well, you know me. Damn Dumb and lucky, that's what I am. I don't intend to leave you any time soon, girl, physically or spiritually. You are stuck with me now and by me forever and a day, maybe even longer than that if I have anything to do with it," Tolbane responded. She held him tighter. Tolbane responded in kind and told her how much he loved her in Vietnamese. That always pleased her. She liked being loved in both languages. They both had some good feeling about making their relationship permanent.

How in the world, wondered Parnell, could he find the right words to inform her about Ba's murder? After a few minutes of silence and contemplation, he decided to just start and let the words come as they will. So, he began. "Mai, there is a reason why I left the telling of the first event for last. It's a very serious situation and I know it will hurt you very deeply, and it breaks my heart to have to tell you about it. There is no easy way to say it. Tolbane knows what it is and as strong as he is, he's been deeply affected by it too."

"What in the world happened that could be so terrible that you find it so difficult to tell me about it?" Mai murmured, thinking of all the difficult and sometimes terrible things she went through in her youth and her escape from Viet Nam in 1975 with Ba, her step-brother. "We've always talked openly about things that were not always good for us or what displeased us."

"This is a different situation, Mai. It's about your Step-brother, Ba. Earlier in the day, the MNPD received an anonymous phone call to respond to his house. He was found murdered there in his home late afternoon today by the responding unit. God, I'm so sorry, Mai!"

"Oh my God, not Ba!" She screamed, threw her arms around Tolbane, and drove her face into his neck. The tears spurted from her lovely brown eyes like a Yellowstone geyser. As she moaned, trembled, and sobbed, Travis stroked her long, black hair and he felt so helpless and at a loss for words, not knowing how to comfort Mai and make everything okay for her again. He understood the Vietnamese bonds of familial loyalty and affection and knew how tragic this was to her and how it would affect her life from then on. His grief over this could never compare to hers and what she was thinking now.

Parnell didn't look like the hardened combat veteran and veteran police officer he was. As he was looking at his friends, he felt like they were his brother and sister, and he had lost a brother too. He was affected by this mutilated body as he had never been affected before. Police officers often become somewhat inured to horrible crime scenes; but this one really hit home for him. His eyes were watering, and he noticed that Tolbane's eyes were watery, too.

Although Parnell knew Mai would not hear him over her sobs, he said once again, "I'm deeply sorry to have had to tell you about Ba. Truly I am Mai. I know how this has affected me, but I cannot imagine how it has hurt you."

Parnell quietly got up from the chair, looked sadly at his friends, walked to the door, set the alarm, walked out, and locked and closed the door. He used the key pad to open the gate and drove out, then closed the gate behind him. The dogs knew it was not an unfriendly presence and remained in their dog houses; always on the alert. He wondered if once in bed he would be able to sleep this night. This was so hard for him too. Having to handle these two crimes against his friends as a cop was one thing, but as a friend to each victim was another matter. It was taking a toll on his psyche already.

Travis and Mai were still in each other's arms, holding each other tight. Tolbane rocked her slowly and softly, whispering in her ear how sorry he was for her and that he understood her hurt and that he hurt not only for her, but for Ba also. He told her that he was there for her, and he would care for her whatever her needs may be. Eventually they both fell into a deep, dreamless, teary and troubled sleep on the couch, still holding each other tightly.

CHAPTER 5

AFTER A LONG CHASE by a police cruiser up and down several streets, the young Vietnamese driver finally shook off his pursuer and drove to a prearranged spot, where he cleaned, wiped down the car once more, and left the car, got into another car and left the area. He drove around the block a couple of times to see if the cops had found the car. They weren't there yet, so he was satisfied. He then used his cell phone to make a call to the Masked Man while driving and received an address to report to. He made a U-turn and drove a few miles to a block from that address, parked the car, placed the keys in a small magnetic metal box under the left rear wheel well as directed, then continued on foot to a small gray ranch-style house with a well-manicured lawn in front and a nice walkway to the front porch steps and covered stoop.

The young man walked eagerly up the steps and entered through the red, unlocked door of the ranch house. He thought of the Stones song about painting a red door black, laughed a little as it was before his time, and wondered why those stupid Americans liked that song. He stepped into a dimly lit living room without any furniture except for a large, four-legged, straight-backed chair, which sat facing away from the front. A set of black curtains stretched across the back of the room, reaching all the way to the ceiling, about six feet from the back wall. The man stopped about three feet in front the chair and knelt down as was the custom.

He was feeling proud of what he had accomplished this night at the mall. His crew had scared the hell out of that American Pig tonight, even though that stupid bastard of a Marine deserved a more fatal dose than what he got. Marines had killed some of his far-removed relatives who had been Viet Cong in the area South of Da Nang in the Quang Nam Province. Additionally, he felt no remorse in losing one of his stooges the Masked Man had assigned to him. They weren't his choice of cohorts. The goose was badly wounded by a lucky shot from the American Pig and was still alive when he killed that pathetic lackey with a head shot. If the guy had been taken alive, he might have talked too much and the Exalted One wouldn't care for that one bit. The guy would most likely have been crippled for life anyhow, most likely for sure.

The police chase had been a lot of fun, driving helter-skelter all over the town, then losing the cops during the chase, cleaning, wiping down, and abandoning the car with no one the wiser about it except himself. "Yes," he thought. Maybe the Exalted One would smile upon him for a change. It was his turn to be praised by the Exalted One he believed. Any job that he had been given to do by the Masked Man had always been properly and speedily executed to a fault. He felt really powerful now and thought he should be rewarded for his effort tonight and for other acts he had carried out for the Masked Man. Not only should there be a lot of money in it for him, he felt, but a promotion in the organization should be in order too. He would be a great asset to the Masked Man's operations. He knew how to operate.

The man still knelt about three feet in front of the chair and waited patiently. He knew that sometimes you may have to wait a while until the Masked Man would appear. After a few minutes, the curtains parted and a masked figure stepped out and quietly sat on the chair facing him. The young man stood and bowed, dropped back to one knee, and lowered his head. The mysterious figure watched the young man for a few moments, in much the same way Hitler would stand in front of masses and not say anything for several minutes, then he commanded the young man to, "Report!"

"Exalted One, Tran Hung Dao," he began. Then the young man carefully related the facts of the ambush of the American Pig in detail, especially about him climbing on top of the compactor. Although he felt no remorse about killing the wounded guy, he feigned a great concern for the man's life to gain respect and favor from the Masked Man. When telling about the police chase, he did it humoredly and egotistically, not realizing the Masked Man did not like that type of humor or those who used it loosely. Furthermore, the Masked Man was not happy about the body of one of his followers being left behind. He really didn't care if the guy was alive or dead; he couldn't care less about the lives of his geese. His Cause was the only thing he really cared about, except for his love for a certain Vietnamese woman. The young man should have retrieved and gotten rid of body. Leaving it there was a betrayal that couldn't be tolerated, even once. One never knows what kind of forensic evidence might be found on the body by the police's CI people. He wanted zero trace evidence left at any crime scene.

"That's a very good report. You report situations in great detail, whereas many followers do not pay attention to details. That is a gift very few men have. You have done a terrific service for this organization tonight. Your actions keep the plan on tract. Well now, you must want my blessing, I presume? Probably a lot of money or maybe even a promotion I take it."

The young man grinned broadly, nodded his head up and down and uttered, "Oh! Yes, my Exalted One. I am your most capable and loyal servant and always will be only your servant. If promoted, I would carry out my duties promptly, fastidiously, and competently as I always have for you. You'll have no greater devotee than me! My loyalty to you is paramount to me." The young man remained in the kneeling position and eagerly waited for the Masked Man's response.

The Exalted One spoke. "Okay, I have decided. You must keep your head bowed and your eyes closed, and I will endow you with greatness and you will always be as one with your ancestors." Thrilled with this, the man missed the hidden message as he bowed his head and closed his eyes. The masked man stood and approached the young man, pulled out a revolver and shot the young man in the top of his head, sending blood, gore, bone, and brain tissue spewing everywhere. The lifeless body of the young man sank to the floor, his blood flowing endlessly, pooling on the floor and filling the cracks in the hardwood. A spray of the young man's blood splatter found its way to the Masked Man's shirt sleeve, shirt front, trouser legs, and of course, his mask. He would burn the clothes at home when he got there this night. He also thought he must be careful of splatter in any future dealings with his stupid geese. He normally had his Number One take care of these trifle things, but tonight he wanted everything to be perfect and the fear of death to be imbedded in the mind and soul of the American Pig. Leaving the dead body behind was an unforgivable sin against his Cause.

The Masked Man turned to the curtain, opened it, and spoke softly to a large Vietnamese man, his Number One, standing behind the curtains: "I don't want this body found, ever. Also, clean up the blood and gore as good as you can. Leave this idiot's car where it is parked, although you should check it out first. There should be no ID, prints, or anything that could lead back to us. Tomorrow afternoon, your wife will find a thick envelope in the mailbox with a little extra Dong in it. I'm leaving here now. I'm very tired after worrying about how the plan would unfold. That silly ass didn't know I was on the mall roof watching everything in real time. It was pathic to say the least about it. I'll let you know tomorrow when you are needed again. I need to go over my plans once more."

As he walked to the door, the masked figure heard the Vietnamese man say, "I shall obey, Exalted One. Everything will be left in pristine condition. Nothing will point to us should anyone discover this place."

The Masked Man knew that the woman to whom he had referred, a middle-aged Korean woman and still hot for her age, was not really his Number One's wife and that she was only at his place part of the time, being when the man was Ba Muoi Lam[25]. The Masked Man knew that, but Number One still referred to her as his wife. He didn't know if she would be at the house when Number One got home or not, but she would get his money anyhow by giving him a sniff of the center of the world now and then. The Masked Man approved of this coupling of the two. As long as she kept Number One satisfied. When she no longer did, she was history.

Walking down the sidewalk, the Exalted One took off his mask and grinned. He thought about the young man's inability to understand how to complete a mission in a

---

[25] Horny as a goat.

properly clean manner. And a thought popped in his head. It was stupid people that always did stupid things. Good dependable men were hard to come by these days. The young man must surely have known that he must not leave evidence behind. He had preached to his geese time and again that the penalty for failure resulted in death. It kept them on their toes. It was very stupid indeed, and to be so arrogant about it was un-acceptable.

When he reached the sidewalk, he turned right and walked a block to his car and departed the area. He would have to burn his blood-soaked clothes and mask when he got home. Being the smart one, he always kept a clean change of clothes and a mask in his trunk, but he didn't have to use them tonight. It was early morning; the streets were dark and deserted of cars and people. No one would see him motoring home. He also kept several masks hidden in the house in case of incidents like this one tonight. He pulled into his driveway and entered his home.

When he arrived home, he put his clothes and mask in the fireplace, lit it, and watched them burn. He made an overseas call to a phone number in Vietnam, and then he received a call and a report from his backup man on the scene, who was sitting in the mall parking lot, about the mall shooting. He received another phone call informing him that the two Americans had been at Ba's house, and then at Waffle House. Later he received a call from a different man letting him know that the two guys had arrived at the Tolbane household. He was satisfied with the info, so he promised money and released the men for that evening and then turned in himself for the rest of the night. He didn't even dream. He slept peacefully because his Cause was beginning to take its desired shape nicely.

By dawn, Number One had cleaned the house and checked the guy's car, making sure it was clean as a whistle.

He had buried the dead goose in the back yard, replaced the turf he had cut out and removed back on top of the grave, and then feeling satisfied, called his girlfriend, waking her up, and asked her to be at his house later in the day. He'd now go home and get some shut eye, and he hoped the Masked Man wouldn't call till the next day. He looked forward to a nice warm body sitting on his face; that was one thing he had on his mind for the next few hours.

CHAPTER 6

EIGHT O'CLOCK AM CAME, and Travis and Mai were still sprawled on the couch asleep in each other's arms. Tolbane's sleep was not restful at all the last hour or so. His dreams seemed to rehash every tragic event that had happened in his life, real or imagined, and even some from mysteries he'd read. When Travis woke, not very rested after the last hour's torment, he looked at Mai's tear-streaked face, his heart went out to her. He didn't know what to do, or worse yet, what to say when she awoke. He knew enough not to wake her yet, so he just held onto her and let himself drift back to sleep, this time a little more restful since Mai seemed to be a little calmer in her sleep.

Ten o'clock came and the telephone woke them. As they sat up, he put his finger to her lips, told her to go back to sleep, and laid her back onto the couch as he got up to answer it. He went to the end table and picked up the phone. "Who's this if I may ask?"

"Travis Tolbane! This is the desk Sgt. at MNPD. Where in the hell have you been? We expected you here bright and early for a statement about last night. I don't want to hear any of your excuses. Don't give me any of your crap. Just get your raggedy Marine ass down here, now, per Sgt. Parnell's orders from last night!"

Looking at his watch, he told the Sgt., "It'll be about an hour and a half before I can get there. If you have any questions about that, just call Sgt. Parnell, wake his dumb ass up, and get my excuse!" With that, Tolbane slammed down the phone and cursed up a storm with an old Marine Corps adage saying, "Fuck 'em all but seven. Six for pallbearers, and one to count cadence!" At least the guy didn't call him a "raggedy assed Marine." Of course, that ringing phone got Mai up and she was on her feet. She ran to Travis, threw her arms around him, and began to quiver and cry again.

The phone rang again, so Travis moved Mai with him to the ringing phone, picked it up, hung it up, then took it off the hook and left it on the end table. He picked Mai up and carried her back to the couch and pulled her close and comforted her. Soon Mai began to get control of her emotions, and her sobbing and trembling subsided. After a while, she dabbed at her eyes, looked into his eyes and uttered in a desperate manner, "Oh my God, Travis, make love to me." He picked her up and took her to the bedroom. He did so, very caringly.

After he finally showered, shaved, groomed, and dressed, Travis told Mai that Carly was waiting on a call. Once outside, he called the dogs off and petted them, and then put them on guard once more. He left home and arrived at the MNPD headquarters desk about 1500 hours. Sgt. Parnell had arrived at Metro not more than fifteen minutes before Tolbane and had received an update briefing on the two cases. He went to the desk when informed of Tolbane's arrival by the desk Sgt.

Parnell greeted him with a firm hug and a pat on the back. They went into the office area, got themselves some black coffee that was a couple of hours old, and sat at

Parnell's desk. Parnell shuffled some papers, put them into a folder, then slid the folder into his top right desk drawer. He looked at his friend for a moment and then offered, "The powers to be are allowing me to take your statement today. Before we do that, let me give you an update as we know it.

"First, there were only about five projectile marks on the dumpster. The rest were above it. All the signs point to high shooting, probably on purpose. I would guess some one sent you a message. The crime scene techs found 97 spent cartridges. The lab is going to examine them for fingerprints just in case. There are no leads on the guy that got away or the getaway car. It was probably cleaned before the incident so it could be sanitized very quickly. There is no other info as to who or why as of yet, except that it was done by Vietnamese.

"Secondly, the coroner will start the autopsy on Ba's body in about thirty to forty minutes from now. I'll be there to observe. It'll be hard for me to watch him carve Ba up. I understand it was hell trying to free his body from the floor, but they did it by chopping out portions of the wood floor. The coroner will remove the nails and pieces of the floor of course. Ba's house was squeaky clean. It was a good wipe down job. The guys couldn't even find any of Ba's fingerprints there. They did find a lot of fine blood splatter on the wall in his bedroom and bathroom. The bed linens were missing too. They took samples of the bedroom splatter, the blood that we saw, and blood from the drain in the bath tub and sent them to the lab. The neighbors that were questioned didn't hear any commotion from his house. Other neighbors that were missed will be checked out today. Our leaders believe, as you and I do, that yours and Ba's attacks are connected in some way, but we still don't know the reason why."

"The CI guys went through Ba's house with a fine-tooth comb. All of the paperwork in the house has been brought in for evaluation and interpretation. That's all we have about the scenes so far in a nut shell. Not very damn much. One of my guys entered what we have from both crime scenes into the VICAP (Violent Crime Apprehension Program). After we get DNA from the blood samples, both Ba's and the Vietnamese it will be matched against Ba' and his, I don't completely know how it works. If there is any DNA not matching Ba's, it will be entered into CODIS.[26] So far there is no hit on the VICAP entry."

Tolbane had sat quietly and listened while Parnell updated him. Then he questioned Parnell, "Damn! What in the hell is going on here Parnell?" Travis added, "This crap has got my mind all fucked up to hell and back. It makes me feel like a damn mental midget. By the way, what did you get from the mall cameras if anything?"

"I was about to tell you that we are going to let you review the tapes first. We called the mall and the guard on duty will have them ready for you. Then you can bring them to me. Give me a call on the cell when you're done scanning the tapes in case I'm out."

After Parnell took his statement and it was signed, Tolbane stood, informed his friend he needed to get to the mall and said, "Thanks! I don't know what I'd do without our friendship Parnell. I know Mai appreciates your help too. You saved my bacon informing Mai of Ba's death I'll check you later." He left and Parnell just waved him off.

Tolbane sped and ran stop lights in his Marine Corps Green pickup, and when he arrived at the mall, he went straight to the camera room. The first tape was ready to view on one of the five tape recorders and monitors. He grabbed a seat and pushed play. The images—slightly

---

[26] Combined DNA Index System database.

blurry and grainy, a jumble of multiple shades of gray, and clearly taped from distance—came to the screen. One by one, Travis reviewed the three tapes. The three cameras were mounted at the East mall entrance/exit doors, the main vehicle entrance in the West, and the South entrance/exit closest to the intersection of Harding Place and Nolensville Road.

Tolbane could only see the Vietnamese driving in, shooting AK-47s on single shot. On another tape he saw the killing of the guy he had injured, and then the Vietnamese guy getting in the car and escaping from the mall. He couldn't identify the vehicle makes or any license numbers. The tapes were of no use. He sat there and cursed and cursed in the strongest Marine Corps language he could muster, all in reference to those "damn old cameras and outdated tapes they had. They had been used over and over again." He called Parnell on the cell and made arrangements to deliver the tapes. He gave the tapes to one of the mall security guards and sent him to the Criminal Justice Center to give them to Parnell and to see if he could obtain copies of the police reports on both crimes.

Tolbane sat in his office, with his feet on the desk, pondering the events of the previous night when the Guard Captain came in. The Captain handed Tolbane a letter and told him, "This came for you a couple of hours ago. The girl at customer service found it lying on the counter. She brought it straight to me. I would have gotten it to you sooner, but I was having a late lunch. I heard about the murder. I know you two were close. You have my deepest sympathy! Bull shit like this should never happen here."

"Thanks! That's okay about the letter. I'm really not with the program right now." The Captain then asked for an update on the shootings and about how Mai was taking it. Tolbane related what he could to the Captain about both incidents and Mai. The Captain gave his best wishes for Mai and was as stumped as Tolbane was to the happenings.

The Captain briefed him on the day's security efforts so far in the day. Nothing exciting had happened so far. After that, the Captain left to tend to his crew, and Tolbane put the letter in his desk drawer and went back to la la land. He soon nodded off. He napped about a half an hour, and when he woke up, he wondered if he would ever dream about the woman doing her back flip ever again.

The phone rang and the mall manager, who was in Pigeon Forge, TN, on a vacation, was on the other end demanding, "Why haven't you called me? I've been waiting all day on you. Worrying about the mall and my wife's attitude has about done me in today!" The manager had no knowledge of the previous evenings events so Travis took the next half an hour to explain. The manager was not too pleased, and advised Tolbane not to do anything drastic. The manager was more concerned about the mall's image and his own future. He didn't want the mall's consumers to think that Perkin's Mall was not a safe place to shop. He wondered seriously if he should end his vacation a little earlier than he had planned, and return to do any damage control to preserve the Mall's reputation.

Tolbane walked around the interior of the mall, going in and out of the stores, greeting sales associates and assistant managers on evening duty. Having good rapport with them was essential to a good and successful mall security operation. The personnel in the stores knew that when needed, mall security would be there and the situation would be handled professionally and with the best outcome. If physical force was needed, they were certainly up to the task also. The security personnel benefited from their performance too. Sometimes a guard may need a favor from a vendor.

All that walking around the mall a few times tired Tolbane more than usual because of the way he was feeling, and he made his way to his office and sat at the desk with his feet upon it as usual. There were copies of the police reports on his desk. He'd have to thank the security guy that picked them up for him. He quickly scanned the reports and placed them in his in basket to check the next day.

It was nearing the time he should go home to Mai. He'd phoned her three times during the day and she was more than anxious for him to come home to her. She had told him that Carly had come over after she called her and they had a really good cry together. She had said, "I feel just a little better, but what I really need is you! I'm alone and lost without you Travis. I don't know what to think or do."

He tarried some more, wondering if he'd get the same shooting treatment again this night on leaving the mall. The security camera man knew the ongoing situation, and was monitoring the outside areas closely as possible and hadn't called about anything strange in the parking lot, so he felt that might be a good omen for him. Travis, who had considered taking a nap was just rising from his chair when Parnell strolled into the security office.

"I got some no good news and some bad news," he stated, then, "Oh, by the way, Hi." Tolbane nodded and responded with, "So what else is new, that's not bad or whatever.?"

"The coroner has ordered the standard tests on the organs and blood but said he'd give me a briefing sometime in the AM on his post mortem of Ba. That's the no-good news. Here's the bad news. Remember the Battalion Scout that always took point and we called him Light Foot? His name is, or was, James Strong. We got a hit on VICAP. He was murdered like Ba about a week ago up in Missouri, some place between Springfield and Joplin close to the Wilson Creek Civil War National Park. He was cut up and nailed to the floor like a cross the same as Ba. The only other info was that neighbors saw a couple of Asians around his house the day before he bought it.

At first, I didn't recognize the name. After a while it came to me that we knew him. This shit just gets deeper and deeper. It seems strange that you three and I served together in Nam on a couple of patrols, and that it's Vietnamese doing this."

"Oh my God, what hell are we in for! The Vietnamese conflict all over again, only here in Nashville? It looks like we'll never get that friggen monkey off our backs until they are broken," Tolbane quipped. "Man, this is some terrible stinking crap. It smells worse than the odor from burning the four-holer crapper tubs in the Nam. I'd rather smell Napalm in the morning. Damn! Wasn't there something about that in a movie? Shit! After all those close calls Ba and I had in Nam, I can't believe it ended with this happening. Damn it! Damn it! Damn it!"

The two discussed what little they knew for a few more minutes and then they parted ways. Parnell went wherever, and Tolbane called home to make sure Mai was okay, found out she was hungry due to not eating all day, and then he went home. On the way, he called Carly at Waffle House on his cell phone and had her fix a couple of BLTs and iced teas to go. When he got to the diner, he and Carly hugged and greeted each other and talked a little about the events. He picked up his order and left for home. Carly couldn't believe he didn't have his usual because he was the typical chowhound Marine with an extended appetite.

During the drive from the mall and then the Waffle House, Tolbane kept his Colt Model 1911A1, .45 cal. ACP close at hand, and his eyes were always vigilant. He did his best during the drive to scope out passing cars as he kept the legal speed limit of 55 mph on his cruise control all the way to Mount Juliet. Arriving home, he was relieved that it was a peaceful and safe trip. He pulled into his driveway, and as he was tending to the dogs and the gate, he could not know he was being observed from the same area as the night before. It was a different observer this night, and that the guy was reporting Tolbane's arrival.

Mai greeted him at the door with a big hug, a kiss, and tears in her eyes, nearly knocking the boxes of food from his hands. He waltzed her into the kitchen and sat her down at the table, placing one of the boxes and a cup in front of her, then he took a chair. He looked at her and commanded in a joking way, "Eat!" to which she responded, "Yes Sir My Master!" and took a couple of bites and then just sat.

"Then eat some more!"

"Yes sir, my commander, sir," was her response with a bit of a teary smile. Suddenly she did feel hungry and finished her sandwich and tea in quick time.

He could see that her beautiful brown eyes were still a little red, moist, and cloudy. He hated seeing her like this. "I'm so sorry, Mai! I'm at a loss for words. I haven't even talked to myself out loud since it all happened."

Mai grinned a little at him, saying, "You not talking to yourself is just a thing I can't believe either. Not even a Mike Hammer quote?" He nodded in the affirmative manner.

"Travis, I called the funeral home by the railroad tracks in Mount Juliet today and told them what had happened. I think we can use them for Ba's memorial. I explained that I didn't know when Ba's body would be released. Do you know?"

The coroner will talk some more about Ba's body to Parnell sometime in the morning. I have no idea what it's about. Maybe he'll find out when the body's release is. I'm sure he'll let us know right away. It'll take a while before all of the blood tests are back. We'll know even more about his death then. I'll tell you the latest on the situation in the morning after you get a better night's rest. But, let me tell you right now that you're the best looking broad in the whole wide world. You're the sexiest one, too. You've got the most beautiful eyes, the nicest legs that run all the way up to your sexy butt, the perkiest boobs, the most kissable lips, and that other really nice thing that takes me to heaven going for you. I'm really glad you're feeling a little better tonight. I've never seen you gobble up food so fast."

"Well, I must say, that flattery will get you everything your little ole heart ever desired tonight," she said with a southern drawl and a sheepish grin, still having tears in her eyes.

"What we need tonight is a good night's sleep," he answered. "Afterwards."

"Travis, I know you're being kind by not pushing me to talk about Ba. You're always there for me. It's really hard for me right now. Never could I ever imagine anything like this could happen. After you give me your version of the real facts tomorrow, I may be able to talk to you about Ba. We went through so much together. Thank you for being you!"

"I'll do anything for a beautiful and buxom Vietnamese broad with gorgeous legs, tasty boobs, and a beautiful smile, my beautiful buxom Vietnamese broad with the luscious thighs." She liked being his beautiful buxom Vietnamese broad with luscious thighs. It had the most-worthy benefits any girl could ever ask for.

After slow and meaningful lovemaking, Mai, weeping once more, fell asleep in Tolbane's arms. Tolbane woke a few times during the night and could feel her body shudder in a fitful sleep against him. His heart went out to her. He loved her so much and wished he could make her pain go away. He also wished he could kill the ass that had caused this pain to her. As a matter of fact, thinking on it, he had a few books on medieval torture. There were a few things he'd like to try out before the ass's final curtain. Oh yeah, that would fill the bill. It wouldn't pay the whole bill, but it would be a little bit of justice.

The inquisition knew how to prolong death, and he wanted to be able to do the same to Ba's killer.

CHAPTER 7

THE OLD ABANDONED CEMENT block building sat back in a clearing in a wooded area close to Lavergne, TN, not quite 20 minutes, depending on traffic, South of Nashville, just off Murfreesboro Road. No one really knew what it had been used for. Maybe it was some kind of business or a work shop at one time. It was one large room, about 70 by 80 feet, with three windows on each side and with double doors on the east side. Tonight, there were 30 chairs set in three rows, with enough room between rows for the occupants to kneel, facing North, and a podium about ten feet in front of the chairs. All of the chairs were occupied by Vietnamese men who were members of the No Name, a secret society, except two of the chairs were empty. One large Viet, the Masked Man's Number One, stood by the door, disgusted by the din of the chattering geese.

Suddenly the man at the door shouted, "Quiet! Kneel, you undesirable Geese!" The room suddenly became still, and all of those seated got off their chairs, kneeling and bowing their heads. "The Exalted One, Tran Hung Dao enters." The door opened and the Masked Man entered and moved straight to the podium. He stood quietly, looking at the group as he had at the man at the house. One could hear the proverbial pin drop. He slowly moved his head from side to side, looking at each man. He remembered seeing footage of Hitler using this same tactic and hoped he was as effective as that insane man. After ten minutes he bade all, in Vietnamese, to return to their chairs and listen up.

The Masked Man continued in Vietnamese, "Tonight we have two empty chairs. There would be three empty chairs except that we have one new member joining us this night. Welcome to our Cause, new man. One man that's absent is following orders and is observing one of our enemies. One peon was killed last night while serving our Cause at Perkin's Mall. The last missing one disappointed me by his actions and will never be seen again. I will not tolerate failure of any type that would interfere with my Cause.

"Two of you have returned from extracting information from the one known as "Light Foot," who lived close to the site of the Civil War battlefield called Wilson's Creek, near Springfield, MO. He had nothing at all to tell us. I believe he told the truth. He was found staked down like a cross as was the other unworthy one. You two have served me well. Tomorrow you will each receive a thick envelope of Dong. In two days, these two patriots will return to the state of Missouri. They will go to the Immaculate Heart of Mary Shrine in Carthage, MO. There at the Marian Days gathering, they will find another, whose name they have, to question in relation to our cause. I've already wished them well. Let us all now praise our successful brothers."

In unison, all of the No Name members stood and shouted, "Praise You Brothers!" After the shout, they all sat again.

The Masked Man continued. "Before I relate to you what our cause really is, I want to remind all that each of you received a little card with a number on it when you entered this room tonight. I want you to look at your numbers now. I'm going to call out two numbers. Do not tell anyone if you have the either of the numbers called. Twenty minutes after you leave this meeting tonight, the two with the numbers called will return to this room to meet with me. I have a very important task for you to perform for the Cause." The Masked Man took two small cards from his pocket, looked at them for a moment and called out, "The numbers are fifteen and three! I'm sure you will be delighted in your assignment."

He paused, then looked at each member one at a time and made eye contact with each. "Now I want to tell you a story about a Vietnamese patriot whose name was Troung Van Ba. He and his guide, Tran Thi Mot, who later became his wife, went on a vital journey in the late 1500s, and their story relates to our Cause. It is also about our history, the history of the No Name. It is about our very being."

Before starting that story, he told the group about Tran Hung Dao, a Vietnamese general who fought the Mongols at the end of 13th century twice, and about how he defeated them twice and became a Vietnamese hero. Dao was the Father of guerilla warfare and booby traps. He wrote a text book on these things, which was later used against the Japanese and the Americans by the Vietnamese. The NVA, the Viet Minh, and the Viet Cong." The Masked Man spoke of the festivals honoring Tran Hung Dao held in present times in the northern provinces of Ha Nam and Nam Dinh and of the Tran Thuong Temple Festival.

Then the Masked Man asked the group who he was, and they responded as one, "Tran Hung Dao." The next statement really awed the group. "Yes, I am the Exalted Tran Hung Dao reincarnated. I am the hero who defeated the Mongols. I wrote the war book on how to beat the

Mongols. I invented the punji pit, as well as the pit with the two revolving timbers spiked with sharpened bamboo stakes driven into them. I taught the men to sharpen long posts and put them in the waters just below the surface to disable Mongol ships at low tide. I live again for the Cause. Many things I drew up in my book were used to defeat the French and the Americans during the Indo china and the Vietnam conflict. I and the book I authored defeated the Mongols, the French and the Americans. This book is so valuable that it is kept under lock and key. It will be used to fight Vietnam's next enemy, and the ones there after." The whole group was wide eyed and amazed. They believed in reincarnation but had never known even one soul who had returned to the living. What a miracle they were observing. The Exalted One thought to himself, "These geese will believe anything I tell them."

The Masked Man then related the story of Troung Van Ba and Mot, then about Nguyen Hai and how the No Name Society had begun. He told about the American Marine Patrol, the Marines who were a part of it, and how they had found a missing Jade Cross and reburied it, but then it disappeared again. He told of the importance of the Jade Cross's disappearance once more, and deduced that one of the Marines on that patrol, or one of the Vietnamese Army unit, must have returned to the site and taken it. He emphasized how important it was that the cross be returned to its rightful place. Finally, he told them about the Cause, which was to oust the communists and reunite the people of Vietnam North and South once more, and how he had vowed to recover the Jade Cross to that end to be the Cause's Icon. The group was sworn to keep the tale secret or else there would be severe repercussions. Violations of any sort could only end in death to the violator. Any word being leaked to an outsider could lead to disaster for the cause.

"Are there any questions any of you would like to ask about my presentation?" he queried after he finished speaking. He could only see the side-to-side shaking of their heads indicating no questions.

He then praised the groups' performance as a whole. He must keep them interested in the Cause. Then the Masked Man had them kneel with their heads bowed once more. He looked at each bowed head. A good leader must know and recognize his minions. When he felt they had knelt long enough, he dismissed them. They arose slowly on sore knees and filed out one row at a time, starting with the first row. When they were gone, he told his right-hand man, Number One, to bring Fifteen and Three to him as soon as they arrived back. He had an important mission for them.

While waiting for Numbers Fifteen and Three, the Masked Man made a couple of calls on his cell phone. One was to a local weather line to check the next day's weather, and the other was to a man watching Tolbane's home. He hoped the man's cell phone was set on vibrate as ordered. It wouldn't do for a ringing cell phone to be heard where there should be none. Sound does carry a long way at night. Talking with the man and finding everything secure there, he put his cell phone away and called the other man to come to him.

"Have you heard from the two extra men that had a mission yesterday and today?"

"Yes, Oh Exalted One. The three letters were delivered, and that Sgt. Parnell's bedroom window was shot out while he was sleeping. They got away clean, ditched the car in the Cumberland River, and went on their way. I was called by them while you were speaking. I believe they would like to know when their payday is. They are awaiting my call."

The Masked Man thought for a moment then instructed the man, "Call them and arrange a meeting to get paid. To be sure they are prompt, you should promise them a bonus for a job well done. That should do it. After you finish with them, leave the bodies where they will be quickly and easily be found. We can't afford any witnesses that might know too much."

"It will be done Exalted One. I don't like those two punks anyhow. They are dirty, scraggly, smelly, and foul mouthed. I am glad they are not regular members of the No Name. I will enjoy myself once more. I know just where to leave them."

"I don't know what I'd do without you, Number One. You are so loyal to me. Great rewards will come to you for your endeavors in the cause. You have served the Cause so well," the Masked Man said as he patted the man on the back. Number One smiled a satisfied smile and started to return to his post at the door.

Just then, there was a pounding on one of the double doors. "It must be Numbers Fifteen and Three. I'll get the door and send them straight to you," the man said back to the Exalted One as he let them in. The Masked Man stood and waited while the two walked towards him in an unknowing manner. When they were close enough, he told them, "Please sit! Relax! You have nothing at all to fear from me or Number One.

"I have a task for you two. If you perform it well, there will be a generous payday for you. I think you will enjoy doing what I have in mind." The Masked Man pulled an ASP, an expandable baton, from his hip pocket and handed it to Number Three, telling him he would be in charge of the task and would be the user of the wand. He instructed him to only handle it with gloves on, leaving no prints. He turned to Number Fifteen and explained, "You'll assist Number Three, and you will be his look out too. This assignment must not fail. Failure is never an option for anyone! Don't fuck it up!"

The task ahead was then explained to the two men in great detail because information on the Jade Cross's whereabouts must be known, and a clear message must be sent to some people, and there must be no forensic evidence left when the beat-up American Pig is found along with the ASP. Once the task is completed and the message is received, they will act in a manner that will assist his Cause.

After he explained the task, the Masked Man complimented the men once more, shook their hands, wished them well in the task ahead, and sent them off with a warning not to fail. As he watched them amble towards the door, they were chattering excitably and he smiled under his mask. He hoped they were smart enough to do as they were told. At this point in time, he couldn't afford any more screw ups by any of his geese.

Waiting a few minutes to make sure the two were gone, the Masked Man removed his mask, patted his Number One man's shoulder. "I hope these two geese don't screw up. Even if Tolbane doesn't know anything about the Jade Cross, he deserves what he will get. I want you to observe closely what happens in this building tomorrow with those two and Tolbane, and report to me immediately anything you feel is not going right. Have a good rest of the night off and have fun with your wife." They left in silence without locking the door. The two followers will need the building the next morning to complete their task.

CHAPTER 8

ABOUT 6:15 AM THE next morning, the phone rang incessantly. Tolbane stirred awake and grabbed the landline from the nightstand by the bed and barked, "Who the hell is this! Whoever you are, don't you know that some people do sleep in the mornings?"

"Well, fuck you too," Parnell answered. "Time to get your ass out of bed. Guess who's going to the Big Mo with me."

"Jesse and Frank James, Bell Star, Quantrill, Harry Truman, or who in the hell gives a shit this time of day. I can give you seventy-five cents, or the equivalent of three quarters, to call three people who really gives a flying fuck today," Tolbane bitched back while trying like hell to get his brain fully awake. He felt like he had cobwebs in his eyes waiting on spiders and flies, and only the good lord knows what was going on in his brain housing group at the time.

"Listen u, Dude! I just got a call from the desk Sgt. At the station. Someone upstairs, for some reason or other, gave permission for me to go to the Big Mo. to see what I can find out about Light Foot's death. You'll never guess what! If you want to go along, you can accompany me as a driver! How's about that info for a wakeup call in the early morning hours of a beautiful day?"

Suddenly, Tolbane heard over the phone what sounded like shotgun blasts, glass breaking, buckshot hitting a wall, and Parnell cursing up a storm hollering, "What the fuck!" Then all was quiet.

"Parnell! Parnell! You OK! What in the hell's going on over there!"

"Right now, I'm OK. Someone just fired about ten rounds of buckshot through the bedroom window. I'm under the bed with my 9 mm. I'll call you back. I'm calling back up right now!"

Tolbane's shouting into the phone woke Mai. She awoke trembling with a scream on her lips and called out. "Oh my God! What is it Travis?"

He hung up the phone and said, "Somebody just shot up Parnell's bedroom window while we were talking on the phone. He's calling for back up. I'm getting dressed and going over there. I wonder if this is more of a warning like my shooting was." Just then the phone rang again and he answered.

"Travis! As I was calling the station, I heard a car peeling rubber. I checked and it seems to be all clear. I'm sure you're about to get dressed and come over here, so don't. Right now, Mai needs you more than I do. Got that? I'm OK. A unit is on its way and you'd just be in the damn way as usual. I'll call you later." With that, Parnell closed the connection.

Travis looked at Mai and informed her, "I guess he doesn't need me in his life any more. I think I'll go cry my eyes out. Now, where were we before we fell asleep?"

"I think we were horny!" she smiled. Her eyes were a little clearer now.

After finding out where they were before succumbing to sleep and complete the situation, they slept once again. About 8:30 AM, the cursed phone rang anew. Of course it was none other than Parnell checking in again. He said he was alright, not harmed and asked if they would they meet them at the Waffle House in Mount Juliet shortly. Breakfast was on him. Tolbane wondered aloud how much breakfast could Parnell get on himself.

Tolbane couldn't resist telling him that, "Your clothes must be pretty messy and smelly with all that food on them!" In response he got another curt, "Fuck you, and the boat you came over on," from Parnell. He and Mai showered and dressed together, and since they had to meet Parnell they didn't mess around as they usually did. They finished their grooming and getting dressed, fed the dogs, and then went a-waffling at Waffle House to see how much waffling they could waffle. Within Ten minutes after closing the gates, they were at their destination. The early breakfast crowd had thinned out and they got a good booth right away, ordered coffee from a chunky, dark-haired waitress, and waited on their friend before ordering.

When Parnell arrived and was seated, the chunky waitress brought coffee for him and asked for their orders. Mai ordered a Western omelet and toast, Parnell wanted a ham and cheese omelet with scattered, smothered, and covered hash-browns and toast. The chunky waitress looked at Tolbane and said, "You don't come here often, but I know what you want, with a bucket of syrup on the side," and went to turn in the order.

Mai looked at the two men's glumness. She decided they needed a little cheering up. She got their attention easily and said, looking very seriously, "I've got some important news for the two of you. Hold on! I'm pregnant!" The eyes of the two got big and they looked dumbfounded. Travis gave out a, "Oh my God!"

Then she burst out laughing, almost splitting a gut. "Looks like I got you both good! Ha! Ha!" The guys laughed and relaxed somewhat. Tolbane wondered, "What, me a father? How in the hell do you change a shitty diaper on a baby anyway?"

Mai retorted with, "Just hold your nose you big Dumb ox!"

While waiting for their food, Parnell explained what had happened at his place to the others. "The neighbor across the street had just got up and was stretching in front of his upstairs bedroom window when a dark-colored, four-door car, he didn't know the make, didn't get the plates, pulled up in front my house with at least two people in it. He couldn't see what the driver or shooter looked like or the weapon, but he heard what sounded like ten shotgun blasts. He said the car sat there for a minute or two more, then peeled out. That's it in a nut shell folks. Outside of damaging the window pane, busting out the glass, and peppering the side of the house and the wall with pock marks, no harm no foul. The crime boys dug out the buck shot. There's nothing else to check on. These guys are really sick and slick. Like your mall shooting, the rounds were high. I guess I've been warned too. About what I, like you Tolbane, have experienced, I have no earthly idea, or why for that matter."

"Yeah, your right, but warned about what?" asked Tolbane. This whole thing is really sick, sick, sick, and it's getting me on edge. I'm not so worried about this situation myself, I got a silver spoon up my butt. I'm more worried about Mai than myself. Speaking about you, Mai, you seem to be a little better today, a little cheerful in fact." Tolbane looked closer at her, "Mai, are you sure you're OK?"

"I'm hurting in my heart over Ba. Losing him has really hit me hard. I'm trying to get a grip on it and accept it. Ba was not only a wonderful step-brother to me, but sometimes he was like a father until I grew up. I am doing my best to cope with this, so don't worry. Someday I'll be at peace over it. Right now, I'm worried about you two. Right now, you're the only two guys in my life, and I can't lose either of you. I'd be so alone and terrified to be alone. There would be no one I could ever to turn to for help. I know there's Carly to lean on a little, but she's not like you two. You two are mentally and physically strong and you are my family now, my only family."

Parnell said, "Scouts Honor Mai. We'll always be here for you. You can always depend on us, always and forever." Tolbane nodded his head in agreement, "That's for damn sure." Then they were quiet till the food came.

After they ate, Tolbane looked at his now-clean plate and said, "Wow! We must have been hungry!"

Mai shook her head side to side, looked at him, and quipped, "We? What's the matter? You got a mouse in your friggen pocket? I thought sure you were going to lick the damn plate till it disappeared!"

"I don't think so," he responded. "The plate wouldn't be as tasty as you are my sweet." Mai turned her head away and her face turned a bright red. Parnell did his best to ignore the comment, but smiled inside. It was pure Tolbane nonsense.

The waitress served more coffee to them, cleared the table, and they talked. Tolbane and Parnell related to Mai everything they knew about the crimes, first about the mall shooting and then how Ba's body had been so horribly mutilated. Several times, she winced and shed a tear over some of the details. She couldn't really visualize it, but she tried to. Tolbane was proud of the way she was taking the details in stride. He also knew that after he left for work that day she would let her emotions out and cry her head off. She'd been holding back too much for now. He wished he could stay home and be there to comfort her, but he had work to do at the mall. Plus, he had to keep busy in order to keep his own sanity.

After the coffee had been drank, Parnell put a generous tip on the table and they left. Parnell told Tolbane, "I'm coming to the mall a little later. I should have more info on Light Foot and we'll discuss our going to the Big Mo then." They said their good byes, Sgt. Parnell went his way and Travis took Mai home. He thought that sometime or another he heard something about, "One more kiss and say good bye." So, he kissed her one more time and said good bye. He wondered if it was in a song or in a book, or what.

Tolbane pulled into the mall parking area, close to the South entrance. He left his personal statement pickup truck and was almost at the doors as a man, about 35 to 40 years, was running out of them with two security guards chasing him. He was looking back at the guard when Tolbane reacted, launching himself, right shoulder first, into the man's right knee. They both went flying hard and skidding onto the pavement. By the time Tolbane was able to get up, the guards had caught up and had the man cuffed and lying on his side so as not to interrupt his breathing and keep him from aspirating his body fluids. When someone is left lying on his stomach with his hands cuffed behind his back, it puts too much pressure on the chest cavity and hinders the respiration process. The subject could die. That could cause a nice law suit, so the guards are careful to avoid it.

Desoto, one of the guards kidded Tolbane," Hey Master Gunny, you're getting too old for that kind of shit, you know what I mean? You're not playing in the NFL with the big boys, you know. Seriously though, you OK? You gave me a scare there for a minute or two. The tackle was poetry in motion though."

Tolbane laughingly quipped back at the guard, "You're fucking 'A!' It was both poetic and text-book. I'm OK. By the way, I'm not old, I'm a Marine and indestructible, remember? What's happening with this joker?"

"We were assisting a sales associate in Dillard's with a mouthy customer when this guy walks up to a mother and daughter about 12 years old and grabs the young girl's breasts. We both witnessed this, and then we took off after him when he ran. I think you know how the chase ended. I'll take this worm to the security office and call MNPD, and this clown, pointing at his partner, will go into the store and escort the mother and daughter there to await a patrol unit." The security guards then gave a high five to Tolbane.

Tolbane smiled, patted the guard on his back, and complimented him for a good job, well done my man. "Only next time, please run a little faster so I don't have to break these bones with a poetic, text-book tackle." With that, the security guards smiled and left, taking the cuffed man with them. He was very glad that this was now the security captain's problem and not his. He walked slowly to his office, trying to ignore his bones aching all the way. He made sure to glance into each store window as he passed by to make sure all was good, and that there was no visible trouble.

When he sat down at his desk again he relaxed somewhat. He kind of put himself into a semi-trance to see if he could come up with any answers. After a few minutes he remembered the letter the captain brought in the previous night. He took it out of the drawer and laid it on the desk. Before opening it, he decided to call Mai. He used the mall's landline this time to save on his cell's overage on minutes charge. The telephone rang at home about five times before Mai could move to answer it.

"Oh good, it's you" she answered. "I'm so glad you called. I was sitting here crying and feeling sorry for myself for about a half hour when I began realizing how lucky I am to have someone who cares for me the way you do. I think I fell in love with you the moment you rescued little ten-year-old me. I'll never regret giving all of my love and myself to you. I think after realizing how lucky I am, I feel better and more like accepting all that has happened. I am so very lucky to be in love with you and you with me! Oh! By the way, I called Carly as soon as I got in the door. I think I woke her up. We'll have lunch somewhere later on today. I'll let you know where. Then I had my cry. I feel I can cope with it a little better now."

"I'm happy for you that you're somewhat better. I'm the luckiest guy in the world having you at my side. You've made me so happy. I'm very much in love with you! In fact, I love all, and I mean all, of you. You are very tasty. Well, I've got to go. I'm just glad you're alright. Just call if you need me. I'll let you know if I find out about Ba's body release. Bye." He hung up and opened the letter. He then took the paper from inside the envelope, unfolded it, and as he read it, he expounded, "What the fuck!"

UNWORTHY TOLBANE!
You know what we want!
You have been warned!
And so has Parnell!

Tolbane laid the paper on the desk, picked up his cell, and hit the speed dial for Parnell. This sounds like some really deep kind of Oriental shit. Once again, he exclaimed, "What the fuck, over!" After a couple of rings, Parnell answered. Tolbane asked, "Are you busy right now? I'm still at the mall. Something else came up you need to see right now. Do it pronto, if you can."

"I'll be right there in about ten to fifteen minutes," he answered and ended the connection.

Tolbane looked at the lettering and decided it was computer generated and printed on a dot matrix printer.

It was probably typed on WordPerfect, one of the popular computer word processing applications of the day. It didn't look like the style of WordStar or Microsoft Word to him. Tolbane took out a pair of latex gloves from his bottom desk drawer, put them on, picked up the letter, and walked to his copy machine and made four copies. He put two copies in a manila folder in the bottom desk drawer and laid the other two copies with the letter and envelope on the desk top. He took his little memo book from his pocket, noted the delivery details of the letter, the time and date he opened and read it, the time of the call to Parnell, and the time of making copies. On a second thought, he made the same number of copies of the envelope and dispersed them the same as the letter. He sat and waited on Parnell to arrive.

When Parnell entered the office, Tolbane told him, "Put on some latex gloves and read this! It was delivered yesterday. I just opened it today." Then he handed the letter to Parnell. Parnell complied. After reading it he said, "Jesus H. Christ on a crutch. What the fuck are they talking about, we know! I don't know shit from the Shinola, a brown shoe polish!"

"Don't feel all alone Mein Gruppen Fuhrer. The mouse in my pocket doesn't know the difference between the two either. This whole situation is making me think even more about Vietnam. I'm wondering, my good buddy, do you think this has anything to do with the day we were ambushed by the ARVNs on that patrol with the prisoner? So far, all four of us were on that one patrol. That was the only time the four of us ever served together in Vietnam, as Light Foot had rotated home before others we were on, and there is definitely a Vietnamese twist to this whole damn affair. Damn it Parnell! Remember that Jade Cross with all the beautiful jewels that was buried there by that old worn-down hooch? God, it was so beautiful. I've never seen anything like it in my entire life."

Before Parnell could answer, a lady from customer service came in the office. She greeted them with, "Hi guys! I hope I'm not interrupting you two from anything. I've got another letter that was left for you. I found it on the service counter just now. I don't know who left it. I was on the phone with a customer and my back was turned to the desk."

"You're not interrupting a thing. We're just telling sea stories as usual. Did you know that Parnell and I won the Vietnam War; all by ourselves? We killed them all in the name of Ho Chi Minh, or Buddha, or somebody, and bade them to visit their ancestors and have a joyful reunion with them. Oh yeah! Thanks a lot for the delivery Bea. Are you the one that found the other letter yesterday?"

"No! That was Goldie. She told me about it. She got her letter the same way I did. Her back was turned to the counter and someone just snuck up and placed it there. I got to get back to work now. If you need me for anything just holler. Bye! Bye!" She left the office with a smile and a jaunt.

"Damn Parnell! I'm almost afraid to open this one." He put on another pair of latex gloves and tore it open. He read the letter out loud.

DON'T WORRY UNWORTHY ONE!
MAI WILL NOT BE HARMED!
MAYBE YOU WILL BE!

He went to the copier, made copies of the letter and the envelope as before, stashed his copies in the bottom desk drawer, and handed the rest with the envelope to Parnell who, still having his gloves on, took a plastic baggy from his sport coat pocket and placed this one and the other letter and envelopes in it, commenting, "I'll bet there will not be any finger prints of interest or use on these. I'll ask the lab people to check the seal for DNA. With the way our luck is going now, whoever it was probably used a wet sponge or something to seal the envelope. This is fucking asinine!"

Tolbane was stumped again. "Yes, it is asinine! What's this crap about Mai? How the hell does she fit into this situation? That bothers the shit out of me. You would think the pressure would be put on her to convince me to give up something of which I am totally ignorant. I'd sure like to believe that she's in no immediate danger. She's too precious to me. Someone is being predictable by being unpredictable, if you can understand that. I sure the hell can't. I'm no fortune teller. Could this really be about that Jade Cross we found in Nam and then re-buried?"

"You may have hit the proverbial nail on the head for once Dumbo. It's definitely a possibility when the bad guys and those victimized all seem to be connected to the Republic of Vietnam. I remember that patrol very well. It stands out from others because it was so different. The ambush by ARVNs and finding that Jade Cross were both a complete surprise to me. I had thought we would find most anything buried there but that. I was initially afraid of a booby trap of some kind being buried there. We could have all bought the farm. You know! Don't bunch up. One round will get you all!" Parnell thought a little more and added, "I wonder if it's still buried there or if someone dug it up and made off with it. Maybe that's the problem."

"I remember that too. I wanted to strangle that lieutenant at the S-3 at the time for his ignorance and disrespect on the field phone to me. He probably was a newbie and didn't know his ass from a hole in the ground yet. He hadn't yet learned not to fuck with a Gunny. Especially not me. At the least, I wanted to cut his balls off and stuff them down his craw. When we got back to the enclave, I went to the S-3 and taught that shave tail the Marine Corps four don'ts:

Don't call your rifle a gun.
Don't piss in the wind.
Don't shit in your mess gear.
Don't fuck with me.

"I think he got the message. But really, I don't know what made me think of Vietnam and that patrol just now. I guess I reasoned it out because of my superior knowledge and superior intellect. I'm good at doing that, you know."

"Yeah, OK, right Tolbane! Define the word 'that!' Only the good Lord knows how you can sometimes come up with even a partial answer to the dumbest questions, let alone an answer to a good one. I guess with your superior knowledge and superior intellect, you would say that this is a, 'superior hypothesis' based on your super-duper pooper-scooper active brain power."

"Ten Four, that's an affirmative, Marine. I got you five by five, long, wide and deep, and I've also got your six on that crap. Could that patrol possibly be what this is all about? If so, someone must want that beautiful Jade Cross awfully bad, and for some reason or other thinks that one of us four either has it or knows where it's at. That's crazy, really inane. How would we have gotten it? Oh, I know how we did it! We must have dug it up. Do you dig it! Duh!"

Parnell thought about it for a moment. "When I get back to the station, I'll have one of the troops run background checks, criminal and financial, on all the members of that patrol I can remember for as far back as they can. They will also run a check on you and me. Then by cross-checking the data, we might come up with other connections such as a trip or trips to Vietnam, etc. Right now, Ba is the only one of us, to my knowledge, who has ever gone back there. He went to Ho Chi Minh City to see if he could find either of his brothers a while back, and that's a long way from the Hoi An City area. He could easily have gone to visit the Hoi An City area and we would never know about it. Maybe Mai might know if he brought a strange package back with him. We can ask her about it later on.

"I was on my way back to the station to get an update on going to the Big Mo. when you called me, so we'll have to talk about it later. I don't think you should tell Mai about these weird letters at least at this time. Right now, she has enough on her plate having to come to grips with Ba's brutal murder and the attacks on you and me. I sure hope it's a stone-cold fact that they, whoever they are, definitely do not want to harm Mai for some reason. It would indicate to me that she might be known to them, or she may know them, and they respect her enough that they wish her no harm. Either that, or whoever it is just wants to fuck with our brain housing groups by the numbers. Got to go Buddy! Got things to do to protect and safeguard Nashville's populist and safe guard the ambience of Music City, USA. I'll check on you later gator when your legs are straighter gator! I'm leaving now. Semper Fi!"

"Semper Fi!" Tolbane responded as Parnell left the office. He remained in his chair, put his feet up on the desk, and while contemplating his and Mai's fate, he dozed off and dreamed. Just as the woman was in the middle of her back flip once more, the phone rang.

"Travis! I don't know what to say," Mai began, sounding upset. "I just received the most disturbing and irritating letter in the mail. It came by the regular mail. It had only one sentence IN it. It said:

"MAI, DO NOT WORRY,
YOU WILL NOT BE HARMED!"

"My God Travis, what in the world is happening to us? I'm about to go crazy over this. This whole mess is stupid and unsettling. It's really got me on edge. I've got the dogs on guard, the alarm on, and my 9 mm by my side. Damn it, Travis come home! I need you here with me!"

"I know! I know! My heart goes out to you Mai. I'll be home shortly. Right now, let me explain to you what I think. Parnell just left here. I had received a warning letter about him and me, so I called him and asked him come to the mall. It seems that someone, somewhere, thinks one of us has something, maybe a Vietnamese Jade Cross, and whoever it is, wants it. While he was here, I received another letter saying that you would not be harmed. With two letters saying the same thing, I'm hoping that you will be safe. That's what I always worry about. Your safety is above all else to me. I'll show you copies of the letters when I get home. Right now, I want you to call Parnell on his cell phone and tell him about the letter you received. Don't forget lunch with Carly! I love you bunches and gobs!" They ended the call and Tolbane sat and thought about how he could put what little he knew about the situation on paper.

Mai thought that among other things, he was going crazy also. He didn't even know the time of day as usual. It was later in the day and she already had lunch with Carly. She also knew that his "shortly" would actually be longly as usual. Then giggling she thought, long dong.

Tolbane felt he needed to put down some facts and questions so that he might make a little sense of what was happening. He needed to get his brain in gear, so he retrieved a lined legal-sized tablet from the desk along with a pen. He wrote "Factors" at the top of the page, then thought out loud to himself, "What Factors do I need?"

CHAPTER 9

TOLBANE KEPT THINKING ABOUT how he could factor the events together and get some idea of what the situation was. "*Factors*!" he reasoned aloud, even though he was by himself. "What would I do if I were still in the Corps and working in an S-2 or G-2?" he continued. "How would I develop any information collection then process it through evaluation and interpretation. But of what?" Then it struck him smack in the middle of his brain. "*Order of Battle Factors*!" First, he would develop questions, apply them to the order of battle factors he knew, and then look for indicators on which to make assumptions. Once again out loud he exclaimed, "Why not try it. It'll give me and Parnell questions to answer." He picked up his pen and tablet and began to write.

1. <u>Composition</u>: The attackers are composed of Vietnamese. It is not known if there are any other ethnic groups involved. Are the Vietnamese from the old North Viet Nam? Are they from the old South Vietnam? Is there a difference now? The dialect sounded like the Sai Gon dialect. Do not know how they are organized or if there is a rank

structure. What kind of leadership do they have, strong or weak? Where do the members come from?

2. <u>Disposition</u>: No general idea where they may be located. Most likely somewhere around the Nashville Vietnamese Community. Could they be from someplace else? Need to have Parnell check with that Vietnamese MNPD officer and see what he knows of the people there. Maybe Parnell has already checked with him.

3. <u>Strength</u>: Do not know how many there are. At least four, one dead, three escaped, and there must be a leader. They have AK-47s, shot guns, and hand guns. How many guns? We know they have knives. What other kind of weapons might they have? What type of communications do they have? They have at least one computer and one dot matrix printer the letters were printed from.

4. <u>Training</u>: If they were not shooting high on purpose, then they had little or no training. If they were aiming high, then there was some marksmanship training involved. As for getting around the Nashville TN, area, they could be trained by memorizing maps or by driving around and through the city. Do they do any escape training?

5. <u>Tactics</u>: They use ambushes. There must be some escape and evasion training, judging by the manner the guy got away and ditched the car. Probably the same with Parnell's shooters today. Don't leave wounded alive. Shoot high to intimidate. Intimidation by letters? Note: don't know how one shooter got away. They had to know the area well, as the attacks and getaways were well planned. Leave the woman alone? Is that a tactic? They aren't sticking

to one place, ref: the Big Mo. Will there be other places? Also, there's death by a thousand cuts and cutting the throat with significant exsanguination.

6. Logistics: How and where do they get their weapons and ammo? Steal from people's homes? Who steals the cars for them? What other types of transportation do they have to move themselves around in? What other supplies and resources do they have? Do they have some type of FM radios? Do they use cell phones, and if so, who is the carrier? What other kinds of supplies do they receive and how?

7. Morale: They seemed to be in good spirits a couple of nights ago, and today's shooting at Parnell's must have given them a big high. Don't really know much about it.

8. Miscellaneous: What are their reasons for murdering and intimidating? Is it about the patrol members and the Jade Cross, or is it something different? Was it the same guys all three times?

When he got done writing, he tore off the sheet of paper, and looked at it, thinking. "Well, it's a lot of questions to be answered," he voiced aloud to no one in particular. "There's not much we know to evaluate. There are no indicators at all. There is no way to make any assumptions or conclusions except that those Vietnamese clowns are most likely well organized." He wondered if he had just wasted his time writing these things down and trying to make sense of it all. He'd still show this list to Sgt. Parnell. The good pal of his would probably say something like, "Evaluate this Tolbane!" Maybe even, "Indicate on this!" He then remembered he had not written a report for the mall manager.

He got the pad again and started to write. After three pages of thinking and writing, he took the report to one of the mall security officers to be typed and the appropriate number of copies made and disseminated. The mall manager's secretary usually did his typing, but she was on vacation too. Tolbane giggled over the vacations. She was shacking with the manager in the same motel as the mall manager and his wife was staying at. He couldn't help but laugh at that situation. How did the manager manage to schedule both women without the other finding out? The guy must be a genius. Lucky with the secretary too! She's a fox for her age. Were back flips part of her repertoire, he wondered.

Tolbane then did one of his daily security strolls through the mall, checking the stores and sales associates as he went down one side, through the wings, back up the other side, and finding nothing out of the ordinary, ending up back at his office.

The damn phone was ringing as he entered, and he made a big jump for it, nearly falling onto the desk, and got it just in time to hear, "What the fuck took you so long to answer Dumbo?" Recognizing Parnell's voice Tolbane responded, "Do you really care, Jungle Bunny, or maybe it is Dip Shit to whom I'm speaking?"

"Screw you too, Leather Head! I got the release date for Ba's remains. I have a couple of other odds and ends of info too. Give me a call when you are ready to leave, and I'll come by and follow you home. Somebody needs to protect your dumb ass anyhow. We can discuss things there and maybe make some plans." Parnell continued, "I've got a package of frozen hamburgers, a package of buns, two six packs of Bud on ice, and a big #10 can of Bush's baked beans. Yes! Of course! You can have the grilling duty tonight. I'll have the double six pack duty, and Mai the Bean duty"

"Sounds damn good to me Bro. Better than having to burn the four-hole shitters in the out-house. Oh, what an aromatic aroma that brings forth! It makes you relish having the sense of smell. I'll give Mai a phone call when I get ready to leave and she can put on the charcoal for us and set up the patio. Maybe she can round up a small salad too. She'll have the oven hot, and she'll doctor the beans with catsup, mustard, brown sugar, sautéed onions, and diced and braised bacon, and then throw those puppies in the oven for a little while. Do you know what you get when you mix beans and pineapple together? Beautiful Hawaiian music, that's what my friend." Parnell groaned his usual groan.

"As an afterthought, about your house and window, did you know that that Mike Hammer would have had his Colt Model 1911A1 .45 cal. APC out and blasting away at those turds? He would have killed them all and let some god somewhere sort them all out." Parnell knew enough not to egg him on farther about Mike Hammer, Mickey Spillane's fictional detective. Tolbane would carry his tales on and on forever, and Lord only knows what else he'd bring up from his fantasy world.

"Also, my fine feathered friend without feathers, I've got something to show you! It's nothing but questions I put down on paper earlier, maybe something we can measure this crap from. By the way, I wonder, do you know any good-looking girls with good legs who can do back flips? Never mind. It's just a thought."

"Back flips? Have you been daydreaming again? I swear, you are one strange nut. The squirrels wouldn't even stash you away. They'd call the nut wagon instead. Bye for now!"

Parnell cut the call off, and then he called the station again. This time, he was able to hook up with MNPD's only Vietnamese Officer. He had a few questions for him. After exchanging pleasantries, Parnell asked, "Do you know of any new or weird individuals running around the Vietnamese Community area that just don't seem right?"

"I don't think I've seen any," the guy said," Although I've heard that there is some crazy bastard running around thinking he's a Vietnamese old-time hero reincarnated. He lives a few doors down from Ba's place. A real kook, that one is. He comes and goes all times of day and night, I hear. I know there is a rumble out there of something going on, but I can't get a handle on it. I'll look into it some more tonight. If there's anything hot, I'll call your cell phone. Otherwise, I'll see you at the station tomorrow morning. Have a good day."

As Parnell was saying, "You too, and take care of yourself," the officer said, "Wait a minute! Looking at my computer screen, I see someone found two bodies that appear to be Vietnamese over by the racetrack at the fairgrounds. There are units responding. Let me check it out and I'll give you a heads up. It might be as much as forty minutes or an hour, OK!"

"OK! Thanks!" Then Parnell wondered what the hell would happen next.

As promised, the charcoal was blazing, and the oven was hot. The patio table was set with dinnerware, salads, and dressings. Mai placed a lot of honey mustard out for Tolbane. Parnell gave Mai the beans, and she hastily mixed the ingredients she had prepared and put the results in the oven. The two guys were having a beer at the table, and they handed her one when she sat down with them. Tolbane asked her, "Do you want me to go over things we now know or after the food, fun, and games?"

"I think afterwards would be just right. I don't want to spoil a good mood before we chow down, let me see now, is it chow or mess? I know! When Travis does the burgers, it'll be a mess!" she answered and they all laughed.

About 45 minutes later, Tolbane put the burgers on. The coals were just right. They had already eaten the salad Mai had fixed and were still hungry. As expected, Tolbane had drowned his salad with honey mustard. Tolbane topped the burgers with cheese and put them on a plate, then he sat it on the table and they began topping off their burgers with their favorite junk: mustard, catsup, onions, tomatoes, relish, lettuce, and what not. The beans turned out terrific, as always, and Mai was complimented on them. After the stuffing of food into their craw, they moved to the living room with a fresh brew and sat down. Now was the time for the discussion with Mai. Even though Tolbane and Mai were both on the couch, she sat a cushion apart from him so she could concentrate better. When sitting too close to her man, she sometimes got horny and would forget to pay attention to things being said. She knew Tolbane liked it when she got horny, and she did too, but this was not the time for it.

Tolbane had retrieved his copies of the letters he had received and was about to show them to Mai when Parnell's cell phone rang. He'd forgotten to put it on vibrate again. It was the Vietnamese patrolman calling him. It was about the two bodies found by the race tract at the fair-grounds.

"The two Vietnamese guys had been stabbed several times over, and their throats were cut from ear to ear, clear to the vertebrae. It looks as though they had bled out from it. The bodies are headed for the Davidson County Morgue. Both were laid out like a cross, but not nailed down like Ba's. A homeless guy was walking around the outside of the racetrack at the fairgrounds looking for lost coins when he found the bodies. He said that the only reason he called it in to MNPD was because 'Some cop did him a favor once.' Dig this! He has a cell phone! Who would have thought so? One of our guys took his statement and let him mosey on. If need be, he can always be found wondering around in that area."

The patrolman continued, "The area was checked for blood and other signs. No go! They were killed someplace else then dumped. The assistant coroner said that marks on their wrists and ankles look liked like they may have been bound when they were mutilated. That was really cruel That's all the info I have on them now. Hope I didn't disturb anything important."

Sgt. Parnell said it was OK, then thanked him and told him, "Have a good night." He terminated the call and related the details of the call to the other two who were patiently waiting for the update.

Mai took the copies of the letters from Travis and read them. They made no sense to her. After reading them and looking up without saying anything, Parnell and Tolbane related to her all that they knew up to that point in time. Mai asked a few questions to help her understand what was going down the last couple of days. The three agreed they didn't know much. Then Mai, with tears in her eyes, asked Parnell about the release date for Ba.

"The Coroner said that as soon as you finish making the arrangements at a funeral home to give him a call and he'll release the body to whoever picks it up for them. He asked me to give you his condolences. He knows how difficult this is for you and that you are in his prayers. He also told me that Ba had been beaten as well as tortured with knives, and his death was from bleeding out."

"Oh shit! I didn't want to hear that." She commented with tears in her eyes and a little choking. "Thank you,

Parnell, for telling me the truth. I was hoping it wouldn't be that bad. He must have suffered very much. First thing in the morning, I will make the calls. It will be hard to do, but I'll do it any way. Now, promise me that whenever the tox screen comes back, you will let me know the results right away! I don't really want to hear it, but I must know! I'm hoping he was drugged and unconscious when it was done to him, but I guess that's too much to hope for."

"You have my solemn promise!" Parnell replied.

Tolbane then handed Parnell and Mai each a copy of his mental exercise in prognostication from the afternoon. They both studied it a minute then looked at Tolbane. Mai spoke first. "This doodling doesn't really say anything for real. You spent the whole afternoon doing this Travis? It seems like a mess of mumble jumble or however you say it."

Parnell defended Tolbane's endeavor. "Mai, please think about it for a moment. This doodling of his tells us exactly what we don't know about this crap and what we need to find out for it to make sense. It is like a guide for us to follow. Travis used to do things like this at his job in the service, and he was always good at it. It helped a lot of commanders. Reread it and you will see what I mean." She reread the paper thoroughly, thought about the content some more, and changed her mind. They did need to answer these questions.

The trio of friends discussed the questions as well as they could with so little evidence to go on. Every now and then, Mai would ask a question or offer her thoughts. They were running out of things to discuss when Parnell's cell phone rang again. After answering he stood and walked a few feet away from the pair on the couch. When he ended the call, he went back to his seat.

"That was the Assistant Chief of Detectives. He wants me in bright and early and wants me to take over the investigation of the two Viet bodies. He believes, as we do, that there is a Vietnamese connection to all of this crap. The detective who caught the case will remain on it with me and will do most of the leg work, giving me some flexibility. He said I could even let you tag along to Missouri with me. He even said that you could drive too, old buddy, and I agreed with that even though it had already been cleared for you to accompany me to the Big Mo. I guess I need to move on home and get a little sleep before I go in."

"OK! I'll catch you tomorrow." Tolbane hollered back. "Wait a minute! Gee, I was thinking, yes thinking once again, that's why my shoes are smoking like crazy. What about the ARVN soldiers who were there at the scene? Any one of them could have returned to the area and retrieved the Jade Cross and did whatever with it. Does that mean there will be even more deaths if that's what this is all about? How in the world would we ever find them to ask?"

"You have a valid point there. How in the hell would we find them? It's just another couple of questions to add to the list. I'll call in the AM and let you know what time we'll leave for the Big MO. Good night Mai!"

Tolbane escorted him to the door, they said so long. Tolbane took care of the dogs, put them on guard, secured the gates and the door, and set the alarm system. Mai was standing behind him as he turned from the alarm pad with teary eyes once more and put her arms around his neck, stood on her tip toes and, pulled his head to her and planted one big sloppy kiss on him. God, how he loved this woman. He picked her up and started toward the bedroom with her, him saying, "I think we should call it a night. We'll make it a great night to remember forever."

Mai responded with two words, "A night!"

CHAPTER 10

TOLBANE AND MAI AWOKE early, talked, and made a little love. Then Tolbane took care of his morning toiletries and dressed for work. Mai had fixed breakfast while he got ready, and they ate heartily when he finally sat at the table. After they finished, Tolbane left for work. Mai did her thing and got dressed, and put on some tea to drink while waiting for the time to call about Ba's arrangements. She also gave Carly a call to see if she would be free any time during the day.

When Tolbane turned onto the I-40 West on-ramp from Mount Juliet Road, a four-door sedan with two young Vietnamese males in it pulled out of the park-and-ride lot at the corner of Belinda Parkway and South Mount Juliet Road and on to I40 overpass, right behind him. The car also took the on-ramp to I40 West but made sure they stayed well behind Tolbane's Marine Corps Green pickup. The car's occupants knew where Tolbane was going, and that made it easy to keep their distance while following him so he wouldn't notice.

Arriving at the mall, Tolbane turned into its southwest entrance, and the pursuing car pulled into the southeast one by the creek. The two Vietnamese watched Tolbane as he parked his truck, then they put on ski masks and pulled up behind him. They hurried out of the car and jumped him as he was walking to the mall doors. One of the men put him in a sleeper hold, closing off the carotid artery's blood and oxygen flow to the brain, while the other grabbed his legs and lifted him off his feet to keep him from having any height advantage or leverage to escape from the hold. Everything soon went black for Tolbane. The two quickly threw him into the back seat of their four-door sedan and hightailed it out of the mall lot, going east on Harding Place. The car turned South on Murfreesboro Road and headed for the building where they had received their orders the previous night.

Before long, Tolbane started to wake up a little by little. The one guy should have held the sleeper hold a few more seconds in order to keep him asleep longer. At first, he felt really groggy and his head seemed like it was swimming in circles and throbbing like crazy. As he became more awake, he kept his eyes closed and listened to the two in the front seat. They were speaking in Vietnamese about how they would take turns standing guard and getting his attention with the ASP while disobeying the Masked Man's orders. Neither one of them was aware that Tolbane was awake or that he still spoke some Vietnamese too.

Tolbane lifted his head a little and quickly peeked out the window since the two weren't paying attention to him. He had an idea of where they were on Interstate 24. Then he thought about jumping them while the car was moving. He decided that was too risky, and a very bad idea since the car would lose control, so he decided to continue to feign sleep and see what happens. Maybe he could find some answers to some of the unanswered questions on his factor sheet. His head was still throbbing from its temporary loss of oxygen. He thought it may burst any second. He kept his eyes closed and relaxed as much as possible. Little by little, his head cleared of its fogginess.

They arrived at the building, and then the two carried Tolbane, clumsily due to his size and weight, inside and laid him on the floor. He listened while one of the guys told the other that since he was in charge, he would use the ASP on the ass first. He instructed his partner to stand guard outside the door, then they would switch off. Grumbling, the man, Number Fifteen, went outside and assumed a position by the door.

Number Three pulled the ASP from his hip pocket, gripping it firmly, then raised it in the air and made a hard, downward swing, which extended the ASP to its full length. As he took a step towards Tolbane and raised the ASP to strike, Tolbane jumped up, grabbed the ASP with both hands, pivoted, and shoved his backside into the guy, hard. He jerked the wand from the man's hand, causing the guy to fall, and spun around and smashed the ASP on his head with a back swing. He looked down at the guy and thought, "What the hell!" and gave him another whack. If Lizzie Borden could give extra whacks, so could he. He pulled out his cell phone and called the MNPD desk sergeant. He quietly explained what he could about the situation and about where the building was. The desk sergeant said he would call the La Vergne Police Department right away and notify Parnell. As he ended the calls, the door opened and the other guy looked inside.

When Number fifteen saw his partner lying there all bloody and Tolbane with the ASP, he turned and ran. Tolbane chased after him but was too far behind to catch up. The man jumped into the car and tore out of there, throwing up dirt and debris and leaving two deep ruts in the dirt. Tolbane stood there stomping his foot and cursing him out loud. He didn't see the man standing in the tree line observing the entire situation. That man turned and moved back through the woods and hurried to his car. He needed to leave the area and personally report this stupid idiot to the Exalted One.

Tolbane returned to the man on the floor. It was good that he wasn't dead and looked like he would survive. The guy was moaning and trying to move his limbs some but not having much success at it. Tolbane tried asking him some questions. About all he could get from the injured man were some words like, no, name, masked man, cause, exalted, beat up, and something that sounded like ass. Most of what the guy said in a mixture of Vietnamese and English just sounded like a lot of gibberish to Tolbane.

Now he could hear police sirens. Evidently the La Vergne police knew about the building. Throwing the ASP off to the side, he walked outside to greet them. As two patrol cars pulled up to the building. he could hear an ambulance coming in also. He thought out loud as usual, "Good! Maybe Numb Nuts might not die on them." The officers got out of their cars with their guns drawn hollering, "Get down on the ground asshole!" and a few other choice words. Tolbane complied. He was cuffed and searched before the officers would even talk to him. Tolbane found them to be very proficient at what they did. One of the officers waved the ambulance in after clearing the building, and the medics, one Caucasian and the other Asian-looking, entered it with a gurney and medical kits.

As one of the officers started to ask Tolbane questions, Sgt. Parnell pulled up to the building. While holding up his gold badge, his first words to the officer were, "Hey! How're you doing today? I'm sure glad you caught this guy. He's a real bad ass. He's wanted in three states. You name it, he's done it, Bank robbery, murder, and whatever. He's a hard-core dumb ass to boot. Make sure you keep him cuffed."

From the ground, Tolbane spat at Parnell, "Fuck you too, bitch!"

"Actually," Parnell explained to the Officer, "He's my buddy. Tolbane's one of us good guys and my good friend. He's helping MNPD out on a case. You can turn him loose like a long-necked goose, as the Big Bopper used to sing. He's real goosey anyway," Parnell kidded. The officer looked cockeyed at Parnell and said, "Are you shitting me? I guess it takes all kinds of clowns like him to make the world go around and around." He then un-hand cuffed Tolbane and turned him lose.

"Thanks a lot for the praise, Dip Shit. Even Ho Chi Minh wouldn't want you as a buddy!" was Tolbane's curt answer to Parnell. The La Vergne officer asked Tolbane, "What the fuck's going on here! I want some answers!" Tolbane explained everything except the pause before the second blow and the words the guy spoke. Then he and Parnell filled the officer in on the recent events with some Vietnamese, except for the Jade Cross theory. While they were discussing the situation, two more patrol cars pulled up, one from La Vergne and one from MNPD, as well as a forensic unit vehicle. Parnell greeted them and let them get to work sealing off the crime scene and doing their thing. The MNPD unit would only assist the La Vergne PD.

Tolbane, Parnell and the officer watched as the medics came out of the building pushing the gurney with the suffering Vietnamese on it. They hurriedly shoved it into the back of the ambulance and sped away with the strobe lights and siren blaring. Tolbane said aloud to no one in particular, "I sure hope that little fuck-head doesn't die on us. We need more answers than what we have up to this point. We need him to talk."

"I need you to come down to the station with me and make a statement," the Lavergne officer explained to

Tolbane. Parnell interrupted and explained that he and his buddy had police business at MNPD, out of state, and if it was alright with the officer, he would get the statement and have it delivered to the La Vergne PD in the morning.

After the officer gave it some thought he yielded, "If you're on the level I can do that, but I will check up on you."

"I wouldn't have it any other way," Parnell replied.

"OK! Go on and get out of my friggen sight then! Good hunting!"

Parnell and Tolbane got into Parnell's unmarked vehicle and left the scene and headed for the mall. Tolbane told him about the second blow with the ASP and the questioning of the guy. They both thought about the words, no, name, masked man, cause, exalted, and ass. Try as they may, neither could make heads or tails of them except maybe the ass was really about an ASP. Masked Man? It's something else to add to the puzzle and the questions, along with the fact that the building with its stacks of folding chairs looked like a meeting place.

Arriving at the mall, they went straight to Tolbane's office. Parnell said he couldn't stay long. The two buddies sat and thought some more about things. Then after discussing it, they decided that most likely a guy wearing a mask was giving orders, and the cause must relate to the Jade Cross, and that the masked man, whoever he was, must know about them. The other words made no sense unless no and name meant the masked dude had no name. It's another question to ponder. Then Parnell received a call from the MNPD desk sergeant on his cell. "The guy your friend beat the crap out of kicked the bucket on the way to the hospital. You two are stringing bodies all over the place. I don't know how the hell you do it! Have fun boys," and he hung up.

Parnell related the news to Tolbane and Tolbane replied, "Shit on a stick! That makes at least seven in the group.

Four dead, two got away—the one today didn't look like the one from the mall shooting—and a masked man. How many more are there? Oh! Two from the Missouri scene makes nine. Damn! How many more are out there? How many more might be attending meetings in that building?"

"I'm afraid to ask. I wholeheartedly agree with you. This could be a much larger group than nine. We could be facing thirty, forty, or fifty guys. I sure in the hell hope not. I really wished we could know what the hell we're facing. It's beginning to be nerve wracking and irritating for me. This old shit of our not knowing what to expect next is for the birds. It's been a huge dung heap for us. It makes a land fill look like Disney Land or Disney World in all its glory and glitter."

Tolbane thought for a moment before commenting farther, "You got that right. When those dickheads got me in that hold, I thought I was finished for good. I was really surprised when I woke up in the car's back seat. It's a sure bet they definitely were not pros. A pro would have made sure I would stay out cold and would have placed me in the car trunk. We are probably dealing with mixed talents and expendables. When that guy was running for the car, Mike Hammer would have pulled his 45 and dinged the turd in the ass before he got to it, so he would catch him and have knocked the truth out of him."

"Oh shit," complained Parnell, "Not him again. Why don't you stick Mike Hammer where the sun doesn't shine? Then you can shit him out!"

Parnell continued after a pause, "Before I forget. I got the final go ahead for the trip to Big Mo. If we leave about 2200 hours tonight, we can take turns driving and be in the Springfield, MO area around 0800 tomorrow. When we get around Rolla, MO I'll call the State Police HQ. in the Springfield, MO area. This is their case. They'll send the trooper in charge of the crime scene along with the case file, not the murder book, to meet us at the Wilson Creek Battlefield Building in the morning. He'll lead us to Light Foot's place and give us an onsite sit rep and let us look around till our hearts are content. We'll use your truck and split the gas and the food costs even Steven. Is that OK with you donkey dork?"

"I guess it will have to be alright with me. But, I'd rather that you, the real rich guy, pay for it all. I'm just a poor underpaid peon being used by an unsympathetic and abusive jerk of a cop. I'm so broke, I can't even afford to get up in the mornings, and you want me to pay for half of it. I'm so bad off I'd have to pay to move up to be poor and destitute. You're a heartless prick, you are!"

"That's the way the pretzel or the Mercedes bends old buddy!" Parnell chortled. "Hip! Hip! Hooray! for me and fuck you so very much! Speaking about food, do you think Mai would make us some of those good tuna salad sandwiches she makes to take along? She always makes good tuna salad sandwiches, no matter what kind: tuna, chicken, or turkey. They always hit the spot for me. Oh! And don't forget the coffee."

"Damn! Before I make a decision, I need to ask Mai about the arrangements for Ba. I know you have to go to Missouri, but Mai would kill me if I missed the last rites for Ba. Let me give her a call. Even if I stay here, I'm sure she'll make you some sandwiches. I know that somewhere around the house I have some arsenic to put in them. Then it's RIP for you Leather Head!"

He phoned Mai and listened to her explain the agenda. "Ba will be cremated the day after tomorrow. We will have a service in that little church-like temple in the Vietnamese housing area next Saturday. If you can't come to it because of these crimes, I'll understand. Getting Ba's killers is number one on my mind. Go with Parnell. Speaking of numbers, you Numba Ten Thousand GI! The MNPD desk sergeant just called me when you didn't bother to. I liked to have died when he enlightened what happened to you. Just so you know, your name is shit, crap, garbage, dickhead and whatever else I can call you when you get home! You got that GI? I no lub you long time, you hear No short time either?"

"Oh God, I'm sorry Mai. Things happened too fast for me today to think straight. My brain was on overload since it happened. I was going to tell you after you explained about Ba's rites. I may be Number Ten Thousand, but you're the Number One in my heart. You are the most adorable, beautiful, sexy, and the best sex partner in the whole wide world."

"Flattery will get you a lot. Why do I think you need something? Your tone of voice seemed to be begging for something more than forgiveness and sex. So, what do you need Big Boy? An acid wash for your crotch or what?"

Tolbane sighed and explained to her that since they had a few days till Ba's service he'd be going to the Big Mo with Parnell. He told her what time they would leave and what they would need, not what they'd like, for the trip. Mai consented to making the tuna salad sandwiches and coffee, then told him, "You need to get your butt home and get a nap right now if you're going to desert me in my time of need. I'll shed many, many tears of joy and sorrow till you return home to me, your most beautiful and beloved wench."

"Thanks Mai! I love you to pieces. Speaking of pieces, I'll see you very shortly as opposed to very longly! I can't wait to hug you to pieces, my piece. Bye!" He ended the call and turned to Parnell with a smile and gave him the diver's OK sign with his thumb and forefinger. "We're good to go buddy, sandwiches and coffee too! I'm following Mai's instructions and I'm going home to get some shut eye."

"All right! I'll see if I can get some kind of police watch on your place while were gone. I have to call in anyway, then I'll get some sleep too. I'll get to your place around 2145 hrs., and then we'll load, and scoot on up the road post haste. I can taste those tuna sandwiches now. I'm sure the arsenic will enhance the flavor. I'm shoving off now. I'll see you tonight," and he left.

Tolbane went to the mall security room and checked with the officer on camera duty. The officer showed him the tape of the kidnaping. Tolbane could only shake his head. Then the two checked the monitors. The parking areas seemed to be clear of any thugs on the cameras. He checked in with the officer about the day's happening around the mall. The officer said it had been very quiet all day, except for a kidnaping that morning, and he was sure that Tolbane already heard about it. Tolbane shook his head again from side to side. "Wow! You're real informative today as opposed to yesterday.

He then told the man to pass on to the others that he would be gone to the Big Mo for a few days. "And if anyone wants to know where I'm at," he told the officer, "tell them to become seduced by themselves!" He said goodbye and left the mall building, then he hopped in his pickup and was gone. His only thought was to get home, get a little, and then get some sleep, maybe. He actually drove seven miles an hour over the posted speed limit, savoring the thought of jumping Mai's bones. The going-home-after-work eastbound traffic had not begun to crowd the highway yet, so it was no problem.

Tolbane pulled onto his driveway. Instead of getting out of his truck and opening the gates, he sat in the pickup and thought some more about the morning. How did these clowns know when he was on his way to the mall? Was his house being watched? Then he remembered all the clustered trees along Beckwith Road. Could someone be watching him from there? His first thought was to get his .45 and go check it out. No, that wasn't the way. He called the MNPD desk sergeant and explained the situation to him and ask if he could call the Wilson County Sherriff's Office and request a search of that area. The sergeant. said he would call, but it would be up to the Wilson County guys to decide if they wanted to do it and when. Then he called off the dogs, opened the gates, and went in.

As usual, Mai met him at the door. They did the hug and kiss routine, carry her back in, then sit together on the couch. As Tolbane told her about the morning, Mai had a bunch of questions, some of which he had no answer to. The conversation turned to the trip to Missouri. He told her all he knew about it at that time, including Parnell trying to get a watch on the house while they were gone.

After talking about forty minutes or so, they heard what sounded like gunshots coming from the Beckwith Road area. He stood up and exclaimed, "Son of a bitch! I was right." Sitting back down, he told her about his idea on the house being watched and the call to MNPD. They speculated on what happened in the woods. Soon they heard the sirens of police cars and maybe an ambulance. A few minutes later the phone rang. Tolbane answered it.

"You were right on Tolbane," the Desk Sergeant informed him. A couple of Wilson County deputies checked out the road, found a car hidden there, then they initiated a search of the woods. Some Vietnamese-looking guy spotted them and tried to shoot it out. It didn't work for him. He's now with Buddha, his ancestors, or whomever. The deputy said the guy used a .38 Police Special and the other deputy got a slight flesh wound on his thigh and is being treated. The two deputies each got three shots into him. Then they searched farther, and found a hiding spot on a rise in line with your house, with a bolt action rifle, an old starlight scope, and binoculars. When I hear more, I'll update you through Sgt. Parnell. Check you later. Good luck on your trip!" After the Sergeant hung up, Tolbane briefed Mai on the situation. He added one more Vietnamese to the count, making it at least 10 of them in the group for sure.

He took off his clothes and leaped on the bed, and Mai only gave him a 2.2 for style and 1.1 for his technical form. Mai kept her clothes on and lay beside him. "No sex right now big boy," she said as she rubbed his chest. "You need a Numba One sleep for a Numba Ten Thousand guy. If there's time before Parnell arrives here, maybe. But I am thinking about the old Hawaiian adage, 'Comeona wanna layya!'"

"Her Highness hath spoken and I shall obey!" he quirked. He put his head on the large firm pillow and immediately fell dead asleep. Mai just grinned, covered him with a blanket, closed the door, and went to the kitchen to make the tuna salad. After opening three cans of tuna, she took out a large mixing bowl, mustard, catsup, mayo, relish, an onion, a loaf of bread, and chopped boiled eggs and went to work, humming "Paint it Black" by the Rolling Stones the whole time.

Sometimes while busy, she would start thinking about when she and Ba found things going bad in Vietnam, their country being overrun by the North, and when they had to leave there, so she would hum the old American tune that went something like, We got to get out of this place if it's the last thing we ever do. When she had first heard it as a young girl back home, she didn't care for it very much. As time went by, she could relate to it as did Vietnam veterans, and also the one about a "Bridge Over Troubled Water." She and Ba certainly had troubled waters before they knew they had to get out of that place and flee their homeland. It was funny to her that she never thought about the Vietnamese songs she learned as a little girl in the makeshift school in Saigon she had attended.

When she finished mixing the tuna with all the junk in it, as she thought of the ingredients, she made the sandwiches and placed them into the refrigerator. These guys will eat anything, no matter how raunchy. Having a second thought, she put some diet cokes in there too. She knew the guys well enough to know they would tire of drinking the coffee about half way there. Oops! She forgot to set out the large coffee pot and coffee, so she took care of that along with two thermos bottles and a canister of coffee grounds.

Seeing that she had everything ready for now, she went to the living room and turned on her favorite soap and relaxed on the sofa. She decided to call Carly and update her on the happenings. Mai got out her cell phone and made the call while leaning back on the sofa. She informed Carly about the ceremony for Ba, the day's event with her hunk, the shootout over on Beckwith Drive, and the guys' trip to Missouri. Carly said to tell them to stop by Waffle House on the way, suck up some chow and she'd take care of the bill. Mai ended the call after telling her that the guys would love that. There was no bigger chowhounds than those two, especially Tolbane the human vacuum, especially if it was free. Then as she started to watch the TV, her eyes felt heavy and eventually closed, and she went to dream land too.

It was 8:15 PM when she awoke. She turned on the living room and front door lights. She went into the bedroom, took off her clothes, and leaped on Tolbane. It scared the hell out of him and he jerked up like he was ready to fight. She pushed him back down and asked him, "Is this, maybe, time?" He looked at her and said, "You fucking 'A' lady, you fucking A!"

Afterwards they showered together then dried each other off. When they were dressed, they went to the kitchen for a snack. She made each a fried egg sandwich with a slice of American cheese and mayo and served them each a glass of milk. They rehashed that morning's and afternoon's events over the food. Mai told him about Carly's offer of the free meal for him and Parnell, and there was no doubt in her mind that he would eat more there, and she made a comment about how she hoped they had enough syrup and bacon at the Waffle House for you know who. She started the coffee after they finished their chow and the phone rang. Parnell called letting them know he was on the off-ramp to South Mount Juliet Road.

Tolbane opened the front door and worked the keypad that opened the gates and called off the dogs. Mai took advantage of this and took the bowls of food out to the dogs, which they gobbled up promptly like there wouldn't be any more tomorrow and each gave that "I need more look!" Parnell drove in and the gates closed behind him. He entered the house, closed the door, and the three greeted each other.

"I've got an update for you all plural. That means more than one person to you Travis," he said in his best Southern accent. "We have an ID on the Vietnamese the deputies killed this afternoon. Unlike the others, he had a wallet with his driver's license on him. His name is Nguyen Tam. Some detectives from the Department visited his wife with the bad news and a search warrant. His wife told the detective that her husband had been working odd hours, days and nights, for the last two weeks and she would always receive an envelope with a lot of money in the mailbox after each time he worked. The woman had no idea where the money came from because her husband refused to tell her anything about what he was working at. As of yet, I have no idea what was found there. It was all sent to the lab for evaluation. If there is anything important to know, I'll be called and briefed on it. The coroner will autopsy the body tomorrow. A preliminary check he made found there was petechial hemorrhaging in the eyes. How did that happen if he died from gun shots? Well, who knows!"

"Score one for the good guys," Mai offered to them. We got something solid out of this affair, finally. The guys agreed with her. She told Parnell about Carly's offer for free food and he said, "I guess I won't have to hit you up for a sandwich now, will I?"

"You mean I don't have to make you one? Thank goodness!"

Mai just grinned after she said it. The three went to the kitchen and packed up the sandwiches, cokes, and coffee, then lugged the stuff to the pickup. Tolbane gave her a big hug and kiss, and then they said goodbye. After they drove off, Mai secured everything, set the dogs on guard, grabbed her 9 mm, chambered a round, and went to bed early.

They guys were chattering about Carly and free food along with other things, but they were still aware that they could be followed and were very vigilant. They reached the I-40 off-ramp in Hermitage with no problem and pulled into the Waffle House parking lot, parked, and entered. Carly hugged and kissed each on the cheek in turn and told them how concerned she'd been for their safety. She seated them and brought them coffee after she gave the cook their order. They didn't have to order. She knew just what they wanted to eat. Those two clowns would eat shit if she served it to them on her bountiful bosom, in an instant.

After sating themselves with all the good chow they were fed, Tolbane having had an extra couple orders of bacon of course, the two guys hugged Carly tight again, thanked her for the chow, got another hug, said their goodbyes, and left the Waffle House and headed West on

140. The two had visually checked out the surrounding area before getting into the pickup, then they got back on the road in a cheerful mood.

Parnell stuffed his service weapon beside the seat and fell asleep right away. Tolbane turned on the disk player to hear more of *Phantom of the Opera* music, thought about a beautiful Christine, back flips, and relaxed enough to enjoy the drive. He had decided he would go out I-24 to I-57, then I-64 to 55 in Saint Louis, and then I-44 west to Springfield. From there, it would be wherever the MO State Patrol directed them.

CHAPTER 11

AFTER FLEEING FROM OBSERVING the screw up at the building in La Vergne, the Vietnamese man, the Masked Man's Number One gofer, jumped in his car and immediately sped off. He went to the Exalted One's secret house. Along the way, he had called the Masked Man on his cell phone and was instructed to meet him there. The Exalted One was pissed off big time. Thank goodness it wasn't him, Number One, that the anger would be taken out on. Those stupid guys deserved everything they would get. He could only guess at what happened inside the building. They both should have been inside to take care of things. He wondered if Number Three had been killed, and if not, did he talk about the Cause? If they'd followed their instructions, none of this would be happening. Once inside the house, he called the stupid one, Number Fifteen, on the phone as he'd been asked to do, and gave the guy the address of the house and told him to get his ass there right away to get paid. He knew what the pay would be and that was alright with him. The stupid one deserves whatever pay he gets.

Number Fifteen arrived forty-five minutes later and entered the house hurriedly while huffing and puffing from running. The Masked Man's aide told him that the Exalted

One wanted to thank him personally for his efforts. "I don't know when the Exalted One will arrive with your pay, so you can sit in his chair until then. Just relax and take it easy. No harm will come to you. You couldn't help it that Number Three screwed things up. He was the one the Exalted One put in charge, and he didn't follow the man's instructions. I think you will be well rewarded."

When he sat down apprehensively, Number Fifteen started to think about the morning's event and what had gone wrong at the building that the ass got the jump on Number Three. That big dude almost caught him. He knew he was lucky to get away.

How did they know about Number One's screw up so damn soon, and how much did they really know about it? Someone must have been watching them. He knew that looking at that huge mad man with the ASP and the bloody body of Number Three would cause anyone to run. He opined from what this man said that the Exalted One wasn't mad at him per se. That was a big relief because he had been scared of being penalized for the screwing up of Number Three. Maybe he would leave town after receiving his pay. There are a lot of places he would like to visit that have nice beaches and beautiful white women in skimpy bathing suits. He could really enjoy living that kind of life.

Now, after waiting patiently for what seemed forever to him, Number Fifteen was starting to feel a little nervous again. He'd been sitting in the man's chair for about an hour. Looking around the room, the only things that he could see were an empty living room, the curtain, and that big Vietnamese guy still standing by the door. Was this so he couldn't leave if he wanted to? Now he really felt scared. He stood up and started to walk to the door, and the big man said loudly and briskly, "Sit back down Goose! The Exalted One will be here to see you before long! He won't be happy and will throw a hissy fit if you're not here." He sat back down and fretted some more. Number One liked the term hissy fit. He thought it another funny American saying that gave him a big laugh.

Half an hour later, the big Vietnamese told the young man to get out of the chair and kneel three feet before it and lower his head. Number Fifteen complied as he was told. The Exalted One, masked as he usually was, having put his mask on outside the door, entered and went straight to his chair and sat quietly observing the now trembling, kneeling figure before him. He liked it that he could see the trembling in the man's body. Finally, the man was told to rise and stand before the Exalted One.

"I was told that the task you and Number Three were to do today was fouled up beyond belief. You must tell me all that happened, and be truthful, because I must know the facts in order to plan other tasks against that American." The Exalted One continued, "Relax now, and don't be so nervous. No one will harm you here. I know that Number Three was in charge and was responsible for the screw up. I already made plans for him, he no longer exists. Now please, start your report at the beginning!"

Number Fifteen began with the cell phone message informing them that the American was leaving his home and how he and Number Three followed the American at a safe distance because they believed he would go to the mall that time of the morning. He explained how they accomplished the kidnapping, put the unconscious American in the back seat of the sedan at Number Three's order, and drove to the old building and dragged the American inside it and threw him down.

Feeling a little braver, he prattled on boldly, "Number Three ordered me to stand guard outside and wait until he came to get me after passing on your message. I waited outside for a while, and then I heard noises like someone being beaten coming from inside the building. I believed that Number Three was completing his task. It suddenly got quiet, and I waited a long time, and when Number Three didn't come out to get me, I entered the building and saw Number Three's bloody body lying on the floor. That's when I was attacked by that American Monster, and I fought him off, leaving him lying on the floor. Then I kicked him a few times in the head to give him the message you had ordered. Then I checked on Number Three. I thought he was dead after checking his pulse, so I walked to the car and left the area." The Masked Man knew that this turd was lying big time. He had the report from the big Vietnamese, his Number One man, and he had additional information on Number Three's being taken away in an ambulance from another source. Knowing Tolbane, it was for sure that he got some information from Number Three before the police and ambulance came. What information exactly was extracted; he didn't know yet. Thankfully the idiot died in the ambulance, per his instructions, before he could be questioned further.

"You have reported the situation with vigor and confidence. I therefore commend you for being a big stupid fucking liar. I have many people observing everything that happens in pursuit of the Cause. I know everything that happened there and your cowardly action of running away while being chased by the American. Because of the incompetence of you two, the American was able to realize that his home was being watched. He called law enforcement and my observer on his home was shot and killed. I lost a good man and a good source of information. You disgust me, you are an ignorant ass!"

The Exalted One was really angry now and with a loud, sharp tone told Number Fifteen, "Kneel. Put your head down and close your eyes while I consider how much to pay you." Number Fifteen complied. The Masked Man, disgusted with this stupid ass and the day's failure, pulled his hand gun and shot the guy in the top of the head as he had done to another screw up before.

He walked to his Number One and told him, "You know what to do with that piece of shit. I'm still too angry at him to think straight. I'm leaving for home now. When you're through with this task, go on home to your woman. I'll call you in the morning to let you know what is next on the agenda. I need to relax and rest awhile. I've got a lot of thinking to do tonight." The big Vietnamese answered as usual, "Your wish will be done, oh Exalted One, and with a great amount of pleasure as usual! If anyone deserved death for his deeds, it was this dumb, cowardly turd. He'll never be found Exalted One."

"Thank you, Number One! You are my faithful rock!" With that being said, the Masked Man took off his mask and left the house. He still had a lot of anger raging inside his body. He didn't need any more screw ups like today's folly. He needed some geese that were dependable and could follow orders. While he was walking the couple of blocks to his car, his rage subsided somewhat. He was tired from the long day and looked forward to a having a long night' sleep. He got into his car, closed his eyes for a moment, shook his head, and then drove off. He made sure he didn't let his anger make him drive too fast. There were some MNPD speed traps between this location and his home, and he didn't need any pigs on his case this day.

Arriving home, he decided he needed to get things moving along. He called one of the two men who were going to Carthage, MO to get at the Priest. "Get your partner and head out to Carthage now. Things aren't going as well here as they should. I need answers from that Priest ASAP!" he ordered, then he hung up. He hoped the answers they got there would be what he needed to locate the Jade Cross. It was driving him crazy, trying to find that icon and include his hatred for the two Americans without his geese finding out he didn't believe either of them had it. He just wanted his vengeance against them.

He showered and got ready for bed. He checked all the extra door and window locks and turned in. The book he tried to read wasn't very interesting, so he laid it aside and turned off the bedside lamp. He lay there a long time trying to sleep, but his mind wouldn't let him. All of his life's events were replayed in his mind time after time. His thoughts were of the war, escaping the communists in Vietnam, hating the Americans, all of the pretending he had to do, and his life in this hated country. He must, as in his fantasy, reunite Dai Viet, Annam, and Cochin China back into Indo-China as Nguyen Hai would have done. After all, he as Tran Hung Dao, had set things in motion. After a long time of tossing and turning, he fell into an exhausted and dreamless sleep.

He awoke feeling groggy and stiff and did his morning rituals at a snail's pace. Toast, butter, jelly, peanut butter, and hot coffee made him feel better. Now he could think clearly, plan well, and get things going his way once more. He hoped the two in Missouri didn't screw up too. Those two knew a little more about him and the Cause than the other dumb geese. When they returned, he needed to have a heart-to-heart talk with them and find out how serious their dedication is to the Cause. If he didn't like their answers, he would have his Number One man take care of them for good.

He took his cell phone from the charger and called the MNPD. When the desk sergeant answered, he asked to speak to the Vietnamese officer. The Desk sergeant wanted to know who he was, and he answered, "I'm his cousin, Nguyen." He thought to himself that the name Nguyen always worked with Americans. It was probably the Vietnamese name they heard the most. When the Vietnamese officer answered, the Exalted One ordered the officer, "I need an update now. Things haven't gone too well the last couple of days and I must redo my plans somewhat. It is essential I know exactly what the Americans know or don't know about my search for the Jade Cross and for their demise. You have given me much valuable information in the past that was useful and I thank you for that."

The officer gave him an update on how Number Three died in the ambulance by his man, how his surveillance man was killed by the Wilson County Sherriff's Department Deputies, an officer being wounded in the process, and the man's wallet and ID had been found on him. When asked about Tolbane and Parnell, he offered, "Last night they left town and are going to Springfield, MO, to check on the body your men left there after questioning the guy. They're going to meet a MO State trooper there at the crime scene. They'll probably be back tomorrow night or the next morning. It most likely will be the latter. If there any updates come in for them on the situation, the MNPD Desk Sergeant will call me and update me. That's all the info I have for now. I'll contact you later on when they return, if they do return."

"Thanks!" the Exalted One said. He ended the call and put the cell phone in his pocket. He sat in his recliner and contemplated things anew. After some thought, he took out his cell phone and called the two guys in Missouri on their cell phone again. He warned them about the two Americans going to Springfield area, gave them a slight change to his plan, and told them that he may have additional instructions for them later. He reemphasized their need for secrecy and caution and warned them not to screw up this important task. He pocketed his cell phone, laid back, closed his eyes, and nodded off.

He awoke feeling dopey and drugged out. Shaking his head to clear it, he got up and stretched with his arms over his head. Suddenly, relaxing some, he knew what to do. He walked out to his car, and while just sitting behind the steering wheel, he called the two in Missouri on their cell phone. After giving them additional instructions about the two Americans, he started the car and left the house. He was going to check out the area on Beckwith Road where his man had been killed if there was no police presence with their stupid yellow crime scene tape that they had surely placed there.

Maybe while there, he could take a quick look at Tolbane's house from the wooded area too. He might even see the beautiful Mai if she came outside to check on the dogs or whatever. He hoped so because he missed her very much. He knew she would be alone, and that suited him. Even though he could care less what eventually happened to Tolbane or that Parnell on his orders, he would never let any harm come to her. He hated the idea that she could share her bed with any American, let alone the hated Tolbane. She should have had a nice Vietnamese husband and several kids by now. She would be worshiping ancestors if her head and her ass were screwed on straight. He was going to fix that for sure. She was his true love. He knew she loved him too and she would realize that when he would bring her to her senses. Also, he still couldn't understand why she would want to live in the middle of nowhere in the old Belinda City area of Mount Juliet instead of in a nice city area amid her own Vietnamese people and the one who truly loved her.

Arriving at the wooded area on Beckwith Road, he could see no sign of law enforcement or yellow tape, so he parked the car, got out his binoculars, and wandered into the tree line. Several meters in, he found the observation spot on a rise and sighted in on Mai and Tolbane's house. Everything seemed quiet and serene, and the dogs were grabbing at a cloth toy and chasing each other around the enclosed yard, each trying to take the toy from the other. They were both beautiful dogs. He'd never hurt them either. Dogs were like children. They just wanted to play ball, chase sticks, and please their master or mistress.

He suddenly got the idea to place punji pits around Tolbane's house then thought better of it. Mai or the dogs could become impaled in one of them. That he couldn't live with. He'd rather cut off his right arm than hurt one of them. He considered ordering his next man, maybe Number Five or Number Six, who would be watching the house to make a lot of different traps around the house's area, but he gave that up for the same reasons. Besides, Tolbane and Parnell may not make it back from Missouri if those two geese got the job done right and with a little extra pizazz.

Suddenly he had to rethink what he'd ordered. He hoped that the two men would miss Tolbane and Parnell. Damn! One of those two may have his answer to the missing Jade Cross. What was he thinking, wanting to send them to hell before getting his answer? He must learn to keep his personal feelings out of the plan. He tried to call the two in Missouri, but there was no answer and his call went straight to voice mail. He hoped they were busy with the Priest as he left a voice mail.

Having watched the house for a time, and with no sighting of Mai, he decided he may as well go back to Nashville. He sighed and then wandered back to his car on Beckwith Road. On the way back to Nashville, he drove a little below the speed limit, trying to think, and the traffic was passing him like he was sitting still. For whatever reason, his mind seemed to be a bit foggy and blank. When he arrived at his house, he felt relaxed again, checked his mail box—no mail—and then lost no time in sitting in his recliner and falling asleep.

The Masked Man didn't know his presence had been noticed in the tree line by Mai and that he'd barely left when a patrol car arrived to check the woods.

Mai wanted to give the dogs some treats, but she was cautious. She got her binoculars and looked at the tree line through the closed blind slats. While scanning the tree line where the Vietnamese had been killed, she saw what looked like the sun's reflections on binoculars. "Shit!" she cursed in a loud voice. She went to the phone and called the County Sherriff's Office and reported what she saw in the tree line. She was assured a unit would be there post haste. Twenty minutes later, she received a call from the County Dispatcher and was given an update. The dispatcher told her the woods were clear now, but it looked like someone had been there in the same nook the earlier observer had been using. She also indicated that a patrol unit would check that area periodically and would inform Mai of any change of the status.

She felt a little better now, put on her side arm, and took treats out to the dogs and joined in their playing. Sometimes, she thought, she would go crazy if not for the dogs. They were a big part of her and Tolbane's family. Someday maybe there would be an addition to it also. Lately, for some reason, she felt like she would like to be a mother, and she knew just who could make that dream come true. She could just see Tolbane cringing while changing a smelly, dirty diaper and trying to hold his nose at the same time. Maybe if it were a boy, he'd get the golden shower he so rightly deserved. She laughed out loud at the thought of him getting drenched by his offspring. She would laugh and rib him about it until the cows came home and the chickens went to roost. She could call him her "Golden Boy" after the golden shower. She giggled a bit and went on with her daily tasks.

She wondered what Carly would think of her having a baby or two. Would she think that her big lug would be too old to father a child or be a part of a child's life, or would she think he would be a great father to their child? She thought a little more and decided that based on the way he treated her and the dogs, he would be the greatest dad their children could ever have. Even though they had talked about having children, they had not done anything toward it. Maybe she should take the bull by the horn, or should she be thinking of grabbing him by his horn. Maybe even toot it a little bit. The idea sounded okay to her.

She called Carly to ask what she thought about it. She valued and trusted her input on things very much. Carly is a knowledgeable and experienced woman.

CHAPTER 12

TOLBANE AND PARNELL MADE good time driving, even though Tolbane stopped at each rest stop they passed. They would relieve themselves, drink a little coffee, chat some, and hit the road. At a rest stop on I-64 in Illinois, about 26 miles, give or take, east of Saint Louis, MO, they stopped and took care of their bladders and then had their trip's treat. A couple of tuna salad sandwiches apiece and ice cold sodas. Parnell really dug into his. Mai's tuna salad sandwiches were worth dying for two times over. Her mixture of mayo, catsup, mustard, relish, diced onions, diced peppers, and chopped boiled eggs was top of the line for any self-appointed tuna salad connoisseur such as himself. He had hoped Tolbane wouldn't want any of the sandwiches, but he was completely shit out of luck about that idea.

After they were done eating and Parnell took the wheel. Their next stop would be a Quick Mart off Hampton Road on the west side of St. Louis, MO, just off I-44, to get gas and some fresh Krispy Kreme delights. As early in the morning as it was, the traffic was very light going through the big city and the stop came quickly. The next stop after that would be at a small rest stop about 57 miles west of St.

Louis, MO, on I-44. Then it would be a very long drive to the next one. The State of Missouri did not have but two rest stops on the route to the next state. After that rest stop, Tolbane put his seat back and slept.

Just past Rolla, MO, Parnell pulled to the side of the road and made his call to the Missouri State Police Department in Springfield and made the arrangement for meeting the trooper at the Wilson Creek Battlefield National Park. The call woke Tolbane up, so he got out a couple of sodas and filled donuts, and they munched out while they continued on their way. After his snack was gone and his soda drank, Tolbane drifted back to sleep and with a smile on his face dreamed of back flips once again. Parnell looked at him sleeping with a silly grin on his face and just shook his head.

Around 35 miles past Rolla, Parnell looked in the rearview mirror and saw flashing blue & white lights. He pulled to the side of the road and stopped, and the flashing blue lights pulled in behind them. Parnell nudged Tolbane in the ribs, waking him, and told him to get out the registration paper and insurance card. He got out his driver's license and gold badge. A Trooper left his car after a couple of minutes and approached the driver's side. Parnell put down the window and said good evening to the trooper and asked if there was a problem. The trooper said, "Yes there is, and as a matter of fact, you're really driving too damn slow!" Parnell and Tolbane both had a stunned look on their faces. "I'm Trooper McCabe, and I'm your escort to Wilson Creek Battlefield Park. I was told before my shift that you'd be coming through here. I was sitting at the top of the on-ramp back there and got the call just before you drove past me. You guys must be pretty important to get a high-speed escort!"

Parnell showed the trooper his badge and ID and introduced Tolbane to him. He explained that they were investigating murders around Nashville, TN, that they believed there was a Vietnamese connection to them, that they were being targeted, and that they might personally be connected to the one here in Missouri. Hearing their story, the trooper said, "Sometimes you think you've heard it all, but this takes the cake. You two follow me. We'll be doing about 85 or so, and I'll slow a few mph at a few curves. I'm damned sure this crate will keep up." Remembering he saw a USMC sticker on the rear window of the pickup beside the gold Eagle, Globe, and Anchor painted on the two doors, he said, "By the way, Semper Fi, Jarheads! Do or Die! Eat the apple and fuck the Corps and all that horse shit. I love it." After those comments, the State Trooper got in his car, pulled in front of them, turned on the strobe lights and siren, and took off like a bat out of hell, leaving smoke and a couple of tons of rubber behind. He didn't care at all. The state paid for the tires.

Parnell looked at Tolbane and said, "How about that! Can you believe all this crap we get into sometimes? We found another screwed up Jarhead like you." Then he put the pedal to the metal of the 5.9 and it took off like a rocket, and sped off after the trooper. After nodding up and down, Tolbane just put the seat back again and was immediately in dreamland once again.

When they came to exit 70, they turned south on 1-60, took it down to Road FF, then road 182 to the Wilson Creek National Battlefield Park, which was about three miles east of Republic, MO. They arrived at the Battlefield entrance about 8:00 AM. Then Trooper McCabe turned around, drove slowly by them, saluted and waved, and was gone with another screech of tires and a blink of an eye.

The National Park Service protects, oversees and controls visitors to the bloodied grounds where Union troops, commanded by Brigadier General Nathaniel Lyon, who had divided the force at the urging of Col. Franz Sigel, attacked a larger Confederate force, Commanded by Major General Sterling Price, at Wilson Creek, about 10 miles southwest of Springfield, MO, on August 10, 1861. One purpose of the battle had to do with control of the state and the pro-Union stance of the governing body of the state of Missouri. The battle turned into a disaster for the Union force because Sigel had convinced Lyon to split his force and attack from two different areas. Sadly, General Lyon was killed in the battle and Sigel was lucky to make it back to Springfield alive, then on to Rolla where the Union troops had a camp.

Parnell drove on into the lot by the visitor's center building and saw another state trooper sedan parked by the entrance. He parked in a visitor slot. They got out of the green machine, stretched, stomped the stiffness out of their legs, and then went inside. The two were surprised. The trooper was a good-looking lady, about five feet six or five feet seven, raven haired, with a chest any man could dream about. Her uniform was neat and well fitting, her Smokey Bear hat was tilted slightly, and she had a big grin on her face. After Tolbane, his mind wondering about back flips, told her that they were her guys, she reached out her hand and said, "I'm Trooper Sgt. Candice Brown. Sorry for the grin. The park ranger over there just told me a dirty story. It's the kind of story that's not for virgin ears." The two guys knew they were going to like this trooper. Once again, Tolbane wondered if she really could do back flips.

Parnell showed her his gold shield, then gave her their names and briefly explained the weird circumstances leading up to this investigative trip. Sgt. Brown took them to the ranger's break room, got out her notepad, and asked for more details after getting them each a cup of freshly brewed coffee. The two guys took turns telling her of their experiences with the Vietnamese in Nashville, chronologically. She nodded her head at the telling of each event while taking notes. When the guys were done, she explained what she could about Light Foot's murder. She indicated she had a written report for Parnell in her sedan and offered to drive them to the scene. They accepted the ride. The house was a few miles away towards Republic, MO, and it took no time at all to get there with Sgt. Brown's heavy foot on the accelerator pedal, the same as Trooper McCabe. Parnell didn't have much time to read the report. It seemed like he no more started reading it and they arrived at their destination.

The house was a small place, it had two bed rooms, one bath room, complete with just a living room and a kitchen, placed on a one-and-a-half acre lot. A 1995 Red Ford Ranger sat on the stone drive in front of the attached garage. Looking around the area, they could see the neighboring houses were far apart, but close enough to see any goings on. Sgt. Brown pointed to one house to their left and stated, "The lady in that house went out to get her morning paper at the end of her driveway, and on her way back to the house noticed two Asian-looking men leaving this house, one carrying what looked like rifles or shotguns. With the sun not very high in the sky, she could only say that their car was a dark-colored four door sedan, possibly a Ford Victoria. Other than that, she didn't know very much more. She's the one who called 911 to report a break in when she saw them."

She took out a key and led the guys into the house, and they followed her into the kitchen. On the wood slat floor were pools of dried blood and holes in the floor where the spikes had been driven in to the hands and feet, and were cut out to retrieve his body. The spikes and pieces of floor had been transported to the morgue still attached to the body as had been done with Ba. "The coroner has finished his difficult autopsy. He died of significant exsanguination from his stab and cut wounds and the near decapitation of the head. The body was picked up by a body transportation service last night. I think it was being taken to Fort Smith or Little Rock, I forget which, to his aunt and uncle's place. They seem to be his only family. I can find out for you if you need that info. So, you two knew him. Sorry for your loss guys."

The two acknowledged her thoughtfulness. Then Tolbane and Parnell wandered throughout the house, checking everything as they went. The living room was really sparse. It had a recliner, a sofa, an end table, a lamp, coffee table, and a console with a 27" TV. There were framed citations for bravery, promotions, and his boot camp picture on the walls. The kitchen had the usual appliances: a microwave, a coffee maker, and a blender on the counter. The cabinets and drawers had nothing unusual in them, just the typical canned and dry foods, dishes, silverware, and what not. The fridge had several items for salads deteriorating, and some drinks that were bio-degrading from age.

The first bedroom held a double bed, a table on each side with one drawer and a lamp, and a large five-drawer dresser. The dresser, as well as the bedroom closet, was filled with clothes. Some things that stood out to the guys were the fact that there were no guns to be found, no landline phone, and no cell phone. "Knowing Light Foot, I'm sure he'd have one or more guns and at the least a cell phone," Parnell mused.

They moved on to the second bedroom, where he must have spent a lot of leisure time. There were two book cases with a variety of books, novels, and keepsakes on top, a few old pictures of him in the Corps, a floor lamp in a corner, and a recliner next to it. On the other side of the room sat a desk with a computer and printer. There were a couple of books for dummies, and IN and OUT baskets beside of it. Leafing through the papers in the baskets produced nothing except bills and correspondence. In the main desk drawer were utility bills, bank statements, and house loan papers. The other drawers just had junk items in them. The closet had odds and ends of clothing and boxes filled with his lifelong memorabilia and an old Marine Corps Dress Blue uniform with stripes and hash marks covered with a clear plastic bag from some cleaners.

Parnell asked about weapons. Sgt. Brown informed them, "Background checks showed he had a concealed carry permit, two 9mm handguns, an imitation AK-47, and a 10-gauge pump shotgun. He did have a cell phone with Verizon, but no land line. None of these items were found in the house, garage, or Ford Ranger. There's not much except tools and junk in the garage, and nothing in the Ford Ranger that provided anything of use. It's for sure the Asians took the weapons and cell phone and probably any loose cash he might have had around. The neighbors on both sides said he was protective of his weapons, had a lot of ammo, and went hunting or fishing sometimes on weekends. One of the guys he worked with said he would go target shooting at a local firing range on occasion. I can't tell you much more than that. We've no leads to follow except two Asians and a dark car that looks like a Ford. No one could identify the license plate number on the car or even what state it was from. That's about it. All I have in one nutshell."

Parnell pondered a bit, looked at his buddy, and asked, "Well Tolbane, you got any questions?"

"I can't think of anything else. I think we're at a dead end here, just like we are in Nashville." Tolbane answered.

As Sgt. Brown was about to suggest leaving, there was a sudden burst of automatic rifle fire and projectiles bursting through the walls, breaking windows, and chopping up the inside of the house. They hit the deck and kept their heads and butts buried in the carpet. They heard a car peel out, and they rushed outside in time to see a dark sedan racing off. Sgt. Brown took her handheld FM radio from her hip and called the State Police Dispatcher and reported the shooting, and as she ran to her cruiser, she shouted, "Come on guys! Jump in!" They piled into her car, and she took off like a bat out of hell with flashing lights and siren wailing. Tolbane in the back and Parnell in the passenger seat lost no time fastening their seat belts and praying for the best.

The car they were chasing was stopped at a traffic light at the intersection of Elm Street and Road ZZ. The driver, hearing the siren and seeing the flashing lights approaching fast in the rearview mirror, swung around the cars at the light and darted through oncoming traffic and made a left turn onto Road ZZ. The traffic stopped and pulled aside for the state police vehicle as it followed the car to the left, nearly tipping over on the fast turn. The pursued vehicle turned left on Road M and then right on Road MM, heading toward exit 70 on I-44. Throughout the pursuit, Sgt. Brown kept radio contact, relaying locations and her direction of travel to the dispatcher. Meanwhile, State and local Police units were responding to the situation.

A local Police and a State unit in the area had pulled across Road MM, blocking access to the east and westbound I-44 ramps and backing up the traffic. The speeding shooter's car was traveling too fast to control, and when the driver tried to swing around the stacked-up cars, he swerved into a wooded area and smashed grill first into a tree, wrapping the front around it, with the headlamps nearly touching each other, the hood springing up, and the motor shoved back into the passenger compartment. Neither occupant had his seat belt on, and they were catapulted into the windshield and blood spattered all over the interior. The passenger was impaled halfway through the window and was still breathing, despite his head and body wounds. The driver's head had only smashed the window, but he had severe head trauma, maybe a broken neck, mangled legs from the engine, and his rib cage had been smashed and penetrated by the steering wheel column so he couldn't inhale or exhale. He was dead as hell. Tolbane, as he looked at the dead Vietnamese, thought about his earlier feelings about being dead as hell when Ba was murdered. He said out loud to no one in general, "What goes around comes around assholes. No Amen will ever be given here for this guy."

Several local and state officers had arrived and were gathering around the totaled wreck now, and the wail of an ambulance and an accompanying fire truck could be heard in the distance. Looking into the wreck, one could see the back seat leaning against the front seats, strewn with empty fast-food containers, a couple AK-47s, spent rounds, loaded magazines, boxes of ammo, clothes, Vietnamese newspapers and other junk.

Sgt. Brown, who was the first Officer involved in the shooting and chase, took charge. She had the local and state cops to get the stalled traffic going to the interchange and block the rest of the oncoming traffic. Her first problems were keeping the crime scene intact, getting pictures until a crime unit could process it, and extracting the wounded Asian in the window before the coroner got there for the other guy. She directed a couple of officers to string yellow crime scene tape a fair distance from the wreck. Tolbane looked at the guy in the window, who had just started to moan, and said to a couple of state troopers, "Hey there, have you guys ever heard Patty Page's song about the Doggie in the Window?" The Troopers gave him a weird look and walked away. Tolbane with his weird sense of humor wondered aloud if he could write a new hit song, "How Much Is that Vietnamese Guy in the Window? The One Without a Waggly Tail."

One local officer was walking around the back of the vehicle and voiced aloud, "Everybody please be still for a minute!" As everyone quieted down to see what was happening, a banging noise from the trunk could be heard. One Officer jerked the driver's door open and reached into the car and retrieved the key chain from the ignition. He walked around to the rear and opened the trunk. To everyone's surprise, there was a Vietnamese Catholic priest, in his black, fatherly garb with the white collar and a large gold cross on a chain around his neck, duct taped by his legs, hands, and mouth in it. The officers pulled him from the trunk, cut him free, and helped him to his feet, a little banged up and shaken, but nothing for the worse. He immediately placed his hands in a praying position in front of his face and started bowing, thanking, and blessing each and every officer for his rescue. He spoke very good English but still inserted a Vietnamese phrase every now and then. As the priest was offering his gratitude, Parnell asked Tolbane if the priest looked familiar. Tolbane took a closer look and nodded affirmatively. Parnell, a little stunned, said, "That's got to be one of the Vietnamese officers in charge of the ARVN unit we wanted blown away when we found the Jade Cross."

"Damn it! It sure does looks like him. Shit, it is him. He's stayed thinner and trimmer than us. I think you've nailed it again. We need to talk to this guy big time. This confirms we're on the right track about the Jade Cross being at the bottom of this fiasco."

Parnell called Sgt. Brown over to them, and they discussed the situation with her and asked permission to talk to him. She was amazed when she learned that the two knew the priest from Vietnam and that they would have liked to have kicked his butt up onto his shoulder blades. They also wanted to talk to the other Vietnamese if he lives. This was one strange happening, and it was getting weirder every minute. Never in her fifteen-year career could she ever dream this shit up. It was like one of those off the wall mystery novels selling for a dime at a yard sale.

"Shit! Damn it all to Hell!" she commented. "This is really all screwed up. You two have no authority here, yet it involves your case and our State's too. The priest is a material witness in an alleged kidnapping and an attempted drive by murder and other charges that other Vietnamese clown faces. I can't legally let you talk to the priest or the other dude. I need to call my supervisor and have her come here. She's the one who's in contact with your department and arranged to allow you to come here and inspect our crime scene and get a copy of the report. It's a good bet she can give you guys permission to speak with the priest in keeping good faith with the MNPD. As for the Viet, I have no idea what can be done. She can work on that angle too." She took her radio from its holster and made the call. She smiled at them and jokingly said, "If you want to, however, you two can interrogate the driver all you want. He may not cooperate much though."

Tolbane groaned, then smiled back at her and said, "Thanks a fucking lot Sarge. I'll need chains, a board, and a few gallons of water, or maybe even a rack and an iron maiden. Maybe even get a lit josh stick to shove up his butt. He'll talk or else!" Enjoying the banter, Parnell agreed aloud with his dumb-assed buddy and even laughed a little bit.

"I don't know what to think of you two jokers. I don't know if you're for real or not, but I think it would be interesting to work with you. You seem to have a penchant for intrigue and adventure. It doesn't seem to bother either of you to step in shit. Whenever you do, you'll come out smelling like a rose I bet. It's for sure we'd have each other's six." As Sgt. Brown finished her sentence, fire and rescue arrived and parked by the ambulance.

They stood and watched as the local fire and rescue extricated the moaning and wailing man from the windshield by breaking it away from the guy. Then the crew broke away as much glass as they could from his body. They didn't try to remove glass shards stuck in the man, leaving that task for a doctor. It was obvious that they were very experienced at their job, probably from a lot of work on the interstate. The guy was then put on a gurney with an oxygen mask, strapped down, and whisked away in an ambulance with the medics treating him as best that they could. The two from Tennessee wondered if the guy would live, and if he did, what kind of info he would provide. They both also remembered another Vietnamese that had head injuries and gored by the post being taken away in an ambulance and expired on the way to a hospital. Parnell remembered seeing the Asian medic getting into the back of the ambulance with that dude. He would check on that medic when they got back. He whispered his thoughts on that in Tolbane's ear.

Sgt. Brown stepped away to take an incoming call on her cell phone. She listened intently and spoke animatedly for a few minutes. After the call ended, she motioned Tolbane and Parnell over and informed them, "That was my supervisor. She's going to check higher up the line to figure out what to do. She wants us to wait here until she can arrive. The dear Lord only knows when that will be. Let's sit in the unit and be comfortable while we wait, and you can finally look over that report."

As they were walking to the car, the Vietnamese priest noticed them, walked over, and stopped them before they reached the patrol car. He looked curiously at the two guys and said, "Please excuse me! You two look very familiar. Have we ever met before, perhaps maybe at a mass or some other place?"

Parnell was in the process of telling the priest that they had indeed met some other place, but before Sgt. Brown had the chance to intervene, Tolbane told the Priest, "You're damn right we met before! I wanted to kill your ass. You and your dumb-assed ARVNs knew damn well who you were shooting at!" The priest's eyes got big and his mouth gaped open. Parnell stepped between them and gently pushed his friend aside. "Cool it Travis! Let's talk to him civilly and not stir up any shit. It has to mean something if these clowns kidnapped him. We need his answers, not his anger."

"I guess you're right. Father, forgive me for flying off the handle. That day has haunted me since it happened," Tolbane apologized.

As Parnell pushed Tolbane aside, Sgt. Brown knew she could not now keep them apart now. She decided she would just listen close, learn a little more, and maybe get a better handle on the situation.

"I don't know your names, but the tall one is right," he said to Parnell. "That day has always bothered me too. I was not an honorable man that day, I lost face with myself. My Captain, who stayed in the background that day, ordered us to fire high over your patrol's heads, and then when you made contact with us, he forced me to meet with you. You see, I knew he was a VC infiltrator who hated Americans and I was weak and unworthy, did nothing, and gave the orders as he wanted. The only thing that went my way was that none of your Marine troops were wounded or killed.

I was really surprised at your fire discipline. Please forgive me for my actions. I've prayed for my redemption of that day and others many times over."

Tolbane thought for a minute then said to him, "I'm Travis Tolbane, retired Marine and a Civilian now, and my partner and friend here is still a Marine at heart, Sgt. Jim Parnell, a detective from Metropolitan Nashville Police Department in Tennessee. I didn't know about your captain's orders. I'm sorry to hear you were put in that kind of situation. Please accept my apology. I think we both have carried a great burden over that day and it's time to put an end to it."

The priest placed his palms together in a praying mode and replied, "I am Father Hung Phat. My son, you are forgiven for your outburst, but I still feel that I deserved it. Later on, in the conflict, during an operation up North by the Khe San Marine Base, I made sure the traitorous Captain, with part of his skull and brains scattered in the dirt, met with his Viet Cong ancestors for eternity, but it didn't ease my mind for all the things I had let him get away with. The incident with you was not the only one. I also think he betrayed other ARVN units too. If I could have gotten more evidence on him, I would have turned him in. I should have dispatched him to whatever great beyond much sooner than I did. Even though he deserved it. I have paid penance for my actions.

"Now tell me how you two happened to be here. You must surely have been a part of my rescue, and I don't know how you fit in, but you deserve my most humble thanks. I will pray for you in all of my prayers and thank the Lord for bringing us together to relieve this burden of ours, and for the rescue of this unworthy one. I was truly afraid for my physical well-being this day, and having been kidnapped, bound, and tossed about in the darkness of the trunk was a terrible experience. I'll have bruises all over my body for a month or more. I'm so happy one of the officers heard me kicking on the trunk lid with my bound feet. It was like Heaven to see daylight and friendlies again. I can't imagine why someone would want to kidnap me. All they said to me was that they would talk to me after taking care of some business up the road just before putting down the trunk lid."

Tolbane and Parnell sympathized with the priest. Then Parnell took the lead and told the priest what had been happening with the Vietnamese gangsters in Nashville, TN, the murders in TN and MO, the shooting at Light Foot's, the chase, the vehicle's crash, and then how they believed the Jade Cross they found and reburied in Vietnam was the direct cause for the mayhem. The priest listened to him intently. He realized he was now a part of this weird fiasco because he was there when the Jade Cross was found also.

"Well," said the Priest, "'It looks like another fine mess we're in with together,' said Ollie to Stan. That's what Ollie always said to Stan isn't it? 'Another fine mess you got us into.' I guess we could say, 'One for All, All for One or something.'" Parnell groaned his usual groan while shaking his head from side to side. Not another quippier like Tolbane.

CHAPTER 13

Sgt. Brown's supervisor, Lt. Jane Jeckel, finally arrived as Parnell was finishing his story to the priest. She looked to be a couple of inches shorter than Sgt. Brown. She had coal black hair, clipped short, and no makeup on. She was becoming a little rotund, and her uniform was getting really tight around the middle and a little too tight in the big butt. Tolbane thought she definitely wasn't nearly as good looking as Sgt. Brown. That's for sure. As a matter of fact, he thought her face had stopped a fast-moving freight train doing 110 mph. No thoughts of back flips came to his mind with this one.

Lt. Jeckel started things off as soon as she left her car, "All right Sgt. Brown, what in the hell's going on here, and who are these weird ass dudes? Oh! Right! I know! You two must be the dicks from Nashville, and you, Father, are you here to give somebody their Last Rites?"

"Calm down, Lt. Jane. Let me take it from the beginning so you get a good picture of the events of today. You're not going to believe what a dung heap we got going here. It's unbelievable, truly. First, this is Sgt. Parnell of MNPD and his side kick, Travis Tolbane, a mall security manager. The priest here, Father Hung Phat, is the kidnap victim from Carthage, MO. I haven't had the chance to hear his story yet. That Ford Victoria over there is a total wreck. It contained one shooter DOA and one shooter badly injured while stuck half way through the windshield. He is now on the way to a hospital in Springfield, but I don't know if he'll make it or not. I'm not sure of the priest's involvement yet, his is a separate crime committed in Carthage, but it started for us while I was showing these two dudes the crime scene house." Sgt. Brown continued to relate the checking of the house, the shooting, the chase, the blockade of the I-44 ramps, and the crash. She described the occupant's positions in the wreck and their apparent injuries and how the priest had been kidnapped and was found in the trunk. "It's a good thing one of the local officers had good hearing, or the priest would still be in there and thrashing around," she concluded.

"Well Father," Lt. Jeckel said to the priest, "What's going on with you? Are you okay from your ordeal?" Father Hung Phat seemed a little nervous and slightly hesitant to answer her. "Just relax Father. Clear your mind and think for a moment. Try to be as precise as you can so we don't have to repeat too much here."

"I had just parked at 1900 Grand Avenue in Carthage," the Priest began. "I was on my way into the Immaculate Heart of Mary Shrine when the guys in the wreck there jumped me and put me in a not-too-good sleeper hold. The next thing I knew, my mouth, hands, and feet were duct taped and I was being put in the car trunk. Then I was being tossed around in the trunk. After a long ride, I heard gun shots and then a chase was on. I could tell we were going fast, and I could hear a police siren behind us. The next thing I remember was a sudden stop and a crashing sound and flying into the trunk wall. I was stunned a bit, and then I heard voices so I started kicking the trunk lid as hard as I could. It worked! I was rescued. That's all I know. I again thank and pray for everyone involved in my rescue."

Finishing his story, the Priest asked of the group, "I have a question. Do any of you know if the deceased individual in the wreck was a Catholic? If he is, may I have permission to give him his Last Rites?"

The other four looked at Father Hung Phat like he was crazy. Being a little more level-headed, Sgt. Brown called one of the troopers over and asked him to check the body to see if there was a crucifix around the dead one's neck, and if not to check for any ID or whatever to see if his religion was stated. While waiting for the officer, Lt. Jeckel explained to the priest that he would need to come to the state trooper's headquarters and give a written account of the kidnapping, and then, after giving his statement, she would get him a ride back to Carthage with one of the troopers. She then informed the priest that someone in Carthage had seen his abduction and had reported it to the police there, who informed the state police, who put out a state-wide BOLO (be on the lookout for) on the Ford Victoria.

That's why the state and local cops were close enough to blockade the road in front of the ramps. They had been looking for the car in case it came this way. When they heard the pursuit on the radio, they knew what to do. Lt. Jeckel asked Sgt. Brown to call the dispatcher and have her pass on to the Carthage Police Department that the victim was safe, sound, in their custody, and she also told her to update them on the status of the kidnappers. Sgt. Brown stepped away to make the call.

Tolbane and Parnell had been quiet and listening closely to the priest's story. Then the lieutenant asked them to bring her up to date on the crimes. The two took turns relating things from present to the past, and when they got to the part about them knowing the Priest from a patrol in Vietnam, and the possibility of the Jade Cross that was found as being the root cause of the troubles, Lt. Jeckel felt like she was going to have diarrhea or, at the least, the vapors. All she could see in her mind were mounds of paperwork stacking up and the possibility of working in concert with the Carthage Police and the case being screwed up big time because of the different jurisdictions. To top it off, she was getting a bad headache again. She just wanted to be home, sitting at beside her pool drinking a beer, any kind of beer, and listening to her favorite heavy metal radio station. Even as far as listening to 'Ina goda Divita' by the iron Butterfly. Sgt. Parnell addressed the lieutenant about their speaking with the priest. "We need to talk with the good Father about the happening that day in Vietnam and the possible connection of it to our crimes here. Sgt. Brown didn't know if it would be in the best interest of the investigation for us to do so. Under the circumstances, she felt we should seek your permission to do so."

"After Sgt. Brown called me about it, I called my Captain and asked what the procedure would be. He told me that if the Priest was a kidnap victim and not part of our shooting incident, it would be my call. Since hearing your side of things, I think it's probably the right thing to do. I have no legal hold on the Father; I only need his statement. He's committed no crime, free of all sin that I'm aware of." She continued, "You guys can talk with him all you want until I'm ready for him to be transported to headquarters. So, be my guest."

Sgt. Brown saw the trooper walking towards them and ambled over to meet him. She returned with the answer to the Priest's question. "The trooper couldn't find anything that would indicate the dead man's religion, Father."

Answering her, Father Hung Phat mused aloud, "He might be a Buddhist, a Cao Die, a Hoa Hau, or a follower of some lesser Vietnamese religion. I'll pray for him just the same." The priest put his palms together, closed his eyes, bowed his head, and said a silent prayer for his abductor.

Once the prayer was said, Lt. Jeckel took Sgt. Brown by the arm and led her away and towards the wreck to check it out. The three veterans brought together during the terrible conflict was left together to hash out some answers.

Tolbane inquired of the Priest, "Do you know anything at all about the Jade Cross at all, Father? We can't understand anything that's been happening to us."

"When I was a child growing up and in school in Hue City, there were stories about a secret Christian Society which had an invaluable Jade Cross for its icon. Today, that would be like an organization's logo, shield, icon, or whatever. It was told to me that the Jade Cross was revered by all belonging to that society and that its members would die with honor to protect it. The stories always pointed to the fact that no one outside of the society knew its name. For all intents and purposes, it had no name."

"One of the stories I was told was of a man and a woman going on a perilous journey to receive the Jade Cross from a Chinaman. They faced, as I can remember, many hardships and fights during their trek. I don't remember where that place was or the hardships they endured delivering it to the society. I don't remember the names of the two heroes either, but they were highly esteemed and rewarded by the society members. I think the society's leader was named Nguyen Hai.

"Also, I heard that Tran Hung Dao, actually born Prince Tran Quoc Tuan, a heroic Vietnamese General who defeated three Mongol invasions twice at the end of the 13th Century, was worshiped by the society as a god-like figure. He incorporated tactics of Ngo Quyen and used guerrilla tactics to defeat the Mongols. Many think he pioneered 'hit and run' or guerilla warfare as well as booby traps. These same tactics were used by North Vietnamese General Vo Nguyen Giap in his struggles against the Japanese, the French, and at the last, the Americans. In fact, there are places in Vietnam today that still celebrate General Trung Hung Dao. When he died, he was posthumously bestowed the title 'Hung Dao Dai Voung'[27] by the Emperor for his brilliance in defending Dai Viet during his lifetime.

"No outsider, as the legend went on, knew of the society's mission, but anyone who tried to find out or interfered would be found dead of thousand cuts and lain out like a cross. That, gentlemen, is about all I can remember from my childhood stories, except that later on there was a rumor that the Jade Cross had disappeared from its secret and sacred hiding place well before the war with the French in the early 1950s."

Now it was Parnell's turn to inquire. "Who told these stories to you? I'm only asking because I'm curious about it."

"My parents and school teachers in Hue, mostly," the priest answered. "And I might have heard some of it from a provincial mandarin speaking on the streets. Of course, the history of the Trung Sisters, Trung Trac and Trung Nhi, who organized a large army around 39 AD and drove out the Chinese and later committed suicide by jumping onto a river when the Chinese returned, was required learning. We were also told about a provincial mandarin in the 11th Century, named Ngo Quyen, who put sharpened stakes in a river bed to thwart a Chinese invasion. We were also taught about the mythical Le Loi in the 15th Century, who was a fisherman who cast his net into a lake and retrieved a magical sword. He used guerrilla tactics to defeat the Chinese who dominated Vietnam at that time. We were given many tales of Vietnamese heroes and heroines to

---

[27] Great Lord Hung Dao.

stimulate our nationalism and our pride in our country, but these are the only ones I can remember."

"Now that you have mentioned these people, I remember them being discussed when I was in Vietnamese language class in the Asian Department at the Defense Language Institute, West Coast Branch at Monterey. CA, but I don't remember what all was said," Tolbane offered. He continued on, "Did you have anything to do with digging up and taking the Jade Cross after our patrol left the area?" Tolbane asked.

"Not on your life, as you Americans say. My unit left the Hoi An area a couple of weeks later to go up North to the Cam Lo area, and I never returned to Hoi An City or the South of Quang Nam area for a few years. I completely forgot about it. I don't know of any of my former troops who did either. Many of them died fighting the NVA up north, and I have no idea what happened to the rest of our unit after the North's invasion and victory in 1975. I made my escape to America and studied for the priesthood. There are many Vietnamese Catholics here in the US who need spiritual guidance."

Parnell asked Tolbane about the words that the Vietnamese had uttered. "What did that clown tell you before he was carted off in the ambulance? You know the words, the ones that didn't make any sense. It was something about a mask, a man, no, and name wasn't it? The Father just said something about the society not having any kind of name."

Tolbane grinned as a thought popped into his head. "I was thinking about that too. He muttered the words 'no,' 'name,' and 'masked man,' as well as a couple others. Could we have a society or cult that has no name, and therefore calls itself No Name and is led by a Masked Man? Damn! That could screw up any one's mind. That would be a very different way to help keep your society or cult secret and mysterious. That's ingenious! I think we could be dealing with some entity that is centuries old and some jerk has resurrected it."

The other two thought about it for a minute or two and then agreed with Tolbane. Father Hung Phat thought some more and offered to the Americans, "You must be right. I think I remember one little tidbit that might have been mentioned. The group might have been known as a society but, it was really a cult. It may even have had a Christian base, as I have mentioned, in the beginning. I truly wish I could remember more. Soon I must leave you and go with the lieutenant to the state patrol headquarters for this area. What I can and will do when I return to Carthage is to research this matter at the shrine and some other sources I use in Vietnam from time to time. If I could have your addresses and phone numbers, I can contact you on the phone and/or send you copies of anything I find that might be relevant." The three were in agreement and exchanged their business cards.

Lt. Jeckel started walking towards them as they finished their conversation and waved to the Priest, "Come on and hop in the car. We're on the way. Bye guys!"

The priest shook their hands vigorously, waved to the guys, and said, "I'm so glad to have met you under these circumstances. I thank you again for being part of my rescue. I'll pray that God's guiding hand will direct you in your quest and protect you from harm." He said good bye in Vietnamese and then he was gone. Tolbane and Parnell felt alone, as if the Priest had been an essential part of their lives for all of the years after that patrol.

While waiting for Sgt. Brown to return from talking with other officers, the two discussed the situation. If they were dealing with a four-and–a-half century old cult led by some fanatic with a mask, what else could they be in store for? So far, all that they had learned seemed to make things somewhat clearer, in regards to what, but not who, they were dealing with. But there was still so much more to learn. After a few minutes of discussion, they stepped apart to make cell phone calls. Parnell called into MNPD to find out the latest info and Tolbane called Mai.

Tolbane and Mai talked for several minutes. After he had told her about the shooting, the wreck, the priest, the patrol and the tales about the Jade Cross and the cult, Mai told him about the reflection she saw in the tree line and calling the County Sherriff's Office and their return call from a deputy that someone had been watching the house again. "I know you're concerned Travis, but don't be upset or worry too much about me. I've got the dogs and, as the old-time gangsters used to say, my gat. The county sheriff's deputy said that they would have a unit check out the tree line periodically, and if anything is wrong, I will be notified by phone and there will be officers checking out our place. So I'm more concerned about you than anything happening to me here. As for you, Numba Ten Thous, you have a penchant for getting into trouble. Damn it, Travis! Take care of yourself! As I told you, I still have the dogs and my gat. Also, I think that letter was true about my not being harmed."

"I hope you're right about that, Mai. I don't want to see you harmed in any way, not even a tear in your eyes. I'll kill any bastard that makes you cry or harms you, period. Oh! That reminds me! Besides saying I love you, have I ever told you that you're really a sweet piece with legs all the way up to your terrific butt? Great boobs too. Just thinking about you makes me horny."

"Yes, you have," she replied, "too many times, you pervert. Have I ever said to you that you have a big and sweet hanging tenderloin? Ha! Ha! Eat your heart out.

It might just get cut off; I mean cut off from your sweet piece." They kidded each other some more, then cut the connection. Tolbane, having that feeling in his groin, knew he'd have to teach Mai how to do back flips from the bed's head board and he could play catch with her. Yes, he'd have to work on that for sure.

Parnell walked to Tolbane and related his conversation with MNPD. "Nothing of interest was found on the body at the autopsy, but surprise, surprise about the one you clubbed a couple of times. You didn't do him in. It seems he was smothered with a pillow or something similar in the ambulance by the Asian medic on the way to the hospital. They have him in custody, but he's playing bad guy and he's not talking. In fact, he even cursed and spat at one of the detectives. Put on your hip boots. This shit is getting deeper by the minute."

Tolbane brought him up to date on Mai's situation. Then a thought popped into his head and he laid it out for Parnell. "If that Asian medic killed him, how did he know he should do it? He would have had to have been informed by somebody that there may be a loose end that needed to be taken care of. He had to know that the Vietnamese dude was hurt and could eventually run his mouth. I wonder, could there be someone in the MNPD that's in on this? Maybe someone who belongs to or is indebted to this cult or whatever it is? I hope not, but it seems likely to me that there's a fink at the clink. Or maybe even a quail in the jail?"

"You and your dumb ass sense of humor make quite a pair of idiots, you know that? That is a real possibility though. I don't know what info the dispatcher passed on to the EMTs or how many patrol units heard the broadcast. Someone had to have passed on the info. We need to step lightly on this if it is a member of MNPD. Damn it all to hell anyway."

Thinking of having a rat in the department was really disturbing. Parnell thought some more then continued, "I'm wondering about the Vietnamese officer I often speak with at the department. He's given me a lot of good stuff. He's been very cooperative and fairly informative whenever I've spoken with him. Shit, I hope it's not him! He's a real nice guy, but after all he is a Vietnamese and that's who we're dealing with."

Parnell started thinking about all the conversations he had with that officer in regards to problems in the Vietnamese community and the recent criminal events relating to Tolbane, Mai, Ba, Light Foot, and himself. Finally coming to a difficult decision, he took out his cell phone, called his lieutenant, and requested that internal affairs look into the situation, including observing the officer and monitoring his phone calls, ASAP. If this guy was on the dole to some crazed asshole, he damn sure wanted to know.

Tolbane heard Parnell's side of the conversation, and when Parnell cut the connection, he told him, "I agree with your decision on this. I don't really know who this guy is, but we do need to check him out, either clear him or arrest him. I never would have thought of any MNPD officer selling us out. That's way beyond belief. This whole mess has been BOHICA[28] all the way since it began."

"You got that last one right buddy. I think we both have symbolically felt it. Right up the old poop chute with sand in the Vaseline."

"Parnell, I'll be so glad when we finally get to kick ass and take some names, and it's all over. This is wearing on all three of us. Right now, I just want to kill a bunch of no-good Vietnamese bastards before they kill us."

"I hope Sgt. Brown is done soon. I don't know about you, but I'm hungry and as tired as crap. We need to get to a motel or something."

---

[28]   Bend Over, Here It Comes Again

"Ditto on that, dude! Once again, I'm forced to agree with you. I could use a head call too."

"You got that right! If I had false teeth, my plates would be floating up to my eye brows."

CHAPTER 14

WHEN SGT. BROWN FINISHED her work at the wreck site, she piled the duo into her unit and took them back to the National Park to get what she thought was an ugly green pickup truck, with an eagle, Globe, and Anchor painted on the doors. She just didn't know about the Green Machine's traditions. If it's not Marine Corps Green, it doesn't exist. On the way, Parnell finally read their copy of the trooper's file on the murder and then passed it to Tolbane. Neither one commented on the file's content. They would talk about it on the way back to Tennessee.

Arriving at the National Park, Sgt. Brown suggested they follow her to a restaurant in Springfield for supper, her treat. The thought of free food got their attention, as she figured it would. After they gave their heartfelt yeses to her, she went on to say, "You two will like this place. It's Lenard's, the home of the thrown rolls. While you're eating, the staff will come out wearing heavy oven gloves and will bring pans of rolls, hot and fresh out of the oven. Then they start throwing them to the diners. It's fun to see people miss a catch and the roll lands in their soup or mashed potatoes and gravy. It does make a splash." She giggled a little bit.

"Then they'll bring out a wheeled cart with several different kinds of food on it and start putting even more food on your plates. Believe me this, if you should leave there hungry you've got a real big problem. I hope you two got appetites." She smiled and laughed a little when all she heard was their growling stomachs. She knew the pathway to a man's heart was through his stomach. They asked her to stop on the way where they could get gas and ice, and she was happy to. They needed to keep the tuna from spoiling and to cool the sodas. The melted ice in the cooler was still a little cool, so they figured the sandwiches were still good.

The restaurant wasn't really busy at the time. Getting a booth was easy. Sometimes tour buses stopped there for meals, and the place would be jammed with people standing in a long line for seats. The two guys sat on one side, and the sergeant sat on the other. They only sat for a minute before a waitress brought menus and took drink orders. She was back with the drinks, took the food orders, and was off in the blink of an eye. While waiting on their food, they discussed the murder, the day's screwed up event, and what they knew about the Jade Cross and a possible cult and a nut with a mask. It was agreed by the three that the root of the crimes was in Nashville or close by there. Parnell assured the sergeant that he would keep her informed of anything he and Tolbane should learn. The three jerked a little as three hot rolls suddenly landed in their booth.

After eating and catching more thrown rolls, they left the restaurant well stuffed. Tolbane thought he now knew how a Thanksgiving Turkey felt after it was stuffed and roasted. All he needed now was to be basted with butter. No room in there for anything else. The guys thanked her for her hospitality and the joy ride and parted company. She went to her headquarters and the guys headed for a motel to get a night's rest before returning to Nashville and Mount Juliet.

The lack of sleep and the day's activities were getting to them. They found the Super 8 Motel Sgt. Brown told them about easily, checked in, and arranged a wakeup call for 0530 hours. As soon as they were in their room with double beds, Tolbane called Mai to let her know how they were and when they would leave. After that, both men were asleep in no time.

When the wakeup call came the next morning, they grudgingly got up, still weary from the previous day. They showered and changed clothes from their bags and went to the free breakfast. After each ate a couple helpings of sausage gravy and biscuits, donuts, and orange juice and fixed coffee to go, they checked out and were on the road by 0630 hours with Parnell driving the first leg. Tolbane called Mai as soon as they got started and begged her forgiveness for calling so early. She informed him that if he hadn't called to let her know he was on the way home; he faced the certain castration and dismemberment of a certain head. Of course, she would make sure it was well used before using the cleaver.

Traffic was heavy until they were about four miles east of Springfield. The speed limit was 70 MPH. They were cruising at 73 MPH and the Dodge pickup was riding smoothly and comfortably. The problem now was the brightness of the rising sun in their eyes. They were happy that they had their sunglasses with them. Before they knew it, they were past Rolla.

A trooper's car was suddenly behind them, and to the pair's surprise, Trooper McCabe pulled up beside them, waved, and flew past them as though they were standing still. Tolbane waved and quipped, "Bye! Bye! Semper Fi, Marine!" Then he put the seat back and began to snore. Parnell wished he had ear plugs.

They arrived in St. Louis and got on route 55 to I-64 east easily. They stopped at the first rest stop on I-64 and made head call and finished the tuna sandwiches. They changed drivers, and Tolbane drove off in a flash. He was anxious to get home and get some use out of something before Mai picked up her cleaver. Parnell called in to MNPD a couple of times during the ride and received no new info. They arrived in Nashville about 5:15 PM during the heavy traffic time, and Parnell called Mai and let her know where they were.

They were at Tolbane's by 6:15 PM. Mai had the gates and the door opened as they pulled in to the driveway. When they exited the car, she ran out and jumped into Tolbane's arms, wrapped her legs around his waist, and lip locked him. The dogs, not wanting to be left out of the action, were jumping on and licking him and Parnell. Tolbane was left with no other choice than to carry her into the house this way with the gleeful dogs following. He put her down, and they hugged and kissed like there was no tomorrow. While the two were embracing, Parnell put the dogs out, closed the gates, and activated the alarm. Now all he needed to do was to pry the children apart.

As Parnell prodded them, they ceased their kissy face and sat down on the sofa, and Parnell sat in the recliner he was starting to feel was his. Mai told them how glad she was that they were home, safe and sound, and the guys replied the same. "I'll bet besides being tired, you two are hungry. I went to the farmer's market in Nashville today and got something special just for you. I bought dried fish and nuoc mam sauce." The guys nearly gagged. "Ha! Ha! I got you two again."

"That serves you right for abandoning me in my time of sorrow. Boo! Hoo! Hoo! I actually made creamed beef. I sautéed the onions and veggies with diced bacon and added it to the braised meat and made a lot of toast. Oh! Excuse me, Marines. I mean SOS. Shit on a Shingle. I ask your forgiveness for using a civilian term for a type of Marine Corps chow. We can talk afterwards. I'm hungry too, so let's get into the mess hall and get with it. It's chow time, Marines!" The three retired to the kitchen and began loading their plates. They were all sighing with pleasure after the first bite. After three big helpings for the guys and two smaller ones for Mai, they returned to the living room to relax and to rest their overextended stomachs.

Parnell leaned back in the recliner, closed his eyes, and informed Mai, "You should be hired on to train Marine Corps mess sergeants and their chief cooks. You're absolutely amazing in the galley. If I had to eat your chow 24/7, I'd be as big as the MetLife Zeppelin that hovers over football games or whatever it is."

Tolbane couldn't help but put in his two cents worth. He quipped, "I'd be that big myself, but I've got something nice around here to wear the fat off. Besides, sometimes I get put on the no calorie diet too." Mai blushed a bit.

"You only wish it, you big, dumb dork." Mai got her two cents in again. Parnell was always amazed at the jargon Mai had learned hanging around with them. She could rag with the best of the guys. "Ok guys. Give it up! Tell me all about your boring, peaceful trip without anything to do, and don't leave out the part about all the good-looking women!"

They held back about Sgt. Brown's good looks and went over the facts with Mai about the shooting and the chase, emphasizing the gory details of the wreck, enhancing the lieutenant's ugly looks and downplaying Sgt. Brown's good looks. They even mentioned Trooper Sgt. McCabe. Tolbane told her about the restaurant and the thrown rolls, and he made a comment that he'd like to toss and catch her buns, and that they would have to go there sometime. He didn't mention that Springfield also had a large Bass Pro Shop and that Branson was just south of there.

With a tear in her eyes, Mai told Tolbane and Parnell that the service for Ba had been postponed until the next day. There had been some glitch in the funeral home's scheduling. They couldn't do two services at the same time. Those that were interested in attending the service were notified by phone of the change.

Mai then explained what had transpired there at the house and what was done about it. Both guys let her know they were glad nothing happened to her. Tolbane hugged her tighter and Parnell indicated he'd check with the Wilson County Sherriff's Department the next day and find out if there was anything she had not been told about the situation.

Parnell was yawning and decided to go on home and get some shut eye. He knew that these two wanted to hit the sack, but not necessarily to sleep. Mai let him out and took care of the gates, put the dogs back on alert, and set the alarm. She walked to the sofa where Tolbane was still sitting, reached behind one of the pillows, and retrieved a cleaver. She pointed it at Tolbane and ordered, "OK mister! It's in to the bedroom with you!" Tolbane gladly complied. Holding his privates and laughing, he marched into the bedroom. He got used but not chopped.

Tolbane and Mai both slept well and were cheerful and playful when they awoke. After their morning toiletries and such, Mai headed to the kitchen to warm up the left-over SOS and make fresh toast and coffee. Tolbane called the mall to let them know about when he'd be in. He went outside and called the dogs and jumped around with them some, fed them, then put them back on guard. With his mouth watering for some more SOS, he sat hunched over at the table and dug into a big plateful. Mai was always wondering how it always seemed like he just inhaled certain foods like he was a vacuum cleaner. She wondered too if she should tell him he sucked some times.

With his stomach sated and feeling in good spirits for once, even though he really didn't want to go to work he got ready to go. After kissy face with Mai, he got in his Green Machine, changed the disk in the player to one by Nick somebody and he wondered if the Hot Child in the City could do back flips. He was alert all the way to the mall during the drive, and his trip there was uneventful. Too bad it hadn't been that way the last few days. He certainly needed it and could use a break from all this crap.

After checking with the security people, he strolled to his office. He sat in his comfortable desk chair, leaned back, and got into a thinking mode. What info could he add to his Order of Battle Factors? Not a whole lot. He got out his paper and pen and wrote info on five of the factors:

1. <u>Composition</u>: We know now that a masked man is in charge. We know the group could be from an ancient cult called the No Name and composed only of Vietnamese.

2. <u>Disposition</u>: The Vietnamese cop may be able to tell us where they are located.

3. <u>Strength</u>: The group must have many members. They seem to come out of the woodwork. There's no indication of exactly how many there are.

4. <u>Logistics</u>: Now they've lost a Ford sedan, two AK-47s, an ASP, and a few boxes of ammo.

5. <u>Miscellaneous</u>: We know the patrol and the Jade Cross are at the heart of the situation. The Vietnamese priest will do some research on the cult.

Tolbane compared these five to his original list of eight and said aloud to no one, "We still don't know dick about this group. It's like the computer lingo, GIGO, Garbage In, Garbage Out, Crap!"

He'd been sitting back in his chair with his eyes closed trying to understand what was happening when the phone rang. "This is Master Gunnery Sergeant Travis Tolbane, United States Marine Corps, Retired, speaking Sir!" He didn't know why he answered the phone in a military manner.

"This is your ole buddy that's going to castrate your retired ass in about a minute. Listen up maggot. I got some new info to share with you. I'll see you in about fifteen and issue a sit rep. Bye!" Parnell ended the call.

Tolbane uttered aloud, "Fuck you too buddy!" into the dead phone. Placing the phone back on its cradle, he leaned back in his desk chair again and smiled an ornery smile. He thought about how acrobats and pair skaters used a harness while training on difficult summersault moves. Should he get one for Mai to use when he started to teach her back flips? She's going to be pissed when he tells her about her future training.

The phone rang again. It was Mai. "Hey dude! Are you going to be able to come to Ba's service this afternoon?"

"Parnell's coming by soon and we'll both make it. Even if something should come up and Parnell can't make it, I'll be there for you and Ba."

"That's a relief. I know I wouldn't hold up without you. I've got something important to ask you about. I know how you felt about it a few years ago, but I need to ask you again. I have this feeling of loneliness since Ba's gone. It has nothing to do with you. Something different. My biological clock is still ticking and I need a baby, and I want to have it with you! Travis!" No sound from the phone. "Travis Tolbane, are you still there? You better be Jerk."

Tolbane sat with the phone pressed hard to his ear and was dumbfounded and at a loss for words. His stomach seemed to be swirling around and he looked like he would faint. Mai had to raise her voice again to get his attention. "Me? A dad?

Oh my God! Are you trying to give me a heart attack or what? Don't you think I'm a little too old to produce?"

"You, big dumb ass. The way you do things does not show your age at all. You could fill up a five-gallon jug. I've wanted this with you for ages. I know this will fulfill this part of my loneliness, and what's more, I know you'll be a wonderful father whether it's a boy or girl. You may have to cool things down sometimes, but you'll do in a pinch."

"You just caught me off guard Mai. You left me speechless for a minute. I've always wondered what it would be like to knock you up. Damn! I want to do that and have a baby too. It's been on my mind the last couple of years. I think you should get rid of all of our protections, and you need to stand by for a ram tonight."

"Okay, Numba Ten Thous. Just so you know, I'll be standing by for a ram."

"Before you hang up, Mai, would you consider learning how to do back flips?"

"You need to go to a college and buy a new brain. When they passed out brains, you must have thought they said trains and said, 'I'll take a slow one.' Me do back flips? What is this thing about back flips with you?" She hung up.

Looking sheepish, Tolbane lifted his head up and saw that Parnell was standing there. "What's this fixation you have about women doing back flips?"

"It's a long story for a different day. You came early for the service."

"Yes, I did because I've got some new info. Some of it confirms our line of thinking about a cult and the Jade Cross. I'll cover Springfield, MO, first."

The State Patrol was able to talk to the injured one late last night until he was too tired to answer. The guy wasn't as bad off as we thought. He confirmed he and the other guy interrogated, killed, and staked down Light Foot the same as they did Ba, and he also admitted that they kidnapped the Priest and shot at us. They were to interrogate the Priest about the Jade Cross and then kill him and stake him down like they did the other two. It was only then that they were to harass or kill us, but they got greedy. They decided to harass or kill us first so they could take more time screwing with the priest. It seems they were Cao Dai and hated Vietnamese Catholics with a passion. The Masked Man promised these two that they would be richly rewarded for their work when they returned to Nashville with good information.

"He stated that they belonged to a cult called No Name, and its leader is a Masked Man calling himself by two names. One is the Exalted One, and the other is Tran Hung Dao. He claims to be the reincarnation of the famous Vietnamese general who defeated the Mongols. He has a tough assistant called Number One who is his go-to-guy and enforcer. This Masked Man said he had a Cause, and it included recovering the Jade Cross, returning it to its rightful place, getting rid of the communists, reuniting all of Vietnam under one rule, and rescuing his true love from her defiler, Travis Tolbane."

The building in La Vergne, TN, was their meeting place. There were usually about thirty or so members that attended their meetings. Each member has a number. Except these two had no numbers because they were special undercover operatives for the guy. For other jobs, the Masked Man would draw numbers to assign various jobs to the members. The two that took you to the building and were to beat you and ask questions about the Jade Cross were numbers Three and Fifteen. This guy emphasized that any failure of any job or duty would end in death.

"Here's the big kicker. The cult was watching us and your house, but there were direct orders not to involve or harm the Vietnamese girl he called Mai at any time under the penalty of a horrible death. Additionally, they were told that there was only hate that was directed towards Americans, and us in particular.

"We won't get anything else from him however. Instead of an officer outside his room, they had a trooper watching the room on a camera. About four in the morning, a Vietnamese snuck into the room and the trooper responded, but it was too late. The guy was being smothered by a pillow and didn't make it. The killer was taken into custody but has not talked. Sgt. Brown, the one who called us, said he was a pretty tough guy and might not crack very easy. He pretends not to understand English well, and they've sent for an interpreter. That's about the big MO in a nutshell, old buddy."

Tolbane thought about this and took out his paper with the factors and made additions to it and showed it to Parnell. Then he responded to Parnell. "These people are really organized. Just how far are they able to reach out? How did they know about the injured dude and where he was located? These are just more questions to answer. Damn, they're all over the place. One thing that does ease my mind is the fact that this masked ass doesn't want Mai hurt. But why? Did he see her someplace and got a crush on her? Has he known her a long time and is he in love with her or something? If it's the latter, we probably know him from someplace."

"I can't answer those questions, but I think we could know him, or may have seen him, or maybe he just knows who we are. We've been in the Vietnamese area so many times with Ba and Mai. Come to think about it, Mai is a very good-looking woman, and he could be admiring her from afar. Maybe he saw or met her sometime when she was out shopping at the Vietnamese stores or wherever with Ba."

"Well, Hell! You're probably right on that. What's number two on your list?"

"The Vietnamese officer has only offered a little info to IA. He admits being paid to pass on information to some guy, but he does not know who he is. He got caught up in the intrigue because of something his father did during the Viet Nam conflict that could embarrass the family, so he agreed to assist the Masked Man for money. Everything including the threat was all done by phone. The man would call and tell the desk sergeant that he was a relative, and the call would be transferred to his phone. IA is trying to make a deal with him to answer the man's calls and give him false info so that the detectives can trace the calls and get a location. We can only hope he agrees to do it and it works."

"That's good news for a change. We may solve this after all. What we need now are the Little gray cells of Hercule Poirot, Mon Amie, or however you say it Chief Inspector Lestrade. Time, and the little gray cells. With these we always catch the criminal." Parnell still had trouble understanding Tolbane's wit.

"You're pathetic, you know that? Now tell me about that stupid look on your face when I came in the door and your fixation on back flips!"

"Later guy! I'll have to have NCIS run a background check on you first. If you pass, I'll issue you a Top Bull Shit clearance, and after I tell you, you will have to sign a nondisclosure statement. If you disclose the secret, you'll have to commit Hari Kiri with Mai's cleaver, not Beaver Cleaver!"

"Are you for real or fucking what, you dip shit? Something really fucked up your mind some time or other. I bet your mother dropped you on your head a few times and cracked the sidewalk." Parnell with his head shaking side to side again, leaving with Tolbane for Ba's service and noting, "If I didn't know better, I'd swear you have that old Hawaiian disease, Laki Nooki."

CHAPTER 15

Tolbane and Parnell arrived about ten minutes before the memorial service for Ba had started. Mai had taken a taxi and was already there, as were Carly, several Vietnamese friends, a few others, and a couple of policemen who had known Ba. No one knew that the Masked Man's Number One had ordered one of their members to be there also to spy and report on them, feeling safe that the guy he sent was unknown to the three.

Mai had tears in her eyes, and Tolbane took her in his arms and held her tenderly. "I know this is painful for you. It is for me too Mai," he empathized. "Even though I lost a good friend and a brother in arms, I know your loss is far greater than mine, and I'll be there for you when you need me. My heart really goes out to you. I love you so much."

"I know. I've tried to be brave, but it's so hard. I'm so lucky to have you to love and understand me. I love you too. I know Ba was only one part of my world and yours, but it hurts deeply that it affects both of us. I just can't believe that somebody would do a horrible thing to such a wonderful and caring person." Tolbane led her to a couple of seats in the front row and Parnell followed.

They could see the sealed casket with many types of flowers displayed all around it from Ba's friends and Mai. They both wanted to see him again, but they were advised that nothing could be done to reconstruct his face. The mourners were in line passing by the closed casket, some with tears, some saying a silent prayer while doing so. The service had not yet begun.

He looked around the chapel and saw Carly across the aisle with a tear in her eyes. She was dressed in a black business-like knee length dress and looked beautiful. When she saw him, she smiled. He nodded to her, and she nodded back. Tolbane turned his attention to Mai and handed her his handkerchief. She was weeping and sobbing and had only worn a light lipstick so there was nothing to smear on her face or his handkerchief. It didn't matter to him though. She could smear up all of his hankies as far as he was concerned. Tolbane knew he had the most wonderful and the best-looking woman in the whole wide world, one who would be by his side till the end.

Tolbane knew that the next day Ba's body would be cremated, and the following day the ashes would be presented to Mai. He knew he needed to be there when the ashes were presented to her. It would be another very sad day in her life. He knew that of all of the struggles she and Ba had escaping Vietnam, and all of other bad times events she'd been though, this crime had really devastated her more than anything. But the kind of strong woman she is was keeping her from breaking down completely. He held her tighter and handed her his handkerchief again. He also knew that within the next few days she would really break down. Then she would be able to start the healing process.

The memorial service started, and the priest from Ba's church spoke very kindly of him and his accomplishments. He talked about how Ba had lived his life as a good

Christian and how he had adopted the U.S.A. as his own country after fleeing the North Vietnamese onslaught and saving his half-sister at the same time. He dwelt on how Ba would always help his neighbors in need and even strangers in need and how he was a loving and supportive half-brother to Mai. The Priest said Ba had made many good American friends, and he knew if something ever happened to one of them, Ba would be there, offering his help as you all have to his half-sister Mai. After a few more minutes of praise, a few of Ba's friends got up at their turn and spoke kind words about him. Finally, it was Mai's turn to eulogize Ba. Tolbane helped her stand and she moved solely to the lectern.

Mai, with tears in her eyes and pain in her heart, stepped up slowly, paused at the lectern, looked around the chapel, then spoke. "Ba was my big half-brother and always took care of me during the war whenever he was able to. My other half-brothers never tried to help. I don't know where they are today. Ba helped me escape the North Vietnamese onslaught and brought me here to this wonderful land after a long and arduous journey through several different countries. After some years here, he ran into his old American partner from the war, my true love, Travis Tolbane, the very man who had kept me from being raped in Saigon when I was ten years of age, and Ba brought us together again. We three shared our lives as one family. I miss him so damn much. Some dirty son of a bitch took him from me! I want to kill the no-good bastard!" Mai began sobbing with anger and had tears pouring down her face as she said, "I just can't say more right now." She rushed to Tolbane and buried her face into his chest, needing his broad shoulders and strong arms for support.

He pulled her as close as he possibly could. He was glad she finally broke down. She had been in some denial and tried to be strong about the murder and her loss of her half-brother. He knew that in expressing her anger now and letting it all out, she would be able to cope with it better in the coming weeks, even though he felt she would still break down some more in a few days. She would be able to move on with her life, and it would get easier day by day. He was so proud of her. His only job now was to find some way to get her some closure, like killing a bunch of scumbag bastards.

After the service was over, Carly was the first person, besides Tolbane and Parnell, to reach Mai. They hugged, and Carly wiped a tear from her eyes and then from Mai's cheek with her thumb and offered her condolences once more. All of the attendees stood aside as she walked Mai up the aisle and outside with Tolbane and Parnell following, then the mourners followed. The two women spoke briefly and agreed to meet for lunch later in the week. Carly had an appointment before going to work and had to leave.

Mai stood close to the door, still sobbing somewhat. She shook each person's hand, gave them each a half hug, and thanked them for being there and for coming to the service as they exited the building. The two guys stood quietly and slightly behind her out of respect so as not to interfere with Mai's giving thanks to the attendees. This was her time of sorrow, and she needed to express her thanks to Ba's faithful friends herself.

When everyone had left the chapel, the trio walked arm in arm, Mai in the middle, slowly to Parnell's unmarked car. Tolbane and Mai sat in the back seat, and she leaned her head on his shoulder, and he comforted her on the way to their home. No one said a word, each one was lost in their own thoughts.

Arriving at the house, the two guys offered Mai their heartfelt sorrow for her loss, and Mai assured them she would be alright and that she just needed to be alone right now, but she promised she would call Tolbane at the mall later. She went into the house, and they headed back to Nashville. Parnell put on the blue lights, put the pedal to the metal, and they made it to the mall in record time.

Once in Tolbane's office, Parnell called in to Metro to receive an update. He informed Tolbane that the Vietnamese officer received a call from one of the sect members, and it was recorded, traced, and SWAT was on its way to the location to arrest the caller and execute a search warrant for his premises. That dumbass Vietnamese bastard cop was guilty after all.

"There was a message for us. Father Phat had tried to call our cells while they were turned off at the funeral service. He then called the station and said he wants you or me to call him after 9:00 PM tonight our time. It seems he has some information for us from a contact in Hoi An City." It looked like things were turning in their favor for a change.

Changing the subject back to the Vietnamese cop, Tolbane bitched, "That damn little prick, a real jewel. He's a fucking bad cop. I'd like to kick his ass, then use Dirty Harry's .44 Mag to give him another eye socket right in between his other eyes. It would be right on the bridge of his nose. Come on Turd! Make my day! If I were Dirty Harry, I'd have no problem making the day for that whole bunch of bastards. None of them would be around to get any back flips. That's for damn sure."

"Get real Tolbane! Quit day dreaming and get on with the fucking program. I said we have to call the Priest tonight."

"Sorry! This shit has got me brain dead. I hope this is over soon. I'm so worried about Mai and our future together that sometimes I just can't think straight. I'd still like to give him an extra eye socket after I kick his ass up onto his shoulder blades, whoever he is."

Parnell just looked at his friend and shook his head from side to side. Then he smiled and said, "buddy, you're just too much to take. I was also informed that the Vietnamese guy who killed our suspect in the Missouri hospital hasn't cracked yet. He waved his rights but is still playing the hard guy roll. He has a long record, but it's all petty crap. On paper, he doesn't look like a killer, of course paper can be deceiving. Someone here in the MNPD had to get ahold of him. How else could he know about the injured guy in the Missouri hospital as well as the one in the ambulance? It had to be the Vietnamese officer. I'm going in to have a talk with him myself. Maybe he only passed the info to one of the sect members. Either way, he's guilty as shit and he's going to pay for it with his balls if necessary."

"I have to agree with you. When you get him into the little room, pour it on, real heavy like. I wish I could sit in there with you. In fact, I'd like to have an interrogation hut like we had at our Da Nang 3rd ITT site. It wouldn't take long before this clown blabbed his guts out. I'd sure pull a Mike Hammer, a Sam Spade, a Phillip Marlowe, a Dirty Harry, or whatever it took to get to him. I think I'd even ask him how long he's been a VC! You wouldn't happen to have one of those obsolete double E8 crank phones, do you? You could really wire his balls up and give it a few cranks."

"Just keep dreaming! I'll see or call you later."

After Parnell left, Tolbane called Mai to update her, even though he knew he should wait on her call, but really he just wanted an excuse to find out how she was coping, tell her how much he loved her, and remind her that he was there for her. When she answered, he began to apologize for calling her. She stopped him in mid-speech, "Travis, you know you can call even when I don't want you to. Does that make good sense? You know it does. I had a good cry after you guys left. I feel somewhat better now. I just can't believe he's gone. I'm going to need you tonight like never before. Oh, shit! I can just see the smile on your face at that. You only have pussy on your two brains, mainly the one in your pants right now. Well, thinking about it, maybe I have something on my other brain too."

"My brain just stood up and saluted you, your highness. Your other brain is the center of my brain's universe. I'll be there for you, count on it. I love you. I called because I just needed to hear your voice and know you're alright."

Mai responded to him, "Thanks for caring and calling me. I love you too Travis. I'd be lost without your support. You have your' work to do there, so I'll see you when you come home. I'm cooking a treat for you, something I know you like. Well, for now, goodbye, you great big dork of mine." She smiled as she terminated the call. Tolbane had to take a couple of deep breaths to ease his arousal.

When he felt relaxed, he left his office, checked the security office and the camera room, and toured the mall. At one store, he watched while a store security man and one of the mall security officers tangled with a shoplifter and dragged him back into the store's security room. He approved of their actions, even though the crook would have a few sore spots with bruises for the next few days. There really is justice in the world sometimes. He then walked into some of the stores and chatted with duty managers and sales associates about their day. After his tour, he returned to his office, leaned back in his chair, placed his feet on the desk, and faded into dreamland. This time in his dream, he was just ambling along in a green and grassy meadow enjoying the day.

He awoke suddenly by the phone blaring. He wondered if a guy could ever sleep without being woken up by a phone. Mall security wanted him in their office ASAP! Entering, he saw an Asian-looking man sitting in a chair. The mall security captain explained, "The camera man saw this Vietnamese man getting out of a car and looking around, so he dispatched two guards to bring him in here. He knew you'd want to question him. Here's his ID." Tolbane checked the picture and name on the driver's license and just shook his head.

Remembering when he was stationed at the Marine Barracks, Subic Bay Naval Station, Luzon, Republic of the Philippines, he greeted the man in Tagalog. The man answered him back. Tolbane handed him his ID and told him in English to take his possessions and he was free to leave. He explained to him that it was an honest mistake because the guards had never had any dealings with Orientals and they were looking for a particular one. That was a big fib. The guy nodded and left. Tolbane gave the security people there a few tips on identifying Asians. He left the security office and returned to dreamland in his office chair with his feet propped up on the desk once again.

The phone ringing again startled him from his dreams of back flips. It was Parnell. "I won't be over tonight. I've got loads of paperwork to catch up on here, it's unbelievable. I talked to that asshole Vietnamese cop and got no more than IA did. I'll call the priest from here at 9:00 PM. Unless there is something really important, I'll contact you in the morning with an update on the priest and the Vietnamese Police Officer. I'll be talking to him again after I find out more about the SWAT raid today on his caller. Maybe I'll get lucky and will be able to quiz the caller too. Besides, I think you and Mai need to be alone tonight. She really needs you. I don't know why in the world her, or any woman for that matter, would want your sorry ass, but she does. Keep the faith old man."

Tolbane offered, "Thanks buddy! Glad you're on our side. Talk to you in the AM." They ended the call.

Tolbane looked through his IN/OUT basket and found nothing he couldn't deal with later on. Lacking the will to do much at this time, he grabbed the mall security manual he had written and skimmed through it, not really reading it. Feeling tired and useless in his office, he called the security office to let them know he was leaving for home shortly. Then he called Mai once more and spoke lovingly to her, letting her know he was leaving the office and would soon have her in his arms to comfort her. She responded with, "I suppose you will want me naked on the kitchen table so you can eat your supper before you dine tonight?" Tolbane giggled at her and hung up the phone. He would be surprised if he didn't find her just like that, stark naked on the kitchen table when he got home. He waited until his erection subsided before getting up from his desk.

It took Tolbane an extra hour to get home due to a wreck on I-40 close to Hermitage. He used his cell to let Mai know where he was so she wouldn't worry. While sitting idle in the traffic jam, he nodded off a couple of times. He was physically and mentally tired from the recent events. Knowing that Mai would rejuvenate him when he got home was the thing that not only kept his spirits up, but something else too. When the traffic began to move, the car behind him had to toot his horn a couple of times in order to bring Tolbane back to reality and get his ass moving.

Arriving at the house, he went through his entry and lock up routine. Once inside the house, he removed his clothes and walked into the kitchen. There on the kitchen table lay a naked Mai with a big grin on her tear-stained face. "God, you're the most beautiful thing I've ever seen! He commented" She looked up at him and cooed, "Your supper's ready." He greedily attacked his food with vigor. Mai also dined.

Their antics ended up in the bedroom later. After a while, they showered together and put on their robes. Mai told him, "Go pick up your clothes and put them where they belong. I've got your meal in the oven keeping it warm. I'll give you a shout when everything's ready." With a shake of her fine butt at him, she trotted off to the kitchen. Tolbane wanted to swat that fine female butt playfully with a grasping motion, but she moved too fast for him.

He obediently picked up his clothes and put them in the appropriate places. He sat in the recliner and had just closed his eyes when he heard, "Travis, get your tall ugly butt in here this minute. Your supper is on the table. If it gets cold, don't blame me!"

Mai had outdone herself in the kitchen once more. She had made Salisbury steak, gobs of a rich brown gravy, mashed potatoes, peas, and corn. His favorite foods. He said that about all the foods he consumed like a vacuum. He knew that Mai had kept herself busy to help her cope with the situation. He attacked the meal with a gusto that Mai didn't know he had, and she had seen him attack his food many times before. She wondered if he had a suction devise in his stomach that just sucked food straight down his gullet. When she commented on it, he explained to her that some very beautiful, sexy woman had exercised him to his limit and depleted his energy and he needed to rejuvenate himself with food before bedtime, hoping she would exercise him again. Mai's eyes had gotten wide at this and moaned, "You got to be kidding me. After all that tossing around, we just did, and you need more of it? You're incredulous you know that? You're just a damn sex fiend. Well, all I've got to say is that I'll probably be sore in the morning."

After the meal, Tolbane helped her put food away, do the dishes, and straighten up the kitchen. They went to the couch where Mai sat on his lap with her head on his shoulder. He knew by her tears she was still hurting, so he kept still, not uttering a word. An hour later, he stood, gently lifting Mai with him, and carried her to the bedroom. They took off their robes and climbed onto the bed. Then they lay on their sides facing each other. He had an arm over her shoulder holding her tightly, and she had a leg over his body. She sobbed and trembled for a while, then they both fell into a deep, exhausted sleep.

Tolbane woke up early just as the sun was coming up. Mai was still in a deep sleep. He gently eased himself out of bed without disturbing her. He made a head call then put on his robe and went to the kitchen and put on the coffee. After that, he got everything he needed to fix breakfast for her ready. He only needed her warm body at the table to start. Sitting down after pouring his first cup of coffee of the day, he turned his thoughts to the present problem. What the hell would the day bring? Mai woke about an hour later, and he fixed them breakfast. She seemed resigned to what was affecting her and was in a better mood than he thought she would be in. They showered together, then he shaved, and they dressed for the day.

Sitting on the couch waiting for Parnell to call, Mai told Tolbane. "I'm glad we had last night in bed together that way. It was the very thing I needed, and this morning was wonderful. I know you wanted me last night and this morning and I wanted you too, but I needed the comfort of your arms even more. Besides, I really would have been so sore right now. Don't say a word. I intend to make up for your rare Hawaiian disease tonight and give you the proper treatment. I'm a good doctor."

"What in the world is my rare Hawaiian disease, if I dare ask?"

"You know what it is, Lacki Nooki!"

"I didn't know you spoke the language. I can't wait until Dr. Mai treats and cures me."

After a while, Parnell still hadn't called, so Tolbane wiped a tear from Mai's eyes, kissed her goodbye, and left for the office. On the way he thought out loud, "I'm stupid. My ass should be kicked. I should have stayed and let the doctor treat my rare Hawaiian disease." He might even be confined to the bed for a few days. If that was the doctor's order for treatment, Amen, so be it.

CHAPTER 16

AFTER HE FINISHED THE call with Number One, the Masked Man dissected his previous plans to find the weakness of his plots. Some of them had worked and some had failed. "Why, did they fail?" he asked himself. One thing he knew for certain was that he didn't screw things up. It was his geese who were making bad decisions that had caused the problems. They weren't as proficient and dedicated as he had thought and hoped they were. Even though he still had many followers who would do his bidding without questioning him, he needed to do the important things himself. He could bring a member or two along to assist and/or for protection. The hardest parts of the plots must be of his doing so they wouldn't get fucked up. He could only trust himself, or maybe Number One on occasion.

Not knowing what was about to happen to his man, he made a mental note to have Number One find the three best and trusted men left in the membership and give him their names and phone numbers. That way, he could call them at a moment's notice when he wanted to act on something immediately. He would use Number One to help, however he depended on the guy to keep control of the geese and manage day to day operations. He just couldn't do everything himself. Sometimes he felt very lonely at the top. Right now, he was so confused. That's why he needed Mai so very much.

He knew that the service for Ba was today and that Number One had detailed a man to be there and report if anything out of the ordinary happened. He lazed around the house until time to leave for the service and drove to the site. Even though he knew he must be careful and not be seen, he felt brave today and drove slowly and boldly by the chapel, only seeing a couple of stragglers enter. He was thankful he didn't see a tearful Mai. Today it would hurt him deeply.

He drove on down the street till he found a prearranged spot for him to meet Number One's man after the service. He parked the car on an angle where he could see the informant coming in the rearview mirror. He made sure his mask was handy to put on before the guy got to the car. He had brought a magazine with him he purchased at an adult bookstore on lower 4th Ave. and began looking at the pictures to pass the time. He had no idea naked women could look so good and assume so many positions. A throbbing in his groin area began, and he laid his hand over it.

Maybe tonight he would have Number One send a great looking whore over. He would have to decide what ethnic group he'd want her chosen from. Seeing Hispanic, Asian, and Afro-American women in the magazine, he decided he wanted them all. He had a hard decision to make. He'd have to consider what age group she should come from also. He liked them his age, some older, and even the real young ones too. It had been a long time since he had a real-active-young-one. That might be the best plan of the day.

He read through the book cover to cover five times before he saw the informant in the rearview mirror. He had wanted to satisfy himself as he stroked his erection. He looked around, and seeing no one, he pulled his mask on and put down the driver's side window. The guy approached the car carefully to make sure this car was the right one. Seeing the mask on the man, he felt calmer.

"My greetings, Exalted One," the man said to the car's occupant. The Masked Man nodded and bade him to come closer and continue. "Nothing unusual happened during the service. The casket was closed because of the face mutilation. The woman in question raged in anger and broke down and couldn't continue to speak to the mourners, but that is what women do at memorial services I understand. They are so weak and frail. After the service had ended, she stood at the door and thanked everyone who came to pay their respects. When all the attendees were gone, she and the two Americans got into an unmarked police car and drove off. There's nothing else to report on, Sir."

"You have done well." He handed the guy an envelope with money and thanked him for a doing a good job. "Here's a piece of paper and a pen. Write down your name and phone number for me." Retrieving the pen and paper, he told the man, "I sometimes have a need for something to be done right away and must have a person I can count on. I might have another job for you soon. I can assure you it will pay well!" The guy thanked him for the confidence and replied, "I will be eagerly awaiting your call, Exalted One.

With that, the Masked Man started the car and drove off without another word. A half a block later, he pulled his mask off. He took out his cell phone and tried to call Number One's home phone. Getting no answer, he tried the cell phone and still got no answer. He felt a trickle of fear go through his body. Could something have happened, to his Number One? Maybe he's just doing something important like sitting on the john and can't be bothered with a phone call right now, or maybe he and his woman was getting it on. He felt better thinking about it that way. With all the recent screw ups by his geese, he was getting a little jittery. Wondering what he should do to waste time, he thought of getting a drink. He knew of a lounge where he could get a good mixed drink and relax for a bit. That's what he would do. He drove straight there.

He had two Jim Beams with Sprite and relaxed while listening to the piped-in music. He was about to leave when he had what he thought was a touch of genius. His plans were coming together even though he had a few setbacks. He drove straight home and tried to reach Number One on the phone. Once again there was no answer on either the house or cell phone. Now he was almost in a panic mode. He wasn't used to being ignored or brushed aside. He forced himself to calm down and think rationally. Frustrated, he decided to drive by Number One's home. Maybe the guy was sick or injured and couldn't come to the phone. If there was some other problem, he might have left a note on his door. He hopped in his car and left.

He was approaching Number One's house and was shocked like no other time in his life. There was a police patrol unit across the street from the house along with a SWAT unit, and there was yellow crime scene tape all around it. He had gritted his teeth till he thought they would chip and drove as normally as he could past the house and the police unit, keeping his head and eyes to the front. Then he became enraged, pounded on the steering wheel, nearly losing control of his car, and shouting loudly, "Damn you! Damn you! Number One! You dumb bastard, you! What have you done to me, and the Cause? I thought I could trust you? You've always been my strength!" A short way down the road was a strip mall he felt he would be safe at, and he pulled into a parking slot, shut off the ignition, put his head in his hands, and cried. "I hope all is not lost. This is the worst day of my life."

A half an hour later, he had lost some of the rage and he drove on home. He retrieved an address book from his desk and looked up a name and number and called an old friend in Hoi An City, Viet Nam. His friend was a little cranky but he answered the Masked Man's questions relating to the Jade Cross. He thought himself stupid for not making the call sooner. He listened for some time, asked questions, and got answers to them. What he learned from the call was that these people here know virtually nothing at all about the disappearance of the Jade Cross. He still needed to get the hated ones, Tolbane and Parnell, though, and take Mai for his own.

He opened a beer and sat down to consider his options. Number One must be in police custody since he didn't see the coroner's wagon at Number One's place. The police would have his cell phone and would be able to trace his location from his cell and home numbers. Even if his guy lawyered up and didn't talk, the police still might be able to find him through diligent police work. Everything here had collapsed. He needed to leave soon so he could continue his Cause and return later when things cooled down.

His plans here were toast. Even though he could escape the situation, he still had problems with Tolbane and Parnell and getting Mai back. Maybe he could spend a month or so in Vietnam then return and reclaim her. While he was gone, he needed someone to take care of the two Americans. They must be killed very slowly and deliberately. He hated them with his greatest passion. He reached in his pocket, took out the folded piece of paper, and looked at the informer's name and phone number. He had an idea how to solve the present dilemma.

He called Delta Airlines, and they had an early morning flight to Los Angeles. He booked it, then called the Music

City Sheridan and booked a room for the night, all in his alter-ego's name, Tran Hung Dao, not realizing it could be a small mistake. He quickly packed two suitcases with some clothes, his hand gun, his favorite knives, certain drugs, and anything that could reveal his true identity or anything about the Cause, along with a lot of American and Vietnamese money. Satisfied he had gotten everything important, he left for the Sheridan.

He wasn't worried about fingerprints being left in the house or the name on the deed and other documents in the small file box. Every paper had a false name. He didn't think his prints were on file or easily located if they were. He didn't plan to leave much of the house behind anyway, so even if some papers he'd strewn about survived, he needn't worry.

He knew he could get out of the country easily. He had several stolen identities with current passports for each one. Once he was in Vietnam, with what he had learned from his friend, he might still win and find the Jade Cross. Once he reached the west coast, he'd call him again and have him arrange lodging and meet him on arrival at the Da Nang International Airport, or maybe not. He did need lodging for about a month or so once he arrived there. Maybe he'd stay and pursue his Cause there. He'd decide on the way. He happened to think about a different identity for him to use in Hoi An. It wouldn't be cool to have a national hero's name. His friend could arrange a new one for him.

He called the informant on the phone, spoke with him for a few minutes, and arranged to meet with him at the motel later on. Number One had told him that this guy had been an ARVN ranger, had fought in many battles, hated all the Americans, and had a real thirst for their blood. When possible, he liked to torture his victims before going for the kill. This would suit the Masked Man's desire. He liked the guy's bloody résumé, and he had this same thing planned for the Americans he hated.

The Masked Man had planned well for this situation just in case things fell apart. He took his gear to the car, returned to the house, and went to a closet. There were three cans of gas there, and he sprinkled it throughout the home. When this was done, he stood at the front door and set fire to a broom's straw, cast it into the room, and closed the door quickly to avoid the sudden flash of flames from the initial combustion. He hopped in his car and left like a bat out of hell. The house erupted into a fiery inferno in a matter of seconds.

Sitting at the desk in the motel room, he looked at the maps he had. He would get a flight to Honolulu from Los Angeles. Then he'd get a flight on a different airline to Chek Lap Kok International Airport on Chek Lap Kok Island in Hong Kong, China. He'd stay there a couple of days and have a Chinese girl or two. Then he'd book an overnight flight to Hanoi, fly on to Da Nang, and maybe rent a car or a moped and sightsee on the way to Hoi An City. He began daydreaming and couldn't wait to enjoy a couple of Chinese girls, and better yet, get to Hoi An City and get some real good Vietnamese pussy for a change. Maybe some real young stuff. That's what it was all about for him.

The room phone rang. It was the desk clerk informing him he had a visitor. "Send him straight on to my room if you would please." He then thanked the clerk and waited for the man. He pulled his mask on while he waited, and he opened the door on the first knock and greeted the man warmly. He needed to do a good con job on him from the get go. He offered the man the desk chair, and he sat on the edge of the bed. He smiled and inquired of him, "How are you doing tonight? Fine, I hope. It's good of you to come so promptly. I don't like tardiness."

"I am fine, Exalted One, and I hope you are well also. I would never cause one such as you to be kept waiting for any reason. I feel elated to be called upon by you. I hope I can serve you in the best way possible. I have served many men in the manner of which you want. I've never disappointed anyone I've ever served. I'll be at your beck and call."

"My Number One has told me much about you." He didn't let the man know about Number One being in police custody, wounded in a hospital, or dead. "It was all very good. It was a real glowing report, especially about your ARVN service. You're just the kind of man I need for a very special task. I'm very excited to have you aboard. I think we can work well together."

"I am humbled that you have called on me. I will comply with your every wish. I think you'll be satisfied with all of my special skills. I haven't been able to use them for the last few years, and I'm anxious to do so again. I hope it involves Americans so I can have fun chopping them into little pieces. I have no love for them at all."

"Good! It does involve two Americans, and I want you to have as much fun as you can with them. I hate them with all of my heart and soul. I want them to suffer and know there's no hope to live. In fact, I hope you'll make them beg over and over again for their lives. I'll give you a list of questions to ask them and an overseas phone number of a friend to call with the results, as I must leave the country in the morning. I'll give you $25,000 in U.S. cash now, and when the positive report is received, another $75,000 will be sent to your bank account number which you will give me. You may think that's a lot of money for two bodies, but believe this, it's worth it to me."

"It will be as you wish, but why do I think you are talking about the two men who were with Ba's half-sister today? Is it about the woman they were with?"

"You're very perceptive. Yes, it's all about the woman. I not only love her, but she's very important to me in many other ways. She's important, but not in the way you may think. She will fit in with the future of my Cause and the reuniting of a new Vietnam without Communists. Another part of it is revenge served cold. I hate them and I want those two bastards stone cold dead and on a slab in the morgue after they suffer horribly." The man could hear the vindictiveness in the Exalted One's voice and wondered if there was more to the story than what the Masked Man said. That was okay though. It was none of his business anyway.

The man replied, "You've chosen me wisely to perform this task. You can be assured their butchered bodies will be cold and on a slab in the morgue as soon as I can manage it. Your revenge is as good as served up on ice!"

"Very well then. I'm glad I chose you for the task at hand." He handed the man a list of questions to be asked of the two, and with information on the Americans and where they could be found most of the time. He also instructed the man to keep an eye on the woman he loved, after ridding the world of the two bastards, keeping her safe and report on the woman to the long-distance number periodically. "Do these tasks well, and you will have a great future with the No Name."

"You must leave now, as I have to get up early to catch a plane." The man left, and the Exalted One removed his mask and sat on the bed thinking. He got an idea. He called the desk and booked a second night, then called the airline and changed his reservation to the next day. Even though his world was temporarily disrupted, he fell right to sleep and had a restful night, knowing that tomorrow he had one last chore to do before leaving the Nashville area.

He was up bright and early and ate breakfast at the hotel's breakfast bar. He splurged on sausage gravy and biscuits, a cake donut, orange juice, and coffee. It was a satisfying feeling for him. The sausage gravy and biscuits was one thing he would miss while he was in Vietnam. He'd have to teach some nice Vietnamese lady how to make it for him. Too bad it couldn't be Mai right now. Someday he'd have her support, and he might even marry her in Vietnam. He had had a desire for her for a long time. She had always been so beautiful and sexy. She is a real fox. Now there were two different foxes to catch and dispatch with expediency. They were a spear in his back to say the least about them.

Knowing where she resided, he drove straight to Carly's house and parked in front. He knew her son who was staying with her now would be in school at this time. Normally, her son Robert only stayed a week or so at a time; however, his father was on a business trip to three different countries, so she had him for at least a month and a half this time. Brazenly, he put his mask on and knocked on her door. When she opened it, he hit her in the jaw, knocking her ass over tin cups and unconscious. He dragged her into the house then into her bedroom. He took a small leather case from his shirt pocket and removed a hypodermic needle with a sedative in it and laid it on the bedside table.

He went into the kitchen and got a glass of water and poured it on Carly's face. She awoke, sputtering and foggy. He slapped her face. She was scared out of her wits and began crying. He told her, disguising his voice as much as possible, "Be quiet and do as I say, and you might live to see your son come home this afternoon, understand?" She nodded her ascent.

"Now stop crying and get yourself together. You're going to make a phone call for me or else. After you make the call, I will give you a sedative, and you will just sleep for a while." He took out his cell phone and handed her a piece of paper with a message on it, telling her to read it. "I'm going to dial your friend Mai, and I want you to tell her what's on the paper, but in your own words. Don't worry about her. She will not be harmed."

When she controlled her sobbing, he dialed the number. When Mai answered, Carly asked her how she was holding up and if she was doing anything important today. Mai said no, and Carly said, "I've something to show you that could help Travis and Parnell with their case." After she assured Mai that it was true, she requested, "Mai, I need you to meet me at the Hermitage Walmart at 1:00 PM. Stand outside of the food entrance/exit, and I'll give you the information. I need to get to work as soon as I give it to you." Mai agreed to meet her friend there; they closed the conversation. The Masked Man took his phone back and made Carly lay flat on her stomach. He held her down, gave her the sedative in an upper arm, and waited till she went to sleep.

When she was out of it, he undressed, removed his mask and then removed her dress and underwear, then turned her over and stared at her naked body. He was over whelmed at her natural beauty He spoke aloud to no one while staring at her, "You big, beautiful, long-legged bitch! I've wanted to beat and rape every part of your body since I first saw you. If you didn't have a son who was coming home later, you would never live through this. He removed his clothes, climbed in the bed beside her, and fondled himself, making sure he was up and ready, then got on top of her, and for the next two hours, he enjoyed all of her orifices as well as brutally beating her from time to time.

When he was exhausted and cold and could no longer become aroused, he got up and showered and dressed. He found a roll of tape in a kitchen drawer and taped her ankles together, then her hands, then he put a strip over her mouth. He looked at her beautiful naked body again and sighed. He knew that body would soon be showing a lot of bruises and scrapes. He wiped a little blood from her nose with a tissue from the nightstand. That's alright, he thought. It's a shame he didn't have a place to take her to and keep her for a while. As good as she was asleep, he couldn't help but wonder what she would be like conscious while he performed oral sex on her and then raped all of her wonderful spots. Maybe he could even get an array of sex toys to use on her. He couldn't help but want a little more of her someway before he left. So, he crawled in bed with her again. Because she was bound up, he only suckled her large breasts and felt her lovely thighs for a few minutes, then he had her anally once more. He had to cleanse himself again; then he left and drove to the Hermitage Walmart and parked where he could watch the food entrance without being seen easily.

Mai, being very excited had arrived nearly a half hour earlier than needed, then stood in front of the food entrance for over an hour. He watched her grow bored and pace around. She was the loveliest woman in the world, and he wanted her so. He wished he weren't so spent. He'd like to masturbate over her right now. She used her cell phone a couple of times, most likely trying to call Carly to find out what was going on. She finally got in her car and left. When she was gone, he drove back to the motel, removed his clothes and reminisced about sweet Carly while he showered. He soon realized he needed to quit day dreaming about Carly and do some more detailed planning.

Mai drove to the Waffle House and asked if anyone knew where Carly was. Nobody had a clue. She got in her car and called Tolbane and explained the strange situation and expressed her concern for her friend Carly. It wasn't like her to be a no show. She said she was going over there to check on her.

"OK, Mai, but if you knock on the door and no one answers it, don't go in. Get back in your car and wait. I'm going to call Parnell, and we'll meet you there ASAP. With all that's been happening, I'm really concerned that she doesn't answer. It's not like her. Promise me you'll wait on us before going in." She agreed, and he called Parnell just as he was leaving his office. They both lost no time in arriving at Carly's, only a couple minutes apart.

Tolbane walked to Mai's car, and she rolled down the window. "Travis, I'm really afraid for her wellbeing now. I didn't even knock. I could see the door was partway open, so I got back in the car and phoned the house. I got no answer." While Mai was informing him of the situation, Parnell had arrived and heard what she said.

Without any conversation, the two men brandished their hand guns and eased up on the porch. Standing on either side of the door, Parnell hollered in, "Metro Police!" They made a tactical entry and began clearing the rooms. Tolbane entered her bedroom, found her, and hollered out to Parnell, "In the bedroom." Then aloud to himself he bellowed, "Oh my God!" Of all he had seen in his life, Ba's death and this were the most heart wrenching sights he'd ever seen. She had been severely beaten, was bloody, and most likely she'd been raped over and over.

He moved straight to the bed and checked her carotid pulse. He turned as Parnell entered the bedroom, "She's still alive. Get Emergency now. He ripped the tape from her mouth and peeled off the other binds. Parnell had stepped out of the room to make the call for EMTs and Metro back-ups. Tolbane went to the closet to find something to lay over her and grabbed a throw off the shelf and covered her body. That's when he saw the hypodermic needle and note on the night stand. After reading it, he exclaimed, "I'll be a son of a bitch. What a dirty bastard. I'm going to kill some bastard after I cut his balls off."

Handing the note to Parnell, he said, "I'm going to step outside now. I can't help her any further. Besides, now it's a crime scene and needs to be processed. I want to let you and your guys to go to work here. I need to go out and talk to Mai. He left the house wondering just how he would tell her. Someone didn't want to hurt her, but her friend was fair game. Some sick bastard. What was this fucking world coming to? For Carly's sake, he wanted vengeance, Mike Hammer style! Vengeance is mine when I catch the bastard!

Meanwhile, the Masked Man stopped at Ryan's on Lebanon Road in Hermitage and enjoyed their cafeteria-style dining, including the desserts. After sating himself on them, he returned to the hotel feeling very smug. After napping a bit, he lay on the bed and thought about Carly some more. Why did she have to have the kid staying with her now? It deprived him of having his full satisfaction with her. He needed to rejuvenate his sexual desires, and she was perfect. He was still comparing her and Mai to each other in his fantasies. Then he just concentrated on dreaming about being with a Mai that wanted him, and he satisfied himself while daydreaming.

After he washed himself up, he took out another false ID, credit card, and passport. Then he gathered his belongings and snuck out of the hotel and went to a Motel 6. After checking in and entering the room, he called a different airline and booked a flight to Honolulu via San Francisco for the next day. He felt even smugger. He'd left a real good false trail for those idiots to follow. Compared to him, they were mental midgets. "Oh yes!" He thought to himself, he was definitely superior to them. They couldn't think their way out of a wet paper bag that was torn in half.

He took out his travel alarm clock and set it so he could make the morning check-in time at the airport. He lay back on the bed, propped up the pillows, and had a good night's sleep with pleasant dreams after reviewing his new plans in his mind.

While getting ready to leave Motel 6, he wondered if he would be able to get some good Tahitian pussy in Honolulu. He was always amazed at the way those women could move their hips and their ass and make the grass skirts bounce around. What would it be like to slice off their nipples watch them thrash about and scream in their agony? He liked the fact that his old sex drive was returning to him, as it had been almost non-existent the last few years. Torture and sex and death with women or young girls were his thing. How he had missed it.

Arriving at the airport, he parked the car where he thought it wouldn't be found for a couple of days, at least till he was in the air between the U.S. and Hawaii, then retrieved his luggage, entered the terminal, and checked in. He was really feeling pretty smug as he stepped up to the reservation desk to check his luggage and get his boarding pass.

He went to the snack bar and had some coffee and dough nuts, still longing for some good Vietnamese tea, and ate a couple of additional breakfast pastries. In the airport gift shop, he purchased a couple of magazines to read on the plane. He found a seat afterwards where he could wait on his flight. The boarding time finally arrived, and he boarded the 747, got a window seat, leaned back, and reveled smugly in the idea that no one could ever outfox him. He was the best there ever was. His Cause was going to be a reality.

CHAPTER 17

IT WASN'T LONG BEFORE the emergency medical technician crew arrived at Carly's, just few minutes before the police units did, and Parnell met and showed them into the bedroom. They carefully placed Carly on a gurney after checking her vital signs and her injuries, began an IV and an oxygen mask. They covered her up with a blanket, secured her to it with straps, moved her to their vehicle, and carefully inserted the gurney into the ambulance. With the siren wailing and the emergency lights strobing, she was taken to Summit Medical Center, which was fairly close by on Central Pike in Hermitage.

A few more minutes went by, and a crime scene unit arrived and was met at the curb. Parnell briefed them as much as he could about the crime and the scene, and he told them that he had taken some polaroid photos of Carly's wounds. He made sure they knew that testing the hypodermic needle was high priority and warned them about screwing it up, as this one was as personal as one could get. When they went inside the house, he went to Mai's car and got in the back seat.

Mai was leaning on Tolbane from the driver's side, crying, her light makeup a mess, and her man was holding her and quietly telling her that everything would be all right and that they'd catch the dirty Commie VC bastard that did this and string him up by the balls with piano wire.

"Mai, you need to be strong for Carly," Tolbane explained. "Think reciprocity. She will need strong support, not only from a strong woman, but her friend whom she had supported in time of need. She's a very stanch woman, and you will be important to helping her overcome the horrid affair and learn to survive the aftermath." He hugged her tighter and gently stroked her hair. All Mai could do was utter, "It's my fault! It's my fault! Why wasn't it me that somebody had beaten and raped?" Tolbane knew in his heart that this was going to be one really tough time for his loved one, as well as for their friend.

Parnell sat there for a while, being silent and empathizing with his friends. It struck home to him also. It was a woeful sight. Finally, Parnell whispered to his pal, "We need to talk. I didn't get a chance to call you earlier. Sleep and the job took priority. I've got some info on the Vietnamese they arrested, and I still need to tell you what I learned from the priest. I also have an update on the killing in the Big Mo. So, whenever it's convenient for you, come to the car and sit with me."

Parnell left Mai's car and noticed that an additional couple of Metro units had finally arrived and the uniformed officers were stringing yellow crime scene tape. He walked over, greeted them, thanked them for being there, asked them to keep any onlookers away, and then he asked them to walk the property and its surrounding area and look for anything that could be evidence and let the crime scene guys know about it if they found something. Then he sat in his unmarked police unit, laid back his head, closed his eyes, and waited.

When Tolbane finally felt that Mai had gotten herself together somewhat, he left her and opened the unit's door and climbed in. Parnell, who had fallen asleep while awaiting his amigo, suddenly snapped awake and was reaching for his weapon when he realized who it was. "Oh shit, it's you! Can't you ever open a car door a little quieter?"

"Well old buddy, No sense in doing that. Quiet is for the grave yard, dude. You know what I always say, fuck you and the horse you rode in on. That was one poor friggen horse. He has my upmost sympathy. I'll bet he was deeply swaybacked too by the time you finished riding him. You'd never make it with a real bucking bronco. You'd find your ever-loving butt lying in the dust."

"Shit, I should have shot you anyway. You'd have a very picturesque face with another ass hole right in the middle of your forehead. I wouldn't even have to think about Dirty Harry while doing it. Look, Mai's taking this thing pretty hard. Do you think she'll be alright sitting in the car alone right now? She seems really distressed."

"I think she's starting to understand it wasn't her fault even though she's hurting. It was some sick cowardly psycho bastard that set this whole thing up. It was really brutal. I can't understand why it was Carly some prick done this to, or why she was beaten so severely along with the rape either. I also have another problem to contemplate. Why did someone want Carly to call Mai to come to Walmart to meet her? Was she there just for him to see her? Did someone want to take her and didn't get the opportunity to do it? If this is so, what the hell is the idiot's motive?"

"Since we received the notes and know she's not to be harmed, I can think of a couple of things. Maybe someone, most likely the so-called Masked Man, just wanted to see Mai for some unknown reason. Maybe he even got his jollies off watching her and/or wanted her to find Carly as some kind of message to us. It gives me chills just thinking the guy could have been in the parking lot while she was there."

There was a tap on the window right then. Parnell put down the window and Mai stuck her head in. She looked somewhat better having wiped the smeared makeup off. Her eyes were still a little puffy and watery. She took a couple of deep breaths before she spoke. "Travis, I'm going to the hospital to wait till I can see her. She'll need someone to be there for her when she wakes up. She supported me when Ba was murdered, and I'm going to support her now. I would be there for her even if I didn't have to be. You and Parnell need to do something about her son Robert now. He'll be out of school before long. He can stay with us till she can come home."

"OK Mai! He sure can. I know he likes the dogs, which is good because they can keep him busy. And the guest room only gets used when this guy on my left crashes there. I'm glad you're going to the hospital for her. Keep us updated on her condition as you find out. We'll try to see her later on after she's been moved from ICU and is more stable. Give her our best wishes once she wakes up." Mai nodded, left, and headed to the hospital, ignoring traffic laws as much as the traffic would allow. Parnell used his unit's radio to call the dispatcher and arranged to have someone pick up Carly's son before school was out and keep him until Tolbane could come to pick him up and take him home.

"Well, come on Parnell! Give me an update before I blow a gasket. The suspense is killing me!" Tolbane added, "I just can't wait to find out how much more this is screwed up. The worst part of this is that Carly is just an innocent, wonderful, caring person and is so far removed from the situation. That's another big why."

"OK partner. First you need to forget your dumb ass Order of Battle Factors. We don't need them. Now, give me a minute to think about what comes first, next."

"That's easy, either the chicken or the egg. Did the chicken really cross the road? If it did, was it just to get to the other side, or did it just want to get a beer? Maybe it just laid beside of it. Get it? It just got laid beside the road. Another theory is that maybe it was just flying the coop."

"Get serious, you dumb assed jarhead. Now listen up. The killer in Missouri finally gave a statement. It seems he got his instructions from his cousin here in Nashville. This guy was the look out when our buddy was interrogated and murdered. A trace on his phone went straight to calls from the cell phone of the Vietnamese dude that SWAT busted today. That's one question solved.

"We were able to connect phone calls to that same cell phone and to the Vietnamese cop at around the same times as several incidents occurred. The phone also made several calls to another cell phone of unknown ownership. The phone was registered to a John Unknown. Get the last name? It was really original, like, duh! Evidently the cell phone carrier didn't get it. The cop has now admitted his role in ratting us out to the Vietnamese Masked Man or his man whenever information was available to him. Much more information was passed on than we had suspected.

"The guy who was busted today had a few hundred calls to the unknown number. There were also many calls to what could be sect members. They'll all be checked out, and if they participated in anything, they'll be arrested. Here's the kicker on this, the address for the unknown cell phone was burned almost to the ground last night. Investigators are searching the rubble for anything that might be useful to us. One neighbor reported that he saw the owner carrying luggage to his car when he was letting his dog out. Then several minutes later, he saw flames coming from the guy's house when he looked out his bedroom window and called the fire department immediately. No one else saw anything till they heard sirens and looked out their windows."

"Wow! You guys have been busy. That's impressive," Tolbane noted aloud, more to himself than to Parnell. "This is great stuff."

"Moving right along, the Vietnamese prisoner seems to be proud of his service to the No Name society led by a Masked Man. We were right about the group. After waving his rights, he's copped to several murders the two of them committed for the Masked Man's Cause, including the use of his cousin in Missouri, Ba's death, the mall attack on you, and your adventure with the two goons. He isn't really sure what the man's Cause is. He only knows that it has something to do with finding a missing Jade Cross, the No Name society, a Vietnamese woman named Mai, the hatred of two Americans, and the future uniting of and ruling Vietnam.

"Even though he knows what the man looks like, he claims he doesn't know the Masked Man's real name. He's addressed as the Exalted One and has many identities to use when needed. Get this, the Masked Man actually believes he's the reincarnation of the ancient Vietnamese Hero General Tran Hung Dao, who repelled Mongol invasions in the thirteenth century, and that the Jade Cross rightfully belongs to him. That's all we've gotten from him so far, but for one more thing. This Masked Man really seems to be fixated on a woman named Mai, her safety and some future plan for her, and the eventual torturous death for her man and his friend. As we know, he had your place watched and gave orders not to harm the woman to all who are involved with the No Name."

Tolbane spurted out, "I'll be damned. So, the attack on Carly was most likely pointed at us, and there is a fixation on Mai. All this has been aimed to hurt us, bit by bit. I'm going to kill that son of a bitch. But first I'll make sure he suffers. Being interrogated by the Spanish Inquisition would be like a trip to Disneyland and eating an ice cream cone once I get through with him. Maybe I'll even do him the way Ba was."

"I'm sure you will. It's strange that this guy would rat things out so quickly on himself and his leader. He really must be proud of what they've done together for the Jade Cross, the Cause, and the No Name society and whatever else. I think this guy really has a screw loose or something. I just have the feeling he doesn't want a death sentence. We've basically got the general information from him, and now the concentration will be on the details of their organization, how it's formed, its membership, the guy's plan for us, and other crimes they may be involved in."

"Parnell, I'd never tell you and your guys what to do in your investigations, but I think it's very important to press him about the Masked Man's hatred for us and his weird fixation on Mai. There's something much deeper going on here than we first thought. Oftentimes, prisoners give up some information in order to conceal the most important portions of the crime. They think you believe them and think that you won't probe them any further. I think you're right on about him talking too easily."

"We're well ahead of you. I left a list of questions with my guys relating to us and Mai, as well as what plans the Masked Man might have had for hauling ass. If they find out anything important, I'll be called immediately, if not sooner. As soon as we talk about the priest, I'm going back to the station to put my nose into the questioning. One last conclusion on my part of the situation is that this guy, this Masked Man, whoever in the hell he is, had to have known us in Vietnam and was on the same patrol with us, or served with us, or knew us in some capacity and knows what happened with the Jade Cross on that patrol."

"I need to think about this. There could have been some Vietnamese dude over there that didn't like us. None comes to mind right now. We had quite a few ARVN interpreters assigned to us. Ba's gone now, and I don't know how any of those other interpreters could know what happened unless he told them. He probably did. They were a lot like us in having to tell our buddies about our adventures over there. I can't remember any disrespect aimed at me except for some of the Viet Cong Suspects or NVAs. It could have been one of the Viets within our patrol, the ARVN Sergeant, the Kit Carson Scout, or any of ARVN unit that hated us for finding and reburying that cross even though the priest doesn't think so. The Marines are ruled out. None of them knew what we did, as they were too far away from that hut. Now that I think of it, Light Foot was the closest one to us."

"That's a real poser alright. My call to the Priest went straight through, and he was waiting beside the phone and answered on the first ring. He was really excited. His friend in Hoi An City had some good dope for him. Another friend of his in Da Nang confirmed it for a fact. Both of his friends are priests also. Now, this will really surprise you. It nearly floored me. Guess what was learned?"

"Come on, shithead, give out or lose your balls. I'll bet the info gave you a boner." Tolbane still either couldn't or didn't know when not to quip.

"Don't be so irritating. I've got the same feelings about this as you do. You're not making this any easier on us."

"Ok, I'm sorry! I just get too anxious."

"Me too, I was kind of like that also, but I kept my big mouth shut while listening to him." Tolbane made a gesture of zipping closed a zipper on his mouth. Parnell had to grin at him. Him being so intelligent, he was such a dumb ass, but alas, alack, the guy was his dumb ass and there was no other one who could compare to him.

"To continue Travis, It seems that the Jade Cross wasn't really lost at all. It had been removed from its resting place, but by whom he could not say. The real No Name Society, which his friend in Hoi An City is a member of, said that the dilapidated hovel there was torn down and later on a large stucco building was erected on the spot. Politicians in Hoi An City hoped it would be an office and a center for a new community, a new sub-hamlet, a hamlet, then becoming a village over time. Over behind it are five new hovels so far, and it is hoped there will be many more. While it was being built, maybe a watcher for the No Name dug it up and kept it until the building was completed; this he doesn't have any info on. Then it was reburied somewhere in a more protective way. The only stranger that he knows of to visit that site while the construction was in progress was a Vietnamese traveler from the States. The source thinks he flew up from Ho Chi Minh City

"The stranger hired a moped one day and went where the American enclave had been and hid the moped off the road and traveled towards the site. The watcher didn't see what the guy did there, as he didn't stay long and left towards Hoi An. This was reported to the priest. The timeline could be around the time Ba went back to try to locate his brothers in Saigon/Ho Chi Minh City. The friend in Da Nang had received the same information, as he was also No Name. I asked the priest to call back and give them Ba's name and ask his friends if they would try to find out if he visited Hoi An then. If he did, maybe someone thought he may have known the whereabouts of the Jade Cross. That, by the way, sounds like a big phone bill. I had a hard time convincing the priest that Metro would pay the long-distance charges. I finally said 'This is a donation to the church, OK?' Making it a donation, he gladly accepted it."

"Parnell, that sounds very plausible. That could be the very reason Ba was targeted first to see if he had brought the Jade Cross back to the States. Now my question is if these other priests are No Name how do we know they're not in on this crap? We only have Father Phat's word to go by on this."

"Although Father Phat wouldn't tell me how he knew, he guaranteed me that the real No Name had no ties to this group here. In fact, he said, they were pissed that someone would dare to impersonate the No Name for criminal activity in the U.S. The two priests over there know some Vietnamese here in the States that were, and no longer are, members of the No Name in our country. They will contact them and find out if they can supply any information.

"Since we know about the reincarnation bit, we need the priest to let his friends know about it. If they're legit, they'll really be pissed off at this clown's action. It could reflect on their Vietnamese comunity here," Tolbane reasoned. "This real No Name must have quite an organization over there. I'll bet the Communist Government is frustrated over them. That's probably why they have roving gangs attacking churches and Christians around the country sides. Good Guys in white suits against the Bad Guys in black ones. That's like a shoot 'em up B Western. White Hats and Black Hats. Gene and Roy always wore white hats in their crusades against the bad guys in black hats."

"You could be right once more, even though your analogy sucks. I read about those cowardly attacks somewhere. It might have been on the Internet by some guy who reports every few weeks on the happenings over there. Well, do you remember that book from back in the 60s, I think the title was, '*You Can Trust the Communists (to be Communists)*.' I think I read it twice. Never a truer word was written about Communists. They can be trusted to be exactly what they are, Communists."

"Parnell, do you think this No Name group here has been dismantled for all practical purposes?"

"Except for the finding of the Masked Man and the rounding up of the peons, there's not a lot it can do now. It's virtually decimated. It looks like we're down to getting the leadership of it, and we have half of it in custody right now."

The MNPD Dispatcher called his unit and let them know the boy was in protective custody and asked what needs to be done now. Parnell glanced at Tolbane and he responded with a nod, so he instructed an officer bring the boy to this location and let them know that the boy will be in Travis Tolbane's protective custody. The dispatcher gave Parnell a 10/4 and said that the child would be there in around ten to fifteen minutes.

A unit arrived with Carly's son twenty minutes later. The officer with the child was none other than Cpl. Karen Watson. Tolbane and Parnell had gotten out of the unmarked and walked to meet them. "I knew it. Damn it! Tolbane, you just cannot keep your damn nose clean for a damned minute, can you? Who'd you kill this time?" inquired Cpl. Watson.

Tolbane gave her a big hug. "I wanted to kill you, but you wouldn't stand still long enough. Moving targets are harder to hit. Sorry I missed you too. Now then, if I could just get you to pose in front of that tree over there, I can do a much better job on you, with my super, duper, five-round baby. It's not hard at all to hit a still and standing target. Let's see. I'd have to be less than twenty-one-feet away from you wouldn't I?"

Cpl. Watson replied, "Onley in your wildest ass dreams, you, old horny bastard."

While these two were having old home week and Tolbane was giving her an update, Parnell walked the boy to Tolbane's Marine Corps Green pickup. The young man wanted to know what had happened to his mother and why were there so many police there.

"Look here son," Parnell replied. "You're going to stay at Tolbane and Mai's house for a couple of days. Your mom had a problem and had to go to Summit Medical Center for tests. She will be all right and out of the hospital in a couple of days. Tolbane will tell you everything he knows of what happened on the way to the house. Just be patient a while longer." With a long face, the child nodded and mumbled, "OK, if you say so!" Parnell stood by the pickup truck talking to the boy until Tolbane came to it. Robert's watery eyes were getting to him, and he hoped Tolbane hurried up with his bull hockey.

When the two finished their conversation, Cpl. Watson gave him a "Ta! Ta!" jumped in her unit, and drove off, and Tolbane walked to his pickup. Since the boy had rolled down the window, Tolbane greeted him when he approached, "Hi guy! How are things going with you?" He almost said "How's your hammer hanging?" but he caught himself in time. He was going to have to be careful of what he said with the boy around. He hoped Mai would remember that too.

The boy looked longingly at Tolbane, and almost sobbing stated, "I want my mom here Travis. Is she hurt? Parnell told me you'd tell me what happened to her. Did she fall down and hurt herself, did she get in a car wreck or something? I need her!"

"Don't fret yourself, Robert. She's going to be alright. We'll have a good talk about it on the way to my house. Your mom's going to be alright. We'll get you two together as soon as we can. Right now, I have to talk with Parnell for a couple of minutes more, then we'll be on the way to my place. Guess what? Rant and Rave are there waiting for you to play with them." He tapped Parnell on the shoulder, and they walked a few steps away from the pickup where the boy couldn't hear them talk.

"Parnell, what in the hell do I tell him? I'm not used to relating things to kids. Having never had one, I'm completely at sea on this one for sure. I sure as shit wish Mai was here. She'd know what to do. Mai has great instincts about this kind of thing. Mai would just hold him tight and tell the kid what he needed to hear. I can't do that because I just don't know how!"

"Sure, you can do it Travis! Just tell him some bad dude tried to rob the house or something like that and his mom got banged up a little bit and the doctor has her sleeping so she can get better. Let him know about Mai being at the hospital with his mom, and tell him she'll call him when his mom wakes up so he can talk to her. I know it's a little white lie about the beating and rape, but he's too young for you to be explicit about it. Carly can tell him the truth when he's older if she desires. If anyone can talk to Robert on his level, it's you," he grinned, "with the mental capacity of a three-year old stuffed doll."

"Thanks a lot buddy. You'll definitely NOT be on our shopping list for Christmas for at least throughout eternity. Maybe on our shit list you can make number one without any effort at all. I think that someday Carly should tell him the truth about the incident. It wouldn't be very good for him to learn of his mother's beating and rape from someone just talking about crimes or whatnot."

Parnell opined, "Just this once, I think you hit the nail on the head with a good aim, and without using a hammer too. Just your head."

Tolbane got into the pickup and left Parnell, who was standing on the curb waving so long and getting ready to do the investigating on the crime scene. Tolbane looked at Robert and told him casually to hang on and that they would talk when they got on to I-40. Tolbane was still racking his brain as to what he was going to say. He just wished he could kill some son of a bitch right now.

Meanwhile, Mai was in the medical center's waiting room, impatiently awaiting word from Carly's doctor on her condition. She was still feeling guilty about it being her fault Carly had suffered this cowardly attack by some dirty bastard.

CHAPTER 18

Turning onto I-40 and setting the cruise control at the speed limit and wracking his brain, Tolbane spoke as quietly as possible to Robert about his mother's situation. He didn't want to upset the boy any more than he already was. He made a mental note to tell Mai exactly what he told the boy so she and Carly would know not to be too specific when they talked to Robert later. He is just too young to understand the complexity of the crime, the motive behind it, and exactly what had been done to her. He hoped that someday when Robert learned the truth, he wouldn't blame him and Parnell for the fib.

Coming to a decision as to what to say, he began. "Robert, some guy decided to rob your home, and he didn't know your mother was there at the time. She tried to stop him, and he banged her around a bit and she got some injuries, nothing bad. Mai stopped by your house and found your mother hurting, then she called me and Parnell to come help, and we called the EMTs. When the EMTs took your mother to the hospital, the doctor felt your mom needed a lot of rest, so he gave her something to help her sleep for a while. She'll be OK. Mai is there to be with her when she wakes up. She'll call you and me when your mother wakes up to let us know how she is. Maybe you can talk to your mom too. Sound good to you?"

"I guess so. I miss her, and I want to tell her I love her and I want to be home with her."

"I know you do. You're a great kid! We'll be at my place soon and guess what?"

"I don't know? What?"

"Those dumb dogs will need feeding and some play time, and maybe you can do it for me while I find something for us to eat. I'm hungry and I know you probably are too. Mai has a lot of good leftovers in the fridge and freezer, so all we need to do is heat them up. That's a good thing. I'm not a good cook at all. Actually, I'm a very bad one."

Robert came to the dog's defense. "Those dogs aren't dumb, they're pretty darn smart. Parnell always says you're the dumb one. Just like a rock, he said." Tolbane laughed. You never know what'll come out of the mouths of babes.

"Well, I guess I'll just have to talk to Parnell about that, now won't I? He's not all that brilliant either. Sometimes his bulb just doesn't light up and shine, maybe it needs screwed in better. Maybe we should wire him up to a better electrical box. Thinking about the dogs, they probably are very smart. They sure do know how to sleep more than me and eat a lot."

Giggling, Robert said, "I think Parnell was right about you!" Tolbane was glad Robert's mood changed a bit. He needed to keep him even more distracted.

When they arrived at the house and were secure inside the gate, the dogs were each at a front corner of the house watching the guys. Tolbane released them from their guard duty, and they rushed the pair, jumping up on them and trying to lick their faces. One of the dogs knocked Robert on his rear, and he laughed and started wrestling with Rant and Rave. Tolbane watched them romp around and thought that animals could be the best child therapy in the world.

He went inside and checked the refrigerator, set out some leftovers, put them in the oven, and turned it on. Then he went to the front door and called for Robert to get the dog dishes and bring them in. The dogs knew what was happening when the boy was getting their dishes. They halted their playfulness and waited patiently for the food and water to come. When Robert entered the kitchen, Tolbane told him, "You know where the dog food is, so you're on dog feeding duty tonight and every night you're here."

"Aye, Aye, Sir!" was Robert's reply. Tolbane had taught him the Navy and Marine Corps affirmative reply when they first met, and he answered Tolbane with it whenever he could. Robert went about his task and took the food and water out to the dogs. He placed a bowl in front of each dog, and they both sat, eagerly licking their chops and waiting for Robert to step back. Once they attacked their food, Katy bar the door and let no man reach for the dish if he wants to keep his arm. Robert always liked watching the dogs gobble up their food and then look up to see if more was coming. Would Travis let him give the dogs a treat later? The dogs would like that. They'd do anything you asked for a treat. He went back into the house wondering what Tolbane would be cooking up. He was feeling real hunger pains after watching the dogs gobble up their supper.

There was little talk during the meal. When they finished eating, the two cleaned up the kitchen, then went out to the couch and Tolbane found a cartoon channel for the boy to watch. Just as Elmer Fudd was pointing his shotgun at Bugs Bunny, Tolbane's cell phone rang. Checking the read out on it he saw it was Mai, and he answered by saying, "Hold on for a minute beautiful!" He told the boy that he had to step outside to answer the call. Robert was so engrossed in the cartoon that Tolbane could have been talking to the wall. He went outside and continued the call, saying, "OK Babe! What's happening there?"

"Carly woke up a few minutes ago, but she's groggy and not with it yet. The doctor is in there with her right now to check up on her and see if any injuries were missed. As far as I know, she has a broken nose, a dislocated jaw with a couple of chips in it, facial bruises, three broken fingers, a couple of cracked ribs, bruised kidneys, bad bite marks on her breasts and inner thighs, and other marks all over her body. A rape kit was taken from her, and thank goodness that even though she was raped, she didn't have severe internal injuries. They're doing a tox screen to see if she might have been drugged, but as you know that will take a while. The doctor doesn't know yet how this will affect her mental state. My God Travis, what kind of animal could do something like this to another human being?"

He could hear the trembling and the pain in her voice. Why couldn't she be with him right now so he could comfort her and make everything OK? Everything seems to be falling on her shoulders at one time. "Mai, this guy is one sick ass person. He has so much hate for Parnell and me and an unknown fixation on you. I'll explain the latest facts we know about that when you get home. Remember I love you and want you here with me, but Carly will need you to be there and be brave for her. When and if you find out more about her condition, call me back. If she can talk, Robert wants to talk to her. He was really upset that something happened to his mother. Oh, please let her know he's fine here. His playing with and feeding the dogs helped him out lot. We had a good supper together, and he's so engrossed in cartoons right now, I don't even think he knows we're talking." Tolbane then related to Mai what he'd told Robert in regards to his mother's attack so she and Carly would tell him the same. Right now, the little white lie was needed to protect Robert's peace of mind.

"I'm glad he's with you. He looks up to you a lot and tries to imitate you, and I know you're the kind of guy that'll take good care of him. I'm always glad you're my kind of guy. If we had a child or two, I know they'd have the greatest dad in the world. I'd probably have to change two kid's diapers though, a small one and a big one. Right now, I'm in the lunch room drinking coffee and eating coconut cream pie, even though I'm not really hungry. I'm going back up to her room now. I love you Travis! Bye!"

"I love you too Mai. Give Carly my best when you can talk to her. Bye!" Tolbane closed the cell phone and went back in the house. On TV an anvil just fell on Wiley Coyote's head, driving him into the ground, and Robert clapped his hands and hooted. Thank Heaven for animals and cartoons.

Half an hour later, Parnell called to say he was in route to the hospital to pay his respect and to get a statement from Carly if possible. After leaving there, he would drive to Tolbane's and they would talk. He had gotten more info to pass on.

Twenty minutes later, Mai called again. Once again, he took the call outside. "Travis, Carly's awake now, but it hurts her to try to talk. The doctor has put her jaw back in place. She might able to talk a little better tomorrow, but she wouldn't be able to talk to Robert right now, it's too painful. I'm out in the hallway. Parnell just got here and he needed to talk to her alone, officially. She indicated to me she doesn't remember anything after the Masked Man made her call me in the morning. I hope she never remembers anything about it. She was glad nothing happened to me. She feels guilty about making the phone call. I told her it was OK and that I understood."

He heard her sobs and could picture the tears running down that pretty face, and it made him hurt deep inside. Before this was over, someone was going to die like the dog he is. "After Parnell leaves, I'll tell her good bye and come home. The doctor's going to give her a sedative after a while so she can get a good night's sleep. Tell the boy the doctor still has her sleeping and she'll call sometime tomorrow. I'll come back midmorning and hang around as long as the doctor will let me. Oh, before I forget. I told Parnell what you told Robert. See you soon, my love."

"Ok Mai, but Parnell is coming here when he's done there, so please get him to follow you home. I know this sicko promised to leave you unharmed, but it'll make me feel better to know that you are safe with Parnell. I'll try, notice I said try, to have Robert in bed and asleep by the time you get here. That reminds me. One of us will have to take him to school tomorrow and pick him up afterwards. We can settle that chore in the morning. Love you bunches and gobs, exes and ohs, and all the good stuff." After hanging up, he just stood there and hung his head for a few minutes.

Sitting down beside the boy he said, "How's the cartoons going champ? It looks to me like you're having a lot of fun." Robert nodded his head up and down. He put his arm around the boy and explained that his mom woke up, but the doctor wanted her to sleep and rest some more so she'll feel better tomorrow. Robert snuggled closer to Tolbane and asked him.

"Will she really be all right?" Tolbane assured him that his mom would be OK and that the most important thing was that he, Robert, would have to be the man of the house for a few days. Robert then assured Tolbane that he would take really good care of his mother. A few minutes later, after finding out what he wanted for breakfast, Tolbane managed to get the boy in bed before Mai and Parnell arrived.

After the two cars arrived, the three sat in their usual spots in the living room. Mai's eyes were still a little puffy and damp, but she still looked good. Tolbane and Parnell sat there deep in thought until Parnell began the update session. He and Tolbane brought Mai up to date on what they knew at the time when she went to the hospital. Then he began to update the lovey-dovey love birds on what he had learned since then.

"While I quizzed that clown at the station, my guys learned a few things on their own. There was a Tran Hung Dao registered at the Music City Sheridan; however, when they got there, the guy had left without checking out with the desk. They dusted for prints, but everything was wiped down, so no lead there. One of the guys got creative and found that a Tran Hung Dao had a flight reservation for Los Angeles this morning but was a no show. This guy's unreal. He's playing us like a fiddle."

"The desk clerk at the Sheridan could only describe him as an average looking Asian man. He's not one of those 'they all look alike' guys either. He's seen a lot of Asians there and had been stationed in Japan, and he only means that there were no distinguishing features he could identify. The guy looked like an ordinary dude. The desk clerk thought he had an Asian visitor in his room for about an hour or so the night before. One guest that we talked to thought he saw the guy go into his room just before two o'clock PM, so that would be just after Mai left the Walmart. That's the last we know of him. He's always one step ahead."

"The clown SWAT caught says he was named Number One because the Masked Man made him his number one man when he was the only member the Masked Man could trust and rely on. He personally killed the ones who displeased the Masked Man and got rid of the bodies. One of those was the guy driving the car when you were attacked at the mall and taken to a secret building in La Vergne. Believe it or not, but this turd saw you chase the guy to the car when you were kidnaped. Anyway, this 'Number One' guy killed all the ones we know of that're in the morgue, for his leader and his Cause, whatever that is. This guy's a real piece of work. He's more or less the cult's manager and enforcer.

"He also plans the cult's meetings and notifies the members, who the Masked Man refers to as his geese, of the meeting times and place. Right now, there are about 26 members left in the gang, give or take, not counting him and the Masked Man. His cousin in Missouri who killed the shooter and some others there that got him information on the wreck, are not members. They just do favors for him because they are related. You know, family and all that."

"Even though he likes the Masked Man, he thinks the guy is an egotist, narcissistic, sociopathic, control freak, and a cold-blooded killer. He's also basically a loner. He described the guy further as being a man who is not affected by any injuries or death to anyone. He would sometimes get older women, women his age, or real young girls for the Masked Man's pleasure, but the last several months the guy didn't want any women. Evidently, Number One always felt sorry for some of the women or girls because they would be either beaten or tortured by the man during sex. Two women were beaten so badly that he had had to go to the local Vietnamese clinic with them to make sure no one talked.

"In addition, there was also one girl about 11 going on 12 who had an internal injury from him using some kind of sex toy on her, but she was only beaten lightly. He said he felt sorry for her, so he kept track of her treatment, paid for some of it, and started a bank account for her with $10,000 of his own money. This guy said he was devastated when he heard that the girl would be sterile, and he felt like killing the Masked Man over that. As bad and heartless as this guy is, he has a soft spot for children.

"He's very intelligent, so far as he's sound in business practices, handles the geese well, and works hard at any given task, but at the same time he seems not to be the sharpest tool in the shed. A real enigma to us. He seems immune to common sense at times, even with his master's degree in management from the University of California at Berkley. Who would have thought he'd be that educated? It's a sure thing that the Masked Man saw the man's competence in his leadership and management skills and found the perfect dupe for his goals.

"Each time he killed or did something special for the Masked Man, he would receive an envelope with a generous amount of cash in it. Any member of the No Name who performed tasks successfully for the Cause would also receive a generous cash gift, sometimes in dollars and sometimes Vietnamese Dong. If there was any hint of failure in an assigned task, the member would be killed. Most of the time when the Masked Man killed, it was at a vacant house they used for complimenting members or killing them. He's agreed to take us to the house and show us where he hid their bodies.

"Thinking of some of your comments, partner, he reminds me of the hero that tells the bad guy to take him instead of his girlfriend. I discussed this turd with my guys, and we still can't figure out why he's so cooperative and running his mouth to the Nth degree. Maybe he wants to be a martyr. Do you have any ideas on this? Sometimes you come up with some psychobabble that ends up being right on."

"No not right now I don't!" he answered. "It is really strange, though, the way this guy has dysentery of the mouth. Something is going on there with this one. Did you find out anything about any escape plans the Masked Man might have from him?"

"The only thing this guy knows for sure is that the Masked Man will, eventually, travel to Vietnam at some point in time to pursue his Cause. He doesn't know the area there he'll go to, though. He has no idea where the jackass is right now or what he's doing, either. It seems the Masked Man is very secretive regarding his plans. He just acts spontaneously as the situation demands. I really believe him on that point. We didn't ask anything to him about the house burning, the motel, or Carly. Those things happened after he was arrested."

Mai had sat quietly listening to Parnell. She asked him, "Are you saying that this man has all those organizational skills and is still like a big simpleton? If that is so, maybe the guy is just stupid and doesn't know how much trouble he's in. Maybe he doesn't realize the seriousness of what he's done and is proud of his achievements with the Masked Man. Maybe he feels guilty or just wants to help. What do you think Travis?"

"Maybe he's a complete mental midget. It sounds like he could qualify for a run for Congress if he's that dumb. He'd win big time you know. You might have something there Mai. There are people who are exceptionally skilled in one area and completely naïve about everything else. You know what I mean. They could build a car engine but can't tie their own shoelaces. They can't chew gum and breathe at the same time. And some are liberal bleeding hearts at the same time also."

"Now, for a sit rep on Carly's attack," Parnell started, getting Tolbane back on track. "This information comes from our lab and her doctor. The drug in the hypodermic we found is pentobarbital. It comes in pill form too. It's a Category D drug and a Schedule II controlled substance. It's used for relief of insomnia, anxiety, nervousness, and/or tension."

"When I talked to her doctor about it for some time. He said she was lucky to be only having a little of the less serious effects. She has a huge headache, a little dizziness, and maybe some constipation too. She is very lucky that she has none of the major side effects to go along with her injuries. She'd be one sick puppy for quite a long time if she did. He also said he'd give her something much weaker to help her sleep tonight. He anticipates that she'll feel much better tomorrow morning. His conclusions on her injuries are that if more force would have been used in any of the blows by the perpetrator, it would have caused her more severe trauma and longer lasting effects. As for his personal opinion, he thinks that the guy didn't want her to die; he just wanted her to be hurt for some reason or other. I informed the doctor that we believe this was a message being sent to someone by the rapist, but I didn't inform him the message was namely meant only for you and me!

"The question is, where in the hell did this rat bastard get the drug? How did he know how much he could safely administer at a time, and where in the hell did he learn to use it? This guy may have had some type of medical training about it, a connection to get it, and practice in injecting it. He could have overdosed her easily. My guys are working on this too, but we may never know the answer.

"I'm hoping that the airline searches will turn up some information on Vietnamese travelers. We're also checking the bus lines and some trains. It's for sure this guy is going on the lam to cool it for a while, but he'll return some day."

"I'll bet that's right!" Tolbane added, "Mai, I'm glad this guy has a fixation on you, is in love with you, or whatever and doesn't want you harmed, at least for now. Yes, according to Parnell's prisoner, he could be very much in love with you. That would mean he'd have some sordid future plan for you."

Turning to Parnell, he continued to surmise, "It could be that he might go back to Vietnam, maybe even to the Hoi An City area. I'd bet on that, a hundred to one! After all, that's where this crap might have started. If he has any friends in Hoi An, and probably he does, he may have learned the same thing we did from the priest about the Jade Cross. If that Jade Cross is part of his Cause, he'll surly go after it with everything he's got. That brings up another question. Why did the No Name bury the Jade Cross in the first place?"

"That's a damn good question we haven't we haven't asked yet. You've got me on that point partner. Since we were at war, maybe it needed to be hidden for a reason we can't fathom, most likely to keep it out of the wrong hands, whoever those hands might belong to." Parnell responded. Would it be the VC hands or ours.

Mai was the one to offer a suggestion. "Hey guys! Maybe the No Name has plans to run the Communists from Vietnam in the future, and the Jade Cross might be a guiding symbol to the populace to over-throw them. You know, like Joan of Arc and the cross or something like it. It's food for thought"

"How in the world did you come up with that idea? That sounds reasonable." Tolbane looked at her in surprise.

"Well, I read a lot. I've read stories where knights or other kinds of heroes sought out icons in order to reunite kingdoms or a people. Think about the search for the chalice in the King Arthur legends. It sounds very plausible to me. After all, look at how long the Jade Cross has been an icon to the members of the No Name."

Parnell jumped at this. "To think this out a little farther, this Masked Man may have visions of grandeur. Maybe he wants to rule a part of or unite all of Vietnam under his version of the No Name. That's a great idea for us to contemplate."

"I remember galloping at his side when King Arthur called some knight on his cell phone and told him to go find a chalice. That was some call. It was long distance too. He didn't even have to leave a voice mail as it was answered immediately."

Mai couldn't help her reply, "What the shit Travis. Sometimes you just don't know when to keep your lips buttoned up. I swear! Your chalice will never overfloweth."

"I swear to you that I'll not joke about it anymore if you let me teach you how to do back flips off the headboard in one or two easy lessons tonight."

"What are you talking about?"

"Mai, it seems your sour daddy here has some unexplained fixation on back flips that I still don't understand. I feel sorry for you having to be with him. Maybe you could use a soldering iron to seal his lips forever. At least use a whole tube of super glue."

"I might take you up on that very idea. Where can I get a tube of it tonight? Just think of what the world would gain with his lips sealed for eternity."

"OK, y'all! I'll be a good boy," Tolbane surrendered. "I'm sorry Mai. That is a decent scenario you put forth though. Taking into consideration his egotistical delusions and aloof actions here, he might think he's a rightful ruler of Vietnam or something else. His assertion that he's the reincarnation of General Tran Hung Dao could be an infatuation with the general, a real delusion, an alter ego of his own on a large scale, or even a clever deception to fool his followers. In any case, he'll need to get to the Jade Cross in order to accomplish his goals, whatever they are. For us to overcome this ass, we need to beat him to it wherever it's located."

"Oh, crap Travis! That's a pretty far out idea," she replied. "Are you talking about us going to Vietnam to stop him from finding it?"

"Well Mai," Parnell interjected, "Why not? It doesn't sound like a bad idea if it's necessary. Your goofball here does get a bright idea once in a while. I still don't know how he does it. By the way, Mai, you said us. You got a tiny, tiny mouse in your pocket today by any chance?"

The three looked back and forth at each other several times in silence. Mai broke the ice by saying, "This is how it's going to be gentlemen, so listen up and listen good dudes. If it's decided that a Vietnam trip is necessary, I'm going to go with you, and don't bother opening your mouths. It's already been decreed. So there!"

Tolbane responded with, "But Mai…"

He didn't get to finish. Mai cut him off with, "I'm going to be your official interpreter and tour guide. So, Suck it up you two, it's happening like whether you like it or no, comprende." The pair of guys looked astounded and big-eyed, and both of them decided to keep their lips sealed for now. Tolbane figured there would be no back flips or treatment of his rare Hawaiian disease tonight by Dr. Mai if he disagreed with her.

After discussing options a little more, it was decided they would wait till the next day to see what could be learned before they would consider going to Vietnam. Before undertaking a trip that long, they needed to be very positive that it was necessary. Parnell finally left, and Tolbane and Mai were still standing by the door. It was starting to get cooler outside. It had been a mild fall season so far, however the weather they had just checked on TV said it would start to cool some tonight, and their first real cold snap of the fall would arrive in a couple of days.

Mai feeling a little chilled looked up at Tolbane and cooed, "After all Travis, it's my home country, and I do miss some things about it. I just need to see it again regardless of the circumstance." Nodding in agreement with her, he put his hands in her arm pits, lifted her up, kissed her deeply, and then she cooed contentedly in his ear.

"You never did get your rare Hawaiian disease treated, did you? How about you waiting and getting it treated when we get to Hoi An City?" He put her down and she beat him in a foot race to the bedroom, got naked, and was already in the bed by the time Tolbane got nude.

He got up during the night to relieve himself and had thoughts that Dr. Mai, the greatest Dr. in the world, gave the best treatment in the world for the rare Hawaiian disease, even if she couldn't do back flips yet.

CHAPTER 19

Tolbane arrived earlier than usual to the mall, checked with the night security, and sat at his desk and began to reminisce about some of his 30 years of active duty. His thoughts mostly were from his arrival in the Republic of Vietnam in 1965 until he retired and his life after his retirement. During his assignments to the Nam, he had good times, bad times, and terrible times. After the wind down of the conflict, he was high enough rank that he had mostly administrative duties with interrogation teams or with S2s or G2s, or special assignments plus one op by the U.S. Ambassador. He had really enjoyed those assignments.

His favorite memories were after he retired. He retired in 1987 and had enough savings and a big enough retirement stipend that he was able to bum around the country, visiting Civil War battlefield parks, monuments, and other tourist attractions. Somehow or other, he had pulled off of I-40 West into Mount Juliet, TN, on his way to Nashville, TN. After spending the night in a motel in Lebanon, TN, he had eaten a quick breakfast of sausage, two orders of bacon, biscuits and gravy, grits, and coffee. Then he got on the road. Looking at the fuel gage, he saw he needed gas, and the dummy he was had forgotten to fill up in Lebanon. When he pulled off the interstate in Mt. Juliet, he though it seemed like a quiet and friendly little town. He decided to drive through and see what it was like after he filled up his car.

While checking out the town's major road, he saw a small realty company building across the road from what looked like a high school, and for some unknown reason, he decided to go in and see what kind of property might be available. One of the agents there took him to his now present residence, showed him around, and gave him the bottom line. The individual who had lived there had passed away, and his only survivor, his son, put the place on the market. The son lived in Alaska and wanted to sell quickly, so he agreed with the agent to sell it at two-thirds of its value for anyone wanting it. Tolbane looked around, and he liked the house and the fact that it was outside the town and situated on two acres, and he found it to be a very good buy in his estimate. He also saw it as a property he could improve to his tastes on a minimum budget. He agreed to make the purchase.

Now, he needed to find a job to keep himself busy. Back at the realtor's office to sign a contract, he looked through a copy of the Tennessean, the Nashville daily paper, while waiting for the realtor to fill out some papers. Turning to the help wanted pages, he looked under the security column and noticed an opening for a mall security manager at Perkins Mall. The ad called for someone mature, experienced, and trustworthy at handling people. Well, he was as trustworthy as any boy scout. He called and made an appointment at the mall. That's how he got this gig.

His thoughts moved forward to 1994 and the events that made it one of his favorite years and began tons of his good memories. One day, he was doing one of his security strolls through the mall and suddenly he and an Asian man were staring at each other face to face. Neither one could believe his own eyes. It was Ba. It was his friend and interpreter from Vietnam. Ba had been with him on two of his tours. Together, they had been through hell and high waters. What a reunion. After they gave each other hugs and greetings of wonder, Tolbane brought Ba to his office. He served him a stout cup of coffee first thing. They spoke of their war adventures, and Ba told him about escaping Vietnam with Mai and coming to the States and their becoming American citizens. He said that she lived close to him in Nashville's Vietnamese community.

Tolbane Brought Ba up to date on his life, how he came to live in Mount Juliet and work in the mall. They promised to get together, relive the past, win the war, and have a blast. They traded cell phone numbers and talked a little more, but Ba had to leave before long, and when he did, Tolbane felt kind of alone for the first time since he retired, even though he had been feeling a little blue. He just missed the Corps. There was just something about wearing a heavy pack and carrying a side arm or a rifle and moving in formation with the best fighting force. He felt suddenly that he needed some companionship. Being alone all the time seemed to put him in a melancholy state sometimes, even though there were so many people in the mall he had come to know, one would always have a place in his heart.

Two days later, Tolbane sat in his office reading the newspaper and going over some shoplifting reports from the mall security unit, and he couldn't believe it when Ba stuck his head in the door and asked, "Permission to enter Sir!"

"Come on in and grab a seat. Damn! It's good to see you again." Ba returned Tolbane's greeting, then sat and smiled, and they grinned at each other like school kids who had secretly broken some dumb rule together.

After a little banter, Ba asked him a question right off the get go. "Do you remember when you stopped that thug

ARVN from raping Mai in our home in Saigon? She has never forgotten that. You became her hero and idol then, and you always will be this with her, and me to be honest. She has always wondered what happened to you. Many are the times she has commented about how she wished she could have gotten to know you better."

"I've wondered about her too, and of course you too. I really feared both of you were taken by the Bac Viet, and gracious only knows what must have happened to you two. It was rather sad for me losing my relationship with you two. I've thought about her a lot of times too. She was not only a pretty girl for her age, but she was a joy to be around. After I pulled that scumbag away from her, I felt I had done something really good in my life for a change. I will always wish I could kick his ass again and again, then skin his ass with my k-bar. I should have nailed him harder than I did. Dirty Harry would have sent him to a rapist haven, down there with the devil, with his big-assed 44 right up his nose."

"I bet you do feel that way. You always did have a flare for the dramatic. I know I would have liked to have killed him myself. She told me last night that she wished she could thank you over and over again. I think she'd like to see you again. You should know, though, that she turned out to be an almost ugly, kind of fat plain Jane, with straight stringy hair and a body as straight as a board."

Tolbane didn't hesitate with his answer. "That makes no difference to me. Bring her by any time. I want to see her again and let her know it was my humble pleasure to be of assistance to her."

Ba stood up and went to the door and said, "You can come in now Mai!"

Tolbane nearly fell off his chair at the sight he was beholding before him. Trying to stand up, he bumped his knees on the desk with a bang and gave a painful grunt. There coming in the doorway was the most beautiful Vietnamese woman he had ever seen. She had on kick-ass red pumps with three-inch heels, a black leather mini skirt that hugged her terrific hips and buns and showed off her great legs and small waist, and a white V-neck polo shirt that accentuated her great bosom. Her long, sleek black hair framed her gorgeous almond eyes and pouty lips. She undoubtedly had the most unique and beautiful face he'd ever seen. He was awe struck. He stuttered and stammered, "You're Mai? You're the little girl I saved?" Mai grinned and said, "The cat got your tongue there, big boy? You look as smitten as a kitten! Poor baby! I guess you're not used to seeing beautiful bountiful broads around here."

Tolbane couldn't find any words to answer. He was dumbfounded. He had a complete loss of words, his jaw flapping without a sound. In fact, he nearly fell as he took a step back and stumbled on his desk chair. "I'll see you later Travis," Ba said as he left the office quickly, chiding them, "That's nice. Don't fight, kids."

"I see you have a serious malfunction problem under your thinking cap," Mai cooed. "Come out from behind the desk this instant." As he did, she put her arms around him and hugged him tight, pressing those wonderful boobs against him. "Until I got a little older, I didn't realize what you really did for me and what it meant for me that day. I'll never forget you, ever. You are one tall, handsome hunk of a man any woman would give her left tit for. Maybe even the right one too. Maybe even both of them. I fell in love with you the minute you clobbered that turd. You'll always have a place in my heart." She gave him a quick kiss on the cheek.

"There have been so many times that I wondered what you would look like today. I never thought you would be so beautiful, and what a body. I just can't get over it. Is this really my little Mai?" he finally was able to say without a stutter.

She cooed sassily, "It is, and just don't you ever get over it, OK! To be honest, I think you're better looking today as opposed to then. At least you don't have on those baggy military clothes with the weird color schemes. They were ugly. Every guy I run into tells me how good looking I am, but I pay them no attention. I guess it must be true, though, if I'm having that kind of effect on you."

"Mai, I didn't mean to act that way. I apologize. I didn't…"

"Be still. Don't say another word. I thought it was kind of cute, as well as complimentary, to see you show your chauvinistic pig side. I am flattered, and it makes me feel good to know that I affect you this way, but right now I'm hungry. I am now officially your luncheon date today. Take me down to Ryan's cafeteria here in the mall. The pathway to a girl's heart can also be through her stomach, as well as a man's wallet. I'll bet you didn't know that."

Before she could change her mind, Tolbane had ushered her out the door like a quick shake of a stick and took her arm in his, and they were almost prancing down the hall way. What happened after that never ended. He's still awestruck at her beauty and just as horny. He had wanted to walk behind her to scope out those legs and that sexy butt, but they were arm and arm. He'd check out the all of that good stuff later. He took her down to Ryan's cafeteria and couldn't believe what a chowhound she was, like himself, and wondered how she still kept such a fine sculptured body.

All of a sudden, the phone rang, taking him from his revelry. Parnell was calling. "I got going early this morning and have an update for you. There are still no hits on DNA and finger prints, but I got some other scoop to pass on. I don't have much time to do it since I'm on the way to a crime scene. Meet me outside at the south entrance in about five minutes. I'll pass it on to you and then I'm gone. I have a surprise for you too, not!"

"Will do partner. I'm on the way." He went to the south entrance and stood inside the doors, looking out. It was little cool this morning to spend much time outside. There weren't many cars in the parking area. Mostly they were in the far parking slots and belonged to the various store employees, as the mall shops were not open yet; although they were ready to open them. He did see what looked like one employee sitting in his car a little way off with his motor running. Probably the guy was just keeping his ass warm until time to check in. The morning was a little cooler than it had been. Parnell had come from the east on Harding Place and pulled into the lot, pulled his unmarked into a slot near the doors, got out, and walked towards the mall entrance.

When Tolbane opened the door to go out, the guy in the car exited it and suddenly came towards Parnell, pulled a semi-automatic hand gun, and shot Parnell in the leg. Tolbane had his mall issue Smith and Wesson Model 64 with hydro shocks in his hand, and in an instance cranked off four rounds, hitting the guy three times, one in the lower right thigh, one grazing the abdomen, and the third in his right shoulder. The fourth slug had shattered some other guy's car window. By the time Tolbane reached the guy, he could see he was most likely a hardnosed Vietnamese, close to his own age. The security camera guard saw the event take place on camera and dispatched a guard to the scene and called 911. The guard was arriving just as Tolbane was picking up the guy's weapon. "Watch this son of a bitch while I check on Parnell," he ordered the guard, and handed him the turd's weapon.

Parnell's through and through wound was in the fleshy part of his upper left thigh and missed the femoral artery and the femur, but it was still bloody and painful. Parnell was grimacing with pain when Tolbane removed Parnell's belt and made a tourniquet above the wound. He quipped to Parnell, "It'll be OK my friend. You'll still be alive and have your sex tool until you get married. I think. That is if any broad would ever have you."

His friend tried to grin, but winced as he said through gritted teeth, "Thanks for your unyielding support, dumb ass." Tolbane only half heard him though because he was on the phone to an MNPD 911 operator, reporting the officer down incident and calling for EMTs. He was assured that mall security had already called and help was on the way. He removed his light jacket and laid it over Parnell's torso and let him know help was on the way and that he had another matter to take care of.

He walked to the guy's car, turned off the ignition, then walked over to the gunman and knelt hard with his left knee on the guy's wounded right shoulder. The guy screamed at the top of his lungs with pain, and his body thrashed. Tolbane pulled his weapon out again and held it in the raised pistol position where the guy could see it as he spoke quietly, "Look scumbag, you best tell me what the fuck is going on here or I'm going to have a friendly fire accident, right between your ever-loving legs. You'll be the best male soprano in the area. Just so you understand me better, you shot my friend and I'm thoroughly pissed off, and I hate dirty assed scum bags like you anyway. By the way, don't make like a dumb ass and pretend you only speak Vietnamese. I speak it too," he told the guy in Vietnamese. "We'll keep it in English from here on out."

With tears in his eyes, the guy was moaning and groaning from the pain in his thigh, ribs, and shoulder, which was made worse from Tolbane's knee on it. He was also cursing him up a storm in Vietnamese and English both, mainly about Tolbane's sexual relations with his mother. Tolbane pressed a little harder with his knee and got the same response, a loud scream of pain. "Talk to me, and I'll ease up with the knee. I can also press much harder if you'd like. I know I'd like it. I could also do some things to you that would drive you nuts. There are VCs who found I could do a whole lot of things to them and they are not around to tell anyone about it anymore."

"Stop it!" the guy sputtered "You're hurting the hell out of me. Ease up on my shoulder and I'll tell you what I know." Tolbane eased up a little with his knee and told the guy to continue. "A couple of nights ago, a Masked Man called me to his motel room. I had done a small job for him once before. He explained his problem to me and paid me very well to take care of you two and put you six feet under. He wanted me to shoot each of you, just to wound, one at a time, and then drag you off and torture you to death. I think it had something to do with a Vietnamese woman. Afterwards, I'm to call a number in Vietnam to report that I'd completed the job, and I would be sent more money. I'd have got you instead of him this morning, but you beat me here. Oh shit, I hurt. Please get me help. I'll tell you everything that I know, but please help me!"

"Help's on the way. It'll be here soon." Tolbane turned his head, looked at the guard and whispered to him to have the EMTs check out Parnell first when they arrived and had him call the security office to bring the first aid kit out. Turning back to the guy, he pulled out the guy's wallet to check his ID. Before opening it he asked, "I need to know where the dumb assed Masked Man is now, so, give it up!"

"I don't know. He said he would be out of circulation for a while. He did, however, give me a number to contact someone in Vietnam to give updates on you two and said he'd pass on orders and send more money to me. I have the phone info in my apartment."

Tolbane heard the sirens arriving and shutting off as police cruisers and EMTs pulled into the lot. Their multicolored lights were still flashing. He almost fell over when he heard a familiar voice saying, "I just earned $50.00 on a decrepit retired Marine Dork and a half. I bet that this Officer down at the mall call would be you two being boys again. You two are always screwing up, and it's always on my watch."

He looked up at Cpl. Karen Watson and said, "You know what you can kiss, Officer. Please note that I said it politely with no disrespect to gender or to law enforcement. I love you too."

"You know it's sad, but I'm glad you're alright. How bad is Parnell's wound?"

"The wound looks like it's a through and through hole in the fleshy part of the thigh. I put a tourniquet right above the wound. I used his belt, now his pants will probably fall down and make some girl happy. He'll make it OK. It's not his first wound. He's one tough dude," He looked down at the guy and told him, "She's going to read you your rights, which I'm sure you've heard before, but remember, you'll talk to me later at the hospital, or else I'll talk to you my way, get it?" The man still winching in pain nodded his head up and down in agreement and cried out, "I got it." By the time Cpl. Watson finished reading his rights, the guy passed out.

While Cpl. Watson did her thing, Tolbane walked over to Parnell, who was now on a gurney. He put his hand on his shoulder and wished his pal the best. He let him know that it was the Masked Man's doing and said he'd give him an update at the hospital later on this afternoon. "I'm going to call the desk sergeant and ask him to have some security set up for both of you at the hospital. I want to keep both of you alive. I'm keeping him alive because he agreed, with mild friendly persuasion, to talk to me there. He actually got a knee jerk reaction in his shoulder from my mild-mannered persona. I'll bring you some skin books for you to pass the time away. If you're a good boy and take your meds, I might even bring you a little snort later on. The mall manager finally returned and set a jug of moonshine on my desk last night. I think it's called Apple Pie. I always loved Apple Pie. I think he got it from some place around Gatlinburg. I'm leaving you now. I've got to make the calls to the desk and Mai. Mai will cut my good time member off and kill me if I don't let her know ASAP what the hell happened here." The EMTs put Parnell into the ambulance, then went over to check the shooter.

"I'll call you from the hospital when they're done slicing and dicing me," Parnell shouted out the ambulance door. "Thanks for the first aid. I always knew you were good for something." They waved so long at each other, and Tolbane walked to the Vietnamese. The guy was on a gurney too, and EMTs had temporary bandages on his wounds, a blood pressure cuff was on his left arm, and an oxygen mask over his nose and mouth. The EMTs had to work around the cuffs Cpl. Watson had put on his wrists. They were putting the guy in the ambulance. The head EMT took Tolbane aside and said, "This guy wanted me to tell you that the Masked Man has a fixation on some Vietnamese lady named Mai, I think, who is living with you. The prisoner doesn't know the lady himself."

"Thanks man." Tolbane, feeling chilly, put his light jacket back on, which now had traces of blood on it. "If you ever need anything here at the mall, just let me know." The EMT nodded, hopped in the back, and they were off to the hospital. Tolbane turned to the guard, took the turd's weapon, and asked him to clear the onlookers away, and then said, "Get ahold of the gal in charge of the mall cleaning crew and ask her to come in and clean up this mess from the EMT's treatments, all the gauze and blood, etc. We'll pay her overtime for it and if I can arrange it, a little bonus. If she can't come in now, find some other way. Thanks for your quick response. It means a lot to me and Parnell." Meanwhile, another guard arrived with the first aid kit, but it wasn't needed now.

"Hey, you got it, Master Gunny. I'm on it." The guard with the first aid kit started dispersing the onlookers without having to be told to do so and kept saying to them, "No comment to questions today! The show's over! Just move along now."

Tolbane called over to Cpl. Watson where she was pointing out to patrol officers where to string the crime scene tape. Hearing him, she walked over to his position, and he gave her the turd's weapon and the wallet. On the way back into the mall, he remembered that he had forgotten to check for an ID card or driver's license in the clown's wallet. He must be getting really old to forget something as basic as that.

Tolbane hurried to his office and called the MNPD desk sergeant and arranged around the clock security for the two at the hospital. He called Mai and gave her a brief version of what happened and explained he was going to the hospital post haste. He told her to stay home and put the dogs on alert and said he'd call soon as soon as he knew how Parnell was. He looked up as he terminated the call and Cpl. Watson was standing in the doorway. He offered her a seat. "Get your lazy, not-so-petite butt in here and take a load off."

Entering the office, she sat and informed him, "If anyone else made that comment, I'd have to shoot him. Hell, I might just shoot you anyway. You'd make a cute target. I can picture you with a whole bunch of new orifices, one in the long tongue if I aim right."

"Well anyhow, I feel like I've been shot at and missed and shit at and hit and never got cleaned up. Every fucking day we're getting into some kind of shit, and people are getting hurt or killed. It's gone farther than just Parnell and me. It now involves Mai and our good friend Carly. So, what else is new? This whole case sucks from high heaven to low hell. It's one great big cluster fuck after another one. In boot camp, my drill instructor would have called it a CFD, a Chinese Fire Drill! He also used a term like we got hit with a Turd of Hurtles."

"Travis, right now there are no investigators handy. We've got several crime scenes being processed right now, but as soon as someone can be cut loose, they'll be here. I've been following this crap you guys have been into as much as I could, and I still I don't know much about any of it. Everyone at the station has been pretty much closed mouthed on what's happening unless you were working the case. Maybe you could clue me in a bit. I guess it started with that shooting crap on my watch, then at Carly's, now this episode, and I'd certainly like to have some answers, but I'm not getting any input from anyone."

"Watson, I need to get to the hospital with Parnell, but I would like to talk with you about it. I've got your cell phone number, and I'll give you a call as soon as I know Parnell's condition. We'll make an arrangement to meet some place. Maybe you can have supper at our place tonight. I need to give Mai an update too. I can tell you both at the same time. Your fresh eyes and ears might help a lot. So far, we can't see the real beginning, nor can we foresee the end. We've seen only a few pieces in the middle of the puzzle. It's a very convoluted situation, but at the very least, you'll know more than you do know now."

"Sounds like a real winner. I look forward to your call. Please give Parnell my best wishes for me."

"I'll do that; he'll appreciate it. Tolbane answered. Tolbane called Mai once more and let her know he was inviting Cpl. Watson for supper. Mai though it was great; she hadn't seen Watson very often lately. She said, "I just love that cop, not only for herself but for the way she doesn't take any crap from my numba ten thous paramour. Tell her to give Parnell my best if she goes to the hospital. I'll need to leave to pick up the boy a litter later, but I will stay home the rest of the time as per my orders from my commanding officer."

"Whoa up there, Nelly! I'll get the boy from school, and if I can't, I'll have an officer pick him up and bring him to the house. You don't leave there period until I get more info out of our latest prisoner, the shooter." She agreed and Tolbane responded with, "I'll be glad to tell Watson to give Parnell your love and let her know you're looking forward to seeing her; she's in the office." He hung up and tried to relay Mai's message, but Cpl. Watson had left the office to go out and release the other officers to go on to their patrols. He quickly called the camera room and informed them of his plans, locked his office, and ran out to catch Watson. She just finished sending off the other officers, except leaving one to mind the crime scene, keeping everything intact. When Tolbane caught up with her as she was opening her cruiser door, he gave her Mai's instructions, informed her that a plate was set at his place for her, and told her to call him when she's ready to come over. He then hopped into his pickup, which had an alter ego of being a Marine too, and peeled out to get to the hospital.

He arrived at the hospital rather quickly and had to park at the far side of the lot and walk back to the emergency room. A nurse stopped him when he walked in, and he asked her about Parnell's and the Vietnamese man's rooms. She was giving him the usual song and dance about not being able to give out patient information, so he showed her his mall badge quickly and put it away. She didn't know the gold Mall badge from a gold Police badge, so she thought he was with MNPD and gave him the room number for Parnell. She said the other one was still in surgery and she wasn't sure what his room number would be yet. He thanked her and went looking for his best bud.

He found Parnell's room easily. He looked really calm in the white bed with a white sheet thrown over him. He looked like he was half asleep. His eyes became fully opened when he saw Tolbane enter. "Before you ask Dumbo, it was a through and through in the fleshy part, and the X-ray showed no serious damage. They packed it with gauze and taped it up. I have a slight fever along with some pain, but I'm doing OK. I think after a good night's sleep, I'll get discharged tomorrow. I'll have a crutch to use, but I'll still out run you, any day of the week. Please tell me that that clown's not dead. I need to know what the hell I'm doing in this bed with a hole in my leg. It is kind of comfortable though. Maybe I'll steal it and take home when I'm discharged from here. Mine's getting a little lumpy."

"And what army are you going to use to hold me back during the race?" quipped Tolbane. "I'm glad it's only a through and through wound. Just think what would have happened if it had hit the femoral arty, or smashed the thigh bone, or even both of them. You're sure a lucky one, I think. The turd, by the way, is still in surgery.

"Yeah, that I am, and I do count my blessings. So, what can you tell me?"

"I don't know any more than what I told you at the ambulance. I'm waiting for that maggot to get out of surgery. I think he'll tell me all he can. Oh, I remember now.

He's about our age and Vietnamese. The one EMT told me he said the Masked Man had a fixation on Mai and for some reason he wanted us to be wounded, kidnapped, and then tortured to death. This joker really loves us bunches and gobs. Exes and Ohs. I guess he must want to tuck us in to bed at night too. I'm really pissed off as hell about this Masked Man's obsession with Mai. I just can't figure how we all fit into his sick scheme of things. His killing of two people, kidnapping a priest, beating and raping Carly, then trying to intimidate us, all the while putting Mai on a pedestal, is just mind boggling to me."

"Well Travis, I've racked my brain ever since this madness began, trying to figure out the connection among us. We know about the Jade Cross and our patrol, and we know a little bit of history about the No Name and can't come up with any one we know, but somehow we're known to him. It's stupid. You don't get this much confusion during a fire drill, or a good old fire fight with an enemy for that matter."

"Amen to that pal. I called the desk sergeant. There will be security on the rooms for you two shortly. He needed to dig up a couple of bodies to stand watch. They'll be live ones at that. Mai and Cpl. Watson send their best regards and hope for a fast recovery. Evidently there's a lot of shit going down son. You know Cpl. Watson. She will be dining with us tonight, and I'll update her and Mai, then the three of us will hash things out as much as we can. Watson is very much in the dark about these things too. These things have happened on her watch, and she's been kept in the dark on them.

"Right now, I have to go pick up Carly's boy Robert and take him to the house. I've got Mai on lockdown for the time being. As soon as I drop him off, I'll get back here and hope I'll be able to talk to that scumbag also. Also, when I get back, you can give me the scoop you came by the mall to give me before you decided to catch that guy's bullet. It was a real good catch too, so, I'll see you later when your legs are straighter, gator."

Parnell threw his pillow at him and said, "Go on and get the hell out." Tolbane grinned and threw the pillow back at him and left.

He made good time in traffic going to the school. He only had to wait about five minutes, watching all the kids leaving before the boy came out, hurried to the pickup when he spotted it, and climbed in. His first words were, "Is my mother coming home now? Is she alright yet? I miss her a lot, Travis."

Tolbane said, "Well hello to you too. Here's a factoid for you champ. You should always say hello or hi or something before asking questions. That always shows your respect to the person your meeting with."

"I'm sorry Travis. Hi. I guess I got a bad habit from watching you and Parnell greet each other all the time. I'm just not thinking very well at all today because I just need Mom so much, and I just want her to be well and with me again."

"The first thing for you to know is that Parnell and I have been friends for a long time. We've been through a lot together, and we are like that only between us. It's just a thing between mutual friends.

"Secondly, I know you do love your mother very much. A lot of things have happened today, and I haven't had time to check on her, but Mai has, and you two can discuss it at the house. When she's ready to come home, we'll bring her to our place for a couple of days. That way we can all help her to get better. She'll be safer there too. I'm going to drop you off with Mai, and I'll have to leave right away. Sgt. Parnell was shot in the leg today and I have to get back to the hospital post haste. He'll be OK though; it's not serious.

"Travis, you guys are the best friends we've got. Well Mai too. And don't forget Rant and Rave. I don't know what we would do without you all to be there for us. Oh, I forgot, please tell Parnell I said I hope he's okay. Can I ask you why all these things are happening to us? I'm kind of scared over it. I don't want anybody to get hurt!"

"I can't give you any good answer to that question, but we're trying to find out why for all of our sakes. There is one more thing for you to always remember son. It's the most important one in the whole wide world, and that is, 'The Marines have landed and have the situation well in hand.' OOH RAH!"

"OOH RAH! back to you, but I still think you're silly as a goose."

Tolbane took out his cell phone, "Here, take my cell phone and call Mai. Tell her where we are and that we'll be at the house in fifteen minutes or so, and ask her to have the gate opened. We'll fly in to the driveway like a hurricane blowing through South Florida." The boy laughed and made the call.

Mai opened the gate and called the dogs off as Tolbane pulled into the driveway. She walked to the car window, and he reached for her head, pulled it through the window, and kissed her while the boy got out and started romping with the dogs. Tolbane told Mai what he needed to do and left. She closed the gates and took the boy and the dogs into the house, and she and the boy had a talk about his mom. "We will bring her home on the morrow, maybe in the afternoon, but she will want you to be the man of the house until she gets better." Mai gave him one set of instructions. "She's going to need a lot of hugs and kisses, and that will be your primary job. You can help me prepare the food and such, and then you can serve it to her. Your payment will consist of your mother's hugs and kisses. Let me see, oh, yes, you need to tell her, "I love you," as much as possible too. Are you ready for your mission?"

"Aye! Aye! Ma'am! I understand the mission and I shall obey. I love Mom's hugs and kisses."

"Good for you! For that, maybe there will be an extra piece of banana cream pie on your plate tonight. I baked one earlier today."

"It's my favorite pie; YEAH!"

The policewoman Cpl. Watson will be our guest tonight, and she will be eating with us too, so let's go to the kitchen to see what we can cook up. Oh, and I just happened to think. You didn't bring any homework with you tonight."

"Our teacher didn't give us any homework tonight. She's going to start a new unit of instruction tomorrow, so I'll have a few new books then. Let's go to the kitchen, and you can show me what I have to do."

"We're off to see the kitchen, the wonderful kitchen of Tolbane," Mai sang. "Too bad we don't have a yellow brick road to walk on." Mai locked her right arm around his left elbow, and they skipped into the kitchen, both singing the Wizard of Oz. Mai thought how wonderful it would be for her and Travis to have a son or daughter of their own.

She'd have to work on that. She supposed he would have some dumb comment about back flips in relation to that request. Someday she needs to find out what the story really is about doing back flips, although she knew it had to be something stupid, or sex related. Maybe she'd even have to put up with some superhero comments. You never knew what Travis might come up with. They were in the kitchen now and were scouring the refrigerator, freezer, cupboards, and pantry for the evening's fare.

"After supper tonight, I'll let you take my cell phone in the bedroom, and you can talk to your mom while we adults talk together. You'll like that, won't you?"

"My gosh, I sure will! Thank you! I love you Mai. You're the nicest person I know. Well, maybe Travis is a nice guy too." He walked over to her and put his arms around her waist and his head on her bosom and held her tight. She put her arms around his shoulders and held him tight. She told him, "It'll be okay, just you wait and see." Mai had tears of joy in her eyes.

Tolbane decided he should have let the mall manager know what he was doing, so he stopped by the mall to inform him. The manager was sitting at the secretary's desk, and Tolbane asked where she was, and he replied, "She and my wife had a spat about the affair, and she quit. I've got to try and get her back. I have no idea what to do with all this damn paperwork." Tolbane shook his head and grinned, thinking about playing with fire and getting burnt. After thanking him for the moonshine, he and the manager had a long talk about what was happening and what plans they may be making for the next few weeks. When they were done, Tolbane took off for the hospital.

When he arrived there, a different nurse was on duty on Parnell's floor, and he went through the Mall badge routine again. He was glad to see that there was a policeman sitting between two adjacent doors. He knew the cop and greeted him and thanked him for being there. He entered the room and Parnell and a nurse were joking about something, so he quipped, "Hey dude, I can't leave you alone for a minute, can I?" The nurse's face turned red, and she quickly left the room. As Tolbane watched her slither out the door, with a great wiggle, he wondered if she could do back flips. Hell, he would settle for front flips too.

"You are a worthless turd, Tolbane. I almost had her ready to treat my third leg in the manner it has been accustomed to, and that I would like to continue the practice here and to the great beyond. You never have had very good timing have you, spoiled sport?"

"You don't need a nurse to do that job. You can handle the extra leg on your own. You're a 'handy' man with great big hands." Tolbane put the package he brought from the mall on the nightstand.

"The bag's got Apple Pie moonshine and some paper cups in it. On the way here, I stopped at an adult book store over on 4th Avenue and got you some educational materials. If you're a good boy and give me the latest scoop, maybe Papa Tolbane will give you a sip, and later you can handle your thing all the while you read the porn books like any good boy would."

"I wonder why I put up with you Dumbo. OK, pull up the chair, sit your dead ass down, and lend me an ear like the Romans and Countrymen did. The odd Vietnamese dude told my guys about some geese, as he called them, who screwed up and the Masked Man wasted. He had promised them a reward for good work, had them kneel down, lower their head, and close their eyes. He then pulled out his pistol and shot them in the top of the head. He always felt that those guys had screwed up and deserved what they got. The Masked Man always had him clean up the blood, bone and gore afterwards and hide the bodies as instructed, and he did it to the best of his ability. Without any coaxing, he has agreed to lead the guys to the house and where the bodies are buried. Before I forget, this guy is a sociopath, and the powers to be are going to get him a psych exam. He needs one, he's definitely dingy.

"There was a no show on a Delta flight to Los Angeles yesterday. The agent there described the missing passenger as maybe being an Asian. She was the one who booked the flight for him. There was also an American Airlines flight to Honolulu via San Francisco that left Nashville this morning that a person described as a Vietnamese got on. I was updated a while ago that it made one stop in Denver,

CO. The police in San Francisco were notified, but there were no Asians on the plane when it landed there. He must have debarked in Denver. We're back to square one, I guess, on that issue.

"The department has authorized me a trip to Hoi An City. If you and Mai come along, they will only pay your way to Honolulu and back. I'll keep all receipts and will be reimbursed for my cost when I return. The rest of the trip will come out of your pocket, so you best dig out those old, dirty, smelly socks full of moths and money, wherever you got them buried. Tonight, ask Mai to research the town and get information on reservations at a decent hotels at our layovers."

"It'll be a few days before I'll be ready to go. I'll let Mai know the dates, and she can reserve the airlines and a hotel in Hoi An City and the other stops along the way. Oh, by the way, the priest will be coming with us too. He feels he has a personal interest in the outcome of this crap since he was kidnapped and bounced around in the trunk of that car. Besides, he reminded me that he will be the contact with his friend there. We'll link up with him in San Francisco."

"Gee Parnell," Tolbane quipped, "Now we have a large posse, and we can head them off at the pass just like Gene Autry and Roy Rogers. Of course, I'll be Roy, and I'll also substitute for Trigger, you'll be Gene, and Mai can be Dale Evens. She can ride Trigger to her heart's content." Parnell cringed at that ridiculous comment. Tolbane took a quick look outside the door to make sure no medical personnel were around. He stepped to the table and poured a couple of drinks, and the two were awed at the first sip and enjoyed their shine in silence for a few minutes. They even had a refill. "Damn, buddy, we need to hide the shine and cups someplace away from the friendly medics," Tolbane commented.

"No problemo, señor. One of the patrolmen went to my place, packed some of my stuff, and brought me a bag full of clothes and goodies I might need here. It's in the closet. Just stash the stuff in the bag." He did. They discussed the situation until the same nurse came in and interrupted them.

"You'll have to leave the room now, sir. In a few minutes one, of the interns will be in to check his wounds, and I have to check Parnell's vitals before his arrival."

Tolbane thought, "I'll bet she'll check his vitals with her best bedroom manners!" But he didn't say it aloud for a change. Holding his tongue, he bid his friend goodbye and went to the next room where the shooter was recovering. The guy was really out of it, so he decided to leave and talk to him the next day, so he left for home. He figured it should be a relaxing meal and a nice evening with the boy and Cpl. Watson being there. These last few days had been so stressful for everyone that was involved in some way with all of this crazy crap happening. Relaxation would be a good thing.

He stopped at the mall for a few minutes to check on things, hoping it would be quiet there. At times, nothing would be happening, but at others, he couldn't take a breath before another incident happened. Finding it a quiet afternoon, he didn't stay long. On his way home, he stopped at a Kroger store and made sure they wouldn't run out of beer, chips, and dip before the night was over.

CHAPTER 20

HE ARRIVED AT THE hospital rather quickly and had to park at the far side of the lot and walk back to the emergency room. A nurse stopped him when he walked in, and he asked her about Parnell's and the Vietnamese man's rooms. She was giving him the usual song and dance about not being able to give out patient information, so he showed her his mall badge quickly and put it away. She didn't know the gold mall badge from a gold Police badge, so she thought he was with MNPD and gave him the room number for Parnell. She said the other one was still in surgery and she wasn't sure what his room number would be yet. He thanked her and went looking for his best bud.

He found Parnell's room easily. He looked calm in the white bed with a sheet thrown over him. He looked half asleep. His eyes became fully opened when he saw Tolbane enter. "Before you ask, it was a through and through in the fleshy part, and the X-ray showed no serious damage. They packed it with gauze and taped it up. I have a slight fever along with some pain, but I'm OK. I think after a good night's sleep, I'll get discharged tomorrow. I'll have a crutch to use, but I'll still out run you, any day of the week. Please tell me that that clown's not dead. I need to know what the hell I'm doing in this bed. It is kind of comfortable though. Maybe I'll steal it and take home when I'm discharged from here. Mine's getting a little lumpy."

"And what army are you going to use to hold me back during the race?" quipped Tolbane. "I'm glad it's only a through and through wound. Just think what would have happened if it had hit the femoral arty, or smashed the thigh bone, or even both of them. You're sure a lucky one, I think. The turd, by the way, is still in surgery."

"Yeah, that I am, and I do count my blessings. So, what can you tell me?"

"I don't know any more than what I told you at the ambulance. I'm waiting for that maggot to get out of surgery. I think he'll tell me all he can. Oh, I remember now. He's about our age and Vietnamese. The one EMT told me he said the Masked Man had a fixation on Mai and for some reason he wanted us to be wounded, kidnapped, and then tortured to death. This joker really loves us bunches and gobs. Exes and Ohs. I guess he must want to tuck us in to bed at night too. I'm really pissed off as hell about this Masked Man's obsession with Mai. I just can't figure how we all fit into his sick scheme of things. His killing of two people, kidnapping a priest, beating and raping Carly, then trying to intimidate us, all the while putting Mai on a pedestal, is mind boggling."

"Well Travis, I've racked my brain trying to figure out the connection among us. We know about the Jade Cross and our patrol, and we know a little bit of history about the No Name and can't come up with any one we know, but somehow, we're known to him. It's stupid. You don't get this much confusion during a fire drill, or a good old fire fight with an enemy for that matter."

"Amen to that pal. I called the desk sergeant. There will be security on the rooms for you two shortly. He needed to dig up a couple of bodies to stand watch. They'll be live ones at that. Mai and Cpl. Watson send their best regards and hope for a fast recovery. Evidently there's a lot of shit going down. Cpl. Watson will dine with us tonight, and I'll update her and Mai, then the three of us will hash things out as much as we can. Watson is very much in the dark too. These things have happened on her watch, and she's been kept in the dark on them.

"Right now, I have to go pick up Carly's boy Robert and take him to the house. I've got Mai on lockdown for the time being. As soon as I drop him off, I'll get back here and hope I'll be able to talk to that scumbag. Also, when I get back, you can give me the scoop you came by the mall to give me. So, I'll see you later when your legs are straighter, gator."

Parnell threw his pillow at him and said, "Go on and get the hell out." Tolbane grinned and threw the pillow back at him and left.

He made good time going to the school. He only had to wait about five minutes watching all the kids leaving before the boy came out, hurried to the pickup, and climbed in. His first words were, "Is my mother coming home now? I miss her."

Tolbane said, "Well hello to you too. Here's a factoid for you champ. You should always say hello or hi or something first. That always shows your respect to the person your meeting with."

"I'm sorry Travis. Hi. I guess I got a bad habit from watching you and Parnell greet each other all the time. I'm just not thinking very well at all today because I just need Mom so much, and I just want her to be well and with me again."

"The first thing for you to know is that Parnell and I have been friends for a long time. We've been through a lot together, and we are only like that only between us. It's just a thing between friends.

"Secondly, I do know you that do love your mother very much. A lot of things have happened today, and I haven't had time to check on her, but Mai has, and you two can discuss it at the house. When she's ready to come home, we'll bring her to our place for a couple of days. That way we can all help her to get better. She'll be a lot safer there too. I'm going to drop you off with Mai when we get to my place, and I'll have to leave right away. Sgt. Parnell was shot in the leg today and I have to get back to the hospital post haste and talk to him. He'll be OK though; it's not serious.

"Travis, you guys are the best friends we've got. Well Mai too. And don't forget Rant and Rave. I don't know what we would do without you all to be there for us. Oh, I forgot, please tell Parnell I said I hope he's okay. Can I ask you why all these things are happening to us? I'm kind of scared over it. I don't want anybody to get hurt!"

"I can't give you any good answer to that question, but we're trying to find out why for all of our sakes. There is one more thing for you to remember son. It's the most important one. 'The Marines have landed and have the situation well in hand.' OOH RAH!"

"OOH RAH back to you, but I still think you're silly."

"Here, take my cell phone and call Mai. Tell her where we are and that we'll be there in fifteen minutes or so, and ask her to have the gate opened. We'll fly in to the driveway like a hurricane blowing through south Florida." The boy laughed and made the call.

Mai opened the gate and called the dogs off as Tolbane pulled into the driveway. She walked to the car window, and he reached for her head, pulled it through the window, and kissed her while the boy got out and started romping with the dogs. Tolbane told Mai what he needed to do and left.

She closed the gates and took the boy and the dogs into the house, and she and the boy had a talk about his mom.

"We'll bring her to our house on the morrow, maybe in the afternoon, but she will want you to be the man of the house until she gets better." Mai gave him one set of instructions, "She's going to need a lot of hugs and kisses, and that will be your primary job. You can help me prepare the food and such, and then you can serve it to her. Your payment will consist of your mother's hugs and kisses. Let me see, oh, yes, you need to tell her, "I love you," as much as possible too. Are you ready for your mission?"

"Aye! Aye! Ma'am! I understand the mission and I shall obey. I love Mom's hugs and kisses."

"Good for you! For that, maybe there will be an extra piece of banana cream pie on your plate tonight. I baked two of them earlier today."

"It's my favorite pie; YEAH!"

The policewoman Cpl. Watson will be our guest tonight, and she will be eating with us too, so let's go to the kitchen to see what we can cook up. Oh, and I just happened to think. You didn't bring any homework with you tonight."

"Our teacher didn't give us any tonight. She's going to start a new unit of instruction tomorrow, so I'll have a few books then. Let's go to the kitchen, and you can show me what I have to do."

"We're off to see the kitchen, the wonderful kitchen of Tolbane," Mai sang. "Too bad we don't have a yellow brick road to walk on." Mai locked her right arm around his left elbow, and they skipped into the kitchen, both singing the Wizard of Oz. Mai thought how wonderful it would be for her and Travis to have a son or daughter of their own.

She'd have to work on that. She supposed he would have some dumb comment about back flips in relation to that request. Someday she needs to find out what the story really is about doing back flips, although she knew it had to be something stupid. Maybe she'd even have to put up with some superhero comments. You never knew what Travis might come up with. They were in the kitchen now and were scouring the refrigerator, freezer, cupboards, and pantry for the evening's fare.

"After supper tonight, I'll let you take my cell phone in the bedroom, and you can talk to your mom while we adults talk together. You'll like that, won't you?"

"My gosh, I sure will! Thank you! I love you Mai. You're the nicest person I know. Well, maybe Travis is a nice guy too." He walked over to her and put his arms around her waist and his head on her bosom and held her tight. She put her arms around his shoulders and held him tight. She told him, "It'll be okay, just you wait and see." Mai had tears of joy in her eyes.

Tolbane decided he should have let the mall manager know what he was doing, so he stopped by the mall. The manager was sitting at the secretary's desk, and Tolbane asked where she was, and he replied, "She and my wife had a spat, and she quit. I've got to try and get her back. I have no idea what to do with all this damn paperwork." Tolbane shook his head and grinned, thinking about playing with fire and getting burnt. After thanking him for the moonshine, he and the manager had a long talk about what was happening and what plans they may be making for the next few weeks. When they were done, Tolbane took off for the hospital.

When Tolbane arrived at the hospital, a different nurse was on duty on Parnell's floor, and he went through the mall badge routine again. He was glad to see that there was a policeman sitting between two adjacent doors. He knew the cop and greeted him and thanked him for being there for security. He entered the room and Parnell and a young, good looking nurse were joking about something, so he quipped, "Hey dude, I can't leave you alone for a minute, can I?" The nurse's face turned fire red, and she quickly left the room. As Tolbane watched her slither out the door, with a great wiggle, he wondered if she could do back flips. Hell, he would even settle for front flips too.

"You are a worthless turd, Tolbane. I almost had her ready to treat my third leg in the manner it has been accustomed to, and I would like to continue the practice here and to the great beyond. You never have had very good timing have you, spoiled sport?"

"You don't need a nurse to do the job. You can handle the extra leg on your own. You're a 'handy' man with great big hands." Tolbane put the package he brought from the mall on the nightstand. "The bag's got Apple Pie moonshine and some paper cups in it. On the way here, I stopped at an adult book store over on 4th Avenue and got you some educational materials. If you're a good boy and give me the latest scoop, maybe Papa Tolbane will give you a sip, and later you can handle your thing all the while you read the porn books like a good boy."

"I wonder why I put up with you Dumbo. OK, pull up the chair, sit your dead ass down, and lend me an ear like the Romans and countrymen did. The odd Vietnamese dude told my guys about some geese, as he called them, who screwed up and the Masked Man wasted. He had promised them a reward for good work, had them kneel down, lower their head, and close their eyes. He then pulled out his pistol and shot them in the top of the head. He always felt that those guys had screwed up and deserved what they got. The Masked Man always had him clean up the blood afterwards and hide the bodies as instructed, and he did it to the best of his ability. Without any coaxing, he has agreed to lead the guys to the house and the bodies.

Before I forget, this guy is a sociopath, and the powers to be are going to get him a psych exam.

"There was a no show on a Delta flight to Los Angeles yesterday. The agent there described the missing passenger as maybe being an Asian. She was the one who booked the flight for him. There was also an American Airlines flight to Honolulu via San Francisco that left Nashville this morning that a person described as a Vietnamese got on. I was updated a while ago that it made one stop in Denver, CO. The police in San Francisco were notified, but there were no Asians on the plane when it landed there. He must have debarked in Denver. We're back to square one, I guess, on that issue.

"The department authorized me a trip to Hoi An. If you and Mai come along, they will only pay your way to Honolulu and back. I'll keep all receipts and will be reimbursed for my cost when I return. The rest of the trip will come out of your pocket, so you best dig out those old, dirty, smelly socks full of moths and money, wherever you got them buried. Tonight, ask Mai to research the town and get information on reservations at a decent hotel. It'll be a few days before I'll be ready to go. I'll let Mai know the dates, and she can reserve the airlines and a hotel in Hoi An and the other stops along the way. Oh, by the way, the priest will be coming with us too. He feels he has a personal interest in the outcome of this crap since he was kidnapped. He'll meet us in San Francisco."

"Gee Parnell," Tolbane quipped, "Now we have a posse, and we can head them off at the pass just like Gene Autry and Roy Rogers. Of course, I'll be Roy, and I'll also substitute for Trigger, you'll be Gene, and Mai can be Dale Evens. She can ride Trigger to her heart's content." Parnell cringed at that ridiculous comment.

Tolbane looked outside the door to make sure no medical personnel were around. He stepped to the table and poured a couple of drinks, and the two were awed at the first sip and enjoyed their shine in silence for a few minutes. They even had a refill. "Damn, buddy, we need to hide the shine and cups someplace away from the friendly medics."

"No problemo, señor. One of the patrolmen went to my place, packed some of my stuff, and brought me a bag full of clothes and goodies I might need here. It's in the closet. Just stash the stuff in the bag." He did. They discussed the situation until the same nurse came in and interrupted them. "You'll have to leave the room, sir. In a few minutes one, of the interns will be in to check his wounds, and I have to check his vitals before his arrival."

Tolbane thought, "I'll bet she'll check his vitals with her best bedroom manners!" But he didn't say it aloud for a change. Holding his tongue, he bid his friend goodbye and went to the next room where the shooter was recovering. The guy was really out of it, so he decided to leave and talk to him the next day, so he left for home. He figured it should be a relaxing meal and a nice evening with the boy and Cpl. Watson being there. These last few days had been so stressful for everyone that was involved in some way with all of this crazy crap happening. Relaxation would be a good thing.

He stopped at the mall for a few minutes to check on things, hoping it would be quiet there. At times, nothing would be happening, but at others, he couldn't take a breath before another incident happened. Finding a quiet afternoon there, he didn't stay very long. On his way home, he stopped at a Kroger store and made sure they wouldn't run out of beer, chips, and dip before the night was over.

CHAPTER 21

AFTER THE PLANE WAS about halfway to Denver, the Masked Man started fretting a bit about being caught. He shouldn't have underestimated MNPD or those two that he hated so much. On the off chance that his man didn't get them and they figured out that he was on this plane, they could notify the police in San Francisco and nab him when he deplaned. He checked his carry-on bag and retrieved a map. If he got off at Denver and took a bus to another town, he could fly to San Diego and then on to Honolulu, Oahu. Thinking about his stowed luggage, he could retrieve it at Honolulu International Airport.

Thinking more on it, when he landed at Denver, he'd tell the stewardess he had to lay over a day and would continue on the next day. That way she'd have the correct passenger count. Yes, that's what he'd do. He studied the map and decided on a town to go to. He'd check at the reservation counter and find out if that town had an airport; if not, he'd ask where he could find one.

After two days, he finally arrived in Honolulu. He was able to retrieve his luggage from the airline and was able to get a room at a plush Waikiki hotel, the Ala Moana Hotel to be exact. It was a little expensive, but it was worth it. He checked in, and had his luggage brought up. He showered, changed clothes, and went for a stroll on the beach. Scoping out all the gorgeous young ladies sun bathing, running, or swimming in their skimpy bikinis made him horny as a goat.[29]

The Masked Man finally made up his mind that he'd go down on Hotel Street that night and find himself some sexual gratification that night, but not in the manner he normally desired. He left the beach and strolled around the myriad of shops on the main drag for an hour. Then he had an early supper of sumptuous Mahi Mahi at a crowed restaurant and returned to his room sated and had a nap.

He napped about an hour and a half, woke up, relieved himself, and washed his face. He opened his luggage and removed a small bottle that contained oral tablets of phenobarbital. Oh, yes! He was going to get some tonight. He'd have his kind of fun with someone, only he wouldn't use his knife. Just looking forward to it reminded him of how wonderful it was with that fine broad, Carly. Damn, that was some fine piece of ass. Oh, those long gorgeous legs, especially the thighs, and sumptuous breasts. She's the kind you'd like to cage and keep for a while.

He hurried down the elevator, left the hotel, and caught a cab to Hotel Street. He'd never been to Honolulu, but he thought about all the things GIs bragged to him about the adventures they had on the street after they returned from R&R on Oahu. So, he inquired of the cab driver, "Years ago a lot of GIs coming back from R&R told me about a lot of places they had fun here on Hotel Street, but the only name I can remember is the Huba Huba Club where they had Oriental dancers. So, does it still exist," he asked the Driver?"

"It closed down a few years ago," was the driver's reply. "If they were there and didn't get caught, they were lucky.

---

[29]   IN Vietnamese "Ba moui lam" means horny as a goat.

The place was off limits to the military. If they were straight, they wouldn't even consider going there anyway. There were no women there. The dancers were all Asian female impersonators. I can drop you off a couple of blocks from where it was and you can walk that way. There are still a lot of the old Asian dancers and some younger ones, and also good-looking women working along there, if you know what I mean." The cabbie snickered to himself. If this guy was for real, he was looking for a gay bar and female impersonators that did the big nasties for a modest fee.

"That sounds really good to me. I always like to take in the scenery and make my own choice. I've even been places where it was hard to make a choice because of all of the beauties that were on parade."

"AH! You're a wise man. Good hunting tonight."

When the cabbie dropped him off and explained where that club had been located, the Masked Man gave him a generous tip and began walking casually along the way. There were people mingling along the street, there were people going in and out of bars, and there were people standing in small groups talking and pointing different directions trying to decide where to go next. He went into a bar and had a cold Primo beer, which represented all the beers brewed in Hawaii at the time. He decided if he got another beer while on the island, it would be mainland brewed. He finished his beer and continued his walk.

When he got to the next block and looked up both sides of the street, he could see some women here and there talking to guys. The farther he went on the block, the better they looked. He could feel that old sensation in his groin telling him he was in the right area to find a good broad for the night. As he crossed the street to the last block described by the cabbie, he couldn't believe what his eyes were seeing. There was a really good woman walking towards him.

As they neared each other, the woman kind of cooed to him, "Hey handsome, you looking for a good time tonight or are you going to do yourself by hand again for your kicks? You look like you've got real strong hands."

"I might just be looking for the right woman for the night, depending on what's she's willing to do," he replied, looking at the woman's ample bust trying to escape from her bra. The top three buttons of her white blouse were undone, and he liked the sight. From there, his eyes checked out her waist, hips, and good legs begging to get out of the mini skirt. "I came to Hawaii to have a real good time and have a good broad for a night. You look like you fill the bill just right. You stay near here."

"I'm your girl. I usually go back in the alley for a quickie, but if you want to stay a while and have a lot of good times in one night, I'm the one to do it with. I've got a small pad just up the street we can go there if you like. It's very expensive though."

The Masked Man pulled a small roll of bills from his side pocket, showed it to her, and said, "Expense is not a problem for me. I think I'd like to stay a while and have a really good time. I can be horny for hours at a time, and I like to please the ladies."

"Well, come on, you horny old devil. I've nothing but a good time for you." She looped her arm in his and led him to her pad, which was on the second floor of a seedy-looking building. She climbed stairs ahead of him, and he admired that great butt wiggling with each step up and couldn't resist squeezing her buns. She stopped, wiggled it some, and he groped it some more.

Her pad had a small bedroom, a small living room, a bathroom with a shower, and a small kitchenette. After he looked around, he picked her up and carried her to the bed, laid her down, got in beside her, and began kissing and hugging her and feeling her thigh. He nearly gagged when he grabbed a handful of what shouldn't be there. Enraged, he hauled off and belted the transsexual in the jaw, stunning the guy.

The Masked Man got off the bed and quickly took out his knife and opened it. Then he took out the vial with the pills. There was a half a bottle of white wine left on the nightstand, and he pulled the cork on it. As the faux-woman was coming around, he pointed the knife at her when she stated at him, and in a very belligerent way said, "Here. Take three of these pills and down it with the wine." She was scared completely out of her wits, she did as she was told to avoid getting cut up.

"What kind of pill did you give to me? Will it kill me? I don't want to die," the transsexual cried out. "I'll even give it to you for free if you want!"

"The pills will only put you to sleep, then I'll do you. Why, of all those good-looking women on the streets, did I have to get you? A weird ass damned transsexual, you!"

"I don't what you were thinking. All of the skirts you see along that area are all men. Some are homosexual transvestites, some are pre-ops like me, and some are those who are done transforming. Years ago, all of us in this area were required to wear a badge stating, 'I'M A BOY!' I thought you knew what you were getting here in this area." The Masked Man could see this faux thing's eyelids getting heavier.

"That fucking cabbie who brought me here will suffer for this too. At least while I'm here, I'm going to let you show me how good you are at oral sex." It was satisfying. By the time it was over, the prostitute was even drowsier.

When the sleep finally came, the Masked Man took the clothes from the victim's body and raped him anally. He cleaned himself and went back to the bed. He retrieved his knife, cut off the victim's genitals, and beat him from head to toe. He enjoyed some more anal intercourse and used the victim's mouth, then slit the victim's throat, nearly through to the spinal column. His rage was now satisfied for the time being.

He cleaned himself up again and then left the pad after wiping down anything he might have touched. After walking a couple blocks and fending off a couple of other so-called women, he caught another cab to his hotel. As an afterthought, he had the cab leave him off a way from the hotel. He needed to walk off his anxiety. He was almost at his hotel when the first cabbie of the night pulled up beside him and rolled his window down and asked, "Hey, did you get what you needed down on Hotel Street, and was it good?"

The Masked Man couldn't believe his luck. He wanted to punish this guy in the worst way. He climbed in to the back of the cab, all while he grinning a large smile, and told the driver, "Yeah man! That was some good stuff. Do you know where there's some that's real classy?"

"Sure, I do, I know a lot of them. If you've got the money, I know just the one for you. It's the top-of-the-line stuff, real classy, brother. She costs a lot more than any of them hopeless ones on Hotel Street."

"Good, I've got the money, let's go man!" As the cabbie pulled from the curb, the Masked Man reached over the seat and put his knife to the cabbie's throat. "Just keep going and pull into some dark quiet place where we can't be seen, or you're a dead man!" The driver drove a short distance and pulled into a very dark alleyway, shut off the ignition as instructed, and handed over the keys. Then the Masked Man slit the guy's throat, pulled him out of the cab, took all the money he could find, and put the body in the trunk. Since it had been easy to get where they were, he was sure he could drive back towards his hotel without a problem. When he was almost there, he spotted a parking garage. He drove in, parked the cab, wiped the cab down as good as possible to erase any trace evidence he may have deposited, and left. While walking to his hotel from there, he put the keys down a drain.

When he was alone in his room, he discovered his luck was holding out. No one had noticed him enter the lobby and get in the elevator. He had blood on his clothes from the spurting of the cabbie's neck and on the back of his shirt and trousers from the cab seat. He stuffed the clothes in his bag and showered for a long time. He lay on the bed contemplating his next move. He hadn't planned on killing anyone here and possibly calling attention to himself. He only wanted to use a pill and do a little rough stuff. He'd call the airlines in the morning and book the first available flight to Hong Kong. That stupid cabbie ruined his dream of having a couple of days of good sex and relaxation, and he paid for it. Damn him! He won't steer another tourist the wrong way. The Masked Man knew he would have to be more careful in Hong Kong. He could taste that Chinese pussy now. Rubbing his crotch, he dropped off to sleep.

Waking up, his first thoughts were to get the hell out of Dodge as quickly as possible. He called the airlines and learned there was an afternoon flight that had some first class and passenger seats left. He booked a first-class seat and cleaned up and went for breakfast. Returning from breakfast, he got his luggage, called a cab for the airport, wiped down the room, and went to the lobby where he checked out.

The hotel rep asked if he was dissatisfied with the stay or anything at the prized hotel since he was checking out early. It was that his boss needed him back, the Masked Man had stated. A worker was injured on the job and couldn't work for a while, so he needed to fill in for the worker. Of course, he would use this hotel when he renewed his vacation, he told her. He was actually thinking about using another hotel if he returned, until the desk clerk offered a room discount for when he returned. He wouldn't have accepted the offer it if it wasn't for the discount. Returning to the scene of any crime indicated guilt, and it would be very stupid to return to the same spot. But he figured he should be in good shape because he would probably be a year or so away from returning to Honolulu. He walked over to a book stand and purchased three Adult type magazines, to read on the flight, that seemed to have scantily clad women in them, during the trip. The Masked Man really loved looking at real Porn Magazines, especially when he could rub himself.

His cab came and picked him up and put his luggage in the trunk, and away they went. He took in the sites on the way, and soon he was at the airline reservation desk getting his ticket and boarding pass. Then he went to the cafeteria to wait. He had a Budweiser beer and two donuts. Before long, his flight was called, and he boarded and got comfortable in his first-class seat. The plane taxied shortly, took off, and was circling the island when he finally breathed a sigh of relief. He had made good his escape.

There was nothing for him to worry about now, Honolulu and his victims were behind him. His only problem he knew about now was whether he should stay on the Kowloon side or the Victoria side of Hong Kong. Maybe he could ask about availability of women on either side when he landed. He leafed through the magazines until he felt his eyes wanting to close. He laid his head back, and drifted off to sleep, dreaming about those nice, long slits in the Chinese ladies' long dresses and a show of nice legs all the way up to their shapely butts. The next ten hours in the air to Chek Lap Kok Island, Hong Kong, China, International Airport wouldn't be over soon enough for him.

He woke about four hours later and felt rested. A few minutes later, a pretty Asian stewardess, who looked Japanese to him, appeared with a food cart. While she was serving the other passengers in first class, he was admiring her body, from her nice legs on up. He wondered what it would be like to have his kind fun with her in the restroom. He knew it would be great. It would be his kind of Mile High Club. He had to remind himself to get rid of those thoughts. Taking that kind of risk on a plane would be utterly stupid. Finding out where she would be staying was a no, no, too. Either one could deprive him of his Cause. He gave her a big smile when she served him. She said, "Let me know if you need anything else." He kept smiling and thanked her. If she only knew how lucky she was, he thought.

After the food trays were removed, he turned to his magazines again. He read every word of every story, even the advertisements, and mentally devoured the pictures with good looking ladies in them. Damn, but he was horny. Being bored after reading the magazines, he fell back to sleep. The Asian stewardess came in to check on the first class passengers, and when she saw him sleeping, she laid an airlines blanket over him. The next thing he knew, he was startled awake by a grating noise and realized it was just the landing gears being lowered into place. Stretching and shaking his head to fully awaken, he felt a moment of joy. "Hong Kong, here I come! Ladies, your worst dreams are about to come true, and my best ones a reality," he thought.

Before retrieving his luggage, he went to the money exchange and talked to some of the clerks in the shops about a good hotel to stay at on the Victoria side. He had decided since he would have to take the ferry to the Kowloon side, it would be best to be close to the airport in case he was running late the day he left Hong Kong. As soon as he retrieved his luggage, he'd check in to a recommended hotel, shower, get a good meal under his belt, and then head for the ferry, cross over and find a good woman. He was sure a rickshaw man could steer him in the right direction. He wouldn't make the same mistake he did in Honolulu. He would stress that he wanted a real woman. Little did he know, his plans would change in just a few minutes.

There was an information booth on the way to the baggage claim, and he noticed a pretty Chinese girl behind the counter. He thought, "It won't hurt to take a look," besides there were a lot of brochures on the counter. He picked up one in English that said, "Transportation Schedule to Kowloon and Hong Kong." When he read about the duration of the bus ride, he was a little shocked that it went to Kowloon first then Hong Kong, and he got a puzzled look on his face. The young lady saw this, and from her experience she believed she knew what was wrong. She approached him and began speaking in Chinese, and he asked her politely to speak in English.

"Oh, you're not Chinese?" she replied in perfect English.

"No, I'm Vietnamese! You speak very good English, I compliment you"

She introduced herself. "Sir, I'm called 'Ling,' short for linguist. I speak three languages and a little of a fourth one. I never had a chance to study Vietnamese. I grew up in Kowloon and learned the King's English from British troops. When I studied in America, I lived with one of my instructors and her husband. They were German, and I learned that language as well. My teacher drilled the American English into my brain because she couldn't stand the accent I had."

"That's OK. I'm called Bao. I'm a very distant relative of the former puppet emperor Bao Dai, who would rather be a playboy in France as opposed to running his country. I've come all the way from New York City to see the wonders of Hong Kong I've heard so much about."

"That's wonderful. I can see by your face that you don't understand the schedule. Let me see if I can use my ESP and solve your dilemma. You have been to Hong Kong before, yes?"

"I have."

"You landed in Kowloon at Kai Tak Airport?"

"Yes, I think that was the one."

"Due to a lot of variables, that airport was closed when this one was built. When you heard there was an International Airport in Hong Kong, you surmised it was on the Victoria side?"

"Yes."

"We are not in either one. Chek Lap Kok Airport is on the Island of Chek Lap Kok, not Hong Kong." She pulled out a small map from under the counter and showed him the layout of the islands and the transportation routes. "From here, you must cross to Lantau Island and then the road link across to Kowloon and then to Victoria. Were you planning to stay on the Victoria side?"

"Yes. I thought I'd get a hotel there and take the ferry back and forth from Kowloon the few days I'm here but looking at your map I'm at a loss."

"When were you here before?"

"During the Vietnam conflict I came here with a US Marine on R&R, and we partied day and night with the loveliest of ladies in Kowloon."

"I hope I'm not being too nosey, but are you looking for another good time with the ladies of Kowloon? If you are, maybe I can offer you a little tidbit."

Slightly embarrassed, the Masked Man's face reddened a bit, and he said a little sheepishly, "I was hoping to enjoy my stay. Chinese ladies are very beautiful and very talented in any kind of bed, if I remember correctly."

"Don't be embarrassed. You'd be surprised of the things I get asked about and the propositions I get. Everyone thinks Chinese pussy is the best in The world."

"Here's the deal. I'll write the name of a bus stop in Kowloon on the back side of this brochure. When you get off at that stop, there will be several taxis waiting, all trying to flag you down. Any one of them can get you to a reasonably priced, clean hotel with a restaurant, not the expensive big named ones. Once you've checked in, all you have to do is ask any rickshaw man in front of the hotel, and you can be guided to any number of party ladies. Just tell the man what you're looking for. Only use rickshaws from in front of your hotel. They can be trusted. Never take one on a side street or a distance from the hotel. It could be dangerous to your physical health."

"Thank you Ling! This has to be the most informative information booth I've ever encountered. It's the most beautifully manned one too." Now it was her turn to blush. "I hope you're well paid. You do your job very well."

"Thank you for the compliment. It was a pleasure to be of service to a nice man. I do get some real jerk offs here. You wouldn't believe some of the stupid asses I've had to put up with from time to time."

He bid her so long and made his way to the baggage claim. He thought about making out with her. She is the kind of girl he could never hurt. No, she would never be a victim of his kind of fun. After retrieving his luggage, he went to find the bus stop. It wasn't hard to find. There were about a dozen people waiting in a line with their baggage. When the bus arrived, it took nearly ten minutes to load the passengers and their luggage. During the bus ride to Kowloon, he nodded off, not worrying about missing his stop. When he boarded, he had shown the driver the paper with the bus stop he needed, and the driver assured he would let him know when they arrived. He did.

As he got off the bus, he automatically turned to the baggage hold where the driver was retrieving his luggage. Then the driver pointed to the taxis, and he went over to them. The first driver in line greeted him in Chinese, and when the Masked Man frowned, he changed to English. "I'm very sorry. I thought you may be Chinese. My English not very good. Only know enough to help passengers. Please tell me where you need go and I, your humble servant, will give you a discount."

"No need to be sorry. I understand you completely. I'm Vietnamese." He told the taxi driver about the conversation with the lady at the airport and that he was indeed looking for a nice, moderately priced hotel, a good meal, and then some evening female enjoyment.

"Not to worry," replied the taxi driver, "I will take you to the Hotel Sav on Wuhu Street. When we arrive, I will show you the rickshaw to look for when you are ready for your night out. Let me get your bags, and we are on the way." The Masked Man got in the cab as the driver put his luggage in the trunk, and they were on the way.

Arriving at the Hotel Sav, the taxi driver asked the passenger to wait one minute. Outside the hotel, along the road, were four rickshaws. The driver pointed at one and motioned for him to come to the taxi. When he did, the driver told him to take a good look at his passenger. "This man was directed to me by our lady friend at the airport. Later when he is ready for a night out, he will look for you. Make sure you take him to the very best, and don't over charge him. Is that understood? He received an affirmative nod from the man as he returned to his rickshaw.

"Okay! You can get out now mister." The driver retrieved the luggage from the trunk, set the luggage on the curb and turned to his passenger for his fare and pointed to the Rickshaw man and said, "that's your man.". The Masked Man paid him and gave him a generous tip to boot and thanked the taxi driver.

As the Masked Man turned around to head for the entrance, a bell hop was approaching with a cart to shuttle his luggage. The bell hop nodded a welcome to him in Chinese and loaded the luggage on the cart, and the two moved into the hotel. He was greeted by a middle-aged woman, not half bd looking, working behind the desk. They discussed his length of his stay, the room cost, the maid service, and other trivial things that could come up on the spur of the moment. When they agreed to terms, he surrendered his passport to her and paid in an advance for three days. He was assured that since it was not the busy season, it would be no problem if he decided he wanted to stay a little longer. The woman gave him an electronic key card and a room number and directed the bell hop to see the gentleman to his second-floor room.

He showered, shaved what light bead he had, then rested a short while. After dressing he then went down to the restaurant and had a New York Strip steak, a loaded baked potato, asparagus tips, and a chef salad with ranch dressing. The one thing that amazed him was the dessert: hot apple pie topped with a slice of cheddar cheese and a dip of vanilla ice cream. Who would have thought that would be on a menu in far off Kowloon? He never heard of it in Vietnam, but when he tried it in the U.S. for the first time, it became one of his favorites. He lingered a while at the table having an after-meal cup of coffee, a rich, and thick French blend, and daydreaming about how nice a Chinese woman was going to be that night. His stomach was feeling full and satisfied he got up and he found his way to the lobby restrooms, then went out front and contacted the rickshaw driver.

He explained to the driver exactly what he wanted to get from a beautiful Chinese woman. He hoped that this guy wouldn't be like the idiot taxi driver in Honolulu. His desires were for a real woman, not a pretender. He must keep his feral side inside him at least until his last night in Hong Kong, maybe even then.

The driver assured him that he knew not only the right place but the right woman to please every one of his wanton desires. The driver also told him, "I'll bet 500 Hong Cong Dollars you'll want to go back to this place again tomorrow night. I'll be waiting in front of the hotel to take you there as I did tonight."

Now the haggling over the cost of the buggy ride began, and the haggling was in earnest. When both parties were finally satisfied on the price for that night and the next two nights, the Masked Man climbed into the rickshaw, and the driver took up the buggy's arms and began pulling it at a slow trot. He pulled the rickshaw up one street and down another for a good twenty minutes or more.

He finally pulled up in front of a two-storied building that seemed to blend in with the rest of the neighborhood. The driver told him to go directly inside, not to linger out in front of the place, because it might be too dangerous for his, physical health and well-being, and he would be taken care of.

He paid the man the agreed-upon fare and entered the building. At the far end was a small bar with three customers smoking and drinking. There were tables and chairs on each side of the room, with an aisle going to the bar. He could see a lone woman sitting at one of the tables facing away from him. As he approached the woman, she turned around to face him and said. "Welcome to my abode. I've been waiting for you." The shocked look on his face betrayed his surprise at the woman sitting there.

CHAPTER 22

Tolbane was feeling a little solemn during his drive home. Sometimes he felt all alone and despondent driving the lonely divided highway home. He was about halfway there when his cell phone rang. He pulled to the side of the highway and answered it. Before he could say hello, a voice blurted out, "Hey you butt wipe, I just pulled up to your place and Mai's opening the gates for me. Bye!" Then the call was terminated. He grinned and wondered what kind of a Sherlock's Watson, his Watson would have been for Sherlock Holmes when he had a case that had become very singular and the game was afoot.

His gates were still open when he pulled into his more than adequate driveway. The dogs were sitting on the lawn by the drive. They would not egress the gates unless they were commanded to or were walking on a leash. They sat quietly until Tolbane exited the pick up and said, "Come on boys!" Then he got the usual friendly dog mugging, nearly falling on his butt when they jumped up on him. He patted both on the head, and they romped around for a few minutes.

While he and the dogs were going at full tilt, Mai had closed the gates and looked on with pride at her man. She knew she'd made the right choice and to be with the right guy. Sometimes she even wondered why she always felt so damned horny around him but never around other guys. Other men just didn't seem to have it like Travis Tolbane does. Carly was probably right when she once informed Mai that not only was Mai deeply in love with Travis, but also that she had to be the horniest woman ever and living with the horniest guy ever put-on earth. What lovey, dovey pair they made. She thought that watching them sometimes was the, cutest and funniest thing ever.

Mai met him at the door which was customary for her and when he entered the house carrying his dearest and good lady in his arms, he heard the raggediest greeting of all times.

"Well, well! Pecker Head finally got home. Three cheers for the Mental Midget" Watson was sitting in the recliner, which Parnell had basically proclaimed as his, with an ice-cold beer. Tolbane noticed she was wearing a very conservative, blue with white trimming, dress for a change. She looked so much better in it than in her uniform, but he had to rag her too. "Which friggen Goodwill Store did you get those seedy assed rags at? Joe's Junk Yard?"

"Tolbane, you best be real nice to me tonight or I'll get Mai to cut you off. Maybe even cut IT off, Bobbit style."

"She's right Travis," Mai entered into the ragging. "Tonight, we women here in this house rule the roost. If I have too, I'll do the Bobbit-style cutting off. Then you'll be Peckerless Head. Dig it Bro?"

Watson retorted, "You go girl! I'll even hold him down while you operate on the poor soul, Dr. Mai"

Tolbane responded with, "Damn, I've got to put up with two of you tonight? I've been ambushed before I even get an ice-cold beer. There's no friggen justice in this wacky assed world of ours."

Carly's son came out of the kitchen and ran to Tolbane and jumped up in to his arms, and they both fell back onto the couch, laughing. "I talked to Mom on the phone," he said, "and guess what? She's going to let me get a dog like Rant and Rave. Isn't that great?"

"It sure is guy. I know a man who raises German Shepherds. If you're a real good guy I might just talk to him about getting one for you, that is if your Mom approves of it. She'd have to take care of it while you're with your Dad. The next thing is if you got one, what would you name it, Parnell?"

"First I guess I'd have to know whether it's a boy or a girl dog first, wouldn't I?"

"That sounds like the right plan dude."

"Well, if it's a girl dog I'd name it Mai! I know it'd be just like her."

"What if it's a boy dog?"

"Maybe I'd name him Semper Fi! Or maybe even just name him Marine." Tolbane thought they'd got him well trained.

"Kid, you're a guy after my own heart. Now, let me get up so I can go get a beer and get away from what these two feminists are plotting for my demise."

Both Mai and Watson stuck their tongues out at him and gave him raspberries. He went to the fridge, retrieved an ice cold brew, took a long satisfying swallow, and returned to the couch. Just as he sat down, his ever-loving love said, "Sorry to spoil your worldly comfort dearest one, but get your rear end back to the kitchen; soup's on! I didn't spend all that time slaving in the kitchen today for nothing. I need rewarding in bed tonight."

"Oh crap!" he moaned getting up slowly as if his bones were stiff. The group headed for the kitchen. Tolbane was the only one grumbling about his having to leave the comfort of the couch, but he didn't grumble for long. Mai had a feast laid out within a couple of minutes. The fare was Salisbury steak drowning in a rich, dark brown gravy, along with garden peas, whole kernel corn, a tossed salad with lots of honey mustard, and the coup de grace, a huge bowl of garlic mashed potatoes. After grace was said by Robert, Mai informed her bigger infant.

"If you're a good boy and eat your supper tonight Travis, your momma will give you a surprise dessert!" Watson and Robert both giggled over that one. Of course, the young lad had to rub it in to Tolbane by informing him that he knew what the dessert was because Mai told him and already promised him an extra dish of it, and if Tolbane didn't like the dessert, Robert would eat his share too.

Tolbane knew when he was out-numbered by this clan, so he said, as casually as possible, "Can we please begin passing the dishes of food around?"

Everybody at the table, except Tolbane of course, laughed and started passing the food dishes. The salad came first, and Tolbane doused it with a thick and rich honey mustard dressing and shredded extra sharp cheddar cheese, and he seemed to inhale it as opposed to just chewing. He was happy as a pig snorting in slop. The mashed potatoes were passed to him next. He liked that because when the meat and gravy got to him, he was ready to drown his potatoes in the rich, dark brown fluid. He just hoped there would-be room left on his plate for the peas and corn, he might have to drown them in gravy too. Watson was watching him build his plate of food. When he had his plate loaded and it was looking like Mount Everest, she said, "I can't believe you're going to eat all of that!"

He smiled at her and replied, "You're darn tooting I am." Mai groaned and commented that his kind of tooting was not allowed at the food table unless they had gas masks. Watson nearly choked on her first bite at Mai's quip.

They ate in silence, savoring each and every bite. They were sating themselves much more than usual, but Mai, Watson, and Robert took occasional breaks to look up and grin at the human vacuum cleaner inhaling his dinner. After the dishes and food were cleared from the table, Mai served them coffee, milk for the lad, placed dessert plates on the table, and retrieved a couple of pie pans covered with foil from the refrigerator and set them on the table. When she removed the foil, Tolbane was elated. She had made two delicious-looking banana cream pies topped with an inch and a half of a meringue and vanilla cookies. She grabbed the plates and began to dish dessert up, making sure the two guys both received good-sized portions. Tolbane's was about three to four times a normal serving.

After dessert, Robert went to his room to call his mother again, and Tolbane went to the couch with a fresh beer, plopped downed, patted his stomach, and closed his eyes. He nearly fell asleep and spilt a little beer on his trousers, leaving a large wet spot. He spilt it on his crotch to be exact. He set the beer on the coffee table, leaned back, and nodded off again. The two women rinsed off the dishes and placed them in the dishwasher and then washed the pots and pans. Tolbane snapped awake again when the women came back to living room and Watson shouted, "I'll be damned! Hey! Look at this Mai. He actually peed in his damn pants!"

"Come on now ladies," he complained. "I fell asleep here and spilt my beer on me. Honest to goodness!"

Watson and Mai both glared at him, and he could see that no matter what he said, he was in Shit City. Mai of course came up with a comment. "The only thing honest you ever knew was most likely a pet rock!" Both ladies giggled at Tolbane's expense.

Eventually all three got comfortable, and Tolbane and Mai took turns updating Watson on the situation, each one spoke chronologically. Watson was really surprised about the patrol and the Jade Cross in Vietnam with Parnell, Ba, and Tolbane the No Name, and all the rest. She had been at a loss for words over the whole situation on her beat from day one. They were nearly complete with the task when the phone rang. Mai answered it, and after listening a minute, she handed it to her paramour and stated, "Someone wants to talk to the Bone Head of the house."

Tolbane, knowing he was the Bone Head, also knew who it had to be, so he answered in kind: "What's up, limp along? Or could that be hop along, and I don't mean Hopalong Cassidy hop, hopping along the bunny trail."

"I'll limp along on your friggen head with my crutch! I took care of what you forgot to do. I talked to the shooter for you. He finally woke up about an hour ago. For your enlightenment, he said he was glad it was me talking to him instead of that, and I quote, 'Dirty crazy bastard!' Everything he told me we already knew or suspected except for a phone number in Hoi An City he was to call to report our demise and receive any other orders. He would be paid accordingly to what he had accomplished. One of the detectives is in with him now and will find out what he can about the phone number tomorrow.

"He was hand cuffed to the bed rail was arrested and read his rights once again, only on some new criminal counts. Our guy is not a real nice guy at all, it seems. He was an ARVN soldier, but , he stated, he never served any place near Hoi An City, nor did he know anything about the No Name. He had, however, heard of Tran Hung Dao running some crime gang. So, that takes care of that problem. I also got an update from one of my guys on the trail of our Masked Man."

There was a long pause and Tolbane blurted out, "Are you going to tell me about it today or what? YES!"

"I thought you'd never ask me. It seems as though a lone Asian, possibly a Vietnamese dude, landed at the International Airport at Honolulu. That's one thing that's being checked out as we speak. The next thing is that our crazy confessor guided my guys to a couple more bodies in the ground behind a house used by the Masked Man. It's getting a forensic going over now. Using the list of names, he gave up, there have been eighteen arrests made so far and a few more are being hunted. So far, all those dudes seemed to know is what was said at meetings by the Masked Man. Seven of them have owned up to some petty crimes they were ordered to do. It looks like the No Name whatever it is in Nashville is now defunct. Hocus Pocus and Presto.........! Now you see it, now you don't.

"Moving along my addled brain one, my prognosis however, is pretty good. The doctor said he might clear me to leave for the good old RVN, which isn't the good old RVN anymore, in about four or five days if I'm a good boy and follow his orders here and there. Of course, I told him I was never bad and I always followed orders from mine Fuhrer. He didn't care for my quip. After the doctor left the room, the nurse informed me that she would see that I wasn't bad as long as I was in her care."

"I'll bet that just broke your heart knowing that she's going to make sure you aren't bad," Tolbane quipped. "You are a poor, poor, bad guy forever. Mai and I are updating Karen Watson on the Vietnamese situation right now as we speak, so I'll give them the latest scoop, without the poop. Tomorrow we'll get to bring Carly here, so I don't know what time I'll get to the hospital to see you. So, I'll see you when I'm able. Bye! Bye! Hop Along." With that, he terminated the call.

The girls were all ears to get the latest scoop from Tolbane. After a couple more beers and friendly chit chat with Watson, Mai had to relieve herself, so she stood and excused herself to go to the toilet. She quipped to Watson, "Keep an eye on the brain-dead clown. Make sure he doesn't pee his pants again." Tolbane tried to swat her on the rear end, but she was too quick for him.

When she was gone, Watson noted to Tolbane that, "You two are really in love like no others could ever be, aren't you?"

"Well let me put it to you in Marine Lingo, my dear Karen Watson. I'd crawl over ten miles of broken glass laying com wire just to hear her fart over the field phone."

"That's what I like about you Travis. You speak so fluidly and elegantly. You must have studied real hard in English Lit 101 for dumb, dorkless, dorks."

"Thank you so very much my dear, Sherlock said to Watson. Real friends are hard to come by now days."

"You're welcome, oh hairy lips of wisdom."

"Watson! Just think! The game's not afoot! To be serious though, let me explain where it all started. I liked her the way you would like any ten-year-old child when I kept her from being raped. She was cute and seemed to be very bright and friendly for her age. You knew she would be a heart breaker when she grew up. After leaving the Saigon area, I had always wondered what had happened to her with all of the to-do relating to the evacuation of the people and the Bac Viet (North's) takeover of her country. The day Ba brought her to my office, I was dumbstruck and couldn't speak, not only because of her Asian beauty and magnificent sexual appeal, but her presence and her self-confidence. She really had me by the short hairs. I fell hook, line, and sinker for her right off the bat. The most astonishing thing to me was when she told me she had loved me since I became her hero. I never thought I could or would fall in love with any woman the way I have her, especially after the affair with

Kaila. I had always pictured myself as a miserly old hermit. We've talked about marriage and having children a little. Maybe after this affair is over, we might get more serious about our life together and having a family."

"I hope you two do tie the knot and have kids. I've never met a couple more deserving of each other. Of course, any baby girls you have must be named after me."

"I'd never, ever name a girl, Cpl. Ermintrude."

"Travis, you are one lucky dude. If I didn't have two swallows of beer left in this bottle, I'd club you with the damn thing."

"Go ahead and throw it at him. Whatever he said, he well deserves it. Maybe it would cause him to rise from the living dumb dorks," Mai interjected as she returned to the living room.

"Do you hear that Watson? Did you hear what she had to say? She loves me."

"Yeah, you're right as crap, as usual."

After Mai returned to the room, seated and comfortable again, they discussed their planned trip to Hoi An City and their hope of ending the Vietnamese situation and the monster once and for all. Ridding the world of this serial killer, the masked monster that took her half-brother's life so brutally and assaulted Carley would be the greatest achievement of their lives. Watson felt a little cheated that she couldn't go to Vietnam also. Besides, the dumb turd thug screwed things up on her watch and she wanted a piece of the action on this one.

After a while, Watson told them reluctantly that she had to leave, as she was still on days again and needed to get some shut eye. Mai and Tolbane wished her well, gave their goodbyes, and hit the sack after putting the boy to bed. After discussing what they needed to do the next morning and bringing Carly from the hospital to the house, they engaged in a little fooling around, then they were dead asleep in each other's arms. Neither one tossed or turned or dreamed during the night. They both awoke bright-eyed and bushy-tailed, ready to whip the world.

Tolbane called Parnell on his cell phone first thing and discussed their schedule for the day, barring any unforeseen incidents. Mai would call the hospital and find out the release time, and they would take the boy with them to pick her up. After getting Carly to their house, Tolbane needed to get to his office and arrange everything with the mall manager and the security guard captain for the Vietnam trip. He'd probably have to use his stored-up vacation time to go. When he was finished there, he'd visit Parnell at the hospital. Then he'd relate to him what he called the Watson Files, from the previous night's visit with her and Mai. He would leave out the peeing in the pants joke, though. When he completed his call, Mai had lots and lots of bacon, three eggs over medium peppered, orange juice, milk, buttered toast topped with black berry jam, a full salt shaker, and good hot coffee ready. That was good. His stomach was growling like a pissed off tiger as usual. This was his favorite breakfast meal, ranking only after Mai and waffles.

After breakfast, they showered together and donned their clothes for the day. Then Mai woke the boy, got him cleaned up and dressed, and then fixed him breakfast. When he was done eating, she cleaned up the kitchen, got food out of the freezer for the day to thaw, and then waited with Tolbane and the boy for time to call the hospital. The boy was as excited as a guy with ants in his pants. He couldn't wait to hug his mom again. Right now, she was his whole life. He didn't want to live without her.

Finally, at nine o'clock, after feeling like the time would never come, Mai called the hospital. She was informed that the Doctor would give Carly a final checkup around ten o'clock AM, and she would be released right after the doctor was through with the check-up; if he okayed it. She most likely would be ready to leave by ten thirty or a few minutes after that. Mai told the boy the time and he jumped up, pumped his fist, and shouted, "Yeah!" They decided they would leave at ten o'clock. Barring any real heavy traffic, the timing would be just about right, and they wouldn't have to wait long. Waiting at a hospital always seemed so drug out and weird.

Finding out the release time, Tolbane called the Mall Manager and the Security Captain and let them know about when he'd be in. He no more than hung up when Parnell called. Parnell relayed the same information that Mai had gotten from the hospital. He also told him that their "friend" in the next room talked a little more. Not very informative, though. He only said that he had heard rumors about a Vietnamese cult doing bad things around the town, but he had never associated the rumors with the Masked Man that contracted him. He thought the guy was just a little far out in left field, and maybe little nuts, but he didn't mind taking the guy's money and doing the job the guy wanted him to do. Partner, I think the well has gone dry there for them. He knows less than we did at the beginning. When you get here, don't stick your head in his room. You'll scare him half to death. He definitely doesn't want to see you, now or forever."

"Shucks, Parnell. I was looking forward to manual strangulation and the ruptured blood vessels in the whites of his eyes, and the broken hyoid bone. His eyes would look adorable with petechial hemorrhaging don't you think. As Sherlock might say, 'It was a very singular incident Watson.' Come! The game's afoot."

"I'll give you a foot Dumbo. I'll put it right where the sun doesn't shine. It'll go right up your old wazoo, my dumb ass buddy. They, whoever, will have to operate to get my #12 out of your butt."

"I love you too. Bye!" Tolbane hung up the phone and laughed. Mai wanted to know what was so funny. Since the boy was there, he told her he'd tell her later. It was five minutes to ten when they pulled away from the house. The boy was on pins and needles in the back seat.

The trip didn't take any longer than they hoped. The traffic was light and it was a pleasant drive for a change. Tolbane parked in front of the double doors, and they entered. When they checked in, they were informed that hospital regulations stated that the patient had to be taken to the vehicle in a wheelchair. They waited only about five minutes, and the elevator doors opened, and an orderly pushed Carly out. Before she was pushed very far, the boy practically jumped on her lap, hugging her tight, and she returned the hugs. The orderly said he had to escort her to the waiting car, but he allowed the boy to push her, which delighted him to no end to help his mom. Both Mai and Tolbane were glad to see she looked good considering she still had facial bruises, and seemed to be in good spirits. Arriving at the car, the orderly said goodbye after Carly was helped into Tolbane's pick-up and left with the chair. Then Carly hugged her two friends tightly, with tears of joy. Mai tried to hide her happy tears, but she was not very successful.

After dropping off the trio at the house, Tolbane immediately left for the mall. Traffic was light going west on I-40 into Nashville, and it allowed him to think about the upcoming trip to Vietnam. He was bothered by what they didn't know about what the Masked Man's activities in the Hoi An City area had been. He began formulating a plan and decided to discuss it with Parnell when he visited the hospital. It was a little unorthodox, and it involved their favorite loony tune in the lockup.

The guy has not hesitated to rat out everything he was involved in when asked, but did anyone ask him what he knew about activities in the Hoi An area? He finally arrived at the mall and met with the Mall manager and the Security Captain for nearly an hour, and they discussed the necessary arrangements that were to be made for his leave of absence, which would start when Parnell was able to travel during the next day or two. Then he spent the next hour catching up on his paperwork, then doing a dutiful check on all the stores, doing his customary inquiries. Then he had a quick cup of coffee with Gerta at the Thai Café, then returned to his office. When all of that was completed, he called Mai to check up on them and felt good to hear that Carly would be OK. At least she had no memory of the actual beating and rape. Feeling a little better, he then headed for the hospital, hoping Parnell would help with his idea.

After he and Parnell had greeted each other with some stupid remarks, they got down to the business at hand. Parnell considered his friend's request. Although he agreed with it, he didn't know if he could make the arrangements. But he thought you never know if you don't try, so he made several phone calls calling in some favors.

When he finally got a green light, he called the public defender who had been assigned to the Masked Man's Number One clown. He promised the attorney that Tolbane would not try to elicit any incriminating statements from the guy, only information about what arrangements and support the Masked Man might have in Hoi An City. The attorney pondered for a few minutes, then he and Parnell established rules for the sit down with Tolbane. Parnell explained the deal to Tolbane, then made a call giving the green light. Then he told Tolbane to be at the justice center in about an hour, and the desk sergeant would get him an escort to an interrogation room where the Masked Man's Number One and his attorney would be waiting for him. They said their so-longs and Tolbane left.

The desk sergeant had an officer escort Tolbane to interrogation room #4. The public defender was just exiting the room, and he laid down all the rules to Tolbane and left. He entered the room and sat down on the other side of the table from the burley Vietnamese and looked him in the eyes. Number One smiled and said, "So, we finally meet. I am honored to meet a true and honorable warrior such as yourself." Tolbane didn't say anything; he just continued his stare.

"Mister Tolbane, I know you probably don't like me at all, but I have no animosity towards you. I was obligated to do things I didn't agree with. I didn't like the Masked Man all that well, but he was all I had here, and he would have killed me if I hadn't followed his orders immediately. I might add that I was well paid for being loyal to him. He paid anyone who did a good job for him a generous sum. He gave me the impression that he had somehow gotten ahold of a large amount of money, Vietnamese Dong and US dollars, before fleeing from Vietnam. That is my story and I'm sticking with it."

Tolbane finally spoke, "I'm curious, did the Masked Man know something and held something over you?"

"Yes, he did."

"I won't ask you about that or things you've done for him. I just want to get some answers about the jerk and what you know about him and Hoi An City," Tolbane replied.

"I will answer what I can, and I will be truthful. I have always admired strong people who can overcome difficulties and win. I knew you were that kind of man when I saw you burst out of that building and chase that dumb goose to his car." He then explained why he was observing the building and reporting to the Masked Man.

"Well, you seem to be that kind of man too, only on the wrong side of the law." Tolbane decided to change the original approach he had decided on. Maybe playing on his vanity a bit would soften him up. "Not many people could handle your job as well as you did. It takes a good, strong, dedicated man to carry out his responsibilities when he doesn't agree with them. You don't find many people with those traits. Although I don't really like you for various reasons and for the things you've done, you seem to be an honest man, and I respect your abilities."

"I thank you for the compliment. Ask me what you will, and I will answer you truthfully as best as I can."

The most important thing for Tolbane was not Hoi An City right then, but was about Mai. "What is the deal about him and my woman, Mai?"

"All I know or can remember is that he said he knew her very well in Vietnam at one time. It was in Sai Gon I believe. Yes! That's right! I think that was where he said it was. He said he knew her for a long, long time and he had loved her right from the start. He spoke often of being madly in love with her and he believed that she rightly belonged sitting beside him and ruling Vietnam after the No Name succeeded in its quest to oust the communists and reunite the country once again".

"He definitely did not want her to be hurt in any way or by anyone. He would have tortured and killed anyone who hurt her. That is one of reasons he came after you. He felt you were keeping her against her will and you were defiling her."

"Did he ever say how he met her?"

"No, he didn't"

"Do you know who he is?"

"I only know him as Tran Hung Dao reincarnated and/ or as the Exalted One. He gave some people different names for himself depending on what he was doing at the time, but I don't really know what his name really is."

"You seem to be a sincere guy. I believe you. The first thing I need to know is why he wants the Jade Cross."

"It is because the Jade Cross is a legendary uniting symbol, a great Icon, for the No Name society. He feels it has mystical powers and will make him a great uniter and leader. He believes it was made from a piece of jade that Tran Hung Dao had been given by a Mongol prisoner in the late 13th century, and since he was that man reincarnated, the Jade Cross rightly belonged to him. He never said too much about it, except that it was one of the two most important things he needed for his Cause. The Jade Cross and the woman, Mai, were his obsessions for the Cause being successful for him. To top it off, he thought you and some of the Marines had taken his Jade Cross from its hiding place to foil his plans and aspirations of a united Viet Nam, and he was determined to recover it from whoever took it."

"That is very illuminating. Thank you very much! The next things I need to know are who his contacts are and any plans he may have hiding out there, for Hoi An City."

"Aah! Let me think on it a moment. I must try to remember what was said." After giving it some thought for a few minutes he offered up the following. "Most everyone he knew here in Nashville or other areas here in Tennessee, are in jail here now, I think. I believe he said something about having an ally on or near Tran Hung Dao Street in that city, and that was where he stayed the last time he visited the country. I do believe that he once commented about having several No Name members there also. I don't know if he went there to find the Jade Cross or not. I think he just ran off to save his everlasting butt, as you Americans say it. I've thought several times that if he ever had a real confrontation with someone, he would turn tail and run for his un-honorable life faster than he'd ever ran with his tail between his legs."

As I ponder about him a lot. He is egotistic, narcissistic, sociopathic, and a big asshole to boot. Also, he has psychological tendencies. He thinks he's really strong, but he's not the kind of physical man you and I are. He's not a warrior. He's very temperamental, and he loses his cool very easily. The least little foul up and he would get a bruised ego, would want to kill the screw-up, and I would suffer his justice some way or another. He doesn't have our temperament, and he explodes easily art the least little thing."

"That's good information to know. What else did he say?"

"He said he had enough money, Vietnamese and US to live on for a real long time, and his friends there in Hoi An City would always help him any time."

"He told you this before he left for Viet Nam?"

"No! He didn't. He would mention it from time to time when he'd become bored. I think it was his contingency plan if he ever needed to take it, as you Americans say, on the lam. Also I believe now, very firmly, that he thought maybe the Jade Cross was still there too since he didn't find any trace of it being here. If he would have really looked further into it, he wouldn't have needed to kill anyone at all. Mostly, for some reason he would still want to kill you and Parnell and take the beautiful Mai."

"Did he say where he thought the Jade Cross might be located in Hoi An City?"

"He wondered if it was back at the spot your patrol found it or someplace near it."

"Do you know exactly where his friend lives close to Tran Hung Dao Street?"

"No! I do not, he never said one way or another."

"Do we know about all of the killings he was responsible for?"

"I don't think so. He spoke about taking care of several people who didn't perform up to his standards before he and I were connected. I don't know of any names or where the bodies lay. He could have been bullshitting me, but I don't think so. He could be very cruel."

"Thank you for being frank with me. I can't think of anything more to ask at this time. I may need to speak to you again."

"If you find him, be very, very careful. Protect yourself. He's a very dangerous individual. He only cares about himself and the beautiful Mai. Please tell me, is she really that beautiful Mr. Tolbane?" Tolbane nodded his head.

As the prisoner's attorney turned to the door to knock for the guard, the prisoner turned toward Tolbane. "It just struck me that there were a few times I heard him kind of talking to himself in a low voice. He said things like, 'No more Mr. nice guy,' and something about, 'I've pretended to be a good and decent person, and that's all over now.' I'm done and I will leave you now." He bowed to Tolbane, the officer opened the door and took him back to his cell.

Tolbane left and drove to the hospital thinking about the interview with Number One turd. He discussed the interview with Parnell, and they came to the conclusion that Parnell should contact the priest and ask him to have his friend in Hoi An City see what he could find out about the Masked Man's cohorts on or near Tran Hung Dao Street. Then Tolbane called the mall and informed those who gave a damn that he was on his way home if there were not any pressing matters. Leaving Parnell's room, he stuck his head into the shooter's room. The guy started to cringe at the site of him, and Tolbane only told the guy to have a nice day and heal soon, and he continued on with a big smile.

Arriving home, he was greeted by the dogs and Robert who were playing in the yard. Stepping inside, he received a big hug and a kiss on the cheek from Carly and her thanks for everything. He blushed a bit and Mai, patiently waiting her turn at him, felt proud to be his woman, now and forever. After another big hug, this time from Mai, and a seductive kiss, he knew he was hooked on this woman forever and that nothing, or no one would ever unhook them, even if they did do back flips.

The three sat comfortably in the living room, and Tolbane gave an update to the ladies. The two had a couple of questions for him too, which he was able to answer easily. Carly wanted to know if she could go with them to Vietnam with them. He explained to her that it might not be in her best interest at the time. She needed to be here for the boy, Robert, and it could be really dangerous. The only reason he would allow Mai to come was because she spoke the language and they would need an interpreter even though he spoke some Vietnamese, and besides, it was her birthplace. And, besides she would castrate him if he didn't let her go along.

Mai finally announced, "Supper time!" Carly went to the door and called her son in and directed him to the bathroom to wash up. Tolbane went to the master bathroom, washed up a bit, and changed into jeans and a T-shirt. The others were already sitting at the table waiting for him to join them and say grace. When he finished saying grace, he took a good look at what was laid out before him. There was country fried steak, mashed potatoes, rich thick sausage gravy for it, snow peas, corn on the cob, and a tub of real butter to go with the baking powder biscuits and the corn on the cob. Mai saw he was pleased at what he was seeing and added, "There is also a thick banana cream pie with gobs of topping on it."

He looked into Mai's eyes, grinned, and said, "I'm in seventh heaven, put there by an angel. Pass the steak, please!"

After he finished his second plate, he let out a large burp, and the girls looked at him as though he was evil. Carly told Mai, "Go ahead and do it!" Mai reached over and gave him a smack on the back of his head saying, "You! You Numba Ten Thous GI, you no get lubbed long time" with an accent a GI would only hear only in the Nam.

He responded, "And you're the Number One Boom Boom Girl!"

"You got that right, Sunshine," she playfully quipped. "It'll cost you ten thousand Dong for it, GI!" Carly and the Robert giggled over their exchange, even though Robert didn't know exactly what they were talking about.

After the meal, the women washed dishes while Tolbane told the boy some sea stories and about how he and Parnell won the war, over-coming all odds. The more he told, the more Robert wanted to hear. Then they all sat around and talked until bed time. They all had a good night's sleep, but not before Tolbane got lucky. He didn't have to spend ten thousand dong to the Number One Boom Boom Girl hiding under the covers in his bed.

CHAPTER 23

"OH DAMN, ON MY Ancestor's graves, you're the lovely Ling from the airport Information both!" he exclaimed. "What the hell are you doing here?"

"I am the proud proprietor of this establishment. I don't often come here, as I have a good manager who doesn't skim profits."

"You're joking with me, right?"

"I am afraid I am not. I'd never joke about this."

"Look at you. You have on that tight pullover with a deep V neckline and no bra, displaying wonderful breasts, and a mini skirt showing off those marvelous thighs. Oh, and that beautiful face and the long, shining black hair. Wow! You must tell me how you come to own this place. Are you one of the working girls too?"

"My parents owned this place. Sometimes I would have to come here and help serve drinks. I started that at about age eight. It was a busy place then, and I liked helping. My mom only did really rich guys on occasion if they offered the right amount of money. Many rich men tried to buy a night with me, but my father always refused them.

Then when I was twelve, some wretch of a real wealthy guy made the right offer, and my father sent me upstairs with him. It was sickening. I had spied on the working girls before, and I thought I'd never want to do that kind of stuff. It was a nightmare for me. Soon, all the rich guys my father had turned down before were able to get their turn at me whenever they wanted to. I hated it, believe me I did, but I knew it made my dad money and I had always wanted him to be happy and successful. It was on my fifteenth birthday that my mother did me the best favor she possibly could. She sent me to live with my distant aunt in America. I studied hard and long hours at everything I could and finished high school there. I then went to a community college and earned an Associate Degree in Business Administration.

"After that I returned here, and in a short time thereafter, my mother died of a heart attack. Then a couple of years later, my father was hit by a British Staff car and died a few days afterward. He had willed the business and all of his other assets to me. At first, I managed the bar and the girls and discovered it was not doing well these days. We had customers, but they weren't spending much money for the quality of girls we had. Then I got a bright idea. With the new International Airport being built, I might be able to get a job there and guide tourists to the place. I worked hard and recruited bus, taxi, and rickshaw drivers, hotel clerks, and bell boys to help my business. It worked out well. When the locals learned how successful we were with tourists and that I was able to get high class and beautiful girls to work here, they began to frequent my humble place again. That's part of my successful story in a nutshell, as an American might say.

"To answer the second part of your question, I hardly ever work upstairs. Once in a while, an interesting man might come to the information desk who interests me, and I indulge myself. I've never been with a Vietnamese guy before. You interested me, so here I am. I'm your humble servant and the woman who's going to give you the treat of your lifetime tonight. I'm sure you won't mind if I fuck your brains out. Tomorrow night I won't be here, but I have a special beautiful and talented girl who will see to your needs if you come back. I hope you will be here the night after that too. Then you'll have both of us for a threesome." She motioned to the bartender, and he brought over two Budweiser's and frosted glasses.

The Masked Man could not believe his luck. But, was luck really on his side tonight? He needed her to answer a few more questions. "Believe me when I say you can do anything you want to my brains. Wow! Just thinking about it adds fuel to my groin. That's really something the way it worked out here for you. By the way, your name can't be Ling, so what do I call you during this night of wonderment?"

"I don't often give out my real name, but for you, its Shen Wong. You can call me Sue if you would like to. Everyone else does."

"Well Sue, how many girls do you have working here?"

"We have six small rooms upstairs for the girls, and in the back upstairs, there's a two-room suite with a bath for me when I'm here. I very seldom work in the bed. It serves as my office too. There are two nights a week that are slow nights. Tonight, is one of them, and I only have two girls upstairs. They aren't the most popular of my girls, but don't get me wrong, even though they are a little older, they are very good. They just aren't as attractive and as active in bed any more as the others, but they are perfect for those who cannot afford the classier ones. On busy nights, I have eight to ten girls available for the customer's choice. During the daytime, there are at least four, sometimes five girls. All are clean and are inspected by health inspectors regularly."

"Besides my being a Vietnamese, why did you choose me? I didn't come on to you and I don't feel like I'm a chick magnet."

"Well, you're good looking and the fact that you didn't try to come on to me was attractive, and you just seemed like you were a good guy. I must confess that I was feeling a little horny at the time too, just as I'm feeling now."

"Good! I love horny women. I too must confess. I was taken aback by your good looks and super body. You were so competent at your job and you related to me very well." He then fibbed a little bit. "You made me horny too. I wanted to jump over the counter and screw you every way but loose. I felt it was a shame that I could never have you. That's why I was so surprised to see you here. To be that fortunate of a man was not a possibility in my mind at all. I have another question for you. Do you live close by?"

"I never disclose where I live, and I'm always careful to see that I'm not followed home. I also have people who protect me. There have been times the wrong men have tried to get me into their bed, and they suffered. Now the grass grows over them. So, tell me a little about yourself."

"I served with the Army of the Republic of Viet Nam and was attached to American units during the conflict in my country. I escaped the country just before Saigon fell, made my way to America, and became a very rich and successful banker in California," he fibbed some more. "Now I just want to see my homeland that I love; I'm on my way there now."

"I love rich bankers. They always have lots of money to spend. I must say that if they aren't nice to me or my girls, their fee goes way up, sky high. I won't put up with myself or any of my girls being abused by anyone, and our clientele know this and respect it. As I mentioned, there are those who tried and they now live under the grass."

"What's your fee for tonight? I have a lot of cash. I don't use credit cards or checks. They leave too big a trail if you get my drift."

"My good man, You're in good luck. Tonight, is on the house for you; tomorrow night I assure you will pay dearly from your overly thick wallet. The girl tomorrow night will make it well worth your while, believe me. I should tell you so that you can lick your lips in wonderful and gleeful anticipation, the girl tomorrow night could get top dollar in any of the brothels here in Kowloon or over in Victoria. Maybe even throughout the world. She is the best this area has to offer. She's here working for me because of my strict policies and the way I treat and pay my girls, the security I have for them, and the high dollars and tips she earns. They don't have to split their tips here We have become very fast friends too. She's simply the greatest in bed, you can bank on that."

"You can count on that bank money from me. If she's that good, there may even be a really big tip. I'm looking forward to it, and giving her a certain tip, especially the threesome the next night." With that, the Masked Man gulped down the last dregs of his beer and commented, "I'm not tired, but I think I'm ready for bed. What say we turn in for the night?"

Smiling and giggling, she responded, "I thought you'd never ask. I hope you're able to *get up to it*. Come on upstairs!"

They went up the stairs, and he was amazed at the silk-canopied four poster king size bed and the side bar with every kind of liquor he liked and then some. The room was definitely feminine, decorated in pale blues and pinks, even the bedding. What a bedroom, he thought. Even the large desk and file cabinets in one corner matched the décor. While he gazed around the room, she poured them each a drink. After drinking a straight up Beam's Choice, he watched her movements as she grinded her hips and removed her clothes at the same time, making him even hornier. Then she removed his clothes, and he had the most wonderful night of sex he ever had with any woman to date.

That Sue woman was fantastic. She was the most experienced and athletic woman he'd ever been with. The positions and thrills were unequaled on any bed. He not only wished he could take her with him to Hoi An City, but he was surprised he did not get the desire to beat and cut her up he usually did. He knew that he had to have his kind of satisfaction with a woman soon, but not with this one. Maybe he could get one of her other girls right where he wanted her before he left Kowloon. He'd have to be very careful, though. Sue could identify him before he got on the plane and he'd be in a world of shit for the rest of his life. He'd have to find a way to lure whatever woman he could convince to go to a lonely place with hm. Money could be and was always a real lure for most any woman.

Around six o'clock in the morning, he was physically spent and he finally left Sue's establishment. He couldn't believe his eyes. The same rickshaw driver was waiting for him. The streets were pretty empty, and the trip back to the hotel went quickly as he napped the time away as well as could be expected in a rickshaw. As tired out as he was from the night's activities, he went into the hotel restaurant for breakfast. He stuffed himself with a three egg Spanish omelet, a double order of just crisp bacon, an order of toast with jam, orange juice, and coffee. Scooting back from the table to get up, he rubbed is stomach and felt really satisfied and pleased more so than he had the last few months.

That Sue was really fantastic, turning him every way but loose. He was really spent when she was finished with him. When he finally lay on his bed, he began to wonder what the girl would be like this night. He quickly fell into a peaceful slumber and had wonderful dreams of Mai and him copulating to their hearts content.

He awoke mid-afternoon feeling rested and very relaxed. He decided to take a long hot bath instead of a shower. He soaked for a long time, adding more hot water periodically. Finally, after getting dressed, he sat at the small desk and thought about how to get a girl for his kind of fun the day after the promised threesome. An idea was slowly evolving. He would start talking to the girl tonight, but first he must find a place for the deed. He went to the lobby and checked the daily paper for rent ads. He found what he was looking for, tore the out the ad, and went out to the street. He found Sues rickshaw and driver.

He showed the driver the address and a list of items he'd like to purchase later, and he was taken to the apartment. Along the way the rickshaw driver pointed out to him the places where the Masked Man could make his purchases. Having the rickshaw wait for him, he went inside and rented a furnished upstairs two room with a small kitchen and bath for a week using one of his aliases. When he returned to the hotel, it was time to eat supper. By the time he finished eating, Sue's rickshaw, as he called it now, was waiting for him. He closed his eyes during the ride and went over his plans for two nights hence. By the time he was at Sue's place, he was confident in his plan. He only needed the girl to comply.

Entering the building, he had to stand a moment and let his eyes get accustomed to the semi-darkness. It hadn't been this dark in there the night before. It was noisier than the previous night because there were several more customers at the bar and tables, and some kind of Chinese music was blaring from speakers mounted on the walls. He started walking towards the bar, and a pretty girl with long flowing hair, a pale blue tank top covering ample breasts, red short shorts displaying slender legs and gorgeous thighs, and spiked heels approached him.

"Are you Bao?" she asked in a soft and gentle voice.

"That's me and are you my date for this evening? If you are, I'm very lucky."

"No, I am Xuan. I am Sue's manager. I manage the bar and handle the upstairs girls. I keep the old place thriving for her, and of course for the patrons."

"She did tell me she had a very good manager, but not that it was a lady and a very beautiful and sexy one at that."

"You are too kind to this unworthy one. She left me a message stating that you were really a nice guy and horny as hell. We thrive on horny guy here."

"Do you ever work upstairs?"

"I don't climb between the sheets very often. Like Sue, I'm very busy, and it would have to be someone special. Maybe you could be special someday. That remains to be seen."

"I might just do my best to become special for you. I'd like that. It just dawned on me that I didn't see you last night."

"I have two assistants that work when I'm not here. They basically collect money for the girls upstairs and tend to the bar."

"That's nice for you to be able to have some free time. When do I get to meet my beauty for the night?"

"She won't be here for another hour. Something unexpected came up today, so she's a little late. Come, let's sit and have a drink. She motioned to the guy behind the bar, and he called to the back room through an open window, and a decent-looking young girl came and took their order. When she went to the bar to get the drinks, Xuan told the Masked Man, "That girl, we call her Girl right now, is an apprentice here; she's just getting ready to learn the trade. She's not ready to go upstairs yet. We are training her on masturbation and oral sex to start with. If you'd like, she can perform oral sex on you in the back room while you wait for your date. It'll be on the house since you have to wait. Believe it or not, she's still a virgin, but she can really suck the guys say. We have several rich guys who are bidding to be her first vaginal and anal lover. When all of them but one stops bidding, we'll put her and the winner in Sue's sweet for two consecutive days of heaven."

"That's incredible. Too bad I'm not a multi-millionaire. Just to be looking at her sounds like an awfully good deal. Some guy is going to be really lucky." The Girl returned with a beer for him and a non-alcoholic lady's drink for Xuan.

"Girl," Xuan called to her. "Take this guy to the back room when he finishes his beer and get on your knees. Show him your new talent. Make it the best you've ever done. This man rates only the best service we can give offer, okay?"

The Girl responded saying, "Yes Ma'am. I am honored to be selected for this duty. I will make him the happiest." When he finished half of his beer, she took him by the hand and guided him to the back room.

When he returned from the back room smiling, he noted to Xuan, "I think the highest bidder will be one lucky dude. She's a good student." He poured a glass of beer and gulped down half of it and burped. "How much do I owe for that experience? She was worth whatever you charge."

"This one is on the house, as I said before, for three reasons. One, your scheduled date is late. Two, she is on salary and that is part of her job when she's needed. Three, Sue said you are worthy of it. Besides, I'll get deep into your wallet when your date arrives and you are salivating like you never have salivated before."

Finally, his date arrived, strutting into the bar area with hips undulating like he'd never seen before. She put Sue's and Xuan's beauty put together to shame. What a specimen of the female of the species. He was awestruck to even begin to describe her. Even though he was just drained by the girl, he had an immediate erection.

"Bao, I want you to meet Gai Xing, your lovely escort for the night. Xing this is Bao, your night's able paramour, not one of those decrepit old farts that think they are some weirds assed god's gift to women."

The two shook hands and looked into each other's eyes. He was amazed at her deep brown, beautiful eyes and looked deeply into her soul. Also, he felt she was gazing into his whole being also. Her pouty lips were the right shade of red for her, and her body, from what he could see of her as she sat beside him, was fantastic. She was clad in a powder blue business suit with matching heels and purse. He complimented her on her lovely and expensive attire, and she responded in kind to him.

"Thank you for the compliment. Since I'm already promised for the night, I didn't need to wear my working clothes. When I work, I like to wear really skimpy clothes and tempt the customers. I get a kick out of them getting horny when I wiggle my hips as I walk near them or let them put a hand on one of my thighs. Sometimes I'll pull their face into my breasts. It makes more money for me, and happy for him. Some guys even give big tips. It goes with my extreme ego. I love sex and I love money, and I go for as much of each as I and my customer can handle."

"Well, tonight I plan to satisfy your ego and your center of the universe on both counts. Damn, you're gorgeous, and what a body. I can understand why the customers get horny when you wiggle those hips or pull their face into those bountiful breasts. I'll bet you've got creamiest thighs going, or they wouldn't get so excited over them. I know I got an instant arousal the first second I saw you." She reached over, grabbed him in the crotch, checking to make sure he was being honest with her. He was.

"Xing, while Bao was waiting for you, I had the Girl get on her knees and give him a treat. He thought she was great at it." Then Xuan excused herself, quipping, "I need to leave you two love birds alone to get it on. You'll be in Sue's suite tonight. If either of you need anything at all, just call Girl on the intercom. She will attend you promptly. By the way, Sue said you needn't use condoms tonight Xing. Bao, you get the extra pleasure because she is sterile and clean and on the pill as a precaution. You look surprised Xing. I was too when Sue told me that. We've never, ever allowed any of the working girls to go out in the rain without a raincoat before." With that, Xuan left them and went from table to table, talking with the patrons who were trying to cop a feel and make the right kind of offer.

"If you're half as good as Sue told me on the phone this afternoon, I'm happy to go without the raincoat. I have had a couple of boyfriends in the past, and it was nice to get with it and not worry about getting one pulled on. Besides, I really enjoy the warmth when a guy gets his rocks off in me."

"So far, I've had a real rough day today, and I know that's about to change. Can you be patient while I have a drink?"

"I sure can. I always say, 'If it's worth having, it's worth waiting for.' I know you're going to be more than worthwhile to wait for. I can't wait to get my rocks off in you." She caught the bartender's eye, and he sent Girl out with a lady's drink.

Xing explained to him about the billing for the night. "Xuan will bring you a bill before she leaves tonight. All the drinks will be added to it also. It will be a very large one, but Sue says that rich bankers can afford it. I intend to give you your money's worth. I don't have a single virgin orifice, and those orifices are ready and willing to get with it as much as I know you are ready too." When she finished her drink, she took him by the hand and guided him up the stairs and into Sue's suite with that fabulous bed. Her undressing was even more captivating than Sue's, and it was for sure that Sue was no slouch at it.

Later, after a bout of wild sex, they lay side by side conversing as though they'd been friends forever. Each one confessing that neither had ever been with a Vietnamese or Chinese, except for him and Sue, respectively, and how wonderful it was. Gai Xing was especially grateful that Sue had told her she could let herself go and enjoy it to her heart's content. It was not in character for a girl in her profession to enjoy her work, even if she did like sex; only give enjoyment to her customers was the code. Letting herself go, for some reason, she found herself liking the Vietnamese, guy and the best part for her was that she thought he was attracted to her also, not just for her body. As they talked about the next night's threesome with Sue, he was making her get excited and horny again.

Getting an idea in her head to give her and the guy something different, she reached behind the bed post and pressed a hidden button. It took about two minutes for the Girl to arrive. Xing instructed the girl to undress weather she wanted to or not. Then she had the girl do something she'd never had the pleasure of before. She had the Girl sit on the Masked Man's face till she had her first orgasm, then she had the girl prep him with her lips, making him ready for insertion, and then Xing jumped on top of him while the Girl, embarrassed, dressed and left the room. Later on, she would apologize to the Girl for what happened as she was not to have any contact with a man except orally in the back room, and she would convince her not to rat out to Sue what the man did for her.

"Wow! The Girl was really worth it Xing. It was a good idea you had having her sit on my face like that. Squeezing my face with her thighs was fantastic. Knowing what she was like in the back room, and just now, I'll bet she could really sixty-nine. Maybe I'll get a chance before I continue on my journey."

The time for the Masked Man to leave for his hotel was nearing. He was discussing how pleasurable the night had been with her, and the sequence he had with the Girl. He liked her being in agreement with him and guided the conversation to her stated love for money and sex. "Do you ever see any customers outside of here?"

"Sue would not condone that."

"I've already presumed that. I'm curious though, thinking about what you said earlier about liking sex and money, have you ever considered doing it if the sex was good and the amount of money was just right and Sue wouldn't find out about it?"

"Well, to be honest, I have given it some thought from time to time. I haven't done it yet. I've had good money offers, but the sex was not enjoyable enough to consider doing something outside of here with them."

The Masked Man pondered a minute and asked, "Can you keep any discussion we have about this from Sue, especially if I tell you a secret along with it?"

"I've had many conversations that never reached Sue's ears. I value my job." She was getting more curious about what the guy might have in mind.

"First, money is no object, and I can top any offer you've had thus far. Second, for me, sex with you is like being in a heaven. Was it good enough for you to consider a proposition?"

"It sure was. I can't remember when I've been so satisfied. It was great for me too. I can't wait for tonight when we double team you."

"Now, as for my secret, I'm not leaving Kowloon tomorrow. I've rented an apartment, and I want to stay a few days longer. I'd like to have someone like you to have a lot of sex with and to show me around the area. I'm sure there are many sites to see that I've read or heard about. For some reason, I don't know why, I don't want Sue to know I'm not leaving on the plane after tomorrow night." He gave her a pleading look.

"You really do have a place to go to?"

"Yes! It's a nice, quiet place with no one to be bothered by wild sex! It's above a vacant store, and no one would know you were there. You can bet on the fact that I'd never tell." He told her where the address was.

Gai Xing thought for a moment. Then she queried him, "Have you ever seen two girls go at it? I was thinking that I could bring the Girl along and I could teach her a couple of things, since she's in training, while you watch and get horny. She has to stay a virgin, but I noticed you checked out her nice shapely young butt. I think I could convince her that that would be part of the deal to give up her butt, and I'd slip her a little money too. Remember how we got worked up over her during the night? You could get your sixty-nine too."

"You'd do that for me?"

"You bet I'd consider it for the right price." She whispered a price in his ear.

"My dear, I'll even double that and throw in a little extra for the Girl."

"Good! I must talk to the Girl though after I apologize for tonight, and I must decide if we should do it with you. If she won't, I might be there by myself. I'll have a chance to give you an answer tonight when Sue isn't looking. If it's a go, you can slip me the address you told me about and what time you'd like us there.

I have a little secret for you too, Bao. Sue will service customers on the side and she does so. I'm surprised you didn't ask her for a special rendezvous with her. She enjoyed your sex very much too. I really think she'd go with you in a heartbeat." He replied to her, "I had thought about asking Sue, but that was before I saw and had you and the girl. You are my ideal lover, and you're so beautiful too. Every part of your' body is like Sue, Xuan, and the Girl doubled."

The Girl knocked on the door and was told to enter. She brought the bill for the night, and he gave her his credit card instead of cash. Before she left the room to make his payment, Gai Xing told her to turn around and drop her pants. She complied. Then she was told to spread her legs a little, bend over for a moment then to pull up her pants and pay the bill. She looked at the Masked Man and grinning said, "You do like that butt a whole bunch, don't you?"

He just grinned back at her and nodded his head up and down, thinking that an ass like that Girl's ass could bring good money to any brothel. He thought of what the *A Team* leader would say: "I love it when a plan comes together." Then he arrested his thought, thinking that only Tolbane would have a stupid thought like that. That wretched American scum.

He returned to his hotel, had a hearty breakfast, and then hit the sack. He slept peacefully, knowing that during the late afternoon he'd complete his plan for the next day. Two for the price of one would double his enjoyment. If he were in Las Vegas, he would consider it as hitting the biggest jackpot ever.

When he woke, he went for a snack at the restaurant, left there then hired a cab for the afternoon to take him to an area with many shops that would not ask questions. After purchasing the desired items, he needed, he had the cab take him to the apartment where he left his purchases and then back to the hotel.

He took a short nap, then went to have a good supper. While eating, he daydreamed of having both women at his disposal that next night. If Xing and the Girl didn't come, there were always lower-class street walkers he could lure to the apartment and have his fun. He hoped he had figured Xing right about her and the Girl. Even if Xing wouldn't do it, maybe he could lure the Girl. She hadn't had the chance yet to make good money. He left the restaurant and got into the rickshaw that was waiting to take him to Sue' He put the next night's pleasure with the two women out of his mind, then began thinking about what this night promised, and he began to be aroused, almost painfully.

Xuan, Sue's manager, was just leaving for the day when he arrived at the house, and they spoke for a couple of minutes, then he went inside. Sue and Xing were sitting at a table drinking a beer, both skimpily dressed and very pleasing on the eyes. Hot pants and halters were their uniform of the day. Looking at the two beauties, he thought he would get on his knees and start salivating like certain dogs were known to do. He'd need a large bucket for his spittle. Some unknown god was smiling down on him this very day. When Sue saw him enter, she motioned to the bartender, and he sent beer and frosted glass for him with the Girl. Setting the beer in front of him, the Girl was blushing. He felt then that that Xing had convinced the girl to have the threesome the next night. It may be that the Girl agreed to go because she liked doing things with him. He also knew he had to wait for Xing to confirm it.

Both women greeted him with smiles and praise of his sexual potency and of the expected erotic evening to come. It was his turn to be a little embarrassed this time. He did manage to convey to them that his potency was due only to their feminine attractiveness and sexual prowess and that he was very much humbled to be with such ladies, and he told them that some god was blessing him. After more banter Xing said, "Let's cut the horse crap and go upstairs. I'm horny."

Agreeing with her, Sue lifted her bottle to toast both the Masked Man and Xing with, "Here's to a good night of fucking and sucking. May it never end."

The Masked Man not to be left undone gave his own toast. "Here's to heat. Not the heat that burns down the shanties, but, the heat that brings down the panties!"

The three finished their beer quickly then she took both of their hands and slowly towed them upstairs. Once there and undressed it didn't take long for the trio to get down to business. While they were resting after the first bout of romping in the sack, Sue's intercom blared loudly with the bartender's voice. "Sue, you need to come down here now. We have a big problem that needs handling by you." She pulled on a robe and went downstairs.

The Masked Man questioned, "I wonder if she needs some help down there?"

"Not to worry my dear," Xing replied. "I paid a guy with some sex to claim someone stole his money while he was with a girl. I had to get you alone to let you know that the Girl and I will be there tomorrow. I just need to know the time and place."

He stepped over to his trousers and took a slip of paper from one of the pockets and handed it to her. "Everything you need to know is written on this paper. I don't know how to thank you for this."

"You owe me big time and big dollars. I had a hard time convincing the Girl how good you're going to make her bottom feel. I think she's curious about doing that now since you performed oral sex on her. She confessed to me that she enjoyed eating you in the back room more than most guys, and she wants to get ate again. I know you'll be well satisfied with her butt too. If you want to, you can make my bottom feel good right now. It's horny."

"At you service Ma'am." He did just that.

The two had cleaned themselves up by the time Sue returned in a kind of snit. She let him know that as soon as she calmed down, she and Xing were going to blow his mind with a double team, the likes of which he'd never have again. She then explained to Xing in Chinese about the drunken ass downstairs who thought his money was stolen by one of the girls. As it turned out, he was never with any of the girls tonight. He had been at a different cat house. Xing replied, "You never know about some people." Xing then explained the situation to him in English and that that was what interrupted their party. He just nodded that he understood and laughed a little. The rest of the night was spent in pure ecstasy for him. Although he was physically spent, he would gladly try the threesome again. Even after he was too spent to perform, he wasn't too spent to do things for the ladies before he left the establishment that morning.

When he arrived at the hotel, he ate breakfast as usual, went to his room, cleaned up, and called the airport about a flight out later that night or early morning going to Hanoi. There was one leaving out at four o'clock the next morning to Hanoi and then on to Da Nang. That was perfect. He booked it. Then he packed up his gear, checked out, and took a different rickshaw to his apartment to get some sleep after he made sure he had the right tools for the evening.

He arranged for the rickshaw driver to pick him up at midnight or 1:00 AM to take him to a cab so he could get to the airport in plenty of time to catch his flight. If his plan goes well, this will be a night he could never have hoped for. It will be a real dream come true. Two for the price of one or was it two in the hand.

He slept easily and had many wonderful dreams of the young Girl's butt and lips and Xing's center of the universe.

CHAPTER 24

THE MASKED MAN AWOKE in enough time to go out and eat a big supper before the girls arrived. He ate more than usual because he knew he'd need all the energy he could muster before the night was over. Drinking his cooling coffee and daydreaming about what would happen after the meal, he felt himself becoming aroused almost to a mind-blowing state. He realized suddenly that he didn't want to walk through the crowded restaurant with a tent-like erection in his pants, so he forced himself to think of something else. He thought of playing in the streets during his youth in Saigon. Those were happy days before the war broke out and he was pressed into service. He wondered if he would ever be that happy again unless his Cause was a success and Mai was in his bed. His manhood finally stood down, so he finished his coffee, paid the tab, and returned to the apartment to finish his preparation for a most fascinating night of pleasure with two very exciting women.

The two women arrived on time, and he was delighted to see them dressed in very sexy miniskirts, V-neck blouses, and spiked heels. He especially liked the way the Girl was dressed. She was always dressed like a peasant at the house, and it hid her feminine features very well. He greeted each of them with a kiss and had them turn around slowly, one at a time, so he could check out their wonderful bodies and pat their butts. Then he hugged the Girl and whispered into her ear, "I love that butt of yours'. We are going to have a lot of fun tonight." She gulped a little and hoped it would be fun. He then got each one of them a beer, and they engaged in small talk while they sat and drank.

During the conversation, Xing told him, "I think you should call the Girl by her name. It is Le Wong. She is not a bar girl tonight. She's yours, and she must remain a virgin as I have already stated, but she will make your deepest desire of her butt come true! You'll find her other attribute fine also. I forgot. You've already enjoyed that and know what you're getting." He heartily agreed, thinking of the first time she had satisfied him. "Le, tell him about being in the back room with him that night since you've thought more about it."

"I'm not used to talking with men yet, so I may seem shy about it. I had never enjoyed the oral sex I have to perform, but it seemed like I did like it with you a little," she blushed and looked away. Then she looked back at him and continued. "What you did to me in Sue's bed put me on cloud nine. I never knew something like that could do that to me. That's one reason I came tonight. I want to experience that again if you please to do it with me again."

"I enjoyed it too, both times. I really did very, very much. You were very good at it and I think you were created to do so. Don't worry your beautiful head off. I do intend to have duel oral sex with you, called sixty-nine. I promise to blow your mind. I want that butt too! Please don't be embarrassed about it, as it is natural for men and women to do those things with each other."

After the beer they all undressed, climbed on the bed, and fondled each other. He turned his attention to Wong.

"I'm really excited about you. I want to start with you because you are a mystery to me. I know how wonderful each part of Sue and Xing is, but I know nothing of you except that your oral sex on me that night was unbelievable, and I was ecstatic when Xing had you sit on my face. So far, I'm pleasantly surprised. I have a tube of lubricant all ready to help me find out about your magnificent posterior. It will make my entering into you more pleasurable for both of us. I know you'll like the way I move in and out of you."

After performing oral sex on her and letting her know how wonderful her thighs were, he used the lubricant and solved the mystery. They cleaned up and Wong confessed to him, "I didn't know what it would be like tonight. I was a little scared. The first thing that you did to me was wonderful; also, the other was too, even though it did hurt a little at first. What you did with your tongue drove me a lot crazier than it did the other night. I never expected that. I hope you will drive me crazy again tonight. Now I want to see you and Xing do the same things."

He told her how wonderful she was and assured her he would do just that for her before the night was over. Then he crooked his index finger at Xing and ordered her in a flirting way, "It's your turn in the grinder baby. I'm going to punch your ticket good." She smiled, complied, and received the same treatment as Wong.

The two women were relaxing and chatting together, and he took the opportunity to take three glasses of Riesling from the refrigerator. He gave two of them to the women, and their glasses contained a little of the same chemical that he had used on that beautiful long-legged bitch, Carly. There was just enough to make them pass out for close to a half hour, just enough time for him to bind them, hands, feet, and gags. He wanted them to be awake when the real fun he planned started, only one will enjoy.

"Let me propose a toast to you two." The three raised their glasses, and he toasted with, "Here's to the two most beautiful and wonderful pieces of tail in the world! I mean the real tail!" The women giggled, and they clanked glasses and drank a generous portion of the wine. The Masked Man set his glass down and hugged each one, feeling their breasts and nibbling a bit at the same time while they fondled him. The three lay on the bed with him in the middle, and Wong asked how soon he would be ready to do it again. "I really want to know if I like giving my butt to you," she said. His reply was, "I knew you liked it, and I would never disappoint any lady who offered me such a wonderful grand prize again. In just a few minutes, I'm going to be ready to do a lot with you two beauties, the likes of which you've never had." They all laughed.

After finishing their drinks and fondling each other, Wong, not used to drinking at all, passed out first. Xing tried to climb over him to help her, and she slowly passed out too. He moved Xing off of him, got off the bed, and pulled a suitcase with his prurient gear out from under it. All the while, he was smiling to himself at his success so far. His body shivered a bit in sheer delight at the thought of what was to come with these two specimens.

The first thing on his mental list was to bind Xing's arms to her sides, same with her ankles, and tape her mouth shut. Then he propped Xing on a chair where she could see and hear what was happening when she woke. He taped Wong's mouth shut and tied her wrists and ankles to the bed posts. He stared at their bodies and became aroused while admiring the beauty of the two constrained women. Next, he removed his shorts, put on a plastic rain hoodie, and removed a couple of instruments from the suitcase. His plan was to start with Wong because he wanted Xing to see what was going to happen to her when her turn came.

Besides, he always liked taking nice young virgins and deflowering them to start the fun. Nothing else was on his mind now. "Yes!" he thought to himself out loud. "This is going to be the night I can dream about for the rest of my life." Then he took an erection potion tab he got at a Chinese medicine shop.

He got some ice cubes and rubbed it on Wong's forehead and face to wake her. When she started to stir, he then did the same to Xing. As the women began to show signs of life, he started to explain to them what they were in for the rest of the night. He even thanked them for providing their bodies for his pleasure and experimentation on the female body. The women were now terrified, trembling, and struggling with their bindings, to no avail. They knew they would never see the light of day again, and from his explanation, no one would know where they were or ever know who took their lives once their bodies were finally found. Xing finally ceased her struggles and resigned herself to her fate for giving in and trusting a man. She knew she'd never have the chance to trust again. Wong, on the other hand was still struggling against her bindings, and it pleased him to no end.

"This young one was going to be fantastic. Just think," he thought aloud. "Those horny bastards that use the women at the house will have no sweet young thing to bid on." He told her, "Say goodbye to your virginity now sweetheart, and believe me, I really do like your butt and your fabulous lips."

After finishing his lust with the two when there was no more fun to be had, he cleaned up with a shower, burnt the hoodie in the tub, wiped down everything he had touched that was not covered in blood, and left the apartment. The rickshaw driver was waiting for him as arranged and took him to a waiting cab. He gave a generous tip to the guy and also to the cab driver when he arrived at the airport. He checked in at the desk, waited a while, then boarded the plane, once again in first class, and headed to Hanoi and his destination points south of there.

He had never felt this satisfied in his life. Even though he felt satisfied, he also felt he was near exhaustion. The women had really taxed his stamina and had worn him out the last few days. Now that he had relaxed in his seat, his body seemed to ache all over. While daydreaming of the women he left in the bloody apartment, he fell into a deep sleep with a smile on his face. A while into the flight, a pretty Vietnamese flight attendant, Nguyen Thi Bao, woke him to serve his in-flight breakfast. It was like a TV dinner: a sausage patty, scrambled eggs, and a biscuit, along with a cup of coffee. Now he was really pleased because she spoke to him in Vietnamese, and he thought about how lucky he was. He was going back to his native country to retrieve the Jade Cross that rightfully belonged to him, chase out the communists, install the No Name as the rulers of the country, and find a way to bring Mai to Hoi An City and get rid of the Americans, and not necessarily in that order of march.

After he had eaten, he used the restroom and returned to his seat. The Vietnamese attendant came back to check on the first class passengers to see if she could be of any service. Everyone was comfortable and had no needs at that time. For some reason, she sat beside the Masked Man, and they spoke a bit about what he could expect in Hanoi. First, they exchanged their names, then birth places, hers in Quang Ngai City, Quang Ngai Provence, and his was in Saigon, now Ho Chi Minh City, and then she spoke to him about the weather in Hanoi. It had been rainy and a little cooler than normal, and the people there seemed to be content in their every day events. The monuments, lakes, and museums were nice places to visit.

When he informed her, he would only be in Hanoi one night, she recommended he stay at the Asian Legend Hotel Hanoi on Hang Tre Street. He learned that it had a laundry service that he desperately needed, good restaurant service, and an airport shuttle. He asked her why she recommended that hotel, and she smiled and informed him, "I recommend it because that's where I stay when we overnight in Hanoi." At that point, she arose and went back into the passenger compartment to attend the other passengers.

He felt aroused and wondered if he could be so lucky as to see her at that hotel. If they got together, he realized he'd have to curb his real desires for her. He couldn't afford any slip up now. He forced himself to stop thinking about her and instead think about what his plans were on arrival at Noi Bai Airport. He would book a different Da Nang flight under a false name just to be safe. He would call his friend in Hoi An City, and arrange transportation from the Da Nang Airport, which was the third busiest in the country. Then he'd go to the recommended hotel and get some needed sleep. He laid his head back and returned to dream land. The next thing he was aware of, he was being awakened by the attendant and informed that they would land in about ten minutes and he needed to sit up and buckle his seat belt. Soon, he heard and felt the landing gear grinding and being lowered into place, and then the aircraft banked, landed, and was on the taxiway and headed for the terminal.

As he approached the open door to deplane, the attendant smiled at him and asked, "Will I see you at the hotel tonight?"

He smiled back at her and said, "You will if I have anything to do with it!"

She grinned at him as he began stepping down the ladder. He went in to the terminal, cleared customs and followed his plan, retrieved his luggage, and caught the Asian Legend Hotel Hanoi's airport shuttle. He registered with the same name he used on the flight from Hong Kong. If the Vietnamese flight attendant did look him up, she would look for the name which was on the flight manifest. Once in his room, he called the main desk and told the person there he had a load of dirty laundry and was told to put it outside the door and it would be returned early the next morning. He had no trouble falling into a deep sleep as soon as he showered and hopped into bed. When he awoke, his first sensation was of being hungry. He had missed lunch and needed to still his growling stomach.

He called the room service and ordered from the menu posted on the top of the desk and then he called the main desk to find out if the flight attendant had checked in yet. She had, and he obtained her room number, and when she didn't answer the phone, he felt disappointed and left a message for her on her phone, got dressed, and waited on his food. The bellman brought him hot Vietnamese tea, Vietnamese bread, a bowl of boiled rice, and a plate of oven-broiled freshly caught fish broiled in a tasty lemon sauce and a bottle of nuoc mam sauce[30]. This was his first real Vietnamese meal since he had escaped the communists there in 1975. It was good, so he devoured it in record time. He was so glad to be back on his native soil once again. This was indeed as the Americans would say, being in Pig Heaven and loving it!

Now he went over in his mind what his ally had told him about Da Nang. When he cleared the Da Nang Airport, he was to take a private cab seven-tenths of a mile to the Tien Phuc Hotel. He was already registered there, and his room key would be at the desk waiting for his arrival. He was told not to worry about the evening's entertainment. A

---

[30]   A fermented fish sauce.

beautiful young lady of the night who stayed with his ally would be visiting him. Above all, he was to treat her nice, as she was one of theirs. He was to perform no weird sex acts that cause more harm than good. Her name is Thuoc Thi Hai. His ally would meet him around noon time the next day to take him quickly and directly to Hoi An City.

He was contemplating what to do next when there was a knock on the door. He could not imagine who could be knocking. He opened the door, and the airline attendant was standing there with two glasses and a bottle of champagne in an ice bucket. The best part was her short shorts and halter top. What a knock out. She could wear these clothes in the hotel proper, but that type of garb was not allowed on Hanoi Streets. He quickly bade her to enter. His eyes were taking in all of her good physical qualities as she passed him to enter the room, and he became extremely hard. He reminded himself that he had to be on his best behavior tonight. He didn't need to be hunted down for having his kind of fun. He knew his tools of the trade must stay in the bag.

They drank a glass of champagne and chatted until it was gone. She gave him an update on recent happenings around the country and freely gave her opinion on the socialist government and her desire that it change its ways. The two had been sitting well apart on the bed, and when the first class of bubbly was gone, she scooted over till her hips were touching his. He felt a heated impulse at the touching. This girl was hot stuff. They looked into each other's eyes and began kissing and caressing each other. After a few minutes, she stood, pulled some condoms from her pocket, placed them on the night stand, and began swaying her hips slowly as she removed her clothes, then really grinded it. When she was finished undressing herself, she bade him to stand and began removing his clothes, one item at a time, and was on her knees when she removed his trousers and shorts.

Two hours and an empty champagne bottle later, they said goodbye. She needed to sleep because she had an early flight back to Hong Kong. Another girl would take her plane on to Da Nang. She made him promise that if he ever went back to Hong Kong, he would check which flight she was on so they could have another night like this one. He agreed that indeed he would, as this had been a very wonderful and satisfying night with a beautiful broad. One more kiss and she was gone. He wished he could have his kind of night with her again. He didn't tell her he was taking a different plane on to Da Nang.

The next morning, he ordered breakfast from room service, packed up, checked out, and rode the hotel shuttle to the airport. He was early for his flight, so he bought a Vietnamese magazine, then went into a little café and had coffee, a Vietnamese pastry and read until his flight was called. He was ready for this, as he had many memories of Da Nang. That was where he first discovered how to have his kind of sex. It was in Dog Patch, a small group of shacks making a sub hamlet at the base of Hill 327 where the Marine Headquarters was located, as well as a few shops to sell odds and ends to the GIs and a couple of shacks made of tin siding material that had Boom-Boom Girls.

Thinking about his first one he remembered that, she was about thirteen or fourteen years old and was gorgeous. She did Boom-Boom really well, but she refused to perform oral sex on him afterwards, and he flew into a rage and viciously attacked her with the Marine k-bar he always carried. He was real lucky. Hers and the deaths of the few other women he had defiled early on were eventually blamed on the VC. He had a few more of the same sexual episodes in different parts of the country with no one the wiser about him and the mutilated deaths. After fleeing Vietnam in 1975, his sex drive had become dormant little by little. It came back at times, and then regressed again. At first, he was concerned about it, but after a while it didn't matter. He had gotten it back off and on after arriving in Nashville, TN, but sadly after a time it subsided again. It finally awakened just before he left the States. "Damn," he thought, "that long-legged, big-chested Carly bitch was something else."

The flight to Da Nang was uneventful, having no turbulence to speak of, and looking out of the window he could only see a clear blue sky, the ground way below, and only a small passing cloud now and then. He finished reading his magazine and let his mind wonder about the woman he would see that night in Da Nang. He was told she was one of theirs. Would she be in his bed to please him, to spy on him, or both? If she is one of ours, what role would she play in accomplishing his Cause? He had never contemplated having any women in the No Name.

Then he remembered the story of Troung Van Ba and his wife, Mot, and their adventure before marriage. Maybe it would be a good thing. If a woman was young and pretty, besides servicing him when needed, she could probably get information from any guy she wanted to. You could never have enough information. If the guy was high ranking enough, maybe a woman like that could even get the guy in a position for black mail. That would be super. More money for him was okay too!

The plane arrived at the terminal on time; he debarked, retrieved his luggage, and finally made his way to the Tien Phuc Hotel. As his ally had noted, he was already registered there. His room was on the first floor. It was not first class, but it was nice enough. Wondering what to do now with some time on his hands, he found a bell boy and got directions to a place where he could get lunch, then where to get a good massage and oral sex. After eating and being satisfied at a massage parlor, he returned to his hotel room and had a short nap.

When he awoke, he cleaned up, changed clothes and ordered a bottle of Qualitätsweine mit Prädikat, a 1976 vintage Beerenauslese from the wine list—he loved German wines—and snacks from the room service, then he turned on the TV and made himself comfortable on the bed till the promised girl's arrival. After two glasses of the wine, he fell asleep and awoke later by a knock on the door. The girl, Thuoc Thi Hai, was a little earlier than he expected. She wore the customary Vietnamese áo dài, the long Vietnamese dress with slits up to the hips on each side with long pants underneath. It was a nice shade of pink, and the pants were dark blue. It complimented her long black hair that flowed down her back nearly to her waist. She was cute and had a nice smile. They greeted each other, and she informed him that a table was set for them in the hotel restaurant and the food was already ordered, and they could talk and get acquainted with each other there first. She placed her arm in his, and they were on their way.

To his surprise, the waiter poured water into their glasses and asked how they would like their New York Strip steak served, if they wanted their baked potato fully loaded, and what kind of dressing they wanted for their salads. They both wanted their steak medium rare and the potatoes loaded all the way. She ordered vinegar and oil for her salad, and he ordered honey mustard for his. Damn it! Why did he have to like the same salad dressing as Tolbane? She ordered the wine, a nice Riesling for a starter, and the waiter left and she began to explain to him how the night would go.

The first thing she told him was that her real name was Nguyen Thi Hai. She finished her explanation with a reminder that there would be no rough stuff or else she would be gone in a flash. She told him she had been verbally, physically, and sexually abused in her early teen years by her stepfather, which was not her true story, but no one needed the truth of her mission. She never told anyone she stayed with her real father most of the time now and that she would never have put up with anything like that from any man. Otherwise, her whole body was his for the night, and she had nothing against role playing his fantasies if he had any. He could think of a few. She'd erven play a perfect ten-year-old losing her virginity because of her youthful, sexy look.

While eating, he asked her why he had been told a different name for her. "The other one is an alias I use when I'm working for somebody," she told him. Then she explained to him that his usual ally would not be in Hoi An City the next day, or on any day thereafter. It seems that he was suspected of talking to the wrong people and this night would be his last night on earth. The one taking his place could be trusted to do whatever was necessary to see that the No Name was successful in its mission. She then changed the subject.

She wanted to know if he'd like to play the game Lion. She'd be the lion, and he would feed her the meat, or they could play dog and he could feed her the bone. He replied, "I thought you'd never ask! I can be all meat or all bone. Oh, and you could be a hole in a board and I could be the round peg."

She laughed. They finished their wine and left for his room. He thought about the coming hours on the way. He'd have a lion and a ten-year-old. He'd be a dragon and fire her up, and then he'd peg her hole. Maybe she could be a large posthole and he would be the pole. She'd be the pearly gate, and he would have the right key to enter Heaven with.

After a long night of games and exotic pleasures and plenty of wine, the two fell into a deep asleep side by side. They were awakened mid-morning by the desk clerk informing them that there was a limo waiting for them outside the front of the hotel, but there was no hurry for them. The limo would wait till they were ready to leave. The driver knew they could be busy, and that was alright with him. He was being paid well. The two had one more fantasy, this time she took turns being each one of the Troung sisters who defeated the Chinese in 39–42 AD, then they cleaned up, gathered up their stuff, checked out, and caught their ride to Hoi An City. The older Cadillac limo was very comfortable and had a bar in the back seat. They had a glass of port wine and then they fondled each other's body parts.

She told him she was surprised at his sexual prowess and asked if he would like her to be available during his stay in Hoi An City, as she had never been screwed like the way he did it to her. She even told him she very seldom enjoys performing oral sex on any guy, but it was good with him, she fibbed to him big time. To answer, he revealed to her his desires for his visit.

"You know what I like to do with women for my pleasure, but I will not harm you. Even though I have certain needs to experience with a woman, once in a while, I need to have some honest sex without brutality at times, and you fill the bill. I will have you sometimes because you are really a very good piece of ass, and you are very satisfying. I love your breasts, and you've got a great butt and terrific thighs. I would be dumb not to want to do you sometimes. I hope that you may know other girls like you and maybe we can have some threesomes." He was thinking that he hoped she would screw up something so he could really have fun with her. He would have his kind of sex with her whether anyone else objected or not.

"I will bet that would really be awesome to do from time to time. I do know of some former Boom-Boom Girls that very seldom do it anymore, but would do it if they received a really good stipend from you. Vietnamese Dong speaks volumes to them over anything else. I would be honored to pick out a couple of good ones when you request it of me. Just so you know me and my tendencies, I don't do women, ever. We will have great times while you're here. I need another drink, don't you?"

"Yes, I could use a hair of the dog that bit me from time to time. Depending on the type of lady you get for me, maybe I could persuade you to try getting it on with her. I could get some of that good ass of yours while you try it."

"Believe me! It would take one hell of an effort on your part to even get me to even think about doing it with a woman. I just don't chow down on that stuff for love or money! I'm strictly a cock woman!" He wasn't happy with her answer, but he wouldn't let her know it. He smiled at her, knowing he'd arrange it happening someway, somehow whether she liked it or not. He did like her spirit though.

They drank straight whisky, cuddled, kissed, and played with each other in the back seat all the way to Hoi An City until she flat passed out from the booze. The Masked Man had nodded off a little too and was surprised when the driver stopped the vehicle and said, "Hey guys, we're here! Welcome to Hoi An City, Exalted One."

CHAPTER 25

MAI, CARLY, AND ROBERT were up early and prepared breakfast. Mai suggested to the youngster that he take the dogs into the master bedroom and wake the big guy. He brought Rant and Rave into the house and then the bedroom, and the dogs jumped up onto the bed, scaring Tolbane awake, He started to go for his gun under the mattress but then realized what was happening and attempted to hug the dogs. They were trying to lick his face and were pawing at him. He finally got them off his bed, and the boy ran to the kitchen to tell his mom and Mai how funny it was. The women laughed. Then Mai had him put the dogs outside so they could do their thing. Then the big guy joined them in breaking the fast with his usual breakfast fare.

After breakfast, he called the mall security office and let them know he'd be in a little later than he had planned. He wanted to see Parnell and find out what the prognoses for his wound was first. He took his time going through his military Five S's: Shit, Shine, Shave, Shower, and Shampoo. Then he dressed in an old navy blue suit white shirt with a button-down collar, and old red power tie and was bidding the ladies goodbye when the phone rang. It was Parnell.

"Listen up old partner. The doctor is letting me go on home today. One of the patrol officers will pick me up later and take me there. That's not the best news. As long as there is improvement in my leg, I'll be free of the doctor in two more days. I contacted the department, and we're good to leave for Vietnam in four days. I called Father Phat, and he'll meet us in San Francisco at the airline terminal, and we'll be good to go. The tickets will be waiting for us at the Nashville terminal. I'll get you the flight time and number tomorrow, along with the proposed time and day of our arrival in Honolulu, Hong Kong, Hanoi, and Da Nang, and then Hoi An City, and how many days we'll stay at each place; I don't have it now because the department is making the deal. I need you to have Mai call the hotel in Hoi An to make the reservations when I give you the info. Do you have any questions I can't answer, oh hairy lips of wisdom?"

"Probably a lot of questions a third grader could answer, in case you care. Seriously, that's the best news relating to this mess I've heard. We are finally going to do something. I know Mai will be very elated to be finally going there. She really wants and needs to mingle with some Vietnamese in her native country in order to know her heritage better. Maybe we could even get her to Ho Chi Minh City for a day, that would be super. It's hard for her sometimes because she only knew hardship, war, and flight from there, and no one could be trusted not to be the enemy.

Anyway, now she'll be able to relate to her people in a more meaningful and peaceful atmosphere. Also, she, as well as I do, want an end to this farce once and for all, regardless of how it turns out. The end will never come soon enough for either one of us, and I'm sure you to, Carly, and the boy feel the same. I can't wait to hurt some dumb friggen clown's ass. I think somebody once said something about vengeance, or was it revenge being best when served cold. I want it hot! I want my vengeance or revenge served fresh off of the grill!"

"I know how you feel my friend. I'd like to clobber the hell out of some jerk off myself. I'm doing nothing useful here in this hospital bed. I've had too much time to think about this crap, and it's trying to get the best of me. You know me, the super cool, calm, energetic, workaholic cop that I am. Being idle like this is driving me buggy too. It almost causes me to empathize with the jail birds I've put away. I'll call you tonight and let you know how I'm doing, OK?"

Tolbane felt good that Parnell was going home today and knew he needed to do something to help Parnell to feel even better after being cooped up in that hospital room. "Hey, chowder head! I've got a terrific idea. Why don't I pick you up at your place on my way home tonight, and you can dine with us and maybe have a beer or two, or three, or four, whatever, and we can bitch at each other with Mai and Carly being the refs?"

"I thought you'd never ask ding Dong. I'll have to check with the doctor about the beer though. I have some meds to take, and a beer might not go to well with them. Otherwise, it will be down the hatch time. I'll be waiting for you with open arms, not. Don't make me feel like I'm back in the Corps. I never liked the hurry up and wait, and especially the part of it where you wait forever and a day."

"I'll be there, but I won't be any wearing bells. Speaking of bells, remember that poem by Poe, 'The Bells'? Hear the sledges with the bells—Silver bells! What a…"Tolbane was talking into a dead phone. Parnell had hung up. Tolbane thought his bud could take a flying fuck over a rolling doughnut ringing bells and grinned thinking about how it would look.

Tolbane gave Mai and Carly an update on their flight day and informed them the info would be available the next day. To celebrate the news, they each had another cup of coffee and another cinnamon bun, homemade from scratch, no less. After the snack and coffee was over, Tolbane finally trudged off to work, wanting the work day to end quickly.

Around five o'clock, Tolbane was really bushed. There hadn't been much criminal activity at the mall for the few last months, but he guessed the people had the idea that today had been National Commit A Crime Day. There had been ten incidents spread across six stores, plus a severe accident in the parking lot caused by someone ass driving too fast across the parking lanes and broadsiding a car driving in the proper lane. Three people were taken to the hospital, injuries not life threatening. There had also been four chases of shoplifters out of the ten incidents, with three of them ending up in a knock down drag 'em out fight. He was glad he was only slightly involved in them, as he didn't have to go downtown with the prisoners, as the security guards were the detaining parties. It seemed to him that when it came to people committing crime it was either feast or famine.

He straightened up his office, went to his baby, the Marine Corps Green pickup, sighed, and relaxed for a bit. He almost fell asleep, but he finally managed to turn the ignition key on, starting the engine, and put in a different disk. This time, he selected music from Man of La Mancha and the overture began. He thought that the music was right for him. Maybe he was a Don Quixote, a real knight errant that damned the wicked and got his butt kicked by a windmill. He was lucky though. Even though he had a real Dulcinea, she definitely was not all smoke and air. He did have a windmill to conquer, though. This windmill of a cabal by some Vietnamese ass had to be destroyed.

Traffic was heavy for the time of day, but he made decent time getting to Parnell's place in a decent amount of time. It was a different story going east on I-40. Traffic was slow, going only 30-35 mph and nearly stopping at times. They finally got to Tolbane's place and found that the two women were sitting on the patio and the boy was playing catch with the dogs and had only one tennis ball. They were amused at the dogs fighting over the ball. The winner would strut around in a wide circle a couple of times then go place the ball at the boy's feet, and both would get ready for the next round by panting with their tongues hanging out while staring at the ball. Mai greeted Parnell hobbling along on one crutch with, "Hi wimpy gimpy! How the heck are you getting along?" Carly laughed at Parnell's frown at the comment and made a comment about the timely arrival of "Limp-a-long Parnell."

Before Tolbane could say a word after kissing Mai, she informed him, "You won't find anything on the stove or in the oven. We're going to a family restaurant tonight, called Sunset, in Lebanon tonight, so put that in your pipe and smoke it." Parnell quipped that the Almighty Ruler of the Tolbane household has ruled.

Tolbane laughed and retorted, "What Almighty Ruler?" which earned him a kick in the shin and a stern look from Mai.

"I command you all to come on and get in my car right now; I'm the duty driver tonight for a change. I have ruled with finality once more," she commanded. Tolbane and Parnell both groaned aloud, but they surrendered to the higher authority of the Tolbane household and complied with the Almighty Ruler's command. Carly and Robert were amused at the exchange of wise cracks. They all went out and climbed into Mai's sedan.

About 25 minutes later, they were being seated by a rather shy, young waitress who gave them menus and took their drink orders. They were looking forward to the home style cooking and the gobs of food that would be heaped on their plates. All five of them had a hard time making up their minds. There were so many wonderful entrees available. In addition to their meals, they ordered hors d'oeuvres of breaded cheese sticks and chicken tenders with honey mustard and a salsa for dipping. Then, having eaten their fill of the main courses, they each had enough left over for a doggy box to take home. That would give them something to snack on along with their beer while enjoying the evening on the patio.

Arriving back home, the guys discovered in the kitchen two large coolers with plenty of iced long neck beers for the grownups and ice-cold sodas for the young Robert. Tolbane took two ice cold beers out, removed the caps, and gave one to Parnell. Just in time, he remembered the two others and took out two more brews and de-capped them and gave them to the ladies. He knew this saved one of his shins big time.

After a long evening of chatting and joking and having a few more brews apiece, Tolbane and Mai were passed out in their bed and snoring to high heaven, Parnell was asleep, or passed out too, in the recliner, Carly was deep asleep on the couch, dead to the world, and the young man, Robert, was asleep with the two dogs under the covers in bed with him. It had been a long while since they had been able to really let their hair down and not worry about a bunch of scumbags coming for them from who knows what direction shooting or trying to kidnap them. They didn't even talk about the Vietnamese situation that evening, and that was a good thing for a change. It allowed their minds to be free of stress.

The sun had been up for an hour before anyone began stirring. Mai and Carly made it up first and began preparations for breakfast. Mai was really proud of her friend. Her wounds were healing fast, and she was coping well. The one single thing that really helped was the fact that Carly had no memory of the physical part of the attack. The doctor attending her stated that memory loss was sometimes a byproduct of a brutal attack such as Carly had suffered, but she had also been lucky enough to have been in a drugged state and out of it when it happened. Sometimes, he said, the memory loss may be temporary and sometimes it might be permanent. Mai sincerely hoped that she never recovered any memory of the brutality. By the time two men and Robert joined them in the kitchen, the women were drinking coffee, gabbing about nothing in particular, and waiting to start the bacon, eggs, and toast. After the meal, everyone helped clean up the kitchen and dressed as they planned their agendas for the day.

It was soon decided that Mai would drop Carly and her son off at her place so she could get her car. Carly would take the boy to school, then return home to straighten up her house into some semblance of order. Mai had warned her that there would be fingerprint powder brushed all over the place and a lot of things cast about from the investigation, and told her to call if she needed help cleaning up. Carly had not been there since the assault, and Mai hoped it wouldn't bring unpleasant memories to her. Meanwhile, Mai would get new tires on her car, and then she would drive to Hermitage and shop at Walmart, picking up food, beer for the house, and some personal items for the four of them to take with them on the trip to Vietnam.

Tolbane took Parnell home for him to shower, shave and change clothes, and they both went to the mall. Tolbane had to catch up on paperwork and check on what was happening security–wise, then he had to make a quick trip to metro to retrieve some stolen Castner Knott's merchandise a patrolman found in a car trunk when he busted a guy. Parnell made phone calls from Tolbane's office, trying to get as much up-to-date information on the situation obtained from the prisoners as possible, checking out how other detectives were handling his active case load, and also checking on their flight plans. He was done with his phone calls, including one to the priest, by the time Tolbane returned to his place from metro.

The two discussed everything Parnell had learned. Their conclusion was that they were doing the right thing by going to the source of the matter. One thing that really troubled them, though, was the report of two separate brutal and gruesome murders in Honolulu. One of the officers had been surfing the internet and came upon the report. The police there had reported that they believed their suspect was an Asian about 5'6" to 5'8" who landed the day of the crimes and checked out of his hotel early and flew to Hong Kong.

They knew in their gut it was their man that did it. Parnell related that he requested the MNPD to contact Honolulu PD for any information that could be released to them and asked them to inform the authorities in the Hong Kong area about him and alert them to their arrival time. It could be a deciding factor in running this turd to ground. While they were talking, the phone rang. It was the officer who discovered the Honolulu report asking to speak to Parnell. He had called the Honolulu PD, and all they knew was that one victim was a homosexual transvestite and the other was a cab driver. They agreed to meet and update the four when they arrived on the island. Parnell thanked him for the heads up and then told Tolbane what he had learned.

"The detectives there had made no conclusions as to why these murders had happened. The one thing in common with these murders is that the victims were both done in with a knife, possibly by an Asian man. As of this time, they have no connecting motive. They will inform me of any updates, and they are already expecting to meet us four as a courtesy between law enforcement agencies. They are interested in what we can relate to them about this guy. The condition of the transvestite's body really got to them. He was really carved up."

All either of them could think was that this guy was losing it and was becoming even more dangerous. He's a real psycho on the loose. Parnell made his point in a brusque manor, "The bastard is absolutely nothing but a narcissistic, sociopathic psycho. They, or we, need to get this guy really quick, like yesterday." Tolbane echoed his sentiment.

Mai called in to let the guys know she was done shopping for the day and was just getting in her car to leave Walmart. Tolbane updated her on what had happened in Honolulu and gave her the information she needed to reserve the hotel in Hoi An City. She said something naughty to him and he smiled, then he hung up the phone. Not realizing he was quipping aloud he said, "Someday I just have to teach her how to do back flips." Parnell gave him a disgusted look and shook his head from side to side. He knew Tolbane's brain was located in his skivvy drawers.

When Mai dropped Carly off, she immediately took her son to school. Arriving back at her place, she entered the house for the first time since being transported to the hospital. She found the place a disaster. The police had left fingerprint dust all over the place, drawers had been searched and left open, rugs were rolled back from checking the floor, a couple of lamps were tipped over, some of the furniture was stacked on top of each other, broken plates were strewn on the floor in the kitchen, everything had been tossed out of the closets, and her bed linens were missing. She sat at the kitchen table, laid her head on top of her arms, and cried, wondering what had happened to cause such a police search of her home. After a few minutes, she called Tolbane at the mall and asked if Parnell was still there. He gave the phone to Parnell, and she informed him of the mess in her house and how it destroyed her to find her worldly possessions treated in such a manner.

Parnell was pissed off by it too. He assured her that he would get a piece of somebody's ass. He told her where in the phone book to look for a cleaning service that was used for cleaning crime scenes. He swore to her that he would do his damned best to have the department force the jerks that did it, pay for it. He did his best to calm her down and help her realize that the important thing was that she survived and was able to care for her son. She grudgingly agreed and hung up, still upset.

Parnell explained to Tolbane what had happened and he was pissed off about it too. Parnell called his boss and had a very heated conversation with him about the situation and really dissed the forensic team and the investigating detective. It was one thing to leave fingerprint powder in some areas, but really screwing up a victim's home, beyond what was necessary that way, was a wanton act. It made her a victim twice, and it should be addressed in a serious manner, and she shouldn't have to pay one damn penny to clean the mess up. That would make her a victim three times. When he hung up, he told his pal, "Damn! I guess I'm lucky to still have a job. I've never went after a supervisor like that."

Answering, Tolbane paraphrased Dirty Harry with, "You made my day, Mein Herr!" Then he commented, "I wouldn't have pussy footed around either. I'd have used my 44 mag on those assholes. Just who the hell do they think they are?"

Parnell wanted to stay at his own place overnight, so Tolbane dropped him at his place and headed home. Carly had picked up her son from school, and he was outside playing with Rant and Rave. He hugged Tolbane, and of course the dogs needed attention too. Inside, Carly was still in somewhat of a snit over the condition of her home, and it was the first time she had really shown anger at what had happened to her. Seeing her home that way brought home to her the realization of the seriousness of her attack. She still had no memory of the actual assault, though. The women were sitting on the couch. Mai had her arm around Carly's shoulder and was giving her comforting words. Travis leaned over and gave both of them hugs, and he too did his best to help calm Carly down. Things like this made him want to strike out at someone, but he always ended up using his common sense. Besides, who would he clobber? He and Mai let Carly know that if her place wasn't cleaned up by the time they left for Vietnam, she and the boy could stay there until her home was cleaned and livable once again.

The next day was a lazy day full of girl talk for the women, and Carly was in a little better mood. Some of the shock she experienced upon entering her house had tapered off somewhat, but she was still pissed and upset. Tolbane was working at the mall, checking the security and taking care of last-minute arrangements for his absence. Parnell was picked up by a patrol unit and was dropped off at the headquarters. He was getting the latest update and the plane tickets. He even received an advance on his travel pay. While he was there, he went to his boss's office and apologized for his rant the previous day. His boss understood his concern for his friend and sympathized with him.

Since the investigating officer still had a key to the place, a member of Internal Affairs personnel went to the home and checked it out. He wasn't too happy either after entering the place, too much unnecessary bullshit had been done there in this search. Parnell's boss gave his word that everything would be done to make things right for Carly, and she wouldn't have to pay.

It was an even more relaxed evening than the previous night. Everyone enjoyed the banter among the group and the antics of Carly's son and the dogs. The way they were tearing up, Tolbane wondered if he would have to replace the carpet, maybe even the whole damn house for that matter. During the evening, Mai, being a little more astute then her dumb dork guy, noticed what she thought might be the start of some kind of a connection between Carly and Parnell. A woman's intuition! She wondered if she could help it along any. She thought they might just be made for each other like her and her huge mental midget were destined to be.

Finally, the day and time had come to board the plane and enter a new phase of their lives, however, it may turn out. The three were in good spirits. They believed that no matter how things turned out, there would be some closure over the brutal slaying of Ba and Light Foot, the assault on Carly, and the recent mall attacks and the spying on Mai. It felt so good to start the process of getting a cruel, sick bastard off the streets and experience the healing of their souls. Mai hadn't told the guys, but secretly she hopped she could watch the SOB die the cruelest death ever. She had read Tolbane's books on ancient torture methods, and she would like to write each one of them on a separate piece of paper, put them in a hat, and draw out the lucky torture of the day, gather the tools, and have at it with however many scumbags were involved in the fiasco.

They left for the Nashville Airport at 3:30 AM, parked Tolbane's pick up at the long-term parking area, and then they entered and got their boarding passes. The flight would leave at 050 hrs. and with the three-hour difference in time, and a couple of stops, they would arrive in San Francisco at 8 AM, California time. Of course, Tolbane wondered what the difference was between California time and Tulsa time. It seemed to him it would be one hour.

After checking in, they bought books and snacks for their carry-on piece of luggage. Then they got coffee. They were still sleepy enough that they had a hard time staying awake until boarding time. Once they were aboard and in the air, they lost no time going to sleepy land, most of the way, except for the stops, to San Francisco, CA. After landing there, they found Father Phat waiting patiently for their arrival. He was introduced to Mai, and they conversed in Vietnamese for a couple of minutes. Switching back to English, she said, "It's so nice to meet someone from Travis's past, even though it was a dangerous and weird event." She told the guys, making the Priest blush, "I think I'm going to like this guy. I'm glad he's coming along with us." They began the boring wait for their Honolulu flight to be ready. Boarding time finally came, and they sat in the front row of the first-class section. For the first couple of hours, they talked, read, and munched out. Then naptime came very quickly.

Arriving at the Honolulu International Airport, they were met by Honolulu Police Department Detective Sergeant Norman Chau. He was a few inches taller than Mai, a little rotund, and had a big smile that never seemed to leave his face. He informed them that after they retrieved their luggage, they would go to a little kiosk and get their complimentary paper cup of real Hawaiian pineapple juice. Then he drove them into the city and got them checked in and settled at the Ala Moana hotel. He would meet with them on the hotel's lanai after they freshened up, and they would discuss the grisly murders he thinks their joker committed. While on the ride to the hotel, he told them about all the shopping close by, and if they were interested in going to Waikiki Beach, it would be a walk of about a mile. Parnell and the priest would share one room, and Tolbane and Mai an adjoining one.

Upon entering their rooms, the call of nature was the first thing on everyone's agenda and then a refreshing splash of cool water on their faces. Mai found she had to renew her makeup after Tolbane had smeared it all over by playing kissy face and trying to get her slacks and panties off of her, which Mai put off till later. Then after a phone call to the other room to let the other two know they were ready, the group then went down to meet the Detective Sergeant who was sitting under a large beach umbrella on the lanai, drinking fresh pineapple juice and smiling at them like a circus clown.

After greeting each other, they all sat and ordered soft drinks and munchies, and discussed the beautiful weather, the hit series Hawaii Five O that had been filmed there, and some of the best sites for tourists to visit. One of the first things the detective commented on then was how lucky they were for having a stop in Hong Kong and longingly and without a smile stated, "I wish I could get HPD to pay my way to Hong Kong. Poor me, I am a real poor Chinese Man and I have never been to China. Some people are just lucky I guess." The four mainlanders were kind of feeling sorry for him. He sat there with a such sad face, then smiling and giggling at them he said, "Got you guys good, didn't I? I love to establish rapport."

CHAPTER 26

WHILE THE DRIVER TOOK out his luggage, the Masked Man exited the limo and held his hand out to help the woman get out, as she was a little tipsy from the whisky and he had to hold her up with his arm around her waist. That's all she was to him now, just a woman to use or discard if need be. He looked up and down the street, taking in the sight and thinking how appropriate it was that this house was on Tran Cao Van Street near Tran Hung Dao Street; for being back in Vietnam was a part of him and reuniting his people was his destiny. He would build his revolution quietly throughout the country and strike at the right time using the same guerrilla tactics used by the Viet Cong and the NVA and devised by the man of whom he was the reincarnate of. As soon as his revolutionary force begins to enlarge, he would build a central administration building on his namesake street.

Two men, younger than himself, and looking to be in good physical condition, came from the house and approached him quickly with smiles on their faces, anxious to meet their new leader. One of them held out his hand to greet and shake hands with him, but the Masked Man ignored it. Staring at the two men he demanded, "Who are you two, and who's in charge here?"

One man, a little shocked at the manner in which his handshake was rejected and the way he was being spoken to in a demeaning manner, answered, "I am in charge here! I am only known as Huong, and my next-in-line here is only known as Lam."

"From now on, I will not use your given names. You, Huong, will be known only as Number One, my right-hand man, and you Lam, our gofer," he said addressing the other man, "will be Number Two. Now get someone to take this drunken woman off my hands and carry my gear into the house! Then send all other members away; I want no witnesses here for what we do or discuss. They can be sent for any time if needed." When the two looked like they were stunned and couldn't move, he raised his voice somewhat and commanded, "NOW!"

Number One, feeling numb at the treatment from this man, looked at Number Two and informed him to take the woman inside and have her cared for. He also instructed him to get someone out here to carry the gear inside and send all the other members off. Not used to being talked to in such a demanding tone, he found himself speechless. He couldn't comprehend that this was the Exalted One everyone was talking about. What kind of man was he?

"Alright Number One, let's go in the house. We have much to discuss before I familiarize myself with the situation here, especially about why my ally was taken out of the picture, what arrangements you've made for my return, and what progress that has been made relating to the Cause." Number One, not feeling comfortable about this man and without saying a word, followed his new leader into the house wondering what was in store for him and Lam.

Entering the house, Number One showed his leader around. The house had five bedrooms, one bath, a combined living and dining room, a kitchen, and a garage. They settled into comfortable recliners in the main room after the tour. He called to a teenage girl in one of the rooms and ordered her to prepare the tea and serve it to her new master. She moved quickly to the kitchen with haste because she didn't want to be insulted or beaten for being slow, again.

When the girl left the room, Number One was asked to elaborate on the elimination of the Exalted One's friend. He told the Masked Man what he believed was fact. "The woman who met you in Da Nang is one of our best agents when it comes to getting bits of information from various leaders in the area. She knows how to please them and loosen their tongues with rice wine. She had been seeing a high-ranking city policeman and was able to get his confidence over a short time period. One night, he was really talkative and told her about some information he had gotten from an informant about some unknown society that wanted to reunite the country under a new Cause. She didn't press him for further information. Then after two more sessions with him, he revealed, while in a near drunken stupor, that your friend was the informant. We questioned him for three days, and he finally admitted it. He said he was being well paid for his cooperation and that a charge of rape and a couple of minor crimes would not be forthcoming. As near as we can tell, he did not reveal any plans of your arrival, your actions in the U.S., your Cause, or who is involved with the society here. It seems that he was bargaining for a big payoff for everything he knew. He presented a great danger to us, so we eliminated the threat. He was still alive when you called him. We had forced him to oblige you when you called. Then he was sent to his ancestors."

After a moment's thought, the Masked Man offered, "You did well. I was looking forward to meeting my old friend, but the Cause must be our first consideration. A plus is that he's the only one who knew my true identity. So, you say Hai is a good agent? I think after last night I need to change my personal sexual desire about her. That being said, do you know about the man in the States who was to call here with information for me and a request for money to be sent to him?"

"Yes! I know of him, but he hasn't called."

"Then you don't have any information about two Americans and a Vietnamese woman named Mai back there?"

"Not from him. I did have a call from a cousin of mine who's not one of our members. He called to say he met his mother who flew from here to Nashville to live with him. While we talked, he casually mentioned that they saw two American men and an Asian woman getting on a plane bound for San Francisco."

"Damn it!" The Exalted One shouted. "Those two guys are supposed to be dead. I ordered it." Calming a little, he continued, "That means the man I depended on has been caught or killed, and now I have to worry about what is happening with the woman and those two undeserving asses I hate. I'm sure they are coming after me."

"Why would they come for you?"

"It's a very long story to tell, and it doesn't concern you. Let me think about it for a couple minutes." He finally came up with a solution. "It may not be so bad after all. I just need to think of it not as them coming for me, but as them bringing the woman to me. That could settle my personal problem. I won't have to return to the States. I will get my woman, and I will get to torture the two Americans to death very slowly."

Soon they were joined by Number Two. After discussing strategies for a while, they decided to enlist many women to collect information from officials in all of the large cities and in Hanoi, Da Nang, and Ho Chi Minh City in particular. They would adopt a system in the rural areas that the Viet Cong had used after they had recruited and trained men. The Hoa Hau and the Cao Dai went to the Viet Cong side due to the treatment they received during Diem's presidency. It would be worth checking out their feelings about the government and enlisting them if possible.

Then they would recruit or blackmail local officials to set up various associations in the providences, villages, hamlets, and sub-hamlets and indoctrinate the people during meetings and reeducation sessions. The types of associations would be the farmers', old men's, old women's, young women's, young men's, youths', and security, to name just a few for starters, just like the National Liberation Front had done. Instant death to those who refused to go along with the program

Administration of the movement was the first priority. A central location with a large working area needed to be set up on Tran Hung Dao Street. Besides personnel and office furniture, they would need computers and the nerds to operate them. As the movement progressed, they must develop foot soldiers on the sly and train some assassination teams to take out the Communist Infrastructure. Four hours later, the Exalted One assigned Number One to draw up a hierarchy chart depicting their proposed organization and gave Number Two and Hai the task of recruiting some women to train in collecting information by using their bodies.

The teenage girl, hired to cook and clean, had a meal prepared and served it when the meeting was over. The new leader, who she didn't know, ordered her to bring Hai to the table and set another place for her. Not sure what to do, she looked at Number One, and he nodded his okay. She rushed off, wondering what was happening with this person who just arrived. Her life here with Huong and Lam had been horrible enough the last several days. She never knew if she would be berated, beaten, or raped. She liked it better when the other man was in charge, before his murder, for he was very nice to her. She went to her room, woke Hai, and hurried her to the table as she had been ordered to. Then after setting a place for Hai, she went to her small kitchen, sat at the table, and cried.

The four sat, talked, and drank some rice wine during the evening. The Exalted One made it plain to the others that when anyone else in the organization came to the house, he would wear his mask, for he must protect his identity temporarily. He made sure they understood the need to warn him when someone was coming so he could put it on. As bedtime neared, he commented that he might just use Hai's talents upon retiring.

At the Exalted one's desire for Hai, Number One then made a suggestion to him. "Hai really looks like she needs a good night's sleep tonight after her binge drinking today. Take the kitchen girl, Bui, to your room instead of her. I know you won't be disappointed with her youthful body, her agility and her talents." Laughing he continued, "We have trained her well, and she will comply with your every sexual wish and desire. She likes being forced into doing any sexual favor you'd like. Even likes being slapped around some." He and Number Two Laughed too loud.

Although it disgusted him that this goose could make a suggestion like that, he decided to play along. "Ah! You surprise me. That sounds like a good idea. For her age, she seems to have a nice body, and I noticed right off that she has a sweet little ass. You have just earned your first brownie points." He went to the kitchen and grabbed the girl by the wrist and ordered her, loudly so the rest could hear, "Come with me, bitch!" He took her to his bed.

He needed to know how things were really going at this place and needed to build trust in someone to update him on the situation and keep him informed. He'd noticed some marks on the girl that looked like fading bruises, and she seemed scared every time those guys hollered at her. She might be his perfect source of information. Knowing he needed to develop her slowly to gain her trust, he made up his mind to be gentle with her. When he first started fondling her, he could feel some trembling in her body. He assured her she would not be harmed. He kept his promise.

She had awakened in time to go to the kitchen, but first she needed to clean up after the night that just ended. Then she started preparing breakfast for the group. Even though the man had used all of her body, he wasn't as mean or degrading and demanding like the two asses that had ran the house. The thing that really surprised her was that he was kind and gentle and she was not beaten as usually happened during sex with the two turds. She wondered if there was really a future for her working here with this man. Still, how she wished she had a lot of Dong. She would leave here and maybe go to Quang Ngai City or someplace else and be rid of these animals.

After the men were up and did their morning toiletry, Hai met them at the table, and they ate heartily. After the men had their fill, the girl cleared the dishes and cleaned up the kitchen. As she finished a couple of other chores, she was summoned to the men's table at the Exalted One's order. He gave her tea, which irked the other two men, and announced that since he hadn't been in Hoi An for-a while, he'd like to do some sightseeing and that the young girl would be his guide. He looked at her and inquired as to her name. "Nguyen Thi Bui," she replied. He asked her if she could obtain transportation for them. She surprised him saying, "No need to. I have a Moped out in the garage.

I would be honored to serve as your driver and guide. I know this City's streets very well, and also the attractions the tourists come to see." Number One tried to object, but the Masked Man shushed him up.

"That is splendid," he replied. I think that I'll enjoy your service. Finish your tea and do whatever you need to do before leaving, then let me know when you're ready to go." This situation pleased the two men even less than her being offered tea. Number One glanced at Number Two, then remarked to the Exalted One that the girl was a mere servant and should not be treated as one of their members.

"Number One, I'll be the judge of how people will be treated in this house. Just remember that you could end up with the same fate as my friend." Hai sat quietly and uttered not a sound. She approved of Number One's rebuke. She believed he deserved it, as he was a cruel dumb ass and couldn't be trusted. She knew things that she must keep to herself for her own safety for a while yet.

Bui finished some minor chores, then readied herself for the tour. She went to the Exalted One's room and let him know she was ready. As the two were mounting the Moped, he whispered in her ear, "Take us to a secluded little restaurant where we can drink tea and talk quietly first."

"I know just the place," She replied. "Hang on tight." He clasped his arms around her waist, and they were off.

He recognized the little café-type place. During the conflict, there was a brothel on the second floor, and he had eaten and enjoyed himself there a few times. After his tea was served, he began a normal conversation with Bui. She caught him up on her past and things that had happened to her. He easily, after gaining her confidence, steered the exchange to easy questions about the two asses that had been running the show. He learned a lot about their backstabbing ways. This led to the most important questions about what happened to his friend. At first she was afraid to discuss it for fear of retaliation by the two asses. He was able to convince her that she was under his protection and no harm would come to her for being honest. What she told him was enough to enrage anyone.

"Huong and Lam hated your friend and also desired to lead the organization. He was beaten and tortured for a few days until he died shortly after your call. I believe they helped him along. I was told that if I said a word, I would suffer the same fate. That's when they began to beat on me and rape me if I didn't do things right or if they thought I was too slow at a given task. It's been horrible." She now had tears running down her cheeks.

"Right after your friend died, they cornered Hai and gave her the story she was to tell you if asked. It was about seducing an official and obtaining information that your friend was an informant. The two described to her in detail what they would do to her if she ever said otherwise. She and I both are always afraid that we might slip up. I'm not sure how comfortable I am telling you this, but I think I can trust you. I don't know for sure because they whisper a lot, but you may be in danger from them also."

He sat silently for a few minutes, contemplating what he heard. Finally, he spoke gently to her and told her that she had done the right thing in revealing the truth to him, that he didn't trust them either, and that he would see that the situation was taken care of in due time, as he needed the two temporarily. "You needn't be afraid now. Those two will be informed that you're now my woman and to keep their hands off of you. I will talk to Hai also about this conversation too, but before I do, you need to let her know that we talked and she needn't fear talking with me. I have great plans for the future, and you two very well could be a part of them. As for me, I'm always cautious about my physical wellbeing." He handed her a napkin to dry her cheeks. "I want you to know that last night was wonderful and you were a joy to be with." She blushingly smiled at him. "Now, finish your tea. We need to sightsee." He was already thinking how to get at the two asses when he was done using them.

"Okay," she responded. "I want you to know I've never liked doing those things we did last night because I was forced to do them and they hurt, but last night I didn't mind them. You were very caring. Now we'll go by the Japanese Covered Bridge first, and then to the Museum of History and Culture. If we're being followed, we should be able to spot the tail."

Surprised at her comment, he replied, "You're pretty smart for a young lady. I like your idea. It makes good sense."

"I did get some evasion training from your friend. Only a little though, but it helped me when those two asses had me followed a few times. I lost the tails. Come on and hop aboard, and we'll be off."

After sightseeing at the Japanese Covered Bridge, they went to the museum. On the way, she didn't take a direct route. A couple of times, she pretended to take the wrong direction and would make U-turns and return back the way they came. Arriving at the museum, they pretended to just stand and talk outside for a few minutes, but they were actually looking for any familiar motorbikes or cars they'd seen along the way. They spotted one vespa whose rider appeared to be one they had seen and passed about three times. After a couple of minutes, it passed by them again. They now knew for sure now the stupid geese had them followed.

"Bui, now that we know for sure we're being followed, let's check out this place, then you can take me wherever and we won't worry about it."

"That sounds like a good plan. It was fun finding out we were being followed." She continued, "That guy needs a little more instruction on how to be invisible like the legendary Invisible One." He chuckled, and they entered the museum.

Late afternoon, after seeing many features of the City, they returned to the house. Bui promised him she would keep an eye out for Hai's return and talk to her on his behalf. She thought about herself and decided that for some reason she felt more alive than she had been feeling. This new boss was so different. She had gotten some things off her chest about his friend and really enjoyed their outing, especially the part about spotting the spy.

The Exalted One had a serious conversation with the two turds. He demanded they explain why he and the girl had been followed. They hemmed and hawed around and finally came up with the excuse that he wasn't being followed, the tail had been there to protect him. He told them both that was crap and he didn't believe it for a minute. Then he skipped to another subject.

He didn't like the way Bui had been treated, especially the beating, bruising, and raping (That would be his fun at the appropriate time when she was no longer needed). After he laid down the law to them, they got the picture that she was hands off to anyone but him. He then instructed them to inform Hai, upon her return, to put on something sexy and come to his room.

He left them sitting at the table unsure of what they had gotten themselves into. When he entered his room and closed the door, he checked the room for microphones and cameras. He was glad he couldn't find any. As an afterthought, he went back to the two jerks and asked them to set up a meeting of their most trusted followers for the next day, some place away from the house. After the meeting, he and Bui would go to the site where the Jade Cross should be. He returned to his room and crashed. He was tired from the day's events.

He had slept about 45 minutes when a knock on his door woke him. Rubbing his eyes with his fists, he got to the door and asked who it was. Hai's sweet voice came through the door saying, "I'm here at your request, Oh Exalted One." He opened the door for her and upon seeing what she was wearing, he said, "Damn! You sure look good in those pink baby doll PJs. Just look at those full, melon-like breasts of yours, standing tall and holding up the PJ top. I can't wait to see your beautiful naked body again and kiss it all over."

"Wow! That sounds wonderful. Well, aren't going to invite me to come in? We can't do anything here in the hallway with those two nosey asses ogling after me with their tongues hanging out. Besides, there is more comfort on the bed, you know."

He waved her in, closed and locked the door, and had her sit on the bed. He sat beside her and told her they must speak in low tones because he doesn't want anyone's curious ears listening to what was being said; he wanted them to believe he and she were having sex. "Has Bui spoken to you about the situation here that I requested her to?"

"Oh yes. She told me about how you two spoke at the tea house, what she told you about your friend, and about how you played a game with someone following you. It sounded like I missed out on all of the fun. I will tell you all that I know about your friend. I was pumping an official for information, but nothing was ever said about your friend cooperating for money. The two did murder him after extreme torture and humiliation. He died honorably. He told them nothing. He was a very brave man, and I've shed tears for him. He was not a traitor. He had a dossier on those two and was going to present it to you and dump them where they would never be found. I looked for the dossier, but I couldn't find it."

She continued explaining how things had gone down, and it was parallel to Bui's comments, but with a little more detail thrown in. She really dumped on them about how they threatened her to tell a different story or else suffer the consequences. She spoke nearly an hour and finished by telling the Exalted One that she had overheard a plan to get rid of him as soon as progress had been made in establishing the administration of the Cause. When she finished, she looked exhausted but thankful that she trusted that this man would take care of everything, meaning Huong and Lam. She hated them with a passion.

He gave her his promise that she needn't worry any more, as he was developing a plan to settle things with a vengeance. They spoke of just anything for a few minutes, then he explained that as much as he wanted her body, he had promised Bui they would be together this night; however, he wouldn't pass up tomorrow night without her. She smiled, kissed him on the cheek, and left. He laid back on the bed to think more on killing the two asses. It was kind of funny to him that he had assessed them correctly when he first saw them.

Hai sat in her room, forcing herself to remember everything she could about this man and the situation at hand. As soon as she could, she needed to report the situation to her superior. She would have to arrange a meeting in the next couple of days before she was sent off to do what the man wanted. She would also have to remember what she had heard Huong and Lam saying when she peeked at them before going to the guy's room. Something about some Americans coming to Hoi An City and a woman the man loves and wants. She felt that her mission was becoming weirder all the time. She hoped it would be over very soon. She cringed at the thought of the Masked Man touching her again

Meanwhile, Huong and Lam had cornered Bui and tried to find out what she and the Exalted One had discussed during their tour. They were pissed because she more or less told them to stick it up their asses and if they really wanted to know to check with the Exalted One. She turned from them with a suppressed smile and went to her room feeling good. She sat on her folding old surplus U.S. Army folding cot and thought about the lovemaking the night before, the conversations she and the man had, and being followed on the Moped earlier. She had been frightened for her wellbeing since the ruthless torture and murder of her provider. Now she was feeling a little more optimistic about her day-to-day survival. She also wondered if the Exalted One would need her services at bedtime again. She was willing to do him any time because right now he meant her survival, and it was better than being demeaned at the hands of those two turds. When they met their fate, she would rejoice. She lay back and dozed off. Later, Hai tapped lightly on her door and entered. Hai woke her and said, "I believe you're needed by our leader." For some reason at that moment, Bui felt slightly important and knew what room to go to.

After the morning meal was over, everyone was sated and the dishes removed and the table cleaned off, the Exalted One announced to the group that he must talk to Hai about her assigned tasks alone and that Hung and Lam must go to the meeting place, seat the attendees, and instruct them on how to greet him when he arrived. He explained that when he was done at the house Bui would give him a ride to the meeting place on her Moped. The two Geese were not happy about this. It was beginning to seem loke everything was being fucked up by this Exalted one' directions.

The Masked Man and Hai walked outside, and he inquired of her if she knew of two good men, even if they were bandits, who might be good leaders, plus three or four men who could be trusted to follow orders and not be nosey.

"I know two of such men who are dangerous bandits. They can be trusted if the money is right, as can their small gang of hoodlums. They are experienced leaders who were forced to fight with the Viet Cong when they were very young and later they were in the DVR's Army."

"That sounds good to me Hai. I think you were about two or three days from starting the mission I assigned you. Delay that for a couple of days. Arrange for me to meet them tonight, say around midnight. You, Bui, and I will slip out to meet them. Oh, and get yourself a motorbike too. We'll push the bikes a ways so as not to wake the two geese when we start them. As soon as Bui and I leave for the meeting, you can go make contact with them. She and I will be followed probably, but you shouldn't be."

"I'll do my best, and I know you'll be impressed."

A few minutes later, he and Bui left and were once again followed on the Geese's orders. He couldn't believe that Hung and Lam didn't have anyone that knew how to shadow people, unless they wanted him to know he was being followed. He'd have to give that some thought, even though it didn't matter much to him. He didn't think those two geese were smart enough to want him to know he was being followed. They weren't long for this world anyway.

About a half block from the meeting site, he pulled on his mask. The meeting went well, as he had instructed the two lame brains how to do it. It was pretty much organized the way he wanted it to be, and it ran the same as it had been done in the States by his Number One there. He had no assignments to hand out this morning, but he put the eighteen people there on standby. He explained to them that the Cause was in the developing stage, and it could be a few days or more before he'd need hand out any tasks.

After the meeting was over, he made sure all of the members of his No Name were gone from the area before he removed his mask. He was standing with Hung, Lam, and Bui and announced to the group, "Bui and I won't be back to the house for a few more hours yet. We are going joy riding today. I might even get her back into the woods and get some joy for myself. We'll start our work on the Cause tomorrow morning. There won't be much time for any leisure once we get started on it. Gee, I hope we're not followed today, or for that matter, any other day." With that quip he and Bui got on the bike and left.

When they were out of sight of the meeting place, he had Bui stop. "We are not joy riding. I need you to take me just beyond the old ARVN APC School to where a U.S. Marine battalion enclave had been, then into the countryside. We have a couple of things to check out. We'll stop and get some water and rice cakes to take along, as the site's about five miles north of the City and a little east of there." She gave him a thumbs up to his order, and they took off with her gunning the engine for all it was worth.

She wondered what he was going to do to her there. She was feeling very uncomfortable now, and it was hard not to show her concern.

CHAPTER 27

THE FOUR WERE SURPRISED at Detective Chau's humor. The best part of it was that he was breaking the ice and making them comfortable with him. He explained to them that he always wanted to be a standup comedian, and maybe if they behaved themselves, he might do his best James Bond impression for them: You know, Bond! James Bond! Then Chau got serious and began outlining what had happened to the victims, and with Mai's permission, he described the mutilation of the bodies and the coroner's findings. He detailed the canvasing of hotels close to where the cab and driver were found and how Hotel Street was canvased as well.

He continued, "One of the officers got a break at one of them, which is why you were put here in the Ala Moana. It is the one we feel the perp stayed at. The night desk clerk had to come in during the afternoon to fill out some paperwork. Hearing the officer ask a day clerk whether any strange guest or if anyone at all checked out during the night, he told the officer about the Asian man checking out during the night and what his excuse had been. The day clerk looked up the info on the computer and gave it to the officer. He got a good description from the two clerks and gave it to me, and I began checking the airlines and got a hit on the arrival by a dude of the same name on one of the manifests. It matched the name and description of the hotel guest.

"It seems that the perp took a flight to Hong Kong using a different name and is most likely there now. When I got back to the station, I heard some officer talking about the strange goings-on in Nashville and how they had received a bulletin about it. After I read it, I called your MNPD, Sgt. Parnell, and voilà, here you are. Before you ask, I have notified the Hong Kong police. I don't know how seriously they'll take it or if they'll check any incoming flight manifests for him. They have a lot on their plate every day." Then he said in a deeper voice, "Bond! James Bond!" and smiled. Parnell and Mai shook their heads and thought they had another sick ass Tolbane on their hands.

Parnell and Tolbane took turns asking Det. Chau questions, while Mai and the priest listened, then they detailed the events as they happened in Vietnam, Tennessee, and Missouri. They told him everything they knew about the No Name and the Masked Man, and how he was seeking the Jade Cross and Mai. Detective Chau listened and was deeply interested in this story, as he had never before heard of such outrageous criminal activity. Hawaii Five O couldn't have come up with a plot like that in any shape or form.

After all of the events had been described to him and he was done asking questions, Detective Chau gave the group a little more info. "There's been a lot of chatter back at the station about these two killings committed here. Seminal fluid was found in the rectum of the corpse on Hotel Street, apparently deposited after death. Because of the knife wounds, which were numerous and deep along with the castration, the throat cutting, and the seminal fluid, some of the guys have kicked around some theories about the killer.

A lot of cops around here think this maniac is a xenophobe, a piquerist, a sociopath, or a combination of them all. He may even be Dracula arisen from his Transylvania dirt-filled coffin and needs to use a knife because his fangs fell out, or he lost his manhood and his knife is an extension of his penis. Can't you just in your mind picture a fangless Dracula needing to use a knife for his dick?" The others all groaned at the comment except for Tolbane.

"Hey Detective, that was funny! You need to join some comic club. Now I don't mean to interrupt your soliloquy, or your oration, and declaration," Tolbane interjected, "but I know what a xenophobe and sociopath are, but just what in the hell is a piquerist? Never heard of something like that before." Parnell nodded to agree with him.

"I didn't know myself till one of the detectives explained it to me. Then I looked it up in an encyclopedia. The best I can tell you is that it's some kind of sexual pervert who likes to use his knife on his victims, women in particular. He may get his sexual gratification before, during, or after he uses his knife, or a combination of acts thereof. The knife is an extension of his penis I guess. I'm not sure if he actually satisfies himself with his victims, or if the act is completed before, during, or after the cutting. I don't know if there even needs to be penetration at all. Any way you look at it, the guy is a mentally deranged animal and belongs in a cage. That's the best I can describe it. Whether I'm right or wrong, I guess you'd have to find out the real scoop from a psychologist or some other kind of brain doctor. We do think the oral sex was before the cutting this time, and the anal entry was after the time of the victim's death."

Parnell thought for a moment. "To my knowledge, we have no information on our guy using a knife himself. Even though there's two cut up victims that bled out from the death by a thousand cuts, we believe his goons did that. He did drug, rape, and torture a lady friend of ours, but maybe, if it's the same guy, he had a reason not to cut Carly up. He also made it very clear that he didn't want Mai to be harmed, as we already told you about the letters. We came to the conclusion that the assault on Carly was just to screw with our minds and instill some fear into us. To be frank with you, all it did was to piss us off even more. Tolbane, here, just wanted to kill some son of a bitch over it."

"Parnell, think for a minute." Tolbane instructed his friend. That must be what that John Rawlings I killed a while back was. A rotten assed Piquerist that chopped up those people with his girl-friend, Soapy." Parnell agreed with him.

"Aah!" commented Chau. "It must be true what I've come to know about you Marines. 'You F with the bull, you get the horn!'" He chuckled.

Mai, who had been quietly listening, blurted out, "You got that right! Semper Fi do or die!" Then Father Phat added his thought, "Amen to that!"

After giving Parnell a copy of a few police documents relating to the case, and having some more casual conversation around the table, once again Det. Chau told them about the shopping, the beach, and the restaurants, as well as where not to go and what to look out for. He surprised them by saying that lunch was on the HPD and called a waitress in a skimpy high-thigh length sarong, halter, and a lei around her neck over to order. When their sumptuous lunch was over, they said their goodbyes and the detective wished them luck in catching the animal and told them to keep him informed of their progress. He'd see them in the morning when he picked them up to go to the International Airport. The group spent the afternoon strolling along the street, looking in shops and resisting the urge to buy comfortable and colorful Hawaiian wear.

The next morning, Det. Chau picked them up and returned them to the Honolulu International Airport, and told them that he would notify the Hong Kong police that they were on their way and their approximate time of arrival there. Soon they were in the air headed for Hong Kong. Their flight was comfortable and their needs and comfort were promptly attended to by a pretty Chinese flight attendant. Parnell was particularly impressed with her. After a long flight, with only minor turbulence, the landing gear screeching as it went down and they were descending to the Chek Lap Kok International Airport on Chek Lap Kok Island adjacent to Hong Kong.

Before heading to the baggage claim area, they went to the information desk to find out if any policemen had been looking for them. The regular girl Sue, AKA Ling, was not there, but an elderly woman was working, and she had a message for an American police Sergeant named Parnell. He showed her his ID upon her request and thanked her for the message. He turned from the counter and opened the sealed envelope. The message was brief and stated that an officer would be there about an hour after they landed. It also contained an apology that they had to wait. The group claimed their luggage and then decided to get a coffee while they waited. Mai and the priest conspired and decided to have a little fun while they waited. When someone who appeared to be Chinese passed by their table, they would converse a little loudly in Vietnamese. They felt that when the people turned around and stared at them, they were wondering what weird Chinese dialect they were speaking. Fun can be had in any language.

While they were enjoying the coffee, Tolbane drifted into la la land as he sometimes did. This time it wasn't about back flips, but for some reason it was about the first operation he was on in Vietnam. The grunt units involved had already started their sweep of their area of operation. The sub team he was on was choppered to Dai Loc District Headquarters, Quang Nam Province. They landed atop a small hill, and walking down the hill, they could see the horseshoe-bend of the river and upon it, there sat an old French Fort which served as the Dai Loc District Headquarters. The sub team stayed on the roof. They weren't plying their trade in the basement or one of the two floors because of the trash and garbage that was strewn around the main floor office and upstairs billeting area.

Fortunately for them, there was a defensive parapet around the roof. It gave them cover from periodic sniper fire coming from a distant tree line, but not the occasional monsoon rain. One day, a couple of ARVNs got tired of the sniping and fired off one of their two 105 mm Howitzers into the tree line, and voilà, no more sniping came from that area. Suddenly he jerked awake. Mai had given him a gentle slap on the back of his head and told him, "Wake up, Sleeping Beauty. Our policeman is here."

The officer introduced himself as Officer Richard Wei Wong. "I'm called Little Richard because I listen to Little Richard's music all the time. I'm still looking for 'Long Tall Sally' though." The group laughed and introduced themselves to him. "Seriously, I often work as an interpreter or a liaison to English-speaking tourists or visiting dignitaries." He explained that he was late due to an auto accident that held up traffic. He then asked if any of them had ever been to Hong Kong before and when. Both Tolbane and Parnell each gave a short recall of being there for R&R during the Viet Nam Conflict, although at different times. Officer Wong, ordering more coffee for them, then explained the changes to the area since then and how and why the International Airport came to be at this location. "The biggest thing all the previous visitors to the area miss is the Hong Kong ferry ride from Kowloon to the Victoria side and back.

"Now," he said, "about your situation. At this point, we have no probable cause to work on your case officially; however, with the information we have received from MNPD and HPD, be believe there is a possibility that there is a link to the very vile sexual assault and butchering of two lovely young working ladies here. It's most likely the same perpetrator you're looking for. So unofficially, it's in our best interest to work with you and exchange information between us. The detective that is working the case will meet with you tomorrow morning at 10:30 AM. After that, you'll dine at a very nice restaurant on the department's dime. You'll know sometime tonight as to what time you'll be picked up and transported to his substation. If there aren't any questions from you, then it's time to get you to your hotel. I know you must be tired and have some jet lag. That is a long, boring, and tiring trip between here, Honolulu and Nashville. Flying in a cramped-up area is just not my cuppa tea, as the Brit soldiers used to say here."

"Amen, Brother!" Father Phat intoned while making the sign of the cross.

Mai got her two cents worth in also. Smiling at Little Richard, she thanked him and told him how handsome he is in Vietnamese, and then she walked on ahead, wiggling her butt in a way that could topple the tallest buildings or smash the highest mountain if it came in contact with her glorious derriere. Tolbane wondered how in the heck he ever got entangled with this wayward woman. It's okay though. There's no other like her any place on this planet.

Outside, the officer led them to an unmarked deep green minivan with the official Police logo on the doors. When the luggage was loaded and all had their seat belts on and adjusted, he drove off and surprised them as to where their lodging would be. "We cancelled the reservations you had made. We're putting you up in the same hotel that the perp used. You can ask all the questions there you want, and there's a certain rickshaw driver that sits outside you might want to talk to. It seems that he was the only one who carried the guy around mostly. He worked for a very classy Madam who calls herself Sue and also works the information booth here, where she's known as Ling. Here at the airport, she would pick out wealthy men and book them into this hotel. This rickshaw driver would be the one transporting the customer to her place and back from the hotel, but for a few Hong Kong dollars, he has no problem getting diarrhea of the mouth.

"The two women who were butchered worked for this Madam. It seems that the deaths of the two women really got to her. She closed her place down for a couple of days, then sold it to her manager. Don't know if she'd be around to question. This rickshaw driver doesn't have the best command of the English language, but we have covered that for you. During your stay, there will be an interpreter for you to use. His name is Detective Yung Soon. He will contact you after you've checked in. He will accompany you wherever you go and assist you with any bargaining and so on. Don't fret. His job is not to spy on you. He will show you the brothel and take you to the crime scene. I must warn you though. It's pretty gory. It's not been cleaned up yet."

After a long ride in the slow traffic full of honking horns and cars recklessly darting in and out of lanes, the group was glad to finally arrive at the hotel. They were also glad they had a good driver in officer Little Richard. Tolbane was happy he wasn't like those mini-taxi drivers on Okinawa, Japan. He and others swore those drivers were Kamikazes. When they were getting their luggage out of the vehicle, the officer pointed out the rickshaw and driver in question.

He was sitting in his rickshaw, wearing what seemed like black pajamas and a conical hat. Tolbane whispered to Parnell and Father Phat, "He looks like a VCS! We need to detain his ass and get him to a captive collection point, ASAP!" Parnell and the father once again just shook their heads. It was a surprising fact that Tolbane's friends didn't have numerous neck injuries from all the head shaking on his behalf.

They no more than had gotten the luggage out when a bellhop was there with a welcoming smile and a big cart. He motioned them aside and loaded the luggage on to the cart. As he pushed the cart towards the entrance, he motioned them with his hand to follow him into the hotel. He directed them to the registration desk and waited patiently while they checked in. The police officer spoke to the desk lady, said his goodbye to the group, and left. After getting their room assignments, the group went to their respective rooms with the bellhop's aide and crashed on the inviting beds. Soon, the room phone rang. Mai answered it. It was Detective Soon.

He instructed her to inform the group that they should freshen up a bit and meet in the restaurant in about fifty minutes. The table would already be set and the food will be there waiting for them. They would discuss the situation as he knew it after the meal. Tolbane wondered to Mai as to what kind of food was ordered. Mai, being Mai, said, "I don't know what was ordered my dear one, but I do hope you have to eat one of those baby octopuses raw. Or maybe even a raw clownfish sandwich with nuoc mam sauce if they have it, fit for a clown you are." Tolbane's stomach cringed at the thought of eating something so disgusting, and he made a retching sound.

When the group got down to the restaurant, Detective Yung Soon introduced himself and the others responded in kind, and then they were seated at a long rectangular table set with the best china, glassware, and silverware and an ice buckets of champagne at each end of the table. Tolbane wondered aloud, "I wonder who died today and left us to be the Royalty?" He got a good kick in the shin under the table from Mai. She must have read his mind. Soon, Parnell and the priest both giggled aloud and the detective wondered what he gotten himself into.

Two waiters appeared from nowhere and filled their water glasses, checked what type of beverage they wanted, and disappeared into the kitchen. Then two other waiters removed their plates, replacing them with a dish and a bowl for each, one with salad and one with a dressing from a cart. When the salads were served their drinks arrived. The salads were consumed and the dishes and dressings were removed to the scullery, and the first two waiters brought out a cart that had medium-well broiled New York Strip steaks on sizzling platters; baked Idaho potatoes with all the sour cream, chives and diced bacon you could ask for; a side dish of a peas and corn mixture; and lastly, A1 sauce. Of course, Tolbane, not being very happy they had had no honey mustard for his tossed salad, had to ask for Heinz 57 sauce. Parnell told the one waiter that what Tolbane really wanted was nuoc mam sauce. The waiter, never having heard of nuoc mam, looked at him as if he were crazy and went about his duties.

After everybody had eaten their fill and the table was cleared off, two waiters brought hot peach cobbler with a dip of vanilla ice cream for each. After dessert the waiters brought two bottles of Champagne iced down in buckets and Champagne Flutes for all, popped the corks and poured for each one.

Detective Soon stood and proposed a toast welcoming them to Kowloon, Hong Kong, and they clinked flutes and drank. Sitting down, he explained to them that he very seldom got to greet regular visitors in this manner. Normally, he only did for VIPs, but his chief made sure that this group was more important than most VIPs, as they represented brothers of the badge on a quest to nab a criminal that could be responsible for the horrible mutualization and the killing of the two Chinese women.

They then chatted about the case a bit, left the restaurant, went to their rooms to get what they needed, and met Detective Soon outside the hotel. The rickshaw driver was at his usual spot and was sitting in his carriage, sound asleep with his head laid back.

The detective slapped the guy on the leg, and he bounced up ready to fight until he saw who had startled him. Soon handed him a handful of Hong Kong dollars, only worth a couple of American dollars, and spoke to him about their arrangement. About then, a valet brought his large SUV to the hotel front, and the six-climbed in. The rickshaw man sat in front as to direct the detective to the sites. He had learned where the places were from the driver who took the man to them. The first stop they made was the store where the man had purchased a plastic suit and booties, another stop where he purchased duct tape and a couple of knives, and then a small black-market druggist where he bought some barbital and some other sleeping tablets. Then the group was directed to the apartment.

Crime scene tape was still across the door, which the detective tore down. He explained that had this group not have been on the way, it would have been turned over to a crime scene cleanup crew by now. He opened the door, and as the group moved inside, they were horrified. They all wondered if they'd need a barf bag. Not only were the odors of blood and death in the air and still offensive, but the blood splatter on the floor, the walls, and the bed were still dominating the room. He showed them the bathroom and the tub where the plastic suit, booties, and gloves were burnt. He pointed out the counter in the tiny kitchen where partially filled bottles and glasses had sat. All but one of the glasses had traces of a drug cocktail that was only strong enough to put a person to sleep for a while. He informed them, "I'm only allowed to show and tell you this small bit. In the morning at the station, the lead detective will explain more and discuss what forensic evidence we might have. I can also tell you that the young one was found duct taped to that chair and the other one, spread eagled and tied on the bed. This is the most horrific crime scene we've ever had or seen."

Tolbane and Parnell agreed with him. They hurried out to get some fresh air and were relieved instantly when they got outside, although Mai and the priest still looked a little green around their gills. They returned to the car and were off to the brothel.

Soon gave them a short rundown on the place. After Sue closed down the club, as some called it, the girl who had managed it for her, Xuan, was able to buy it from her, and it is still head and heels above most of these types of places here. It's a clean place to go to. The girls get regular medical checkups once a week. The place is honest in its dealings and won't rip off its customers. Best of all, the girls are hot and the beers are cold, what any man alive could desire. Mai looked at Tolbane and informed him he better be on his best behavior and put on his blinders when they go inside. He replied, "You know I only have eyes for thou, only then a glass of wine and a loaf of bread." She gave him one of those "Yeah, right!" stares.

Xuan, clad in a manner to show her assets off as usual, was standing by the bar and saw the group come in. She wandered up the aisle between tables to meet them. She knew why they were there because Detective Soon had briefed her the day before on why the Americans would be checking things out. She knew that if they were able to find the no-good bastard that killed the girls, she would gladly help them any way she could. She smiled her best smile as she greeted them and was introduced to each at a time. She motioned to a young boy who was cleaning tables to put two tables together for their guests. She seated them and inquired as to what they'd like to drink and sent the boy to fetch them along with frosted glasses. Tolbane, Mai's version of being the horniest man on earth, was immediately thinking of backflips at the first look at Xuan. They spoke of the nice weather they were having until the drinks were served, then got down to the problem at hand.

Xuan began, "I came to work the last morning they were here. Xing had gotten some clothes that were loose, but still fit well enough for the Girl to wear to display her wares. She indicated that she was taking the Girl clothes shopping and would have her hair and nails done. I thought Sue had ordered this done, so I didn't question her about it. I went to lunch later, and on my return, my bartender informed me that they had returned with a lot of packages and went to the girl's room. He told me the Girl looked good when they came out. Actually, he said 'Damn it! The Girl looked just as hot as Xing!' She apparently had brand new clothes, heels, and a new hairdo. Then they left, and I never got a chance to see them again.

"I'll show you the rooms now. You can bring your drinks along." She showed them the young Girl's first. It was a small room in back. "Notice the intercom on the wall so she could be paged as needed." It had an old military cot, a small dresser, a nightstand, and a very narrow and tall cabinet that had been used as a clothes closet. "We have all of her new clothes and belongings in storage until relatives can be found to claim them. Follow me, we'll go upstairs."

She showed them a couple of the regular rooms used by the working girls, pointed out the intercoms, then went into Sue's master bedroom which was now hers. It was quite a layout and had a bar also. She pointed out the main intercom and explained that Sue could call any room in the facility and that any of those could contact her. Then she pointed out a small alcove that was Sue's office and said that she has been working time to time to learn all of the records there so she can be as successful as Sue was. There were a lot of files to study because Sue had documented everything she came in contact with, from soup to nuts.

She called down to the bar and was told there was a round of fresh cold drinks waiting at their table. Xuan asked, "Does anyone have any questions?" Mai was first to speak. "How many days did he come here?"

"He spent the first night in the suite with Sue, the second night with Xing, and the third night with both of them. When he was with Xing, the Girl was called to the suite several times. I think that's when the plan to meet him later was planned. Sue had no idea what was going down. She did not allow the girls to freelance. Is there anything else?"

"That will be all we need; you've covered things pretty well. Thank you so much for seeing us," Soon said, bowing to her. After consuming the fresh drinks, they all stood to leave and Xuan remarked, "Anytime you guys get the urge, you know where to find me and my girls. We aim to please. If you use our bathroom facility, you best aim too!"

With a big grin, Mai countered, "They will, but it will be over my dead body and the loss of their useless gonads!" The guys and Xuan laughed and they all filed out. Outside in the car, the rickshaw driver was still waiting patiently, asleep as usual. Before driving off, Detective Soon asked if they wanted to do some shopping. Their replies were all yesses, but they decided not to buy large items as they had no way of totting them around. The detective had the rickshaw driver take them to some decent shops. After shopping and buying small souvenirs, they returned to the hotel.

At the hotel, Detective Soon instructed them to be in the restaurant by seven AM, as the hotel was a little slow at getting food prepared and on your table at breakfast. Then he would drive them to meet with the case detective. After they were done with him, he would take them to the floating restaurants in Aberdeen. "That will be a real treat for you," he said. "You'll even get to pick your own live fish. Off their sterns, they have baskets in the water filled with an assortment of live fish. Just point to the one you want, and it'll be retrieved and cooked to your specifications. It's really a dining treat to experience the restaurants there. See you in the AM."

He drove off, and the group went to their rooms for a nap before supper. They decided at supper that they would sightsee and shop some more after the Aberdeen trip the next day. They gathered in Tolbane's room, ordered beer and snacks from room service, and discussed what they had seen and heard that afternoon. Having seen bloody crime scenes as well as carnage in war, Tolbane, Parnell and Father Phat agreed that they had never witnessed any scene so bloody. It was worse than Ba's. They were glad they didn't have to see the bodies or the crime scene photos of the two poor women. Parnell noted, "Of all the massage parlors and cat houses we've busted, and all the murderers we've covered, I've seen nothing like Sue's suite or the murder room. I thought we'd all gag and puke there."

They rose early and had breakfast—a few waffles floating in syrup and a lot of bacon for Tolbane—and they were standing outside the hotel when Detective Soon drove up. They greeted him, then piled into the vehicle and were off to their case briefing. The streets were busy, and it took several minutes to arrive at their destination. As they got out of the vehicle, Detective Soon told them to wait in front while he parked the vehicle in the police lot, then he'd take them inside and make the introductions.

They only waited about five minutes or so and he was back and led them inside. He directed them to a small office back in a corner of the squad room and bade them to enter. A lieutenant in uniform sat behind a desk with several folders askew on top of it. He stood up and greeted them each with a handshake after giving them his name, Hop WoXuan. There was only room enough for four chairs, and he indicated Mai to take one. She smiled and stated she would just sit on Tolbane's lap for the briefing. She didn't mention she might just feel something probing at her posterior while doing so.

The Lieutenant opened the folder in front of them, and he explained that the information he was about to share with them was confidential and that officially they never received it, but he wanted to share in good faith with those seeking the truth about this mad man and hoped they could help one another to find this dirt bag and bag him up. The group was surprised at his command of the language and slang. He proudly informed them that he had been an exchange student at "*The Ohio State University*" and was capable of speaking in even less than acceptable slang. He was kind of multilingual that way. They all laughed. "Go Bucks! Now," he said, "let's get down to brass tacks."

He continued, "There is something that may have a similarity with your crimes and ours, but first, Detective Soon showed you the crime scene and Sue's place. You talked with the present owner. Do you have any questions about what you've seen or heard so far? No? We interviewed several people and didn't get any solid leads on who the perp is or where he went, but we did ascertain that an individual meeting his description boarded a flight to Hanoi, Vietnam, during the night of what may be right after the women were killed.

We're checking this lead out with Vietnamese authorities. We discovered this guy then flew on to Da Nang, Vietnam, and stayed overnight in a hotel. He was visited by a woman there who stayed the night, and the two were picked up in old limo the next morning. There's absolutely no trace of him after that. We have no idea of his true identity or where he went from Da Nang. We got what was most likely a fake name, Bao. He claimed to Sue that he was a rich banker and was related to Bao Dai, who was once the Puppet Emperor of Vietnam-turned-playboy in France. She had no reason to doubt him at the time.

"The most curious thing about these crimes is that they all seem to be about some Jade cross." He explained, "I understand from reading the reports which were forwarded to me that your victims were laid out like a cross. You may not have noticed, but the blood stains on the bed were in the shape of a cross. One of the mutilated women was tied to a chair. The other was tied down to the bed and laid out like a cross, the wrists were each tied to the right and left bed-posts, and the ankles were tied, together on the middle of the bottom bed board. Both bodies had many cuts from very sharp instruments like a scalpel or serrated knife. Their breasts were chopped to pieces, and their vaginal canals were mutilated. Because of the amount of blood, we feel that the victims were alive while being raped and cut, then died from exsanguination.

"There is evidence of sexual assault on the women, but no DNA. The perp could be a 'no secrete.' I, as well as my fellow officers, feel that the placing of the one victim in a cross position indicates that it probably connects our crime with yours."

The Americans were amazed at this proposed connection. The guy must have a cross obsession. Was he religious or maybe had a disappointment at a church or was it something else? They chatted among themselves for a moment and concluded that this was a logical conclusion. A cross must have become the perpetrator's MO. This has got to be their prey for sure. Each of them related to the lieutenant in turn, including a tearful Mai, their side of the story, beginning with the patrol in 1966, the Jade Cross and ending with what they had learned in Honolulu. He was taken by their story and became quite interested in their reference to Hoi An City, especially to its proximity to Da Nang.

After a short deliberation between the parties, they agreed that the lieutenant would not notify Vietnamese authorities or Interpol until the group could verify the perp was in Hoi An City. The priest indicated that he would contact his friends in Hoi An City when they returned to their hotel and get the search under way for the, he paused and pointed to Tolbane who finished the comment, "Bastard!"

After some more discussion about the cases, the group stood, shook hands with Lt. Hop, bid adieu, and waited outside for Detective Soon to bring the car around. They climbed in, and they were on their way to the floating restaurants in Aberdeen. Tolbane knew he had seen a movie with a man and women at one of the floating restaurants years ago, but he couldn't remember which movie or the year it was shown. He believes that it was just before or right after he joined the Corps.

Aberdeen was a sight to see. It looked as though there were a thousand junks floating in the waters there. It was an amazing vista to behold. They were taken out to one of the restaurants in a little power boat.

The group's spirits were lifted up a little by selecting their own fish from baskets in the water and being able to give cooking directions for their selection. Of course, Tolbane, being at the top of his game, had another inane comment to make about it. Tolbane swore he made his selection because the fish smiled up at him and using mental telepathy said, "Eat Me! Eat Me!" The rest just ignored him this time. Maybe their necks were too sore to shake.

While waiting for the meal to be prepared and served, they shared a bottle of wine and chatted generally about what had happened in Kowloon. There were no words that could describe the fear and horror those ladies had to have endured from the scumbag. When the food finally was served, it was prepared to perfection. They were all too engrossed in their food to think about the case for a moment. About half way through the meal, the priest received a call from his friend in Hoi An City. He listened to the call and hung up. He looked at the group and said, "Well, the good news is that it looks like our guy is in Hoi An City. The bad news I have to share is that he's struck again. This time it's a young girl about thirteen years old."

He prayed for her soul.

CHAPTER 28

Iᴛ ᴡᴀs ᴀ ʟɪᴛᴛʟᴇ after midnight, and Hai was tired from sitting, waiting, and being bored out of her mind. She was still sitting on her moped an hour later, outside of an out-of-the-way hovel outside of the town. The Exalted One was inside having his meeting with the two bandits, Tam and Tuy. She reflected on the early evening hours when Bui brought him back from wherever they had been. Houng and Lam tried to be demanding with him as to what he had been doing, but he put them in their place. She could tell the two were embarrassed, as the spat was in front of Hai and Bui. He made it clear, even though it probably wasn't true, to the two clowns that he had to conduct some business with people that wanted their involvement kept secret for the time being. Later, she tried to find out from Bui where they had gone that afternoon., even though she had been told about the building. She was more or less trying to feel out Bui's loyalty, but Bui was adamant about it.

"He swore me to silence on this matter. I would love to tell you all about it; however, I must think of my own well-being right now." Hai understood. "Whenever I can tell you something relating to what is going on, I will volunteer it to you." Bui continued, "I can say that for now, there is nothing for you to worry about. He seems to be preoccupied with his hate for the Americans and whatever he's planned for those two idiots here. I think he's satisfied enough with our bodies that we're safe for now, as, I believe, he needs us for some kind a plan to work." Hai felt good about that for now.

Hai motioned to one of the posted guards to come to her. She told him, "I'm really bored to death waiting around for the masked man like this. I'm going for a little ride to pass the time away. I'll be back shortly in case he asks." The guard nodded to her, and she left. She found a secluded spot and called her 24-hour contact, related the info about the building, and went back to the meeting place.

The Exalted One had put his mask on for the meeting to preserve his Identity. After the introductions by Hai, he laid out his plans to the two and explained how their participation, along with their gangs' participation, would be of a benefit to the gang leaders as well as himself. They debated mostly about how much and how often the pay would be, what kind of perks would they get and what would be their future be with him and his Cause. Finally, the Two agreed to his terms and became the Masked Man's contract employees. He immediately named them Number Three and Number Four, told them that before too long they would be Numbers One and Two, and gave them some instructions on how he expected them to act when his plan to rid himself of the two Geese and the Americans and get his woman was put into motion. He took his mask off as a gesture of trust.

When the three were satisfied with the deal, they shook hands. Then he inquired of them if they knew of any young bitch or bitches that needed disciplined the good old fashioned way. The two had such a girl in mind, who was about age 13 and was developing into a good-looking girl with nice breasts and hair down to her butt which looked sexy. She had sold them out, getting them in trouble a couple of times because she couldn't keep her mouth shut. She was always talking to the wrong people. He then explained to them his sexual obsession with women and how he handled it. He promised them if they could bring the girl to him now, he would teach them how to have some real fun with a woman. The two agreed, and he went outside and told Hai to return to the house, as his new members would take him home.

Hai left immediately and decided that even though she called and told her contact what was going on, she was going to inform her father about the building. While she had been talking to the Masked Man, the two guys left, and an hour later they returned to the site with a beautiful young girl, gagged with duct tape and her hands tied in the back. Hai was not there then.

The first thing the Exalted One did was take his sharp pocket knife and cut her clothes off slowly and one piece at a time. Her eyes were trying to bug out with fear, and she kept trying scream through her gag as he began to feel her breasts, but only muted grunt sounds could be heard from her. He was enjoying this, as were his new pupils. They discussed between them the fabulous body the girl had for her age. This young girl possessed more sexuality than many grown women did, the Masked Man thought, and he spoke of the things he wanted to do to her. Hearing these things just brought more terror to her; her forehead became sweaty, and her eyes seemed to bulge even larger with fear. Her terror was causing the three to have erections. They took their clothes off, then the fun began. The young girl's cries of pain and fear were still muted from the tape over her mouth and only stopped when she passed out.

Hai rode straight to her father's place at high speed and informed him of what the Exalted One was thinking about the seemingly abandoned cement block building. He assured her, "You needn't worry your pretty head about it. He can dream about it now, but he'll be through with his conspiracy before he has any chance of taking possession of it or even seeing inside of it. Don't worry about any of his moves, my pretty little dove. Time is on our side, not his. His fate is that whatever his plans are, they are doomed for failure. I'm glad you let me know about this though. It's one more piece of info added to what we know." After some more conversation with her father, she hightailed it back to the house and snuck into her room unseen, as everyone there was fast asleep.

The Exalted One returned in time to eat breakfast as Bui was getting ready to clean up the table. He was really hungry after his activities during the night. He had built up an appetite. His food both surprised and pleased him. Bui had scrounged up some bacon and eggs from somewhere. She had done the eggs a perfect over medium, and the bacon was just beginning to crisp and was served with a toasted bread roll, butter, and jelly. The aroma from the kitchen was sheer bacon madness. He thought for a moment, looking at the bacon, that that despicable Tolbane loved bacon too. He made up his mind that he was keeping this young woman. Her kitchen skills should never be ignored. She would never feel his knife. As for Hai, he'd keep her for a while, as she was also valuable to him at this time and her sexual performance was fantastic, too. His stomach satisfied, he went to bed and left a note on the door to not wake him until 1:00 PM.

At noon time, Hai and Bui were sitting in the kitchen listening to traditional Vietnamese music on Bui's small radio as they sometimes did when the local news came on. The first item was a breaking news report. It seems that a very young girl, still unidentified, possibly between the ages of 13 and 15, was found raped and mutilated along the west end of Tran Hung Dao street early in the morning by a Xich Lo driver.

The Hoi An Police were very much affected by the girl's age and her body's condition. She had been mutilated beyond belief, and the apparent cause of death was a slit throat and loss of blood. The police have sworn an oath to find the vicious animal responsible for this terrible crime. The station would give updates when more information was released to them. Instinctively, Hai knew who did the deed because she already knew of the Masked Man's obsession of raping, beating, and cutting up women or young girls. She wondered if Bui knew it was him. He had not come back the night before. Knowing that he was guilty of it and proving that he did it, however, were two different things. Neither one of the women would dare to even give a hint to the police that he was responsible for it, but Hai knew her father and the real No Name would be hopping mad and would do something.

Hai went for a walk and called her father on her cell phone, after retrieving it from the shed, when she was far enough from the house that she wouldn't be seen or heard. She was shook up, and her father calmed her down, soothing her anxiety. "We know about the slaying. We can't prove it to the police yet that he did this horrible thing, but we're working on it. I called my priest friend, Father Phat, who is now in Hong Kong with the Americans. The four of them will be here tomorrow. Very soon, my precious young daughter, as I have said, it will be over. We have a plan in motion that I'm sure will succeed and destroy anything those fakers have conceived, and the Exalted One, or Masked Man, whatever he calls himself, will pay one way or another. Have patience Hai. Hurry and get your rear end back to the house before you're missed and suspected of something. I can't lose you to them!"

Hai terminated the call, and she concealed her phone and returned to the house. When she entered the place, the two jerks wanted to know where she'd been. She was very terse in her answer. She was learning how to be curt. "I just felt stuffy and I had to get a breath of fresh air. Besides, it's a beautiful day to just walk and enjoy being alive, not that you'd know what I was talking about, dick heads." She walked on past them with her nose in the air and went to her room. "Damn," she whispered to herself, "I'll sure be glad when this crap is over with. It's getting harder and harder to put up with these foul minded cockroaches."

She took a short nap, and upon waking began she reviewing the notes she had made on the assignment the Masked Man had given her. She'd ask the Exalted One if she could get started on it. It would get her away from the house. Before she could leave the room, the big man himself knocked on her door. She bade him enter. He informed her that he and Bui had been in bed for a while, and he was amazed at her sexual prowess. He went on to say that Bui had told him that the two women heard about the girl's death on the radio. He said with a smirk, "That was terrible." In a descending manner, he spoke of the teenager, "She was a nice girl, wasn't she?

It took all of Hai's strength to keep her composure and not attack the bastard with everything in her being.

They spoke for a couple more minutes, and she asked if she could start her assignment the next day. When he told her no, she was, without showing it, disappointed in his answer because she was leery of what could happen to her in this house. He told her that she was part of his new plan and would need her for three or four more days. Then she could begin her assignment and make him proud. Then he gave her a request she didn't really want to hear from him. "Tonight, I want you and Bui both in my bed. It will be an amazing time for us three. You two women will really enjoy yourselves tonight." He left the room and went to talk to the two idiots lounging at the table.

Returning to her room, Hai sat on her bed and wept for a short time. She wondered how she could get herself and Bui out of this place before they were found on the side of the road like the young girl that morning. She wondered if she should tell Bui what she knew about the man and the situation, but she had no idea how attached Bui had become to him. The two had been spending a lot of time together.

Bui prepared a large meal for the group, and everyone felt they ate too much. They continued to drink tea and had light conversations. Then the Masked Man initiated the part of his plan which was to piss off the two geese even more. He pulled on his mask and stared at the two and ordered, "Bui will not clean up the table and kitchen tonight. You two mental midgets will, now get to it!" With that, he grabbed the hands of Hai and Bui and led them to his room. When they had entered, he pulled off his mask and laughed like crazy. When his laughter died down, he said to the women, "Did you see the look on their faces? It was perfection for me. Evidently they think I should get their permission before I do anything. I can't stand those two idiots. They don't know it yet, but they won't be around too much longer to stew in their juices. I know that will make you two girls very happy. I know it will make me the happiest guy around. Now girls, shall we shed our clothes and get real comfortable together? We're going to have the most fun we ever had tonight."

Although they weren't physically hurt, the women were disgusted at the way the Manage I Trio went. Neither had ever been with anyone with such a demanding sexual appetite. Where he had gotten the sex, toys was anyone's guess. The session had gone on for over three hours. When he wasn't performing, even rougher than usual, he had the women use the sex toys on each other for his enjoyment. It was really degrading to Hai and Bui. When he finally released them, both went to the little wash up room to cleanse themselves of their vile feelings; neither one could look at the other in the eye, and then they went to their own rooms and cried themselves to sleep. Morning came too early for the two women.

The one calling himself Tran Houng Dao awoke in good spirits, savoring the wonderful sex-filled experience of the previous night. He knew he was going to keep Bui around, but he might change his future plan for Hai. She may just be a keeper too. She was even better last night than she was in the hotel in Da Nang. Though his sexual desire was partly sated for now, he might ask his new members to find a new girl for the following night. Maybe they could get three girls, one for each of them. Three women getting it at the same time might just be the ideal turn on for them. That would really shake up the town. He wrote his request on paper and sealed it in an envelope. He would have Hai deliver it later. He would also have her ask if there was any news on the Americans from the man Number Three sent to watch the Da Nang airport. Now he must think of a new way to irritate the geese this morning. Then he got the perfect idea. He would ask them if they enjoyed the clean up last night.

At breakfast, he did just that. Number Two wasn't too happy about it and muttered something about being treated like a servant. After the meal, he took Number Two out to the rear of the house, grasped his throat with one hand, and shoved him up against the house. "This is your only warning, you insignificant goose. You'll do as I tell you to do and like it, or you might just find yourself beside the road like that girl that was found this morning. So, get this straight. Don't ever mouth off to me again. It pisses me off! Is that clear?" The goose, gagging, nodded in agreement, and the Masked Man released him and went inside.

The two women were cleaning up the table and the Masked Man got a sudden thought. He needed to keep them happy for now, so he approached them smiling and kind of cooing, thanking them for such a wonderful, sex-filled time the previous night.

"I'm sorry if I got a little rough last night. I must be truthful to you. I have never been with two more wonderful women in my life. You two have an amazing inner strength, surpassed only by your beauty! If I were making porno movies, I'd sure want both of you in them." Except, he thought, the two women in Kowloon. That had been pure ecstasy. It was memory for him to cherish forever and a day. Now he wished that Sue could also have been part of that memory. She was another delicious piece of tail that would fit his obsession.

He asked the women to stay close because he would need their assistance in a short while. He went outside and made a cell phone call to the gang leader in reference to a request he had made the night before. He was satisfied with the answers he received and hung up. He reentered the house and asked the girls to be ready to leave in an hour, as he had an appointment to keep. Hai and Bui got out two scooters, filled the tanks from a gas can, and moved them to the front and waited. They voiced their concerns to each other relating to how things had changed and what might be in store for them in the near future. Though she had faith in her father, Hai still feared the unknown tomorrow because she knew what this man was capable of.

He finally came outside and told the women the area he needed to go to and how to find a certain stall in a small market place. "There is a man known as Huang who sells conical hats to tourists as well as other knick-knacks. He has other odd items that he vends on the Black Market that you two will need for future operations. These things have been arranged by my new allies. Let's start the engines, and get going as we have the green flag." The women didn't know what he was referring to, as they knew absolutely nothing about a green flag, let alone American auto racing. He hopped on Hai's scooter, he reached around her and cupped her breasts, pinched her nipples lightly, then hugged her around the waist, and they were off and running to whatever awaited them.

The trio found the right stall and Huang. He let his wife handle the shop and guided them to a hovel not far away. There were a lot of boxes stored there with Vietnam Conflict–era camouflaged uniforms, AK-47s, and some Vietnamese Conflict–era American Military Model 1911A1 .45 caliber semi-automatics, M14s, old M1 Garand rifles, 38 cal. pistols, K44s, and ammo for each type weapon. A few M79 grenade launchers were there too; however, the Masked Man had no need for them now, nor need of any of the old flak jackets piled in the corner. The women were asked to strip and try on uniforms until they got one that fit. They were embarrassed at having to take their clothes off while Huang ogled them greedily.

Then they were each given a cartridge belt with two two-magazine pouches and a leather holster for a US vintage .45, a 45 semi-automatic, four loaded magazines, and four extra rounds for the empty chamber, giving each weapon an nine-round capacity vice eight. Huang showed them how to insert the magazines and load a round into the chamber and how to use the safety. Then he instructed them how to clear the weapons. The Masked Man then paid Huang a generous amount of money for the lot. The uniforms and guns were put in shopping bags and handed to the women, and they departed for the house.

Upon their return, the Exalted One gathered the group around the table and held a briefing on his plan of action. "My two American enemies are on their way here and they hold my true love captive. They will be watched from the time they land in Da Nang, by my new allies, until we get rid of them and rescue her. I know one place they will go eventually and we will be waiting for them. We will consist of just us five, my two new allies, and two of their gang members will be needed also, making nine of us. It will be between two and four days until the hated ones go there with my woman.

The three men, two Americans and one Vietnamese priest, will meet a horrific death, suffering like no others have for a few days before they meet their demise. I'm very competent at torture, and it will pleasure me to no end. I've hated the two American pigs for a very, very long time, and I have recently developed hate for the priest too. Now I will pacify my hatred for them and have my true love by my side while I do it. I'll even let you two girls watch; you'll find it interesting." Then he instructed the two geese how to find Huang and get uniforms and weapons and sent them on their way. His plan was finally coming to fruition.

"Well ladies, I suggest you practice loading and clearing you weapons. You need to be proficient with them. Tomorrow we will have a live fire practice outside the city, and then weapon stripping and cleaning. Don't worry about my needing you two for anything tonight. If you two want to go someplace tonight to relax and enjoy yourself, that's fine with me. I will be picked up by one of the gang members, so you need not worry about me. I now have things to arrange with them, and I have to check out their arms and ammo. I'll see you girls later. I'm going to take a nap now. I'll need my strength tonight."

Hai and Bui took their guns to the shed to practice and to talk. They practiced as ordered and became pretty good at the tasks. Then they checked outside the shed, ensuring it was clear, and had a heart-to-heart talk. Hai informed Bui of her mission and her father's involvement, swore her to secrecy, then insisted that that night they would go to her father's place and give him an update after letting the men think they were going shopping. After that, they would take in a movie. Bui was amazed at Hai's story and was amazed that she was an agent for the real No Name, but she agreed they should visit Hai's father and tell him everything that they knew. She even hinted that she may know a little more than Hai believed she did and was willing to tell. She had learned over time to hear things and not be seen. Then they went into the house and took a nap themselves.

Late afternoon, the Masked Man left to meet his new allies in an old beat-up U.S. jeep that had seen better days, chauffeured by a gang member that drove like shit. A half hour later, the two women told the two jerks they were going shopping and to a movie, and if they didn't like it, tough! They each got a moped and left the house. They rode around a little to make sure they weren't being followed. It seemed like every Xich Lo, pedicab, car, and motor bike in Hoi An City were on the road that night. It made spotting a tail harder, but they were satisfied they weren't being followed. They stopped by a small shop and bought a couple of things, made sure once more that they were not being watched, and sped to Hai's father's place.

Arriving at his place, she gave her father a big hug and introduced Bui as her new friend and confidant who was willing to become a part of the real No Name. He and Bui each placed the palms of their hands together in front of their chests and bowed slightly to each other in greeting. Then they went into her father's little office to tell their story and vent their concern for their physical well-being and fear that one or more young Vietnamese girls may be in danger that night.

He listened patiently and was not happy with the planned involvement of the women and the involvement of two gang members, which, for some reason, caused an alarm bell to go off in his mind, but he couldn't be sure why. He excused himself and left the office to send a message to his watchers about the possible danger to young girls. He returned to the women and they had a short question and answer session, and then he sent them on their way. An hour later, he received a message that his quarry and two cohorts had left the gang hideout and lost their tail when his motor bike was clipped by a pedicab.

Hai and Bui rode around town for a while on their mopeds after leaving Hai's father's place, then they took in a movie. The movie was a supposed to be a comedy, but it didn't make much sense, and they let themselves get into the enjoyment mode and forgot their troubles for a little while. Afterwards, they went to a little tea shop and had tea and sweet biscuits. While drinking the tea, the concerns of what lay before them began to emerge once more and their moods became sullen. The most important thing they discussed was what would happen the day after the firing practice. Between them, they couldn't come up with a useful scenario of what they would have to do in the uniforms, much less what they might be expected to do with the guns. Their worst fears were that the two might have to kill someone or be killed themselves by the Exalted One. Neither one of them could fathom how they could do such a horrendous thing. Finally, with their minds far at sea, they returned to the house, put their rides up, and entered as quietly as possible. They locked their doors and crawled into their beds and had a fitful night's sleep.

At breakfast the next morning, the Masked Man seemed jovial, but determined. His two geese seemed to be exceptionally quiet for a change; therefore he didn't taunt them, and the two women seemed to be only half awake and still tired after a bad night's sleep. When the meal was finished and the table was cleared, he outlined his plan of the day to them. He was taking the four of them outside of the city to an area where gunfire probably would not be heard. They would meet his two new allies there, and they all would practice firing and cleaning both rifles and hand guns. He let them know he wasn't worried that they might not be able to hit the center of a bull's eye; he just wanted them to be able to put rounds into any part of a man-sized target from within about 100 yards with the rifle and 21 feet with a hand gun.

About an hour later, a member of the gang arrived with an old passenger van, a lot of target rounds, ear protectors, targets, other gear, and they all piled in with their weapons and left for their training session. It was a good thing they had worn their conical hats, as it was nothing but sunshine and heat outside the wooded area where they practiced. The Exalted One handed each one of them ear protectors and ammo. Each one fired about 150 rounds at various trees that had man shaped targets on them with both rifle and pistol. The two women didn't do that bad for their first time shooting. They grasped the technique quickly, as opposed to the geese. After the target practice was complete they had a weapons cleaning session. The only break they had was around noon time. The guy with the bus brought rice, dried fish, bread, and tea for their lunch.

When they returned to the house in the late afternoon, they were beat. They stowed their weapons and washed up as good as they could, then they all took a nap for about an hour and a half, except for Bui, who napped only about an hour or so before she started the evening meal, not being very happy about having the two extra mouths to feed. She was a little irritated because she not only had two more mouths at the table, but two mouths that she definitely didn't trust in any way, shape, or form. Her impression of them was that they'd probably eat like pigs at a trough. She wasn't far from wrong. She was very familiar with that kind of men, if that was what you'd want to call them. The Masked Man had invited his two new allies to stay there until they could take action against the hated American group and rescue his true love from further degradation. Hai wasn't fond of that idea either.

Bui and Hai couldn't stand the way his newfound allies would stare at them and the way their hands belied their wanting to grope every part of their warm bodies. Both had hoped they wouldn't have to spend any nights with those two cruds in the house, or for that matter, the Masked Man himself anymore. After the evening meal was over and the table was cleared, the two women breathed a sigh of relief when the Masked Man and his two cruds went somewhere and announced that they would be back very late and told everybody not to wait up on them. Maybe the two women could get a good night's sleep for a change. Sleep, a long and restful sleep, was something they both needed.

The three guys returned before dawn with bloody clothes and some scratches on their arms and faces. They quickly changed their clothes and burned the bloody ones in the kitchen fireplace. Then they crashed, the Masked Man in his room and the other two on the large dining table, till midmorning. The other occupants had to eat breakfast in the kitchen.

CHAPTER 29

THE FOUR TRAVELERS DISCUSSED the present situation in a round table–like manner, whether they should try to get an earlier flight to Hanoi and Da Nang. Detective Soon volunteered to pull some strings and get an earlier flight for them. Looking at the pros and cons of it, they eventually decided not to change the flight time to an earlier one. The deciding factor for them was that the later flight would be the same flight the Masked Man took. Maybe one of the stewardesses would remember the guy and could give a little more insight as to what he looked like and how he acted during the leg to Hanoi or wherever. That also meant they wouldn't have to rush things to catch their flight.

After the meal was over, Detective Soon drove them around a little more and showed them a few interesting sights. Then he dropped them at the hotel because they had changed their mind about shopping some more. They figured the shopping could be done on the return trip when they'd have more time to browse.

The time until the detective picked them up for the ride to the airport was spent rehashing all they knew from Ba's death, Tolbane's Mall ambuscade, to Parnell's shooting at the Mall. Too many questions still remained, especially the

Who and the Why. Father Phat made a call to his friend in Hoi An City to get an update on the situation there, and in relating it to his friends his speech was a little slurred. The three bottles of wine they had killed really didn't help their cognitive abilities to cogitate. They did manage to catch a few hours of sleep before their wake-up call from the desk. They packed up their gear, checked out, and waited in front of the hotel until Detective Soon picked them up and headed for the airport. At the appointed time, they were finally in first class section in the air, on their way to, as the indigenous population would say during the conflict, Viet Nam Cong Hoa.[31]

The Kowloon Police knew what they were doing. The four found themselves on the same aircraft and with the same flight crew as their hunted one had been on days before. After the plane reached cruising altitude and the seat belt sign was off, the flight attendant came to first class and introduced herself, Nguyen Thi Bao. Being one of only two Vietnamese in first class, Mai greeted her in their native tongue, and then the Priest did the same. They had decided they would not question the attendant until all of her initial duties were taken care of. Then Mai would introduce Tolbane, Parnell, and the Priest and strike up a conversation with Bao. A little into the conversation, she would inquire about a relative of hers who went to Vietnam several days ago. Maybe if the attendant remembered him, he might have given her a name or a destination or some other important information. The main thing would be to not cause the attendant to feel like she was being interrogated.

Once Bao had finished her pre-and-after-takeoff duties, she entered the first class section to check on the passengers, and as planned, Mai started a friendly conversation with her. She made an introduction to her friends, and then she

---

[31]   Republic of Viet Nam.

began a little small talk about conditions they would find in Hanoi. She deftly guided Bao to the questions about her uncle's son, who she knew was going to Vietnam. She told the flight attendant that he was to meet them in Kowloon, Hong Kong, but hadn't contacted her in several days and he didn't answer his cell phone. She inquired if a lone Vietnamese man had taken this flight recently and if so, did she remember him. Bao remembered one lone, Vietnamese man.

"I do remember one such man. In fact, he sat in the very same seat as you do now. The reasons I remember him is because his family name is the same as my first name. He told me he was related to Bao Dai, the previous Emperor of Vietnam. Also, he was so nice and so pleasant to talk with. Good looking too. We talked for a long time about many things. I wouldn't talk about this to just any one, especially any of the airline personnel, but I did meet him again in Hanoi."

"Oh yes," fibbed Mai easily. "That's him for sure. He's quite a play boy too. I'm also a distant relation to Emperor Bao Dai. Actually, our relation to the Emperor Bao Dai is very convoluted and controversial due to the playboy antics of Bao Dai, in France. He'd rather party day and night than rule There are always things that are not spoken about in many family circles and the public."

"That's very naughty and nice isn't it. I was very happy to have met him on this very plane; he was a class act. We had a couple of good conversations during the flight. In fact, we even spent the night in his hotel room in Hanoi. I brought the booze, and he had the condoms. We had a real fucking good time. I don't meet many guys who are as polite and respectful to women as he is. He was also very interesting to talk with, and," she added with a blush, "he was pretty good in bed too!"

Mai didn't skip a beat answering, deliberately ignoring the sex part. "Yes, he is always a very good man, and he is always praised for his caring disposition with women and how he cares for and protects them; he's quite a charmer too, according to the Ladies. We share a lot of childhood memories from Saigon together and later on living in the United States. We would go to the popular places in Nashville whenever we'd get together. Did he by any chance say where he was going in country after leaving from Hanoi? We would like to link up with him if we can track him down."

Just then, Tolbane, who had dozed off along with the other two, had been dreaming about the play *Man of La Mancha* with Richard Kiley and James Coco that he had seen at the Honolulu International Center in 1970 or 71. He snapped awake, quickly sitting up, scaring the stewardess, and began babbling, "I should have been Don Quixote de la Mancha. I'd have kicked that windmill's ass, no matter how many times it knocked this knight errant down onto his ass, and I would have risen each time I fell, and it would have been woe to that wicked thing."

Mai give him a love tap on the back of the head and said, "Go back to sleep you big dork!" He looked at her with eyes half closed, laid his head back, closed his eyes all the way, and went straight back to la la land. She smiled at Bao and stated as a matter of fact, "Yes he's a dork, a big dork, but he's my big dork! He does have fantasy problems, as you can see."

Bao caught on, and now she smiled too. "I sympathize with you. I've had my share of them on this run to Hanoi. Your big dork seems to be well trained though." Then she remembered Mai's question. "Oh yes! I remember. I believe your relative said he was going to Da Nang to meet with someone he knew. He said, I think, he was going to meet an old friend and ally, or something of that nature, and go on to Hoi An City to sightsee. He didn't say much about anything else except that I had a nice booty and that it was a fabulous night and he hoped he would catch my flight when he returned to Hong Kong so we could enjoy another fantastic night together."

Thinking a little more about it, she got a big shit eating grin on her face this time. "Oh! I remember what he said now. This flight went on to Da Nang the next day, however, and I went back to Hong Kong on a different flight. Another woman took my place on that plane. The next time I saw her, I asked about Bao and how did she like him. She said he was not aboard that flight, and when she got back to Hanoi, she checked reservations and found out he had booked and taken a different flight to Da Nang. That is a curious thing, is it not? He must be very rich to be able to do that."

"Oh yes! He can afford it ten times over. I'm glad to hear that he got off to Da Nang okay. Yes, he's very rich, and he is sometimes unpredictable and thrives on doing other than normal things. I think he really enjoys messing up people's minds. He's very exasperating to us at times. Maybe I'll find out more about him in Da Nang." Then Mai exclaimed to her in a concerned way. "By the way, did you read or hear about the two girls who were killed so horribly by some Asian man in Kowloon? We heard many people speak of it. It sounded really horrible! They think the hotel we stayed at is the very one the Asian guy stayed at. I was a little un-nerved staying there when I found that out."

"Yes! Wasn't that terrible? My goodness! That shouldn't happen to anyone. I heard they worked for a woman named Sue who owns a brothel and also works at the information booth at the airport and goes by the name of Ling sometimes. She and I have had tea together on a few occasions. She is a very nice woman and really cares for her working girls and would do anything for them. She told me a few times that men found me very desirable and even invited me to work for her a couple of times. I was almost tempted; however, my love is of flying and my job won out. Besides, sometimes I meet really interesting men on my flights, and if I worked for her, I may have to service several guys a night. That wouldn't be any fun."

"Oh wow! Looking at you I can see she has a good eye for lovely and desirable women. It must have been so heart wrenching for her to lose her friends in such a way."

"Most likely it was. She hasn't been back to work at Chek Lap Kok since it happened. We have two planes that fly this route. One is in Hanoi and will leave there for Hong Kong shortly after we land. I thought it odd that the police questioned that crew about any suspicious passengers they might have had but didn't question our crew."

"Yes, that is very odd. You'd think they would question everyone they could" Mai dropped the subject.

The two gossiped only a little more before Bao had to return to her duties. Mai didn't learn anything else that would be of help except the name of the hotel the Masked Man stayed at; the Asian Legend Hotel Hanoi. They would stay there that night to see if they could learn more. She looked over at the three guys who were dead asleep, and she decided that looked like the right thing to do and kicked back and closed her eyes. The next thing Mai and the guys were aware of was the screeching of the landing gears grinding into and locking their down positions and the pilot making announcements in three different languages about moving seats to the upright position and fastening seat belts and being on the final approach to Hanoi. Bao came into first class to check seat belts, then she and Mai spoke a bit, then agreed they would meet at the same hotel that night.

The plane made a smooth landing and taxied up to the terminal. The debarking of the passengers went well, the first-class passengers getting off first as usual. The group got through customs easily and went to the information counter to inquire about contacting the hotel and getting transportation to it. After having their questions answered, they went to the baggage recovery area to wait for their luggage to arrive. Mai called the hotel, reserved a room, and found out that the esteemed Americans would be given a courtesy ride to and from the hotel and would find every amenity they could ask for during their stay. The group went to the front of the building and awaited their ride. The group felt they were getting even closer to their goal.

The stewardess contacted them when she finally checked in and arranged to meet them in the hotel restaurant at 7 PM. Her makeup was perfect, and she was wearing a mid-thigh sheath dress that left nothing to the imagination. Tolbane, of course, fantasized about back flips once again, and Parnell felt hot under the collar. They had a very well-prepared meal and were quite sated, but they still had room for a few glasses of wine.

They spoke in general about conditions in the now-Democratic Republic of Vietnam and how things had progressed since the Viet Nam Conflict. It got around to the topic of the slain brothel girls again, and nothing more was gained, except Bao couldn't shake the feeling that the murderer could have been on her flight as there were quite a few Asian men in the passenger section from time to time. The four most likely felt that Bao may have been lucky not to have been a victim of the sadistic ass, too. The time had passed along with a few glasses of wine and it was getting late, so the group said its goodbye and good night then hit the hay. Mai wondered if Parnell spent part of the night in Bao's room. The two had been kind of chummy and sitting close during the night. She hoped so. Parnell most likely needed exercise for his other leg, the third one, not the wounded one.

They broke the fast the next morning at the hotel's breakfast buffet, then they packed up and were transported to the airport to await their flight. After their arrival there, the Priest called his friend in Hoi An again. They spoke at length. The priest gave him their arrival time, and his friend assured him that a trusted man would meet them and take them to the Tien Phuc Hotel in Da Nang. His watcher had reported to him that that's where the Masked Man had stayed, one night, if it was him. He left the next morning with a good-looking woman in an old, chauffeured limo. Maybe they could get more information from the staff there.

After his friend's man met them at the airport in Da Nang, he would brief them on the situation. The guy they wanted was now active in Hoi An City, that was for sure, and the next morning his man would drive them to his friend's place and then to their hotel on Tran Hung Dao Street in Hoi An City. The Priest terminated the call and pointed to the little coffee and tea shop in the far area of the terminal, and they went there to snack and wait a couple of more hours on their next flight.

The Priest had tea, and the rest had coffee and sweet rolls. Then the Priest updated them on his call to his friend. "It seems there's always good news and bad news no matter where you are. Let me think about which to give first... Ah! I know which to give first." He enjoyed stringing his friends along. "The good news is that—guess what it is!" he kidded. The others shook their heads from side to side, and he cheerfully told them, "We'll be watched from the time we land in Da Nang till we reach Hoi An City by one of the fiend's henchmen. Isn't that nice to be wanted?" The trio groaned, then laughed. It was a real gas. "The bad news is that the bastard has struck again!"

By the time their plane was called, in Vietnamese, English, and French, they were butt sore from sitting on the semi-hard seats of the little shop. They would welcome the soft, cushioned seats on the plane, and they did. The flight was a little bumpy this time with mild turbulence, as it flew through a mild rain storm with some lightning. It was the only flight so far that had any turbulence to take note of due to a storm. The plane seemed to land a little roughly also, and when it taxied to the terminal, they breathed a sigh of relief.

True to the priest's friend's word, his man, Diem Ho, was there to meet and greet them at the baggage claim area, and he spoke good English to boot, as he had worked with Americans during the Vietnam Conflict and had little choice but to learn the language. They introduced themselves and headed for the baggage claim area. On the way, the man said, "Don't look now, but the guy pretending to talk to the information desk clerk is the one assigned to watch and report on you to your prey. There's nothing for you to worry or fret about though. We'll just do what comes naturally to us, and maybe tonight we'll give him something odd to report back to his leader in the morning. I'd hate to see him have a wasted assignment with nothing more to report except, 'They're here,' but wait a minute! Now they've gone, don't know where.' It would be like buying an ice cream cone without the cone, or using a ten-foot ladder with only one rung." This group knew they were going to like this guy.

With their baggage in hand, they went to the terminal's front entrance, waited there while the man went to get their transportation. He pulled up in an old American military bus, the exhaust belching a light black smoke and none the worse for wear. Tolbane couldn't believe it still had chicken wire over the windows to keep grenades from being thrown inside and commented on it to the others.

"It doesn't look or sound good, but it sure gets the job done for me," Ho said as matter of fact. They stowed their baggage in the bottom storage compartment and then found the best seats they could that weren't too beat up or torn, brushed them off, and away they went. They wondered if this driver drove in demolition derbies. He had wasted no time getting to the hotel while using his horn and swerving around traffic all the way. Arriving at the hotel in record time, the screeching brakes didn't seem like they wanted to catch hold, but they finally did the job, to the relief of the passengers.

Much relieved, they debarked the bus, retrieved their luggage, and checked in at the desk. They found out they were already registered there and the rooms were already paid for. After they got their room keys, Mai questioned the Desk Clerk about the Masked Man, using the same story as with the flight attendant. She learned that a man matching that description was visited by a young lady who stayed all night with him. Some man met them the next morning in an old beat up American limo, and the two left with him around noon time. He knew this as he had worked a double shift that day. Getting no additional info from the clerk they went up to their rooms and freshened up then met the man of the hour, Ho, in the restaurant. He had a lot on which to update them.

When the coffee was poured and sweet buns were placed on the table, Ho began, "First, let me welcome all of you back to Vietnam. You had your trials and tribulations here in the past during the conflict. Maybe you have sad, bad, or happy memories; maybe you had some bad experiences or even some good experiences from it. I hope during your stay here, you accomplish your goal of catching this killer and leave satisfied with new and good memories of the country and the people. You will find the atmosphere, the development of the areas, and the attitude of the people so much different than it was back then. The people are happier and a little more prosperous, and their daily fears of life and death from war are now long forgotten."

He continued, "This man you seek, this beast of an animal, is in Hoi An City plotting to start a revolution to reunite Vietnam in his name, and he has already committed foul crimes. He believes he is the great General Tran Hung Dao reincarnated and that he will unite all of Vietnam in the name of the No Name Society, a faux society at that, under his rule. He has issued assignments to his main minions. He will begin his revolt by recruitment, propaganda, building guerrilla forces, etc. in hamlets and then villages, similar to what the National Liberation Front did here. Some of those who will be performing these tasks will be his staff, but he has delayed implementing them until he has destroyed you three men and rescued his true love, which is you Mai." She got a worried look on her face, but she remained quiet.

"He is bonkers to put it in your American terms. We have someone on the inside that reports to our leader, who you will meet tomorrow; plus we do have others that keep watch as much as possible without exposing themselves, but they are limited in what they are able to do at any given time. We have an idea where he will make his move to take you all captive, and we do have a good counter plan in place, which we hope will be his eventual downfall. It will be explained to you later by our Priest.

"He has also joined forces with a rogue band of thieves to aide him in what he refers to as his Cause. Two nights ago, they kidnapped a young girl, raped and mutilated her body, then left it on the side of a road to be found the next morning by someone going to the city to work. Last night, one of our men was following them and lost sight of him and the two main rogues as they were being very cautious. We don't know if they went after a young woman the rouges knew or what, only that a young girl was mutilated and found alongside the road. Earlier in the day, he had our insider and some of the rogues uniformed and armed. Some were armed with 45 automatics and some with AK-47s. The uniforms and arms were all surplus from your conflict.

"As I pointed out to you, the Masked Man is having you watched. He knew you were coming here, but how he knew; we don't know. Beside the man he had at the airport, there was also one who was following us on a motor bike; thus I took us on the wild ride in the bus just to give him something to think about. We'll most likely be followed by them from here to Hoi An. I'll take you directly to the hotel first stop tomorrow, as opposed to taking you first to our leader as he wanted so as not to compromise our operation. When you go to meet our Priest tomorrow night, you needn't look for him; he will find you. He will give you a better handle on the situation than I can. While you were stowing your gear, I called him to let him know you made it here safely, and he anxiously awaits to greet you tomorrow."

Ho asked if there were any questions he could answer. If there were any he couldn't, he would find out the answer. Their answers were all, "No, not at this time," since he had given them a good update. They all decided to do whatever and meet back at the restaurant in about an hour and a half for dinner. Diem Ho went out to pretend to work on the bus in hopes he could get a good look at their observer. Within a half an hour, he had spotted his man and smiled to himself and thought what a dumb ass. He was as obvious as an elephant hiding behind a blade of grass or a palm tree hiding behind a grass shack.

They all met in the restaurant at the given time, and having once more dined on good old American chow in Vietnam, the group retired to the bus for the evening's adventure. They hoped it would be a distraction for them, giving them a chance to relax. True to his word, Diem Ho gave the watcher a good wild goose chase and then some. He would drive the bus around to different monuments or uninteresting sites, and they would get off the bus and he'd act like a tour guide for a few minutes, then they would pile back into the bus and go to another spot. Sometimes he would stop the bus just any place, and they would wander off to a point where the watcher couldn't see them and wait for a while, then they'd return to the bus and go someplace else. This would surely cause the person being reported to wonder what the hell was going on when they could not be observed. They were having a really good time with this charade while trying to screw up the guy's malfunctioning mind in his brain housing group.

Finally, after taking their watcher on a long wild goose chase for a couple of hours, they returned to the hotel and had a night cap at the bar and called it a night after setting a time to assemble in the restaurant the next morning, all packed up and ready for breakfast and travel. Tolbane was already thinking about a triple order of bacon, or may be four orders of it and a couple of big waffles with gobs of butter and plenty of maple syrup. Looking at Mai, he also thought about having a special kind of night cap before hitting the hay, a Tolbane and Mai–style night cap. He wondered if he could get some whipped cream from the room service, or even honey mustard. Seeing the look in her eyes, he decided she was thinking the same thing. Great minds do think alike at times.

The group rose early, showered, shaved, dressed, and packed in record time then met in the restaurant along with their appetites. Ho informed them that he would make their trip as conspicuous as he could. He didn't want the watcher to feel they were aware of him or trying to play tricks. The others agreed that this was the only way to go. The group was ready to get started on their next leg of the journey, except they had to wait on Tolbane, who was in the process of chowing down on his fifth order of bacon, the two waffles and syrup long gone, and chasing everything down with orange juice and coffee. Finally, with a loud burp and a slap on the back of his head from Mai, the others pretending not to know him, Tolbane was ready to go. They hastily returned to their rooms, purged their bladders, got their luggage, and made a last check of the rooms. They stopped at the desk and found out their rooms really were already paid for, they had to check to make sure, and moved outside to await their royal chariot, AKA the wreck waiting to happen that passed for a bus. Ho had had a hotel employee put containers of water, coffee, tea, cups, and bag lunches aboard while they were eating breakfast.

When their luggage was placed in the baggage hold by the hotel's bellhops, they boarded the bus and got into the same seats as the previous day. Ho told them not to look and pointed out where the watcher's car was located and that the guy from the airport was now with him. He wondered if these two had taken turns watching during the night to make sure this group didn't sneak off someplace. It took three tries to get the bus started, but it finally did so with a cough, a puff of smoke, and then a roar of the un-mighty engine without a muffler, and then with a light cloud of black smoke trailing from the exhaust for a few blocks, they were finally on their way to Hoi An City, Quang Nam Province.

The group felt the bus sure could be in better shape than it was. As the bus sputtered and rattled on at about 20 kilometers an hour along Highway 1, the group talked of the scenery this country possessed. The lush forested areas seemed majestic, and the contrast with the open areas and the dried-out rice paddies, not yet flooded from monsoon rains, was beautiful. They also marveled at how they would magically have fish in them when the rains came. Father Phuoc told them about the difference between the dry rice and wet rice, the latter of which was grown in this area. He described to them the method farmers used to irrigate paddies and crops, pedaling little water wheels with scoops on them, and dumping water from one spot to another.

Tolbane and Parnell spoke of some of the beautiful contrasts of the various terrain features seen from the air during many UH-34 helicopter trips in to various hostile sites during their service in the war, especially the beautiful mangrove swamps. They couldn't help but to speak of the awesome Marble Mountain, even though they couldn't see it from this road, and of the internal tunnels and caves utilized by the VC. Marble Mountain is a series of five mountains that were each named after the natural elements, Wind, Fire, etc. They all agreed to make it a point visit the complexes there before their return from Vietnam.

When they reached a point about five miles north of Hoi An City, Tolbane pointed to an area and announced, "There is where the 1/1/1 enclave was situated, and over there is where the ARVN APC training school had been." The driver stopped the bus for all to observe. The old enclave area was over grown with weeds and grass blotches of barren soil There were no clues remaining, except what looked like a few ragged, torn sand bags worn by time, that a reinforced Marine Infantry Battalion was ever there or that its guarded entrance was about 20 feet from the road, nor of the sand bagged barrier or the bunkers that once surrounded the perimeter. The ruins of the ARVN buildings were just barely visible about 150 feet or so from the road, and nearly a third of a mile of no man's land from what had been the CP area. Both Tolbane and Parnell relived the scene in their minds and thought of memories, long ago forgotten, but now returned.

Tolbane informed them that a couple of klicks (Kilometers) or so east of the CP area, beyond the far away tree line, is where the ambush and the Jade Cross crossed paths. They would definitely be back here within the next few days to check it out. Tolbane felt a slight shiver go up his back thinking about the unknown side of it. The Vietnam sun and heat was now readily apparent, and they quenched their thirst and snacked at their bag lunches. A few minutes later, when the guys had seen enough, the driver resumed their trip. The group had felt calm and safe during their travels up till now. Knowing they were about to begin the climax of the sordid affair, they began feeling a little apprehensive and ready to get it started and finished at the same time, with hope that they would survive intact at the climax of it all. Mai was concerned about what the next few days would bring, even as staunch as she was, as she wasn't used to being in dangerous situations like the guys. It was very different in her mind from what the guys knew. When they were younger, Tolbane, Parnell and the Priest wouldn't think twice about going into any number of dangerous situations. They had the attitude of "Bring it on. We'll win!"

About 25 minutes later, after the bus ride over a road badly in need of repairs, the bus finally pulled to a stop with another screech of the brakes and a slight jolt in front of the Hotel Thanh Bin 1 at the corner of Tran Hung Dao and Le Loi Streets in Hoi An City, Quang Nam Province. The group breathed a sigh of relief that the ride was finally over.

"Well! Listen up Pilgrims! That's what John Wayne used to say in the movies," quipped Ho. Welcome to Hoi An City, Quang Nam Province, formerly the Chinese trading port city of Fi Fo, and the Hotel Thanh Bin 1. I hope your stay will be as pleasant as possible." He also couldn't resist saying to his passengers, "This is where you check in and you never check out, just like the roach motel." Seeing the weird look on the four faces, he quipped, "Isn't that a famous American saying from a movie also? We got to see American movies at some of the American bases during the war, and later on here in the City with subtitles too."

Seeing the faces beginning to smile he added, "Seriously, this will be your home away from home while you are here, compliments of the real No Name! You'll have all the comforts of home at your fingertips. Dinning will be at 1900 hours this evening. I'll see you later on today to let you know how the evening's seating for dining will go! I guarantee you won't go back to your rooms hungry, or sober. This hotel has one of the best restaurants in the city, so please take advantage of it. I have to leave you now as I have a few things that have to be checked out. Don't worry about security here. It's taken care of too." Ho left the bus and went inside to get the bellhops to go out to greet them, get their baggage, and then escort them to the registration desk.

CHAPTER 30

THE GENEVA ACCORDS, IN 1954, partitioned Vietnam into two sections, one North and one South, at the 17ᵗʰ parallel making it a demarcation line, and more or less separated Cambodia and Laos from Indo-China. The North was controlled by Nguyen Ai Quoc, AKA Ho Chi Minh. The South was controlled by the puppet Emperor, Bao Dai, with Ngo Dinh Diem (pronounced, Ziem) as the Premier. Estimates of 800,000 to 1.2 million people fled from the North to the South, mostly Catholics. Probably less than 200,000 Viet Minh and sympathizers were allowed to move from South to North. Many of these sympathizers were trained in guerilla and military tactics and began moving down the Troung Son Route, later named The Ho Chi Minh Trail to the South in 1959. Those who remained in the South were mainly Viet Minh, Socialists, or North sympathizers who joined the National Liberation Front (NLF), supported by North Viet Nam and were used as infiltrators into the South's Government, the South's Military, or became part of the National Liberation Front's (NLF) cadre, generally called the VC, or Viet Cong. Viet Cong is a derogatory term given to them by Premier Diem, meaning, Red Vietnamese. Some of these were members of the No Name and played dual roles at times.

The Accords had directed an election to be held throughout Vietnam to decide who would rule the whole country. Emperor Bao Di decided to be more of a playboy in France and Diem controlled the South. He was afraid the election would favor Ho Chi Minh and the Republic of Vietnam (RVN) was born in the South. The United States became a supporter of the RVN. Money was given to the RVN by the U. S. to be used to aid the villages and Hamlets of the South, but it was somehow given to Catholic areas as Diem and family were devout Catholics.

Many of the people were removed from their homes and placed onto what was called Agrovilles. Later on, the Strategic Hamlet program was developed and moved about four million villagers into these barricaded areas which caused animosity between the people, the government and the Hoa Hao and Cao Dai religions. Many of these two religions then united with the NLF. The now President Diem dubbed the NLF members as Viet Cong, or Red Viet. The one-sided distribution of funds and the lack of interest of their government made the Villagers easy prey when VC came to them with good treatment and organizing groups that gave people a little say in how their hamlets and sub hamlets were run. Later the VC would tear down the strategic hamlets sending most to their old areas and begin to use terror tactics on the Villagers.

Nguyen Van Hai who had become a member of the No Name at an early age had also been a member of the Viet Minh during the Japanese Occupation as a very young teenager and had duties as a runner, or general gofer duty. After the fall of Dien Bien Phu and the Geneva Accords, he managed to leave the Viet Minh, but from time to time he'd still help the No Name as his father was a high-ranking member, and went home to Tra Ke Bon (#4), North and East of Hoi An City. He was content to learn rice paddy planting and the irrigation of rice paddies as he enjoyed hard work. He even had his eye on a couple of beauties he'd like to marry.

One day in 1963 a group of Viet Cong from his Village's Guerilla force came to Tra Ke Ba on a recruiting mission, which by now was literally practicing the tactic of the forcing of the area's young men to join the VC or suffer the severe consequences. He wasn't very happy to find out that the one in charge knew all about his role with the Viet Minh. Hai had little choice but to join with the VC or else be imprisoned in a cave somewhere and be given reeducation classes for who knows for how long. That would also mean partial starvation and physical restraints and punishment.

He and the eight other-young men were blind folded, hands tied behind their backs, were marched for two days to the Unit's encampment. Once there he and the others were fed, shown where to sleep and received some propaganda speeches. The next day they were given K44 rifles some ammo and a belt with two WWII grenades.

During the next two days they were given little food, more re-educational speeches, some tactical training and were allowed to fire their rifles a few times for familiarity. On the morning of the fourth day there about half of the unit went on a mission and he was ordered to go with them. He had no earthly idea where he was, where he was going, or what he'd be doing once they arrived at their destination.

The group leaders of the small band were very hush, hush about what their unit was up to. For some reason due to this secrecy, Hai felt a fear in his body that he had not experienced while with the Viet Minh. This was so different. He always had some idea of what was going on because the Viet Minh leaders tried to keep their troops informed as much as was allowed.

The group walked casually, talking and at times some of the men would laugh, prance and strut their stuff. Late afternoon the group arrived at a large hamlet complex with five sub hamlets. The group dived into six groups of five and each segment went into a sub hamlet and the leaders group went to what passed as the hamlet headquarters. The people there had no idea at this time why armed men would enter their community. The people of the sub hamlets were ordered to prepare food and feed them.

After feeding them the, the Peons were gathered together and forced to pay rice taxes. The VC had brought bags for the people's rice storage and they were filled as full as possible. Van Hai was not pleased with this, but he knew he needed to pretend that he was. As darkness was approaching the people were once again assembled in an open area. The leaders group then paraded the hamlet committee's officials through each sub hamlet, informing the people that they would now follow the VC to the death.

In the sub hamlet Van Hai was in a couple of the leaders showed dissent against the VC and they were disemboweled in front of their families and then the families were killed as a lesson to the people. Van Hai nearly vomited as this was repugnant to him. He was not aware that the VC had begun to use some of the same tactics the Government was using, similar ones used with their Counter Terrorist Teams. Those teams were made up of two units; Hunter units and Killer units. The hunters would locate and identify certain important VC's location then pass the info to the Killer Team which would then take action. Sometimes innocent bystanders would lose their lives too.

The last thing on the group's agenda was the selecting of young men for service with the various VC units and the forming of associations with the people. The people in each sub hamlet were broken down in to cells not only by age groups, and farming skills, but by sex also. Some of the younger ones were made unarmed hamlet guards.

Their duties would be to notify the VC if they were in their area if ARVN troops were in the vicinity. Then each of the sub-hamlet groups was formed in to hamlet associations such as Farmers, Old Men's, Old Women's, Young Men's, Young Women's, Hamlet Security and etc. This structure provided over all hamlet control. The VC leaders of the various groups gave propaganda speeches to each of the associations and then chose a leader for each group. Close to midnight the VC's work was done and every one turned in for the night. Early the next morning the VC, along with their conscripts, were fed and they left. The conscripts were blindfolded as had Van Hai been a few days before and each one had to carry a bag of rice. This time the group didn't tarry along the way. It was more of an organized march than the previous day's free march.

During the march back Van Hai reflected on his fate so far and decided that if he tried to escape he would be killed for sure. He resigned himself to be a good soldier for the VC cause even though he felt it would eventually cause his death. He also considered that if he did successfully escape the VC would take their revenge on his parents and maybe a lot of other people in his sub-hamlet too. The group made it back to the encampment in half the time as the previous days march and the conscripts began their indoctrination immediately.

Van Hai was surprised that he and the men from his sub hamlet were called to gather for more training which included the locations of spider holes, tunnels, and storage areas. That night they were informed that the next day they would start digging on the enlargement of a new tunnel complex during the days ahead and during the late afternoons learn to make various types of booby traps, such as punji pits and hand grenade traps with trip wires and etc. The young men taken from the sub hamlets joined

Van Hai's group later in their tasks and training. A month later the two groups of trainees were sent back to their sub hamlets and assumed the role of hamlet guerillas and to oversee the sub hamlets, and would follow orders of the nearest Village Guerilla unit to the death.

Van Hai's group was given the task of organizing the Hamlet Associations, hold meetings with the various groups, and administer what punishment was needed to keep the people under control, and to weed out dissenters. At times they would escort VC tax collectors throughout the Hamlet, and guide them to the next one. Other duties were sniping at government patrols, sometimes ambushing them and turning the weapons and equipment they retrieved from the dead soldiers over to the Village unit. These actions were prevalent throughout rural and farming areas in the South. Van Hai became very proficient at carrying out his duties and before long became the Hamlet Guerrilla leader. Even though he performed well he was still ill at ease because his psychological makeup was of a mold different from the VC philosophy. There had been times when he had talked with Catholic believers that stopped in his sub hamlet for a meal of rice and tea while traveling towards Da Nang. He sometimes wondered if their beliefs would benefit him in his future.

One day early March 1965 a messenger from the Village unit arrived at Tra Ke ba and informed him that U.S. Marines had landed in the Da Nang area, but for now they would only be guarding the airstrip. Van Hai felt a shiver go up his spine. When he was with the Viet Minh he had heard stories about the Marines and their many victories against the Japanese in WWII and in Korea, and that they didn't take many prisoners.

The messenger also informed him that he and his group would continue to harass the Americans if they patrolled in the same manner as they did to government forces patrolling the area. He didn't like where this new order would take them, maybe even to their death, because he felt a deep concern for himself and a responsibility to his men and the people of his sub hamlet, for their safety and wellbeing, but he had no choice in following his orders or die. The Village Guerilla Force could be very cruel to their soldiers as well as the people.

Van Hai Called an emergency meeting with his men and then assembled all of the hamlet people into one area and gave them the news about the U.S. Marines arriving and how they should act if the Marines began to patrol in their area and that they should say nothing of the VC activities in the area if questioned or else!

He dismissed the people, then he and his men began to plot the location of where booby trapped grenades, other explosive devices and punji traps would be set and how to warn the people how to avoid them. The punji traps needed many long bamboo stakes and the older men not capable of working fields, rice paddies, or security were given the task of carving the stakes. A few weeks later he received words that the Marines were now patrolling to the south of the Marine's helicopter airstrip and Marble Mountain, South of the Da Nang Air Strip along highway 1,and they would possibly be in his area before too long.

His orders were to harass any American or RVN units with pot shots, maybe wound or kill some and then run away. Also, another tactic was to pot shot them from someone's hovel in the other sub hamlets then run like hell and let the people be harassed by the Americans for the incident. For some reason the village Force didn't want any incidents in or around Tra Ke #4, he never found out why they only did this from the other three sub hamlets of Tra Ke, and the quick escape was preferred, and leaving the poor peasants to be held accountable to the troops. This later approach would help turn the people minds against the Americans.

Van Hai's group did as they had been ordered. There were a couple of times they had a running fire fight with Marine Patrols. He had lost three of his team killed by Marines and two were captured. It didn't take long for the Village force to replace them.

He was beginning to feel that it wouldn't be much longer till he suffered one of those two fates. In case he was captured he had made a plan. He would resist interrogation for a while then lead Marines to some of the older, less destructive booby traps and then he would ask to be made a Chieu Hoi, more or less a Returnee to the RVN government. Once at a Chieu Hoi Center he would inform his handlers where the most dangerous traps and tunnels were located in his area of operations.

It was firm in his mind that this would be the best way to go if he wanted to live, because he now had a problem of being wounded, killed, or staying alive. He would have to wait on an encounter with the Marines that would allow him to be captured. He wouldn't want to give himself up to the ARVNs because they would be brutal in their treatment of him. Above all, when his father died in midyear 1965 the Jade Cross was passed to him, and no matter what, he must keep the secret and the protection of the artifact and the No Name Society. The ARVN might get him to mention it during a harsh interrogation, but the Americans would not know of the Jade Cross or the No Name, then the torture would really begin to find its location.

During the summer of 1966 he received word that a Marine patrol was moving towards Tra Ke ba. He decided this was his chance to escape the futility and the madness of this war. He sent his hamlet guerillas off to hide in one of their tunnels or rabbit holes, and above all, "Do not snipe at the Marines." Then he hid his K44 rifle, ammunition and grenades and went out into one of the crop areas. He found a young kid tending a water buffalo and he gave the kid a five Dong note and ordered the kid to go back to the sub hamlet, warn the people, go to his mother and stay there for his protection. He slowly rode the Buffalo through the crop field while awaiting the patrol. When the patrol reached him, he pretended to be nervous and acted suspicious when he was questioned; this worked better than he had planned. The Marine's patrol leader, a Sgt. felt that the guy was not what he seemed to be and took him in to custody, bound his hands behind his back, pulled his shirt collar up over his head, made out a capture tag marking him as a VCS[32] picked up in a sweep. The Americans were not allowed to refer to them as prisoners.

Two of the troops guarded him while the rest moved carefully through the sub hamlet checking for VC hiding in various family shelters which were dug into the hovel's floor and covered up. Finding nothing out of place during their cursory search of the sub hamlet the patrol returned to their CP[33] with him in tow. He was fed and kept in a tent with three more VCS for that night. In the morning a two-and a half ton truck took the four, along with two guards, to the Captive Collection Point at the MP CP on the Da Nang air strip which was also the Third Marine Division's Interrogation Center at the time.

That afternoon he met a Marine interrogator, a Marine Gunnery Sergeant named Travis Tolbane. He gave Tolbane a hard time during the interrogation for a while, then gave in, confessed to his VC activities, became a VCC[34] and agreed to lead him and a patrol to some booby traps in

---

[32] Viet Cong Suspect
[33] Command Post
[34] Viet Cong Confirmed

and around Tra Ke ba. He felt he was lucky to get this Interrogator. Even though he was tough and very direct he was a real professional. He could twist your words, confuse you, scare you, he could make you afraid for your life, or be comfortable, glad to be alive, elicit the information he needed and never raise a hand to you. He was fed when returned to the lock up, as it was early evening. As he was falling asleep later he wondered if he was looking forward to going out with an American Patrol in the morning. His last thought was, "I hope we don't get ambushed along the way. I can't trust my VC team at all."

CHAPTER 31

AFTER HO NOTIFIED THE concierge and was walking away, two young Vietnamese lads, around 16 or 17, wearing a semblance of a bellhop uniforms and pushing a large cart, approached and began taking their luggage from the bus. The tallest lad spoke to them in broken English, giving a rehearsed "Welcome to Vietnam" speech and inviting them to enter. He guided them to the registration desk and promised that after they checked in, their luggage would already be in their assigned rooms. The quartet thanked them in Vietnamese and tipped them in 20 Vietnamese Dong notes. They entered the hotel and went straight to the registration desk. There they received another cordial welcome speech and a quick check in, as Ho already had them preregistered, and they got their magnetic entry cards and went straight to their rooms. Tolbane and Mai were in one room, and Parnell and the priest shared another as had been their habit throughout the trip. True to the young lads' words, their luggage was in the correct rooms.

The four were tired, sweaty, dusty, and had somewhat wrinkled and damp clothes from the bus trip. After showering and changing into fresh garb, they read some procedures on the hotel's complimentary services on a sheet of paper which had sections in Vietnamese, French, and English. Per instructions, they found plastic clothes bags in the closet, placed the dirty clothes in them, and set them outside their doors to be cleaned. Shortly after settling in, there was a knock on both of the group's doors. When they answered, they were greeted by employees with carts containing coffee, tea, fresh fruit baskets, and Danish pastries. The employees pushed the carts into the rooms, placed their palms together in front of their chests, gave a slight bow, and left the rooms without even waiting for a tip. They picked up the laundry bags on the way out and were gone. In his room, Tolbane said, "Well I'll be damned!" and Parnell and the priest just kind of "Wowed!" Later they found out that the No Name had already paid for the rooms and taken care of the tips. The goodies were a welcome gesture. They were compliments of the hotel's management for their esteemed visitors.

A good half an hour later, Ho returned and gathered them all in Tolbane's room for a slight briefing. He began by informing them of the surveillance the Masked Man had on the hotel. "There are three watchers outside: one across the intersection, one on Tran Hung Dow, and one on Le Loi Street, and they are communicating by cell phone. So, if you leave the hotel together as a group, in pairs, or alone, you will be followed by at least one of them. Don't worry! They are not a threat. We are watching them too! They aren't even aware of it. Please, if you leave the hotel, don't look for them. Just pretend you don't know they are around and enjoy yourselves."

Parnell asked the expected question, "How do you know they are watching us, and also how are you watching them?"

"Those are very good questions Detective. I was prepared for them! I can answer both your questions with one answer. The No Name has always had an invisible capability, and we know who they are. We also have several pictures of your prey and a few of his cohorts; however, for some reason we have not gotten a good frontal view on the Masked Man. We've gotten only side views of him and cannot make any firm identification on the man. We do know that from now on, he will wear his mask when he is doing something where he doesn't want to be recognized or when he's with the criminal gang members underlings he has working with him."

"If they try to do anything to us," Mai wanted to know, "will we be protected? I don't think I relish the thought of being ambushed, hurt, or killed, especially this far away from our home! We have gone through a lot of strife and grief and traveled too far to fail in getting this bastard off the streets and have our vengeance on his ass."

Ho smiled at Mai, enjoying her moxie, and came up with another old American retort after assuring her of her safety. "Remember your TV series, Laugh-In? I always liked the line 'You can bet your sweet bippy on that!' You can even take it to the bank!"

Of course, Mai smiled back at him and said, "If something happens to any of us, my ghost will haunt and taunt your sweet ever-loving ass the rest of your life, and you'll be another eunuch when it gets through with you."

"Your point is well taken, especially since as I don't haunt well. Nor do I desire to be a eunuch. Now there is one more thing to cover with you about tonight's dining. When you go down to the restaurant at seven on the dot, do not seat yourselves. You will look for an old Vietnamese waiter. He will have unruly white hair and chin whiskers. He will be wearing white pants and an old white Nehru-style jacket. He walks a little stooped over and limps a little too, so you can't miss him. He will guide you to a private dining room and explain your fare for the evening meal, along with why you have a large private dining room all to yourselves this evening, and will supervise the waiters attending you hand and foot. I understand it will be a fabulous meal, and later when you have sated your stomachs, you will receive a more extensive briefing from someone on the situation here. I can guarantee you will not only be well informed, but there will be a big surprise in store for you, Travis Tolbane. So, eat hearty my friends and enjoy. As long as things remain the same as of this time, I will not see you again until tomorrow morning if all goes well."

"Oh! Before you leave, we need to exchange some more money. We only exchanged a little at the Hanoi airport. Where can we do it at here?" Parnell commented. The priest and Tolbane agreed about needing money exchanged. Tolbane quipped, "You never know what may come up that we may need more Dong for." Mai was thinking about saying something like her future hubby would. Like, it would be a miracle if a certain dong came up, but she decided to keep still for a change since Mr. Ho was there, but she did smile.

"You're in luck! There are about 26 ATMs here in Hoi An City. Several of them are in walking distance around Tran Hung Dao and Lei Loi Streets, of which we are at the intersection. The exchange limit is around 20 million VND (Viet Nam Dong), about $100.00 worth at a time, and there's a $20,000 VND charge per each withdrawal fee.[35] If my math does me right, you'll have 19.8 million VND after the exchange."

They thanked him and said their good days, and he left. Mai, suddenly feeling a little tired, wanted to lie down for a bit. Parnell and the priest offered to walk her up to her room, as they needed to grab something from their own room before heading to the ATM, so Tolbane decided to wait out front of the hotel for them.

---

[35] The exchange mentioned here is the 2016 rate of exchange

The two were exiting the front entrance and saw Tolbane standing out front looking around when suddenly a Vietnamese man clad in black pajamas and a conical hat pulled down slightly to hide his face seemingly appeared out of nowhere and bumped hard into Tolbane's left side. Tolbane felt more than a hard bump, and he grabbed the man's left wrist with his left hand, pulling the man off balance. At the same time, he pivoted on his left foot, cocking his right leg, and kicked the back of the man's knee, sending him to the ground. Then he jerked the man's left arm up behind his back and kneeled on top of him.

Parnell and the priest were shocked to see this takedown happen after the guy simply bumped into Tolbane. Both men ran to the scene, and Parnell hollered at Tolbane, "What the hell you doing Tolbane? This guy's no VC! Are you a crazy ass or what? You want to get us arrested? What the hell is your major malfunction anyhow? Let this guy get up on his feet and apologize to him!"

At the same time, Ho and another man suddenly, like apparitions from nowhere, were rushing to the scene. Tolbane was exclaiming, "This clumsy clown stuck his hand in my pocket when he purposely bumped into me! I think he put something in it rather than taking something!" He stood up and released the man, then Ho and his guy grabbed the man's elbows and roughly pulled the clown to his feet. Tolbane checked his pocket and found a small device with a tiny, blinking red light bulb in it. It was something like a cheap mini transponder. "Well screw me blind and call me step and fetch it. Somebody wants to track me down. Can you believe that shit? This guy sure was clumsy, and he's not a very good dip (pick pocket) either."

Ho immediately took charge of the device and the man and informed the group that he would question the guy and get back to them with whatever answers he could get out of him. He and his man took the guy by his elbows and led him, limping and bitching about his knee, away—where to, the guys had no more idea than the man in the moon.

Parnell said to Tolbane, "Sorry about bitching at you. I thought you'd gone ape shit on us. Damn Tolbane! I didn't know you knew how to do all of that martial arts stuff like Kung Fu Panda and the Karate Kid shit, Master."

"I learned it from watching all those Bruce Lee pictures and the *Kung Fu* series, Grasshopper." He bowed with his palms together as a form of respect to his friends.

Then Tolbane and his friends just shook their heads in regards to the incident and went about looking for an ATM without further ado. They tried to make sense of what just took place, why it happened, and how Ho and his man were there so quickly. Tolbane had not seen them when he went outside. They found one ATM just around the corner on Le Loi Street at the Vietcombank, made their exchanges, and returned to their rooms.

Tolbane explained what had happened with the strange man on the street putting a tracking device in his pocket to Mai. She was, and rightly so, a little upset that he had been targeted and gave him a big hug. They were both in awe though that Ho and his man could appear from nowhere in the blink of an eye because, as Tolbane had explained, he saw no one outside the hotel while he was standing and looking around the area. Mai offered, "Maybe they were invisible like the man in the *Invisible Man* movie."

"AH!" Tolbane replied, "I remember it well! If I could be invisible for even a moment, just think how I could sneak up on you and squeeze those magnificent buns." With the look Mai was giving him, he decided not to comment any further on the movie or her buns.

It would still be a while before they were go to the restaurant, so Mai called the front desk and placed a wakeup call with the desk clerk. Then the two lay on the bed and held each other tightly and fell asleep. They awoke at the sound of the room's telephone ringing. Mai sleepily answered it. It was the desk clerk with their wakeup call. She nudged her big brute's shoulder and told him to wake up all the way, get his butt out of bed, and not go back to sleep. She rolled out and went into the bathroom.

Tolbane sat on the edge of the bed looking into the bathroom and watching Mai, who had left the door open, looking into the mirror with just her panties and bra on and applying makeup ever so lightly to her face. He said, "My goodness woman, you've got the finest pair of legs ever put on a woman. And wow! Beside that cute butt, just check out those luscious thighs too." "If you don't stop staring at my wonderful and extremely sexy body and hand me the dress on the end of the bed, those thighs are never going to squeeze you face again! You're still Number Ten Thousand to me. You Dig!" she retorted.

"Oh yes Ma'am. Right away Ma'am. We can't have that happen, now can we?" She stuck her tongue out while throwing a towel at him. When he handed her the dress, he picked her up in a big hug and gave her the kiss of her life. As her feet returned to the floor, he cupped her buns, and she responded, "That's more like it. Sometimes you're almost worth it to have around. Now make yourself useful and get your butt dressed."

Mai and Tolbane were finally dressed when Parnell and the priest knocked. Upon entering, Parnell seemed to be in an extra good mood. "You'll never guess what my dear friend, and I say that lightly because I'm the bearer of more news than the town Crier ever cried to the people while crying his news that had to be cried to the people. Mai, I hope I didn't sound like my goofy pal?" Mai tilted her head toward her right shoulder and spoke to him, "My god. He's rubbing off on you too the world's doomed!"

Tolbane started chomping at the bit. "Okay! Okay! I give up in complete surrender to the Crier who cries good news, so what new good news does my prognosticator have that possibly would be of interest to this most fascinating worldly icon, namely me, in the world today?"

"Remember our talkative friend at MNPD? I checked my emails at the little computer room the hotel has for guests, and I got an update from one of my men. It seems the guy told a little more info about our Masked Man. He had held back a little to me. It seems that the Masked Man had raped and cut up 13 women, mostly young Asian girls, one may have been as young as 9 or 10, over a period of time and buried them in an area past Monterey, TN, along state route 70 and up towards Cumberland Cove. The guy said he was a little sad because some of the victims could have been young girls he got for the Masked Man's pleasure. My guys took our blabber mouth there one day, and he had not only shown him the area but told him a little about each victim. The Masked Man had evened bragged about doing it in Vietnam for several years before coming to the states also, and confessed to him that he was sad that he had to quit raping and killing women because he had suddenly lost his sex drive and wished he could regain it. He really missed the satisfaction of cutting them before, during, and after each sex act. My detectives took the clown to the site, and they have located all 13 graves and will be excavating them sometime this coming week as soon as a jurisdiction snafu between the Counties is taken care of."

Tolbane pondered on this development a minute then replied, "I guess its good news that the graves were found, especially for the women's next of kin if they can be identified, but the bad news is that he got his sex drive back, and the two in Honolulu and those two girls in Hong Kong suffered for it. I still wonder about his vicious attack on Carly. If he had regained his sex drive by then, that would mean that her assault was twofold. He was finally beginning to enjoy sex again, and he was sending a message to us. I can't really understand what the message could be unless he was just horny for her. Nothing that this guy does makes any sense at all." Everyone agreed with him.

It was time to go, so they left the room to go to the restaurant. They wouldn't want Tolbane to be late for chowing down. When it came to food, he was the equal to any mechanical vacuum. Entering the dining room at seven o'clock sharp, they were approached by an old man with white unruly hair and chin whiskers, and he looked almost like Ho Chi Minh, as he was wearing all white clothes with the white jacket knockoff of a Nehru jacket. He was a little stooped over and limping, and after greeting them in perfect English and in Vietnamese with a frail voice, he bade them to follow him. He led them into a small dining area with a slight limp and a shuffle and closed the door behind the group and asked them to please be seated at a large banquet table all set up with proper etiquette. One thing they noticed was odd was that there was a fifth chair at the table, but the place had not been set with dinnerware. After all were seated, another waiter entered at the clap of the old man's hands and filled their water glasses with ice water.

When the waiter left the room, the old man, calmly in a more mature voice, stated, "And now, I have a surprise for all, and, you in particular Travis Tolbane! I am a good friend of Father Phat, but that's not all." He straightened up, pulled off the white wig, revealing his own salt and peppered hair, removed his chin whiskers, and gleefully walked to Tolbane and said, "Surprise my old friend and interrogator. It's me, Father Nguyen Van Hai!" Everyone's jaw dropped so to speak.

"My aching ass, I do know you!" Tolbane shockingly exclaimed. "You were with us as a prisoner when those clowns ambushed us and we found the Jade Cross. If it hadn't been for you, we would never have been on that patrol and found it!" Tolbane rose from his chair, and the two moved together and man hugged for a very long moment. Then they stood apart with their hands on the other one's shoulders and looked into the other's eyes and grinned as though they could not believe this reunion was happening. It was the classic turnaround theme from enemy to ally. The others could not believe their eyes as well. Parnell relished the moment because he too knew the man. Van Hai looked at Parnell and noted, "It's good to see you too Sergeant. Come!" He placed an arm around Parnell's shoulder while gripping Tolbane's. "Ah, what memories we three share from trying times." Mai looked at her man with admiration.

Father Van Hai then gestured with his hand and said, "Please sit my friend, and I will give you all a short synopsis of what has been happening up till now and what we intend to do about it. But first let me welcome you to the Democratic Republic of Vietnam. If you're surprised at my speaking English without an accent, let me say I had a demanding teacher. I'll tell you a little about what's happening, and then we'll dine on some great American fare. I know you'll love it. The chef here, who is one of the best in Quang Nam Providence, is fantastic with American cuisine. When the food is gone, I'll get to the good parts you need to know over some coffee, fine wine, and dessert." He clapped his hands, and a waiter brought a table setting for him.

When the waiter had set his place and was gone, he gave an update on Tolbane's encounter with the man in front of the hotel. "According to the peasant, it seems that a Masked Man, whom he had never seen before, sought him out where he picked the pockets of tourists or stole women's purses for a living and gave him not only a description of you, but a picture of you also. He was paid the sum of 20 Dong to bump into you and place that locator in your pocket. Then he was to get away as soon and as quietly and quickly as he could. He knows nothing more than that. As I listened to Ho question him, I got the feeling that you were meant to find the locator as a message to let you know that the Masked Man knows you're here. I gave him another 20 Dong, told him to hide out for a couple of days, and sent him limping on his way. He was a little mad about your kicking the back of his knee, however. I'm sure you know the words he used to describe you. It had something to with your having an incestuous relationship with your mother five times a day." All five had a big laugh at this.

He clapped his hands once more, and three waiters entered with a cart loaded with pitchers of sweet and unsweet tea; buttered hot rolls; soda crackers; a large bowl of a tossed mixed salad of lettuce, grated carrots, onions, green and red peppers, diced tomatoes, and topped with grated sharp cheddar cheese; and a selection of salad dressings in small cups, along with a special larger one with a lot honey mustard for Tolbane, who thought out loud, "How does this guy know I love honey mustard?" Father Hai smiled, "It's just good intelligence collection and the processing of it, my friend. I believe that you are familiar with that concept." Tolbane grinned. The waiters were into service with a smile after they tossed the salad and as they filled the salad bowls and placed them in front of each diner. When the task was completed, the waiters disappeared once more as if they suddenly became invisible on command.

The group was really impressed with the service they received. Father Van Hai must really have a lot of pull here, they thought. So far, the service was perfection. When the salads had been finished and the bowls removed from the tables, the waiters began bringing the main course, which consisted of a two-and-a-quarter inch thick fillet mignon, broiled medium rare and served with a special au jus the Chef makes; a baked sweet potato sliced in half long ways, heaped with butter, brown sugar, and cinnamon, and chives; a side dish of fresh snow peas with bacon bits and onions in an oblong dish; and a half-ear of corn in a sea of hot, melted butter. Just in case, the waiters also brought A1 and Heinz 57 sauces. After Father Phat gave the blessing, the group quickly dug into their sumptuous meal with almost as much gusto as Tolbane.

When they were done eating, Father Phat commented to them on the food." I have eaten in some really fine-four and five-star restaurants in my travels throughout the world, but this is about the most perfectly prepared fillet I've ever had. The mignon was just perfectly medium rare and the sides were great. My compliments go to the chef, Hai!" The rest agreed with him on that.

Tolbane burped in agreement with them. He was already wondering what kind of dessert they would have. The group's eyes lit up as hot peach cobbler heaped with a gob of vanilla ice cream was served in large individual bowls with a vanilla sauce and whipped cream topping it. Tolbane was elated and laid waste to the contents of his bowl in no time at all, while the rest took their time as their stomachs were nearly full. The waiters appeared magically once more as if from nowhere, cleared the table once again, and served a mild French blend of coffee to top off the meal. Father Van Hai stood once more, stated the wine would come when the coffee was finished, and indicated he needed to relate one enigma before continuing his briefing.

"Viet Nam, as well as the U.S.A., has been actively searching for missing service members and recovering them as well as civilians since the conflict ended. Around Dog Patch just outside of the old Da Nang Air Base and at the bottom of Hill 327, several female bodies were found. Some of these bodies had wounds consistent with war death, but for others, it was evident that they were murdered, and their bones showed signs of knife wounds and stripping of flesh. We have a couple of doctors here who try to keep up on body recoveries in the country and discovered there were remains now in Ho Chi Minh City as well as Quang Ngai City and here in Hoi An City consistent with the knife wounds of those in Dog Patch. The sad part of it is that a young girl was brutally raped and butchered here in Hoi An City in the same manner as the others. We suspect the women and girls were murdered by the same person, who is your quarry. Now I'll continue on my briefing." Parnell interrupted him, relating what he had learned of the murders recently discovered in the States. Van Hai listened patiently and sighed as Parnell completed relating the facts as he knew them.

Father Van Hai then continued his narrative. "A few years ago, there was a man—he always used different names—who was a very kind, nice man, but he was a little off upstairs, or as you Americans say, 'Not the sharpest tool in the shed,' and confused and delusional about belonging to a secret organization called No Name. He was very harmless. We didn't worry that he was a threat to us, as he never did anything untoward to us. One day, an unidentified Vietnamese man came from Ho Chi Minh City and visited him for a few days. They visited the site where the Jade Cross had been reburied by your patrol. After the strange man went back to Ho Chi Minh City, the man began to act in a suspicious manner, trying to organize a unification of the country in the name of the No Name. He recruited two unsavory characters named Hung and Lam to assist him. When he began to develop a conspiracy in some sub-hamlets outside the city, we managed to get an agent close to him, and that agent remains there today. He received and made quite a few calls from the U.S. To make a long story short, the man was brutally tortured and murdered recently by the two idiots he recruited, who then temporarily took control of the organization while awaiting the Masked Man to arrive here.

"We know for a fact that the man who visited him used different names and, in fact, came over from and returned to the States with different passports. The same man has returned here to Hoi An recently and has taken control from the two geese and is preparing to begin a campaign to take control of the country and rule it. He thinks he is the reincarnation of General Tran Hung Dao, an ancient Vietnam hero, and can reunite the country. To do so he needs the Jade Cross as his symbol of leadership and authority and is willing to kill to obtain it. Before he begins his insurgency, though, he wants to kill the two idiots and you three, Tolbane, Parnell, and Father Phat, as well. He also desires to take the fair maiden, Mai, for his own. He believes she is his true love, in his mind, she loves him too, and he believes you've defiled her too many times Tolbane, and for that you must meet your fate at his hands. Parnell, you and Father Phat have also been placed on his hate list for some unknown reason and must meet the same fate as Tolbane. He has had you under surveillance since you landed in Da Nang. But how he knew about your coming and when and where you would arrive, I have no idea.

"We haven't been able to discover the true identity of the man by photos, as his pictures we have taken always have his face in profile. He has aligned himself with a very vicious gang to help him with his dirty work. Since his alignment with the gang, three young boys were found raped and butchered today, as well as the girl earlier this week, the knife wounds were all consistent with the others that were recovered from the conflict era. We know it was this man; however, we just can't prove it yet. We do know that he has a plot to trap you guys and the two idiots at the site where the Jade Cross was buried, as he's sure that your group will visit there in the next couple of days. He has armed his followers and has been rehearsing this plot with his people for a couple of days. I still have someone on the inside, and I know all of his plans as well as he does. I and my associates have a designed counter plan to protect you four and bring him down, and I swear to you this monster will be very shocked when it happens. When I explain my plans, you will have questions about your safety until my counter scheme is enacted. I know for a fact from my informant, a most reliable one, that he will not kill you outright, as he wants to make you suffer the worst agonies possible to satisfy his hate for you. This will not happen. So far, it is still unknown why he has developed this hatred for you.

"Tomorrow during the day, you'll tour the city, shop or whatever, and check out the night life of the city, and the next day you'll visit the reburial sight. Tomorrow night after you return to your rooms, I will explain much of my plan to you. I will keep a couple of things to myself about it, as I want you all to be able to show a realistic surprise and fear at the mad man's trap. I can assure you, our Masked Man, Tran Hung Dao, Dumb Ass, or whatever he calls himself at any given time, will get, as you Marines say, 'The Ram,' and rightly so.

"I cannot tell you much about the real No Name Society, as it doesn't exist in the minds of many, except that it has a long history and most of the people today do not know of it or do not believe it exists, but I assure you, our goals are for peaceful solutions. We don't condone violence in achieving our goals unless during an event there is no other way. Our Society has a long history of being respected by the common people who do know of us and are under our protection. We will not let that image, that reputation known to followers, be tarnished by some fool filled with ridiculous delusions of grandeur. This was the last thing I'll cover tonight. I have many things I must look into before the night is over. Remember to relax tomorrow and have a fun day. It'll be good for your dispositions. The day after, I need you to have clear minds and to be at your best performance level, for that day will be the end game for the Masked Man."

Mr. Hai put on his wig and chin whiskers, once more assumed a bent body, and told the group to drink up and be merry the rest of the evening. "I'm hoping that before you all return to the States Travis Tolbane, we can sit and talk about us during my captivity with you as well as that patrol. It was a difficult and trying time for both of us, as we each had our own agenda. Yours was collecting information and mine was avoiding giving the absolute truth." Tolbane quickly nodded his okay at the suggestion and said he'd like that very much. He'd often wondered what had happened to the people he had to question during that tour.

Father Van Hai bade the group goodbye after informing them to ask the waiters for whatever they wanted and enjoy the rest of the evening. "I have many things to attend to, my friends and the restaurant has an endless supply of fine wines in its cellar. Maybe even some good beers too. You guys might like a Ba Muoi Ba served in a tall glass with a chunk of ice to refresh your memories. Just ask the waiters for it." He waved his arm and hand and in Vietnamese said, "Chao cac ong 'em (good bye)!" Then he was suddenly gone.

The four compatriots were actually awed over Father Hai, his acumen, the meal, and what seemed to be a comradery building amongst them. Over a few drinks, one of which was a glass of Ba Muoi Ba with a chunk of ice, they discussed the present situation, how the information from Father Hai and themselves blended somewhat together to give them a picture of the most vile and despicable killer known to man, and what might be expected from him or what might transpire in the next few days. They agreed that whatever may happen, let it happen and be done with it. The end of this reign of terror must end here and now for the sake of all people who could become his victims. Everyone was OK with this, and they called it a night. Slightly reeling from the last few drinks, the group returned to their rooms and called it a night. Had he thought of it Tolbane might have said, "A Night!"

A few minutes after the group arrived in their rooms, Ho knocked on the doors, one room at a time, to pass on some information about plans for the following morning. He kept his brief short, as he knew the group was ready for the sandman. When he left the last room, the occupants were already sound asleep, dead to the world before they could even count ten sheep jumping a barbed wire fence without setting off flares or hitting a mine.

CHAPTER 32

Bᴜɪ ᴡᴏᴋᴇ ᴇᴀʀʟʏ, ᴀғᴛᴇʀ a slightly restless night, to begin breakfast as usual, not realizing that the two gangsters were sleeping, not only in the dining area, but on the large dining table. She nearly woke them as she traipsed through the area to the kitchen. She got the fire and breakfast going and woke Hai while it cooked. The Masked Man's two geese were up by then and were understandably disturbed that they had to eat in the kitchen because of the Exalted One's two new members were slumbering, farting, and snoring on the dining table. They contemplated complaining to the Exalted One about it immediately, but they decided, rightly so, they would just be making matters worse. They'd save it till they had a couple more complaints come their way and discuss their problems all at once with him.

The two Geese made the women uncomfortable; they were still always staring at their breasts and butts. Bui finally got tired of it and informed them that if they tried anything with her or Hai, their balls and their favorite part of their body would be cut off in no uncertain terms, boiled, then would be jammed down their throats. The geese just laughed at her in a lude and lascivious manner and presented the middle finger at her, and then they went to their rooms. Hai thought they were probably going to play with themselves while dreaming about her and Bui. She hoped they would do it so hard they would pull it completely off.

Hai helped Bui clean up from the meal, and they did a little extra cleaning in the kitchen. After that, they went to do their morning toiletries and met back in the kitchen. Houng and Lam had gone out to take a walk, not saying where they were going or when they would return, and the other three were still asleep. The women were enjoying listening to the radio playing traditional Vietnamese songs and being the only ones awake at the time. The news came on after a while, and they were once again shocked to the point they felt mild tremors. It seemed that the bodies of three teenage boys were found along side of a street, slaughtered in much the same manner as the young girl had been. Both knew instantly who had done this horrendous deed. Once more, they were filled with fear and uncertainty, but they were also glad it wasn't them laying there, mutilated nearly beyond recognition. Taking a very risky chance, they snuck out of the house, took one moped, and went to find Hai's father to inform him of what they believed happened to the boys, hoping to return before the geese returned or the others woke up. It was a quick trip and they had just gotten comfortable in the kitchen once more after returning when the Masked Man woke up, roused the two sleepers, and requested the women fix another breakfast as the three had worked up a voracious appetite the previous night.

The women complied and produced a large breakfast in a very short order. The three men ate and drank hot tea heartily, and the Masked Man complimented the women on their quick response in producing an outstanding meal. He looked sternly at the other two, and they complimented the two women too, only half-heartedly, when they received a stern look from their new leader they apologized. Hai and Bui took the compliments with a grain of salt. They just wanted to be left alone, so they went back to the kitchen to hang out again. They could hear the Masked Man and the two gangsters whispering a lot in the dining room but could not make out what was being said. A half hour later, the Exalted One's cell phone rang.

He answered, speaking louder than a whisper, and he could be heard saying, "That is the best of news I've had lately. You've done very good on an important job. You'll be justly rewarded for your diligence with recognition of many Dong in your pocket." Ending the call, he bade the women to join them in the dining room. They walked in, placed their tea on the table, and sat down, not looking at the two asses they knew were checking them out. They were very suspicious about what might be about to happen to them. The Masked Man had a smile on his face showing a lot of teeth and seemed to be elated over the news he'd just received.

Suddenly, he was almost jumping up and down with elation when he addressed the group: "I have just received the most splendid and satisfying news from Da Nang. It's the news that I was afraid I'd never live to hear. The hated Americans, my sworn enemies forever, their friend the priest, a traitor to Vietnam and to my Cause, and the love of my life are on their way here to Hoi An City right now. They will arrive here, in this very city, within a couple of hours. My plans for our future are coming to fruition as I speak to you. My vengeance is neigh, and you all will be a great part of its success. Yes! Very soon, Vietnam will be reunited under the No Name and I, Tran Hung Dao, and my lady, the beautiful Mai, will rule together, and you will all serve in my court!"

The women, always somewhat tired and a little sleepy after serving breakfast, returned to their rooms and immediately fell asleep. The Masked Man and his gangsters sat around the table drinking hot tea Bui had steeped for them and not really conversing when his two dumb geese returned from their walk. He bade them to sit and have tea with them and remain quiet while he contemplated a few things. Several minutes later, he had Lam wake and bring the women from their rooms. When they appeared, he actually held their chairs for them, one at a time, for them to sit and poured them hot tea. This was something a traditional Vietnamese man would never do for a woman; serving was the woman's job. He smiled to himself as he saw the ugly looks and the disgust on his geese's faces at his actions. The two gangsters could have cared less what they did! He really knew how to push the geese's' buttons. Another reason he was smiling to himself was the knowledge that their buttons wouldn't be around much longer to be pushed. His soon to be Number One and Number Two would make the final push of their buttons for him.

He looked each of the table's occupants in the eye, and when satisfied he had their attention, he slowly outlined the basics of his plan to ambush and capture the targeted ones. He gave them an idea of about when and where it would take place and stressed that he would finalize his plan once he had a chance to observe and learn more of the group's situation. When he finished, he asked for questions. No one had any, so he informed them that he would be leaving shortly and would be gone for a few hours. He needed to post some watchers on the hotel he knew they would use and maybe come up with some kind of a plan to get their attention, to let them know he knew they were here. He might even be able to instill a little fear, keep them off guard and wondering what would happen next.

Now everyone was free and on their own for the time being. He knew the two new ones needed to meet with their cohorts at their gang's hang out, and he could care less what the two geese would do with themselves. They could screw each other for all he cared. He figured that the women would try to get a much needed rest. He had the two geese remain for a moment when the other two men left and the women retired. He cautioned them about harassing the women while he was away and the fate that awaited them should they do so.

He went to his room for a few minutes, then he left, humming the hit tune from *Annie* named "Tomorrow." He got one of the mopeds and looked up several members on the No Name list he'd received from Lam when he first arrived. He found them at home and had them assemble at an empty lot he knew of. Wearing his mask, he gave a limited briefing to them, including descriptions of the targets, and assigned stake out duties, relief times, and the places from which to observe the hotel, and he informed them how to report to him on what they observed.

He left the group and decided to just motor around the city, taking in the sights and enjoying the afternoon while he tried to concoct some type of antic to pull on the Americans. He was sightseeing in a high tourist area when he spied a middle-aged man in black pajamas and conical hat bumping into a male tourist and picking his pocket. He did a U-turn and followed the man, and soon the man turned into what seemed like an alley way. It was a dead end, and he cornered the man as he was removing Dong from the guy's wallet. He knew then and there that the man would be perfect for what he suddenly had in mind for the hated Travis Tolbane, his true love's defiler. It would really be funny when it happened. He just wished he could be there to see it happen. This was a great day for him. Everything seemed to be falling into place.

Meanwhile, back at the house the women were sleeping soundly in their rooms and the two geese sitting at the table were once again bitching to each other about the Masked Man and his deliberate actions with the women to piss them off to the nth degree time and again. Until the two new guys came on board, they had hoped that once the Americans were taken care of and he got his bitch back things would progress to the point they would be able to take care of the Masked Man, take control of what administration he'd build up for the No Name, and have two women to play with, plus his bitch to boot. Taking the two women was something they'd like to do right now, but they did fear the Masked Man as his reputation preceded him.

Presently they were concerned that they would need to rethink the whole situation anew. Tam and Tuy presented another problem, especially since they had a gang of their own. The picture had changed drastically for them. One question they debated was whether they should pack up and get the hell out of Dodge there and now or press forward to take the whole shebang for themselves. Avarice, the root of all evil according to a Canterbury Tale, won out. The decision was to take it all for themselves.

The subject was changed, and it forced a more relaxed mood to take over their angry dispositions. As they discussed several different subjects, they eventually came around to the one thing all men are consumed with; sex! Eventually they decided that thinking about Hai and Bui laying in their beds, and maybe even naked, made them horny, so they decided to go to a cat house they frequented and left the house, hoping the working women there would love them long time.

This particular cat house had been there for a few decades, having been established early in the Vietnam Conflict–era to service ARVN (Army of Republic of Viet Nam). The women were considered too old and useless for the trade by many men, but these two liked it there. The women still had a little shape left and were not yet showing the facial ugliness of age and had never used betel nut, a plus for any city man. The working women didn't have many customers due to their age; therefore, they did not have a great income and would be elated over any business coming along. What the two geese loved about them was twofold. One, they were cheaper than the young, exciting ladies found in the many brothels in the city, and two, the women would leave nothing undone in order to earn a few extra Dong tip for their extraordinary performance on each and every customer. Since money was not a problem for them, they decided that they would both have a threesome at the very least.

Hai and Bui awoke at nearly the same time. Checking that no one was in the house except them, they readily talked about the present situation. Their first concern was their personal safety and then the safety of the Americans. Neither one felt like staying in the house alone right then. They made a plan and felt that would be the best thing to do at the time. They left a note on the table explaining that they were going to a tea shop then would do some window shopping, and in general, just enjoy the afternoon. Bui operated the moped and Hai rode behind her.

They took their time and made sure they weren't followed then rode to an out-of-the-way tea house. Enjoying tea and sweet cakes, they relaxed and had a wonderful time with girl talk. They even talked about some of the handsome young men they'd seen and lamented about being single and, the truth be known, wanting to get laid by a young, handsome guy. After tea, they went to a popular tourist area, parked and chained the moped to a pole, and meandered through the shops, marveling at many of the new things replacing older traditional things. The fact that the tourists really liked buying Vietnamese souvenirs was really strange to them, as the things tourists bought were part of their everyday culture. Their timing was perfect. They arrived back at the house just in time to start the evening meal.

About the time the evening meal was ready to be served, the Masked Man returned; however, he was not alone. It seems he had met a lady and brought her home. The geese had not returned yet, and the other two would be there later in the evening. He introduced his charming companion, Trich Thi Sau, to Hai and Bui but did not elaborate on the real reason why she was there. He told them he had met her at one of the monuments (later he'd confess it was on a street corner where she was selling her ass to anyone interested), and he had confided in her that he had the two most beautiful and finest cooks in the city. Since she sounded interested in good cooking, he invited her to dine with him for the evening meal, and she didn't hesitate to accept his offer. While they were eating, the two geese came dragging in, and he sent them to the kitchen to eat, which enraged the two even more so.

After the meal was over, there was small talk between the four along with a bottle of ice-cold Ba Muoi Ba, and the Masked Man finally informed Hai and Bui why Sau was really here with him. She would be spending the night in his room, earning her money and him getting his money's worth. At this time, he informed Sau, embarrassing Hai and Bui to no extent, "These two lovely women you see here, individually and/or together, have given me the greatest sexual satisfaction in my life, which has made me the luckiest man on this planet. That means, my dear, that you have a lot to work towards tonight. In other words, you'll be working your ass off for me. Do you think you're up to the challenge?"

Sau smiled and answered, "You got it big boy! I love a 'fucking' challenge! My ass works good too." He took her by the hand and led her to his room with one hand while the other hand groped her buns.

The two women couldn't believe this happened, but it did. They waited until the geese finished with their meal and went to their rooms. They cleaned the table and the kitchen, got a few things out to start breakfast the next day, and went to their own rooms and locked their doors, even though the doors would be easy to break through. Both women had old books they had looked through many times, and they spent a while looking through them once again. Later on, they heard the two gangsters enter the house noisily and crap out on the kitchen table again. Sleep came quickly for the women and the gangsters alike when all was quiet except for moans, groans, and an occasional shriek from the Masked Man's room, mostly from Sau. When Bui woke to her alarm the next morning and started for the kitchen, Sau darted from the Masked Man's room with tears streaming down her face and ran out the door. Bui felt sad for the woman. It also startled the two gangsters awake. When they found out what had happened, they laughed at the prostitute's dilemma and instructed Bui to make them hot tea to quench their thirst.

The men and the women were seated and the meal was already served when the Masked Man, in a very good mood after his night of cavorting with Sau, joined the table. He even greeted the two geese in a friendly manner for a change. After eating, he told everyone how a message had been sent to one Travis Tolbane, the defiler of his loved one, and added that he wished he could have been there to see it. He added a little more on his plan. "Later, I will have a drawing of where everyone will be placed when we ambush our targets. I still have to finalize our transportation plan to and from our ambush site and exactly what place it will leave us off to position ourselves. Be patient a little longer for me." He threw out a few things he was mulling over and changed the subject and addressed the two geese.

"I have planned the day for you two. I must know exactly what the Americans and my love are doing today at all times—where they go, what they're doing there, and who they are with; you two know the drill. You will keep me informed throughout the day by voicemail without fail. You will not allow yourselves to be seen or heard by the hated ones, and you will stay at your posts until you're absolutely sure the targets are in for the night before you return here. Now, do not give me any of your lip or ridiculous stares. Go to your rooms now and get what you need to take with you, and get yourselves to a good spot by the hotel to observe from! Make sure you're not observing from the same location our men are using. You may take one of the four mopeds. Go!" The two geese looked at each other, gave each other a little 'no' nod of the head to not complain about their assignment, and went straight to their rooms, put a few things in their backpacks, including a few bottles of water, and were on their way.

The geese left and he turned to the women, took a large wad of Dong from his pocket, and gave each of them a half of it. "Ladies! This will be a good day for you two, indeed a really special day. In a few moments, I'll give you a shopping list of things we will need for a special breakfast tomorrow, an hour and a half earlier in the morning than usual, and a few other things I need. You'll each need a moped for your task. There is a good part to this mission of yours. Not only will you have the rest of the day to yourselves, but there will be a considerable amount of Dong left over; it's all yours. I want you two to shop till you drop, as Americans would say. Buy whatever you want, and don't spare the cost. If you run out of money, just put whatever on a tab and I'll cover it later. Since my arrival here, you two have rewarded me with the performances of your beautiful and wonderful bodies and taken me to cloud nine many times, so this is my thanks and reward to you for a terrific service. Your sex is really terrific." He smiled at the way the two looked bright eyed and astounded at each other and continued, "Off with you two now. All of that good shopping waits for no one else; only for you two, dawn to dusk." Hai and Bui wasted no time getting what they needed and got out of Dodge quickly.

With the women and the geese gone for the day, the Masked Man could get down to business with his new allies. He addressed them: "Gentlemen, and I use that phrase lightly," with a grin, "we are alone now and can get down to the serious side of our business. As of now, I am changing your designations from Numbers Three and Four to Numbers One and Two. This change is between us for now until we capture our targets, then you can take care of business and inform the geese that they are no longer Numbers One and Two geese, but Numbers One and Two Corpses. They will not return here until very late tonight, I'm sure. The targets always stay out late, and they will too, so you will sleep in their rooms instead of on the table, and not only tonight, but any other night you please. The rooms belong to you two now. Anything in the rooms belonging to the geese is now yours too."

He pulled out a hand drawn map of where he decided to launch his ambush on his enemies from. It showed a sub-hamlet, a grove of trees, a grassy field, and an abandoned block building. It also indicated the position of where each member of his team would attack from. He pointed out two extra positions and told them he wanted two more trusted gang members along because he wanted them to serve flankers and also because he needed the superior numbers for a show of strength. He discussed their transportation with them, and they assured him that they would have a large passenger van, a driver, and two additional men in front of the house early in the morning about an hour before sunrise.

Then they got down to specifics about how the ambush would take place, how the two geese would meet their demise, and how their targets would be captured. He wanted to use the minimal amount of force to accomplish the mission. He didn't want his enemies harmed yet because he wanted them to stew over what was to happen to them under his knives. The Masked Man didn't have to tell them that his knife was a phallic symbol to him, an extension of his penis, as it would be with any piquerist. He reminded them that death awaited anyone who should hurt Mai, even accidentally. She was off limits to all beings but himself. They completed finalizing their ambush plans and enjoyed a midmorning beer.

Drinking their Ba Muoi Ba, their conversation, as is natural with most men, turned to thoughts of beautiful women and wild sex. The Masked Man informed the two that he had noticed how his new Numbers ogled at Hai's and Bui's breasts and how they practically mooed over their butts and shapely legs when the women were walking around. He had only one thing to say to them on the subject. "I share your enjoyment watching those women. They are nicely endowed and have great breasts and sexy asses; however, those two are my responsibility. They're my whores, and I will protect them until I have no further use for one or the other, or both. I already have my own party plans for them should I decide I have no further need of their services. I, and only I, will be the one to touch them sexually or otherwise, is that clear?" The new Numbers, a little shocked at the comment, nodded in agreement, not wanting to piss off their new boss, at least not now.

The conversation then turned to what kind of women and what kind of sex they liked to party with best. They agreed that the Masked Man's kind of slice and dice party was great, but just plain recreational sex was fantastic too. They debated about the sexual worthiness of older women, women close to their ages, and of course, really young girls. The two gangsters briefed the Masked Man about the kidnapping and trafficking that was done of really young girls from different countries to brothels in the city. If one went to the right place, one would have a choice of many different races and nationalities, and it could be exciting just trying to pick out the one you wanted the most. Some places would allow you to fondle the girls while deciding which one would be the best choice. It would also depend on what your desire was. There were three different levels of young girls. Some girls would be too young for intercourse but would be available for masturbation and/or oral sex. The next group would handle intercourse as well as oral sex, and then the older set of the young girls would handle anything your little heart desired, as they had no virgin areas of their bodies left. Some guys, so they had heard, may take one from two different levels at a time for a good threesome.

The Masked Man stated that even though he'd like to party with some women, or even with some men, remembering the homosexual transvestite in Hawaii, that night, they needed to get a good night's sleep as tomorrow would be a long day for them. But he decided some good recreational sex with young girls during the day sounded like a wonderful idea. He asked, "Does anyone know exactly where you'd go to find these young wares?"

In answer to his question, his new Number One replied, "Oh yes, Exalted One! We both do. We've been there many times." They then informed their new leader that they knew of two of several such places housed atop of old hotels. The places were managed by older women who had been in the trade many years and were no longer very desirable but knew how to care for the young girls to insure they stayed healthy and clean, were not mistreated by customers, and were well trained at their carnal duties. The main thing to remember though is not to harm the girls. That would lead to dire consequences as these two, as well as other houses, are protected by big crime bosses who frown on the young girls being abused.

The three guys decided to go to both places during the day and sample as many young girls as possible. The Masked Man even decided that he'd pay for everything, and the two gangsters liked that idea; free is something they liked. They then left on foot, holding hands as was a Vietnamese custom, and made their rounds, only stopping to have lunch at a small café at one of the hotels which housed their chosen aged girls. Late afternoon, they returned to their house, dragging their ass so to speak, but sexually sated and in good spirits, just in time to enjoy the evening meal. Then they turned in early to rest their fatigued bodies. The two gangsters couldn't wait to get to their new rooms and see what booty was now theirs.

Hai and Bui talked for a while and turned in early for a change too. Lately for some reason, they had been feeling a little sleep deprivation. The geese didn't get in until late, and their anger really hit the fan when they discovered the two gangsters sleeping in their rooms. They would confront the Masked Man about it and their other complaints early the next morning and had no choice but to sleep on the kitchen table as the others had done the previous two nights.

Bui's alarm went off an hour and an half earlier than usual per the Masked Man's instructions. He wanted an early, special, and big breakfast for everyone that morning.

She got the fire started in the wood burning range and then woke Hai to assist her. It had taken a while the previous day to purchase the things needed for this meal. They went from market to market until they were able to complete the list of eggs, bacon, sausage, ground beef, flour, and baking soda. Bui had been tutored in preparing American style breakfasts at the previous home she had worked at. Hai started the bacon and the sausage while Bui made baking powder biscuits. Hai grabbed a cooking pot and a large serving spoon, went to the dining room, and began banging the pot with the spoon near the geese's heads. She scared the geese awake, and they were about ready to jump her when the Masked Man entered the room. Hai turned around and was laughing while she returned to the kitchen. Bui had started the SOS by then. They listened to the loud arguing in the dining room as they prepared the eggs. It seemed the geese were upset not only at Hai's banging noise scaring them and the Masked Man laughing about it, but about the newcomers sleeping in their beds and what was happening to their belongings in the rooms, the surveillance task they had to do, and several other embarrassments, and they decided that this was the time to confront the Masked Man about all of their complaints.

The Masked Man, fibbing fluently to the two, had the final words on the arguments. "I sent you on that task because I needed someone I could trust to do the job. You did really well on keeping me updated on the target's activities on my voicemail. I really needed to know where they did not go and if anyone else was with them, and if so, who. Now, as far as your rooms are concerned, you have my word that you won't have to worry about those guys sleeping in your rooms ever again. I don't blame Hai for waking you two the way she did. She needed to get your dirty, smelly asses off the table so that the women can serve us the marvelous American breakfast that I have ordered for today. I don't want to hear anything else from you two on these matters or anything else today. I'm tired of your sulky attitudes, your silent stares, and your constant complaints. I hope that's clear to you two because we have much to do today, and I don't wish to be distracted from my Cause." The two swallowed their pride and nodded a yes, realizing further discussion would bear no fruit at this time. They would bide their time until they had a plan of action. Tam was sent to rouse the other two members for breakfast.

When all the men were seated at the table, the women brought out four platters of food and a large bowl of SOS. Each platter had a different food on it, one of bacon just crisping, one of sausage links, one of baking powder biscuits, one with more than a dozen eggs looking just the way the Masked Man liked them, and finally the bowl contained the creamed beef, a real American GI delight, for the biscuits. All ate heartily, having at least seconds, until they were sated, felt their stomachs bulge, and couldn't eat another drop. The women received compliments from around the table, only this time the compliments from the guys were real and well-deserved. It was a crowning moment for them. Something they rarely got. It made their efforts in the kitchen worthwhile for a change, and that was a good feeling. Then the Masked Man had the whole crew finish their tea then help clean up the table and kitchen.

When that was done, he instructed them to change into their uniforms and bring their weapons, ammo, and whatever else they needed back to the dining room and ordered them not to be slow doing it. He would explain his reasons when they were assembled again. Within five minutes, everyone was back and seated at the table, stoically awaiting the Masked Man's instructions. He had also changed quickly, as he had a time table of sorts to follow. He addressed the group in a similar manner any military leader would when briefing troops on an upcoming operation. He stood with his feet about eighteen inches apart, hands behind his back—the only thing missing was a swagger stick for the Patton look—and spoke matter of factually.

"Shortly our transportation, a van large enough to hold us and the prisoners, to and back from our ambush site will arrive here. There will be a driver, who will not participate in our operation, and two additional men with extra equipment, who will act as flankers for us, courtesy of our new allies. We are ready to embark on our desired journey into history." He passed around his drawing to remind everyone of their positions once they were in place.

"I have just a few reminders for you. You all know the signal to attack I've given to you. When the time comes, it must be precisely executed as quickly as possible. Have no fear in your charge at the enemy. Our targets will not be armed as far as I know at this time. We may be in our positions for a long time before our pray arrives. If your body parts get stiff or uncomfortable, flex them slowly, or move them quietly to relieve the feeling. If we have to wait another day there, which is a slight possibility, the van will bring us food and more water, so make sure you have plenty of water for now."

"There will be absolutely no talking when we reach the site. Little sounds can carry a long distance in a quiet atmosphere, and we don't want to alert the targets when they arrive. I reiterate to you, no harm must come to Mai; wound the enemies only if needed. When the enemies are in custody, Mai is mine once more, and we will return here. I'll see that each one of you is greatly rewarded with much Dong for a job well done, and you will all receive a prestigious position in the No Name. Listen! It sounds like our big van is here already. Grab your gear and let's load up!" They grabbed their gear and left the house, for an unknown fate that awaited them.

They grabbed bottles of water from cartons by the door, then the group filed out in a solemn mood. The van looked fairly new, which was unusual for the city. It was most likely used for tourist sightseeing. The gang must have a lot of money at their disposal or good connections, or maybe a little of both was Hai's impression. Upon entering the van, they noticed it was clean, well kept, and the leather seats looked inviting. Usually the seats in most vans had tears, stains, or both. The two extra hands the Masked Man needed were there sitting in the back. There was also more weapons and ammo stored in the van's rear, and there was seating for thirty-two people, eight rows of two on the right and left sides of the aisle.

Hai and Bui took the front two seats on the right side, and the rest spread out throughout the van. With everyone seated, the middle-aged driver started it up, put it in drive, and then van pulled away smoothly. Leaving the city behind, the road was not well kept, so the driving was slow. The two women were trying to sleep resting against each other, but the swerving around bad spots in the road and an occasional bump didn't help their sleep very much. The guys, except for the Masked Man, talked about their sexual escapades the previous day and what they were looking forward to doing that night after the day's business was completed.

A half an hour ride later, they had passed the old Marine enclave site by a half mile and pulled into a slight clearing along the side of a grove of trees that had a beaten foot path that led northeast to the sub-hamlet but stopped a little short of the sub-hamlet area. Before they debarked, they were each given a small plastic squeeze bottle of insect repellent and told to put it on now before the van door opened; then they were to lock and load their weapons.

The Masked Man informed them that the van and the driver would remain there until the entire situation was resolved. He reminded them they must remain quiet in their positions.

He gave them one more very important piece of advice. "If you must relieve yourselves, and I assume you will have to at some point during the day, crawl as quietly and far to the rear of us as you can, do your business, and quietly return to your position. That is a must for us to be successful! Do not under any circumstance fail me! I'm depending on you to do your very best and no less. My Cause is just and right, and it must not fail. The future of all Vietnamese rests on our actions today." He laughed as he looked at the guys and quirked, "No peeking at them guys! Our ladies are extremely bashful! Right ladies?" He laughed some more.

Hung felt really smug and mouthed off about the women. "Then they don't need to peek at us either." His comment wasn't appreciated. The Masked Man let the insult to the women slide because he knew the two geese weren't long for this world and it would just be useless and wasted verbiage to criticize them at this stage of the game. Bui wanted to say it wasn't big enough to spy on and besides she had no magnifying glass and tweezers to use if she had wanted to check it out, but thought better of it.

There was very little moon out. It was barely visible above the trees to the west. The sky was a little cloudy in spots and the night was extremely muggy, but the Masked Man seemed to see cat-like in the dark, as he led his crew through the trees and debris to their positions. As they moved forward slowly into the trees, as quietly as possible, one foot at a time to avoid ground clutter and noise, all of the usual night noises became silent, making it a little more eerie for the women who were not used to snooping and pooping through the trees, especially in the dark. They were all glad they had applied the insect repellent before getting off the van, as they were swarmed immediately on debarking.

The mosquitoes were out in huge swarms large enough to seem a solid mass in spots, and they seemed to be supersized. The Masked Man thought about how the Americans were always joking about mosquitoes big enough to land on air strips and of being refueled and rearmed by mistake. Dracula was another way to refer to them also. They were just miserable little blood suckers seeking their life's sustenance. Everyone knew that the night's mugginess would soon cause their sweat to wash away the repellent they had applied, so they made sure the bottle of repellent was placed within an easy reach and hoped one of those pests didn't fly off with it. The women had bloused their trousers when they had changed into their uniforms as the Masked Man had suggested to them and hoped they needn't worry about what might creep up their pant leg. They had creeped out when they were told what might be crawling around in the high grass. A woman couldn't be too careful with her body. She had too many places that could be invaded by un-wanted pests.

The two extra gang members were posted as flankers to the left and right, about 25 meters each from the main group, in order to keep any one from escaping the trap. The rest moved slowly into their positions and realized they had a good view across the field of whatever would happen between them and the abandoned building. The Masked Man must have had experience, as he had scouted the area and set their positions very well. They would not have too far to run at the targets when the trap was finally sprung.

The first tiny glimpse of light was just becoming visible over the trees far to the east, which meant the heat of the day was not far away. Now the wait had begun in earnest, and it was a more tedious for Hai and Bui than it was for the men. They squirmed as quietly as they could, as their prone positions on the slightly rough ground were not the most comfortable places on the earth.

Hai's biggest concern though, was whether or not her father's counter trap would succeed and carry the day. If it wasn't successful, who knew what fate would await her and Bui. Her body quivered thinking about what the Masked Man might do to her and Bui if he found out their secret.

CHAPTER 33

EVEN AFTER STUFFING THEMSELVES and imbibing the wine and mixed drinks the night before, the Americans all woke early and surprisingly had no hangovers or pounding headaches to speak of. Tolbane and Mai had fooled around a little before going through their morning rituals and later joined Parnell and Father Phat, who were already chowing down from the large breakfast buffet. Looking around the restaurant, Tolbane and Mai could see there were patrons of Caucasian, African, and Asian descents at the tables. All of them seemed to be enjoying their food and the atmosphere.

After their "Good Mornings" and "Hope you had a good night's sleep" banter to their friends, Tolbane and Mai went to the chow line. The large buffet area had two sections of steam lines. One was of American and European style foods, and one was for local fare. Mai got a plate, silverware, and napkins and selected the platter of fresh fruit and filled her plate with several fruit cubes that looked mouthwatering, while Tolbane filled his plate with a gob of bacon, three sausage paddies, a large spoonful of scrambled eggs, a heaping of hash brown potatoes, three pieces of toast, a few catsup and jelly packets, and a glass of orange juice. When the two sat down with Parnell and Father Phat, their coffee had already been poured by a waiter hovering over a three-table area. Once again, Tolbane made like a vacuum cleaner with his chow and Mai ate her fruit in a more ladylike fashion. Parnell and Father Phat couldn't help but enjoy watching Tolbane's food disappear, Hocus, Pocus, now you see it, now you don't.

When the food was gone, the group, the three guys sipping coffee and Mai, hot tea, talked about the sightseeing the day before and of the shopping they'd done. The fun part had been trying on and buying Vietnamese clothes along with conical hats. Mr. Ho had informed them that the best ways to be a little less bothered by the intense sun and heat were sunglasses, wearing the loose-fitting pajama-like Vietnamese garb, and wearing conical hats. Father Van Hai had also heartily recommended they wear them for today's trip to the patrol's burial site of the Jade Cross. All three guys agreed about the sun and heat in that area, as they had experienced it firsthand during the conflict. Mai didn't care for any strong sun and extreme heat; however, she would grin and bear it. Mai had had a good laugh when Tolbane tried on all black PJs and the shop owner giggled and told Tolbane he looked like a Viet Cong. "You VC! You VC!," he shouted, and Tolbane pointed his cocked finger at him and said "BANG!" The owner grabbed at his heart stumbled and laughed. It really had been a fun day for her and the guys, even when Tolbane reminded her why the female Vietnamese peasants along the road rolled up their one pant leg and asked if she would do it for him. The day might not be fun at all if she didn't.

As the four were getting ready to leave the table, Mr. Ho came in, grabbed a chair from another table, greeted the gang, and sat with them. The vigilant waiter quickly brought a pot of tea and a cup for him. The waiter must have been familiar with Ho, they thought. He wanted to remind them of the plans he had shared with them the previous night right before they had gone to bed, especially since they were a little looped. He reiterated the need to take and drink plenty of water and to always walk slowly in the sun and heat, as any unnecessary exertion would drain their strength, their body fluids, and could lead to hyperthermia and a possible heat stroke. The van they would ride in would be left only a little way east of the old enclave site, as the van could not travel well over the rough, irregular terrain. He and the driver of their van would be armed and would serve as their security, as the driver was one of his men and would go with them to the burial site. He assured them once more that the information they had acquired indicated that the trap was real, and was most likely in place already. He knew there was no intent to harm them at the site because the Masked Man wanted to torture them later, which was the key to successfully countering whatever had been planned for them, so he told them if and when they were confronted to show surprise, but not to be afraid.

"I repeat to you," he warned. "Please, do not do anything rash. His cohorts may not care whether you're taken alive or not. We know their players and their capabilities; they don't know ours. It's our terrain also. Remember this, many good things come to those who are patient enough to wait for them. Neither Sun Tzu nor Confucius said this, in case you're wondering about it. It's an Om Ho quote."

Tolbane thought aloud, as was his habit, "Someone's Gala Parade is damn sure going to be rained on today. I don't know who the heck said that!" He received the usual glares and shaking heads. When Mr. Ho was done with his briefing, he left to get ready, and the group went to their rooms to do the same. Tolbane wondered if at Christmas time they could call him, Ho! Ho! Ho!

As they walked to the elevators, Tolbane addressed the group with another of his nonsensical notions. "If we were playing charades and there were three Mr. Hos against the wall, what would you have?" His friends groaned a little and gave up. "You would have a statement by Santa Clause. Ho! Ho! Ho!" The two friends and Mai hurried along to separate themselves from him and pretended they didn't know him from Adam.

When they closed their room door, Tolbane wanted to diddle around with Mai while they were changing into their Vietnamese garb, but Mai gave him a slight kick in the shin as if to say, "Not now big boy" and informed him, "You need to get dressed right now, you big dumb dork!" Tolbane had selected all black PJs at the store, and Mai had chosen black bottoms and an ecru shade top. When she was dressed, she took the band from her pony tail and let her shining, black hair cascade over her shoulders and fall nearly to her shapely buns to protect her neck from the sun. She put on her conical hat and posed the sexiest pose she could and taunted Tolbane with her index finger like a siren while wiggling her hips. "You give me much Dong I lub you long time!" Tolbane looked at her and spoke very earnestly.

"Mai, of all the Vietnamese women, young and old, that I had to question and work with back then, and those I've seen other places, I never saw one that looked as beautiful as you in this type of clothes. In fact, you're the most beautiful and desirable woman I've ever known. If anything happens to me today, always remember that I love you so very much and that I could never find anyone who could come close to filling your shoes." Of course, speaking of shoes, he had to add, "Especially in those kick ass red pumps you lured me with."

Mai's eyes teared up, and she tilted her conical hat back and kissed and hugged him tighter than she ever had, and he responded the same. "I hope nothing ever happens to you Travis Tolbane. I couldn't live without you in my life. You've been my whole life and my love since I was ten years old. You took out my attacker and took my heart all at the same time. I think the tight black short leather skirt may have helped too. You were so horny it was very funny! And also, the way you banged your knee on the desk." They finally separated and Mai had to go rinse her face and dab just a little make up on. Then they went to the lobby to await the others.

Soon Parnell and Father Phat came down to the lobby looking like local peasants in their Vietnamese garb, and they all went outside. As Ho had informed them, the van was waiting in front of the hotel. The driver greeted them and stated that Ho would be there shortly. He loaded them into the van, which was only slightly nicer than the bus they had come to the city in, and then he showed them some large canteens in a pouch, each with a shoulder strap. He informed them that the canteens had been filled with water and placed in a freezer the night before, and by the time they left the van, they would have cool water to drink on their hike. To be on the safe side, he gave Tolbane and Parnell each a six shot 38 mm S&W pistol, loaded, a holster to clip on the inside of their pants in the back, and two loaded speed loaders. They had no problem clipping the holsters on, as the pajama pants sold to tourists had belt loops and they had bought belts with their pants. The two felt a little safer having a weapon just in case they ended ups needing it.

The driver continued, "I will be carrying a backpack, and it has some GI MRIs in it in case we need to eat lunch there. It also has a small first aid kit and some extra goodies in case they're needed. Remember you are not used to the Vietnamese sun and heat, wear your conical hat at all times, and protect your eyes from the sun with the sun glasses."

Ho arrived shortly after the lecture and the game was "afoot" as Sherlock would have said to Watson, and Tolbane reminded everybody of that. Parnell told Tolbane he had his foot cocked and he knew the exact spot where it was about to be placed a couple of times over. The driver started the van, the engine chugging a couple of times, and it began moving with a couple of jerks. The driver said he was sorry over his shoulder to them and related that he was not the usual driver of the rig. Once out of the city, he did his best to avoid bad spots in the road, although sometimes his best wasn't enough.

The group had tried to nap during the ride, but they were often roused by a jerk or a swerve of the van to avoid a rough spot or a bump in the road. It was a good thing the van wasn't driven fast or they would have thought they were riding in a blender set on puree. The driver, who had given his name as Nghia, hadn't told them that the springs were really bad on his friend's van. The suspension system as well as the tires, needed to be replaced also. He believed in that old saying about what you don't know can't hurt you! As he drove along, he also tried singing and old American GI song about "We gotta get out of this place" to cheer them up. Two billy goats in an a cappella duet would have carried a better tune than him.

As they approached the old enclave site, he made sure everyone was awake and informed them it would be a hard bump and a jolt while pulling off the road into the field and it would not be a good ride for a short distance. The group wondered what else was new. The van was good for nearly a bumpy mile when it stopped and Nghia intoned, "We got to get out of this van if it's the last thing we ever do! Guys there's a better path for me and you." Groaning at the driver's paraphrasing of the old song, they dismounted into the already torrid heat, a very bright sun, and a cloudless sky with no breeze at all. The sunglasses and conical hats were put on, and the canteens were quickly distributed. They lined up single file, with Mai third in line behind Ho in the lead and Tolbane second, the Priest, Parnell, and then the driver bringing up the rear, and they began their walk, slow and deliberate, not knowing if it would be their last one. They seemed to be in a determined, and predestined mood, and there was no chatter amongst them. Even Tolbane was mum.

After a quarter of a mile, Ho had guided them to the edge of a grove of trees with long limbs and plenty of leaves, and they walked in the tree shade for a little while until the grove ended. They plodded on, only stopping to swig a little water now and then. Finally, after plodding along slowly for nearly another hour, Ho stopped, gathered them into a group, and pointed to a building a way off and said, "That was to be the headquarters and office for building a village, and that was the village never came to be. That's where we're headed.

"You'll see that it's all boarded up now, as only one sub-hamlet named Binh Thoung #1 was ever formed back in the treed area. The building sits right on the spot where the old run-down hovel was when you found the Jade Cross. We expect the trap will be sprung from the tree line near it as we approach the burial spot, so be on your toes and really act surprised and don't look fearful when it happens. Drink some more water before we leave this spot. We still have plenty of water left in the canteens; however, I don't know when you'll get a chance to drink again till later. When you're ready to go on, just walk along as we have been, except we don't need to be in single file any more; just kind of straggle and poke along. We don't need to look like we're organized. Just walk and talk among yourselves as you normally would. Talk about anything except our plans.

Laughing is a plus for us. We have to look innocent and unsuspecting on our approach to the house. Don't forget. They are the ones who are going to be surprised today, not us." Tolbane and Parnell each gave him an "OOH RAH!" You can never take the Marine out of a Marine.

Before moving on, Father Phat led them to gather in a circle holding each other's hands and prayed that their almighty God would guide the outcome of their endeavor to take down an evil devil and deliver them safe and unharmed at the day's end. When the prayer ended, they all replied, "Amen!" and Father Phat made the sign of the cross. Each one of them then drank a lot more water, and they began to walk slowly onward toward the building and talk among themselves as normally as possible under the present circumstance.

At about a hundred feet from the building, they stopped and stared at it. Tolbane, Parnell, and Father Phat began to revisit orally how each of them remembered the event that brought them there, from the beginning of the patrol back in 1966 to the discovery of the buried Jade Cross and its reburial. This recounting of the events evoked strong emotions from the three men.

Mai listened to their story intensely; she could not help feeling herself becoming somewhat emotional too, even though she had heard their stories before. Being at the scene of the incident brought a realism to it she'd not felt before. Having walked to the spot in the sun and heat, she still could not quite picture how miserable and exhausted the men must have been wearing and carrying all of their arms and equipment in this torrid environment while patrolling several miles at a time, not knowing what destiny lurked ahead of them, life or death. She suddenly felt a new respect for the Veterans who had to fight and survive to fight another day in these elements. The men had started to drift closer to the building, and she drifted along with them, as relaxed as a noncombatant could ever be.

The trap was sprung when they were about 25 feet from the actual burial spot. A round was fired into the air, scaring them, and team of men and women in old ARVN uniforms carrying weapons, rifles, and pistols, led by the Masked Man brandishing a Vietnam era Colt Model 1911A1 45 cal. handgun, rushed from the tree line, shouting for them to surrender and put their hands in the air. Tolbane's group showed their surprise and did their best to look afraid while complying with the demands. They were instructed to sit on the ground with their hands over their heads, and they did. Then they were told to place their hands behind their heads and interlock their fingers.

Checking out the scene, Tolbane looked at the attackers from right to left and noticed that they had a good interval between them and were aligned in a third of a circle, as opposed to a full circle, so if they had to shoot, they wouldn't shoot each other. He thought it was a good tactic on their part. This Masked Man must have had some military training some time or other. Tolbane counted two women with 45 cal. handguns, six peons with rifles, and their masked leader with his 45. He hoped Father Van Hai knew what the hell he was doing.

The masked leader stood defiant in front of them and spoke arrogantly to them. "I have waited for what seems to be an eternity for this day to come, when I would have you, my hated ones, at my mercy, of which, of course, there will be none. I will have my vengeance on you Tolbane, the one who has defiled my true love Mai, whom I'll allow to watch me torture you, and you too, his so-called friends. You'll not be harmed tonight because I want you to think about all of the horrendous tortures you'll be experiencing in the next few days. You will scream and beg to die a hundred times before I'll allow death to spare you from more of my inflicted pain and agony. Your bodies will be broken, and your minds will become delusional, and you'll babble like mad men. You'll be amazed at my techniques that I have developed and savored with my victims for decades. If only the ghosts of those I'd partied with could rise from their graves and speak to you to tell you what you're in for. You wouldn't believe what they suffered until I begin on you. I may even use dull knives just for fun and games. That would be very interesting. I think I'll do just that. It will be a ball. However, before we go any farther with my desires, we have some other business to take care of." As he spoke to them, Tolbane, Mai, and Parnell thought the voice, distorted somewhat by the mask, was kind of familiar, but they couldn't place it.

He turned to Hung and Lam and directed them to step to one side and lay down their rifles, and they did so obediently, wondering what was happening. He spoke to them in a loud angry voice. "I have been displeased with you two geese from the very day I arrived here. Let me state my case against you. You're sloth-like and you're very lazy. You tortured and killed my staunch ally. You mistreated Bui badly by beating and raping her. You've constantly disagreed with everything I've said or done at every step of the way, plus you were overheard talking about getting rid of me and taking over once my Cause was on track. You two are despicable traitors to me and my Cause. You were informed of my penalty for failure or disobedience right from the get go when I arrived. I promised to you yesterday that you wouldn't have to worry about things like your rooms being taken again, being sent on all day assignments, and whatnot after today, and now I will keep my promise to you. As of now, I turn this situation over to my new Numbers One and Two, who will carry out my orders and execute your death sentences. I do not bid you a fond adieu. I hope your ancestors greet you with the displeasure you deserve. Okay Tam and Tuy, they are all yours now. I trust you to take care of our business with them and give them each a taste of our justice so we can proceed here."

Each of the two new Numbers gave an oral OK to him. Tam turned and looked at the loser, Hung, who, with eyes bulging, was trembling. He grinned and spoke quietly to him. "Listen carefully to me. I am now the Exalted One's Number One man. Guess what? You're Number Zero as of this moment! Get it? Oh! Excuse me. I mean, you're the Number One Corpse." He raised his rifle and shot Hung in the head, watched him fall to the ground without remorse, and turned to his cohort smugly. "It's your turn to obey our leader, my friend."

Obediently, Tuy nodded his head and followed suit with Lam, except he didn't state that he was Number Two until Lam too was dead. Then the two Numbers turned towards the Masked Man and bowed with their palms placed together in front of their faces. The Masked Man returned the bow and complimented them for their prompt actions.

The Masked Man now turned to Tolbane's group again. "As you can see, we are very efficient at handling our problems quickly and efficiently. My next problem is rescuing my one and only true love, the beautiful Mai, from he who has defiled her. That's you Tolbane, you the American Pig that I have hated for years. I have loved her deeply for so long, and I know in her heart she loves me too without knowing it. Her mind has been indoctrinated and corrupted over and over, day by day, by you Tolbane, and her body has been continually raped by her American swine, you! She'll come to her senses once she's with me and will soon realize where and with whom she belongs, and she will rule a united Vietnam with me by my side.

She will be the First Lady of the New and True Tran Hung Dao Dynasty. Mai, I want you to stand up, leave him where he's kneeling in the dirt like the puke he is, and walk here to me now."

Mai wasn't having an of it. "I've got one thing to say to you, you masked freak assed murderer. Fuck you and the plane you came over here on," was her staunch and derogatory reply. "You're one very sick bastard, you masked freak. You! You killed my step-brother, and you beat my friend Carly. You're a sick and deranged piquerist. You have to use a knife instead of your deformed dick. I'm not doing shit for you, you got that bitch?! You can go suck an egg, a rotten one, for all I care, or suck one of your male friends there for that matter!"

Taken aback at Mai's attitude, the Masked Man pointed his .45 at Tolbane's midsection and commanded her, "You see where my weapon is pointing? If you don't come here right now and stand beside me, I'll shoot your lover boy in the groin, hoping to hit his balls or something else, and then maybe shoot him in his foot or even his knee if I feel like it. Maybe even both if I so desire, so get your sweet ass over here by me,' NOW!' Woman!"

Mai was feeling really bitchy and angry now, but she had no choice but to comply with his demand. She couldn't let anything happen to Travis because of her anger and stubbornness, so she took her time, slowly and defiantly, and walked to the Masked Man's side, stopping about three feet away. Looking at him even more steadily and directly in the eyes, she spoke up. "Do anything you want with me, but I promise you that if you harm one hair on his head, I'll cut your cock and balls off and shove them down your fucking throat in a heartbeat!"

"My! My! My! Mai! You have turned onto one real feisty and desirable slut. I'll cleanse your mouth with my body fluid and make you come to your senses in no time. You'll be a real woman again when I'm through with your reeducation. Besides, Tolbane's destiny is not for you to decide. His fate has been decided by me a long time ago, and I can assure you that he will meet his fate slowly and painfully over the next few days. I know that you will be pleased to be allowed to observe me plying my trade on his worthless body and soul. I might even have you participate. That's a good idea. You can cut his balls off instead of me."

He demanded she come closer, and she defied him once again, stared directly into his eyes, stood her ground, and gave him a one finger salute. He laughed at her and gave her one back. He informed her that she would be locked in a closet for the night and could think about her future with him and forget the American while in it. He also let her know that she and he would consummate their future relationship the next day in a most pleasant and pleasing manner, many times over, and she would beg him for more.

Once again, she saluted him defiantly, this time with both of her middle fingers, and told him to go seduce himself by sticking his gun up his ass and pulling the trigger. This time, her salute and retort angered him, and he grabbed her left wrist and pulled her near. As she was pulled into him, she kneed his thigh with her right knee, grabbed his mask in her right hand, and began to pull at it. He released her wrist and tried to hold his mask on with both hands, dropping his .45, but he didn't quite make it. With a strong pull from both of her hands now, the mask came off and she looked him straight in the eyes. The captured ones were shocked and at a loss for words when they saw his face.

Suddenly Mai, realizing what enigma was standing in front of her, dropped the mask to the ground and stood there with her tears quickly streaming over her cheeks as she screamed out at him, "My God Ba! You're not dead?

You're alive! You dirty son of a bitch! You fucking ass hole! What the fuck have you done to us? I'll kill you, you fucking piece of shit!" She doubled up her fists and started hitting his face and kneeing him on any place she could. By the look on his face, it was obvious that Ba was not expecting her sudden, vicious assault, and he began backing away from her onslaught. He had already dropped his gun and was trying to block her kicks and grab her arms at the same time. He had forgotten about everything else, which was a mistake.

Then everything began to happen all at once when Mai attacked Ba. Hai and Bui had moved over behind Tam and Tuy while the Masked Man was making a scene with Mai, and when she attacked him, the two women placed their .45's at the base of the two bandit's necks, forcing them to drop their rifles. Several policemen came out of the woods with their weapons at the ready and got the drop on the flankers. The one inch–thick sheet of plywood covering the window of the building dropped down, and two rifles were pointed from it. The two flankers had been taken by the police, and the other two gangsters, not liking their odds with the weapons pressed against their necks, had already dropped their rifles and put their hands in the air and were on their knees. The threat they had presented had been permanently neutralized.

Tolbane, wasting no time, sprang to his feet and ran to help Mai and vent his own anger on the dirty little bastard. When he closed on Ba, he swung a long roundhouse right, catching him on the right side of his mouth, catching and breaking his nose, shredding his lips, and knocking some teeth loose. Ba went down on his back, and Tolbane was instantly atop him with his knee in Ba's gut, pummeling away on him. Mai was simultaneously kicking Ba wherever she could find an open spot, mostly in the ribs, even though she wanted to stomp on and destroy his balls. Ho, Nghia the driver, and three of the policemen moved in and had their hands full pulling the two off of the now-defunct and beaten Masked Man. Parnell didn't move to help break up the fight. In fact, he was cheering them on. He was enjoying watching Ba getting his ass handed to him on a platter as he deserved, especially by Mai. She had a wicked left hook. Father Phat also heartily approved of the beating Tolbane and Mai were dishing out to Ba. Normally he wouldn't condone any fighting at all, but this one was different, and he shouted, "Hallelujah! There is a God in heaven after all."

After the men had a brief struggle with Tolbane and Mai, the two finally settled down. Their adrenaline had subsided somewhat, and they both felt weak in the knees. Mai, still quivering and sobbing, threw herself into Tolbane's arms and cried like her world had collapsed around her. He held her tight with one arm and pulled her conical hat off with the other, stroked her hair, and comforted her as much as possible. He was really proud of her taking Ba down. She truly is a one of a kind woman. Mai, sobbing and trembling, wondered how this shit could have happened to her. Suffering all of the sadness and despair of losing a loved one only to find out she had been betrayed by him was too much to bear. Now her love for her step-brother had turned to a sheer hatred for him.

She had always looked up to him as being kind, gentle, friendly, and willing to help anyone who was in need. He was always the big brother figure. Now she despised him and the ground he walked on. Further hate for him kept manifesting inside of her. She didn't understand how he could deceive her or how he could have done all of these horrible things to people, mostly innocent and defenseless girls and women. She had never known there was a monster in the Nguyen family until now. He was a bigger monster than Vlad Dracul or Jack the Ripper. She looked up at Tolbane.

As her sobs and body's quivering subsided a bit, she suddenly realized something was very wrong with this situation. For sure, certain new facts changed the whole scenario for her. "Damn it Travis! I have a serious question for you. Think about this! Since Ba is really alive, just who the hell was the guy who was tortured, murdered, and staked out in his house? Why was that guy sacrificed like that to begin with? Why would this asshole go to all the trouble to deceive us then try to kill you guys?"

"First off, I don't know why he despised and wanted to kill us. Second, I have no idea who the hell it was or why he was killed, Mai. Parnell and I have made a very big mistake in our identification by thinking it was Ba for sure. The body was cut and the face peeled beyond recognition. When Parnell and I saw the area where Ba's Snoopy Dog cartoon tattoo would have been, we saw that the skin had been sliced from the dead guy's arm to hide his being identified, so we were certain it was Ba. That's why the coroner didn't try to identify the corpse. Everyone relied on Parnell's and my IDs. The coroner can't reexamine the body to ID the guy now since he's now ashes. So, we'll never know who it was unless the coroner kept organ samples he can test. Even then, we may never know who it was. It could very well have been some random guy off the street, a gang member that screwed up, or an enemy of his. Who knows where he came from, or why Ba faked his death! I'll have Parnell email a sitrep to the MNPD to advise the coroner about it."

Meanwhile, the police had rolled Ba over on his stomach and cuffed his hands behind his back then rolled him to his side so he could breathe easier. The four gangsters, aided by Hai and Bui, were already cuffed and on the ground, bitching at each other for being taken by surprise. Two policemen, locked and loaded, were guarding them.

Father Van Hai had moved quickly from the apparently deserted block building and checked on Ba's physical condition. He had already called to the two police medics who were waiting in the sub–hamlet and instructed them to hurry to the scene. He felt no sympathy for the Masked Man at all; in fact, he'd like to cut his heart out and make him eat it, not only for the way he had abused Hai and Bui, but also for the horrible mutilating deaths and crimes he had committed during the conflict. It was Nguyen Van Hai's calling though to care for the sick, injured, and downtrodden instead of seeking vengeance.

Ba was moaning, groaning, and crying out from his pain. Blood was flowing from his nose, and he kept spitting blood from his mouth to keep from choking on it. His face looked like it had gone through a meat grinder at least two or three times. Tolbane had done a thorough job on him. With the blood still running from Ba's mouth, Father Van Hai couldn't tell if he had broken ribs and internal injuries from Mai's kicks or what. He decided that he could leave that decision to the medics. They knew more about injuries than he did. He nodded to the police officers to take over and walked away from the scene. He had other things to address.

CHAPTER 34

Walking away after checking on Ba's condition, Father Van Hai, finding he really didn't really feel concerned about it at all, went to Tolbane and Mai, who were being hugged and congratulated by Parnell and Father Phat in a most emphatic way. Begging their pardon, he joined the group. Grinning slyly, he spoke softly to Mai, but loud enough for all to hear, "I hope I never, ever, piss you off, my lady! I don't want to get my butt kicked or my nuts cut off any time! Those punches wouldn't do my face any favors either." By now, Mai's tears were slowing down. She was gaining her composure somewhat and smiled back at him and kind of giggled a little.

"Seriously young lady," he then complimented Mai on her actions. "I thought you were magnificent the way you handled that psycho, sadistic, and savage beast. That took real courage for you to stand up to him like you did. You're quite something else, as you Americans are fond of saying; an exceptional individual. I liked your saucy verbiage too. There's no way I could have planned your reaction to him in any way, shape, or form. You played him so well. You are one exceptionally strong woman. Please tell me, just how were you able to stand and defy him that way?"

"I didn't want him hurting Travis or the others, and you had told us we needn't worry because we wouldn't be harmed here today. I was expecting you to come to our rescue at any time, so I just let myself go 'Ape Shit,' as my dear hunk of a man would say. I just let my emotions take over any fear I might have had. I hated the no-good Masked Ass and wanted to know what the psycho prick looked like without his friggen mask on. I really did lose it the rest of the way when I saw it was my dearly departed step-brother Ba under the mask. I don't really know why I didn't feel any fear when I grabbed for his mask, nor when I starting hitting him. It just happened because suddenly my love for Ba turned into a ferocious hatred for the worthless rat bastard. I really think I wanted to kill him with my bare hands and chop him up like he did his victims, starting with his worthless balls. Speaking about my bare hands, my knuckles hurt, but it does feel good for my present disposition. There is one other thing though. I'll never forget the punch that Travis threw at him. It sure sent that scumbag flying on his ass." Mai was on a roll now. "I do wish that more of Ba's ribs were sticking out from under Travis so I could have gotten in a few better kicks. I feel bad I couldn't get a good kick at his balls."

"I should have sprung our counter trap much quicker than I did, but it was most intriguing watching you in action. You were like Wonder Woman and Supergirl morphed into one. I kept saying to myself, 'Yes! Yes! You go girl!' You are a great warrior Mai, no matter what motivated you at the time. I'm sure your boyfriend was very proud of you today."

"As it is, you got in some good, solid kicks. He's going to have a few sore ribs for quite a spell. You did a good job on him. So, did Travis. I won't ever forget that first roundhouse punch he threw either. Ba's face and nose look like mincemeat, almost as if he had run it through a grinder. I know you four have many questions to ask me about the situation here. You want to know how today's victory against those geese was possible. So, let's go over there and sit in the shade of the trees, and I will explain to you what took place today."

The four walked to the near tree line and stood in the shade beneath its trees' leaves. Father Van Hai motioned to a couple of guys looking out of the building's window. They nodded, disappeared from the window, and brought out folding chairs, a table, and large glasses of tea with chunks of ice in them that they set in front of each person. They also brought out a dish of sliced lemons for the tea, a tray of sweet Vietnamese pastries, and some napkins. When the guys left, Van Hai explained that they were volunteers from the sub-hamlet here and didn't mind doing any task asked of them. Tolbane felt his old prisoner was on top of everything.

"First let me say I liked the way you three guys kept your composure throughout the ordeal. I know it took discipline as well as patience to do so. I know, Tolbane, that you were tempted to do something, as you say, do something even if it's wrong. It allowed the Masked Man to concentrate on Mai just long enough for her to become enraged and spring into action. It worked to perfection. To trigger our response to the situation, the two women, Hai and Bui, and the police had instructions to intervene at the first sign of violence to any of you. Mai, without your knowing it, you became the trigger that launched them into action. Your temper tantrum did the trick. Their response was even faster and more coordinated than I expected it to be, as the bandits were engrossed in watching you and that worthless piece of human protoplasm. Now, I'm very sure you all are very curious as to how we happened to have tea and pastries in the seemingly vacant, boarded up, and deserted building in the middle of nowhere. Have patience while I spin you my story, and then I shall enlighten you not only about the Jade Cross, and the building, but how my trap was developed and worked to a T.

"The next day after that patrol in 1966, the Americans sent me to the ARVN District headquarters as a VCS, a Viet Cong Suspect, not a VCC. Tolbane, you sent a favorable report along with me. When I arrived there, I chose to go into the Chieu Hoi Program, so I rallied as I wanted to be free of the Viet Cong forever. I had no problem getting into it because of your favorable report and was sent to the Chieu Hoi Center in Da Nang. While there, I became very concerned for the relic because I had become the caretaker of it, and I felt since its location had been compromised, it must be moved. The Jade Cross had been handed down through generations, from father to son. It was passed to my father to be the caretaker for it and he had passed it on to me when he became too old to protect it. I'm the one, by the way, who buried it by the run-down hovel when I decided I wanted to have no more of the VC, the fighting, and the atrocities and allowed myself to be captured by a Marine patrol. I was able to contact some old, close friends I could trust and had them remove the Jade Cross and hide it elsewhere. Once I knew that the Jade Cross was safe, I was able to begin working to build a new life for myself, one with a bright future I had hoped.

"When I was released from the Chieu Hoi program, I married a wonderful woman, and we had a beautiful little girl and named her Hai after me instead of Mot for Number One daughter. My wife became sick about a month or so after the birth and passed on about three months later. Her illness was not caused by giving birth to my daughter, but I never really knew what it was. The doctors we had then had only experiences with war wounds and simple medical problems. They didn't have a long extensive medical training period like they have today."

"I took care of my daughter as best I could. After the conflict with the North was over in the spring of 1975, I searched my soul day in and day out, as I was conflicted as to my calling. I eventually turned to Christ. It was then that my life was at last content and meaningful. My friends helped me raise Hai for a couple of years while I studied theology and until I was ordained a priest and given a small parish. I was then able to care for Hai on my own. Then I was approached by certain elders, whom I will not name, who reminded me of my duties as the protector of the Jade Cross and the leader of many patriots, and it was accepting those responsibilities which has led me to the position I hold today as a leader of a fine organization and great patriots.

As Father Van Hai was relating his tale, he halted midsentence as the two women, Hai and Bui, still in their uniforms and side arms, brought over folding chairs and joined the group. Tolbane and Parnell, as well as Father Phat, couldn't help but notice that both women were very good looking and shapely to boot. They looked really sexy in their uniforms, smiles, and long hair pulled back into pony tails. When they were seated, a young man brought them tea with a chunk of ice also. The two had helped the policemen bind and secure the gangsters and when they were no longer needed there, they decided to join the group and meet the Americans they had seriously risked themselves for.

Father Van Hai greeted them and introduced them to the group. He explained to the Americans how his daughter Hai had infiltrated the faux No Name and supplied information on their plans and activities to him. He explained how Hai had recruited the young Bui to join her in her mission. He told how his daughter, as well as Bui, had to undergo many abuses by the Masked Man, the two geese, his followers, and then his new henchmen. "They are very strong women like you are Mai. Hai endured all the hardships and fears without complaining, and how her endeavors with Bui's help were instrumental in your survival and ending a reign of terror today, not only here today, but in your country too. I'm very proud of her, as a father should always be, and I'm proud of Bui too for that matter. They are a good team; they learned to work great together and have become fast friends. I will have many future plans in our operations for them. I know they will serve with honor."

Hai and Bui were a little embarrassed by Father Van Hai's praise, their faces showing some pride. Their cheeks reddened somewhat, and the thanks offered to them by the Americans caused their eyes to water, even a small tear flowing down their cheeks. Mai, her heart pounding with gratitude, rose from her chair, stepped to the two young women, and greeting them with the Vietnamese custom of addressing them respectfully as "Hai Ba Chi Em."[36] The Trung sisters had defeated the Chinese and reigned from 39 – 42 AD, and gave each a big hug and a kiss on the cheek and let them know they'll always be in her heart.

Continuing, Van Hai related further, "Even before Father Phat called me from Carthage, MO, and told me what transpired there, I had heard of the dastardly events happening to you in Nashville. There are a few compatriots of mine in the Vietnamese community there who keep me informed periodically of their transitions into the American way of life. The things that were happening there were very disturbing to them, and they kept me well informed of the foul events as they happened. Father Phat kept me updated

---

[36] Showing respect to the Trung Sisters

on the situation from the time he was rescued by your guys until you arrived here.

I worked closely with the Hoi An Police Department to trap this monstrous killer by keeping them informed when it became clear from Hai's information that he would come here to this site to ambush you. The police were not able to assist me by instituting a criminal investigation until a crime was committed here. Even though they had the report on the murders from the Hong Kong Police, there was no warrant issued for him by them yet. They had to identify him and then have probable cause for his arrest before charging him with the brutal murders of those poor women in Hong Kong.

When the young girl's mutilated body and later on the three boys' bodies were found, and with Hai's suspicions, they were able to institute an official investigation into him. With their help, we developed this plan for his capture based on Hai's and Bui's information, the fact that he had been here just a few years before looking for the Jade Cross, and what we learned from the surveillance I had instituted. His vanity helped too because he thought he was smarter than everyone else. He never considered that someone's strong emotions could bring him down to the low life he is. I'm so very sorry we couldn't save the mutilation of the girl or the three boys. Those deaths will haunt me and my followers for the rest of our natural lives. At the very least, no other women here or elsewhere will suffer from his obsession.

"According to my sources, Ba will be imprisoned and held here and will be charged with the mutilations of the girl and the boys, your kidnapping at gun point, conspiracy against the government, and whatever else the police can come up with to pin on him. I'm sure there will be legal wrangling from Hong Kong, Honolulu, and Nashville about who will try him first and whether our government will extradite him."

"I don't have the slightest idea when he'll be tried here for the young ones' deaths or extradited to which place. When he is tried, he will be facing the death penalty here and those places when it's all done. Two of the gang members will be prosecuted for kidnapping and the murders of the girl, the boys, and the two geese post haste. The other two will be tried for attempted kidnapping at the very least. I just wish we could just execute the scum bags, but, International Laws will prevail, even if it takes years.

"Now, my friends, for the coup de grâce I want to show you what was at the heart and fervor of his conspiracy to take over the country and his madness about his being the reincarnation of Tran Hung Dao. Come with me now to the seemingly abandoned and deserted building and receive an only once in a life time occasion! Very few people have been allowed to experience what you are about to behold. What you are about to witness I beseech you to never speak of it. I'm sure I needn't ask you to swear an oath!" Each nodded that they understood.

He led the three men and three women to the door of the building and paused, explaining, "There were never any plans for a village to be developed here, and this building was not to be an office for it; it was a major deception on my part. The sub-hamlet, Binh Thoung #1, was formed mainly to protect this building, what it contains, and what it could mean for Viet Nam one day. The residents of the sub-hamlet are mostly former government workers, former military, or former policemen and their families. They have vowed an oath to protect what is contained inside of this door and protect it with their lives if it is necessary.

This morning, the Hoi An Police were already posted in the sub-hamlet waiting when the Masked Man and his crew arrived in the area. At the same time, a search warrant was served at his house by the HAPD. If the Hoi An Police had not gotten involved here, the people in the sub-hamlet would have done the task for us without question. As it is, they stood ready to back up our play and protect you if it was needed.

"Listen very closely my friends. When I open this door, please walk right in and you'll understand what drove your step-brother further into his psychotic and sadistic madness. The instrument he needed to fulfil his cursed Cause, the very thing that has caused many deaths by him and your angst, is right this way"

Mai entered the door first, followed by the rest, and she was awe stricken and short of breath. There were 21 folding chairs set in three rows of seven facing the back wall, a small storage closet in each of the two far corners, a sink and a counter, a small storage cabinet, and a small table in the southwest corner with a hot plate and a cooler. Centered against the back wall was an altar with a row of candles on top. To the right of it stood a statue of Christ, and to the left of it was a statue of the Mother Mary. Above the altar, the Jade Cross was affixed to the center of the wall. Looking at it was mesmerizing.

The Jade Cross had a brilliant green sheen and the jewels sparkled, especially the large ruby in the center that cast out a crimson aura, and it seemed to radiate a peace and serenity for all to behold. It was a magnificent sight that couldn't be imagined in anyone's dream. Mai wasn't the only one left breathless due to its spell. It seemed like everyone in the room had momentarily stopped breathing. Each and every person in the room also seemed to be humbled and at a loss for words in its presence, and each made the sign of the cross and knelt before it. Father Van Hai prayed aloud in the name of Jesus that this Jade Cross would remain a symbol of goodness and mercy in their hearts, souls, and prayers until passing on to the Great Beyond.

They remained kneeling and were very quiet for a long period of time. As they knelt, the Americans felt a calm realization that their quest to stop the mad man was at last finally over, and they could start their lives anew. No more fears of the unknown that had plagued their thoughts and fears for days on end. Now they would be safe to continue forward without concern for their very own lives. They had sought out an evil and they had conquered that evil. Yes! For them, they had their answers now and it was finally over.

After their wondrous experience in the presence of the Jade Cross, they watched as the criminals were stumbling while being hauled off towards several Hoi An Police vehicles waiting at the old enclave site. Once again, they sat in the shade of the trees, drinking iced tea and eating sweet pastries for a while longer, prolonging their time to start their own long walk back to their waiting van. Father Van Hai asked Mai, tongue in cheek, "Tell me Mai, do you want me to call the medics and find out what Ba's condition is for you?"

"Let me say this to you, Father Hai, very plain and simple! If you call the medics to find out his condition, I'm sure I can find a very sharp knife somewhere around here and guess what I'll do with it." Father Van Hai nearly fell off of his chair he was laughing so hard. The rest thought it was funny too. "Truthfully, the way I feel as of now, I don't give a rat's butt about his condition or if he stays alive. He chose to ignore the feelings of those who loved him and killed who is probably an innocent man to further his murderous agenda. He even severely beat and raped a woman who adored him as a friend. He tried to have my husband and our friend beaten and killed. He wanted to make me a love slave even though we are from the same mother. No! I have absolutely no feelings for him as a human being now. He's just a vicious animal that belongs in a cage or euthanized. He can be castrated and eat dog poop and rat turds the rest of his life as far as I'm concerned. He'll never get what he deserves."

The Americans had wondered where Ho and Nghia had gotten to, and Father Van Hai noted that that they always seemed to be invisible for some reason, but if they were needed anywhere they would appear instantly. Suddenly, as if by magic, the two appeared out of nowhere at the table. They could not but help themselves in praising Mai's actions against her step-brother. They also offered their congratulations on the day's outcome. Nghia took off his backpack, took out an MRI for each one, passed them around, and commented, "I thought you might need some reinforcement before we head to the van." It didn't take long before the MRI's were consumed and the group grabbed their canteens and made ready to go hiking. They gave their goodbyes to Father Van Hai, Hai, and Bui.

Then at the last second before they walked away, Tolbane finally put his nagging thoughts together and pulled Father Van Hai a few feet aside from the rest. He hesitated a minute, and, speaking quietly so they couldn't be overheard by the others, he spoke to him, "Father Van Hai, something has been bothering me since we met you at the restaurant and you updated us on the surveillance of the Masked Man your men had conducted. This something kept bothering me, and for the life of me I couldn't come up with an answer until now. It just hit me like a lightning bolt."

"What is it my friend? What's troubling you at this hour?"

"The photos are what bothered me, the ones that were taken of him by your men that you said were profiles and you couldn't make an ID from. You knew what his identity was the whole time, didn't you?"

Father Van Hai grinned at him a bit and did not respond immediately, so Tolbane continued on: "You knew all along the identity of the Masked Man because you saw him at the Captive Collection Point because he was my interpreter, and he was also on the patrol with us! You knew it was Ba, didn't you, and you deliberately kept this from us!"

Father Van Hai smiled at him. "I underestimated you Tolbane. I didn't think you'd ever figure it out. I didn't want to upset Mai at that time by telling her that her vicious step-brother was alive, was a serial killer, and that it was him you all were after. We needed her to be her normal self. Had she known, her whole demeanor may have been different. I knew she would be shocked eventually, and she didn't need that until it was all over and done with. I'll be very truthful about it. Her reaction to his identity was not part of my plan as I informed you. She was not to know his identity until after he was captured for her own peace of mind until then. I believed this was the right path to take."

"You're absolutely right! Thank you, Father! It'll be our secret. Mai will never hear it from my sealed lips. I don't need super glue to seal them."

"Go now Travis Tolbane. Go with your friends, and your' marvelous woman, and God bless you all. See you later when we party tonight." Tolbane moved back to Mai's side and placed his arm around her shoulder.

The group left the building site after one more look at the magnificent Jade Cross, walking very slowly as they had earlier. They were all in great anticipation of the coming evening. Father Van Hai promised them that they would party the whole night through, and they needed to get a good afternoon's rest beforehand. Mai's men were also in anticipation of having a party and of seeing Hai and Bui out of those uniforms and in appropriate party clothes. Tolbane, with his mind clearer now for the first time in days, once again started thinking, even hoping about the possibility, that the two women might wear Daisy Dukes and halters like, Daisy Duke or even like Mary Ann and Ginger wore on Gilligan's Island.

The group trudged away from the building site one step at a time, at an even slower pace than the morning's hike. They were feeling resistance and fatigue from their bodies with each and every step. Nghia was the exception. Even with the backpack on, he seemed to be in excellent physical condition and enjoying the walk as a matter of fact. Finally, to their relief, they reached the van and the hike was over. Once all were in the van, everybody except for Nghia the driver was exhausted from the day's activities and fell deeply asleep. They weren't even bothered by the vehicle hitting ruts and swerving during the drive back and didn't awaken until the van stopped at their hotel with a screech of brakes and a jerk, jolting the occupants awake from their deep sleep, nearly throwing them from their' seats. Nghia explained once again to anyone who might be listening or giving a hoot, "I'm not the regular driver of this van."

The group couldn't wait to get to their rooms. Their first actions were to shed the Vietnamese clothes, as they were dirty, sweaty, and beginning to stink with the foul order of sweat. The next thing in order was to take long, hot, cleansing showers, letting the hot water sooth their tired and aching muscles. Once this task was accomplished, Parnell and Father Phat jumped into their twin beds and immediately went into a well-earned deep sleep.

Tolbane and Mai, having showered together, now lay on their sides facing each other with an arm over the other's shoulder. Their mood was somewhat solemn. First, they discussed how wonderful it was that no harm had come to the other. They then spoke to the issue of her step-brother and the effect his depraved and evil actions will have on their future, long term. Even though they had passed the point of danger by Ba, the betrayal and the shame he caused would always be with them as long as they lived. Tolbane being Tolbane and Mai being Mai, they began kissing and fondling each other slowly and then passionately. Finally, Mai couldn't stand it any longer and let her feelings out to Tolbane.

"Travis! I need you! Heal me, please! Make love to me now!" He didn't hesitate to obey her desire nor her demands.

A while later, after having had a short nap, Mai was thinking about their maddening and mind-blowing lovemaking session between them confessed her recent feelings and her suspicions to Tolbane. She had been mulling over how to tell him for a few days because of the situation and was a little ashamed and felt somewhat guilty for not telling him that she'd missed a period. "Travis, I really need you to listen closely to what I have to say, and don't be flippant about it. This is the most important thing I've ever had to tell you about us. I have felt almost queasy in my stomach the last few days Travis. You need to know that I think I'll be getting sick in the mornings as days go on, possibly for a few months. Travis, I think I'm…!"

"You think you're what? Why do you think so?"

"I'm not a good secretary!"

"What's not being a good secretary got to do with it?"

"Well, my dumb dork lover. Think of it this way. A really good secretary working under a good boss never skips a period! Period!"

"You mean I might be a father?"

"Well, it's not a stone-cold fact yet; however, this time I feel it's for real! If it's real, then you will be a father to beat all FATHERS." She placed his hand on her stomach. Before long you'll be able to feel it kick.

"Oh my god, Mai! I don't know what to say, what to do, or what to say! How the hell do you be a father?"

"Well! My precious hunk of a man, just hold me close for starters! Dads do that to mamas too!" With his head swirling around in the clouds, he did. Tighter than ever before.

Later, not saying anything about Mai's suspected condition, saving it until it could be confirmed, they met Parnell and Father Phat at the party. It started slow with Father Nguyen Van Hai and Father Phat's speeches of their success that day, and even Mai was asked to address the revelers that included people they had not seen before but that had been involved in the success. It turned out to be nearly an all-night affair with food, drink, and a Vietnamese band with two go-go dancers that played 1965-1975 music. It was performed nonstop except for a break for other entertainment now and then. There were some Vietnamese dancers, male and female, who performed traditional Vietnamese dances for the gathering. Although frowned on by the current government, the partiers even danced with each other to different kinds of music. It was a surprise that the Vietnamese knew American dancing.

Parnell and Father Phat took turns dancing slow ones with Hai and Bui. Tolbane and Mai couldn't be separated unless someone chopped their arms off. Tolbane wasn't disappointed that Hai and Bui's choice of dress was not what he had hoped for. No Daisy Dukes and halters this night. They wore the traditional Vietnamese áo dài (long dress). They both wore long white pants, with Hai wearing a light blue long dress and Bui wearing a light green one. The gowns most assuredly didn't detract from their beauty or bosoms, nor did their long, sleek black hair falling from their beautiful faces to their divine derrieres. Tolbane was still on cloud nine and enamored over Mai's condition, and he didn't even dream of the two women and back flips.

The next two days were split between resting, shopping and sightseeing, and festive dinners for the Americans and their new Vietnamese friends. It was finally time to go home and part with a culture they had begun to love. The afternoon they left, they said goodbye to their friends in front of the hotel. The women all shed tears, and the guys shook hands and slapped each other on the back. Tolbane got in the last word as they once again loaded their gear onto the same bus in which Ho had brought them to Hoi An City and would return them to the same Da Nang hotel. He was the last one aboard, and as he waved to his Vietnamese compatriots, he said to them, "Someone once said or wrote, 'Parting is such sweet sorrow!' We are living proof it really is!"

The bus door closed, they were on their way home at last and the adventure was finally beginning to end. This time they didn't mind the damaged seats and the rough ride. Then after dealing with flight layovers in Hong Kong and Honolulu and briefing law enforcement officers in both places on the events involving them in Hoi An City in order that the correct criminal charges could be made along with extradition procedures against Ba could begin, they were flying on their journey's last leg.

After going through customs and collecting their luggage, Father Phat left them in San Francisco, CA, to spend some time with a friend living in San Francisco that he'd met at the Marian Days in Carthage MO a few years before. They bade him a fond farewell with hand-shakes and hugs, promising to keep in touch with each other always, and the trio boarded their last plane for their flight home. They had just flown past the Little Rock, Arkansas, area, a way to the south of them, and were becoming antsy to get home. They were dead tired of traveling and felt fatigued from it.

They were getting so tired of flying they were getting antsy, when at last, there was an announcement by the Captain that cheered them up. "We are now nearing our final approach to our Nashville destination, BNA, about ten minutes away. Please place your seats in the upright position, stash your items in the overhead storage or in the pocket on the seat in front of you, and fasten your seat belts. Thank you for flying with Delta Airlines today."

The shapely flight attendant, that all three guys had noticed favorably, was walking up and down the aisle checking loose items, passenger seat positions, and seat belts. They heard the welcoming screeching of the landing gears lowering into place. It was a sweet music to their ears. Then the plane was on the ground at last.

The plane taxied up the tarmac to the Nashville, TN, BNA airport terminal; Tired as they were, they deplaned, gathered up their luggage, and knew it was all over for real. It was really over. No more looking over their shoulders for real. They left the terminal for the long-time parking area, got into Tolbane's Marine Corps Green Machine and sped off. The drive, with only one stop to drop Parnell off, was only 20 minutes away from home for Tolbane and Mai.

EPILOG OF TOLBANE AND MAI

FIVE YEARS AFTER THEIR return from Vietnam Mr. and Mrs. Travis Tolbane were closer than ever. They had been married by their Priest friend, Father Phat two months after their return from Viet nam. They were happy as two pigs in a blanket. Their daughter, Mai Rose, was born a month early, was four and a half years old and Travis Jr. was three and a half. Mai called them Ding and Ling because sometimes they were ding-a-lings. She was so happy and content. The dogs, Rant and Rave were now house dogs and their replacements, Tried and True stayed in the yard most of the time. All four dogs loved playing with the kids, causing them to howl with laughter. There was no way any woman alive could be any happier than she was. Travis finally retired from work a year and a half before. Now days he just volunteered his time helping veterans whenever he could.

She thought back to the episode in Vietnam. It was so shocking to her about what her step-brother had done to so many people, especially her and Travis, and the kind of monster he became. The betrayal was horrific, the faking of his death in particular. The identity of the man murdered for the farce was never discovered. After returning and marrying Tolbane, the situation really depressed her at times. For some stupid reason she somehow blamed herself because the dumb ass step-brother of hers had made the situation all about her as well as killing those close to her, the Jade Cross and having a revolution in Vietnam.

Before the climax of the situation, she had thought she was pregnant even before they went to Vietnam, but she was waiting to tell Travis when she was sure. She was so torn inside that she feared she would lose the baby. She thanked her lucky star that she didn't. She hated herself too because she was so hurt, moody and of the way she was treating her friends and lover, her Husband. Sometimes she thought about ending it all. When the baby started kicking and Travis refusing to become angry over her tirades and his gentle touches were finally reaching into her soul, it helped her to be come alive and be the whole person she was, anew. By the time Mai Rose was born she realized that she really had not known her step-brother, Ba, at all; nothing was her fault and she should not have put such a burden on herself and those she loved. She had to admit that Carly and Parnell were very patient with her too. From then on, life was peaches and cream again.

She had taken computer courses at Nashville Tech and soon became enthralled with the internet. She bought the best Dell computer and the best HP printer she could and set herself up a small office space. An interest in Ancient Vietnamese History developed because of the Jade Cross situation and she researched as much of it as was available on the net. Hai's father didn't tell them very much of the No Name history as it is a secret society. Once in a while she might find some reference in the library to Tran Hung Dao and a secret society in another century. None of the literature she researched was really explicit about the society.

She was amazed one day when she found the story of two lovers named Troung Van Ba and Tran Thi Mot, on the internet, and their retrieval of the Jade Cross and their journey to deliver it to Nguyen Hai, and of the No Name Society. They had three boy children and died together holding hands. They had thought Ba was blowing smoke about the No Name, Father Hai's indicating he was No Name, but it did exist at one time and was no longer viable, according to the data she amassed, but she knew better, it was still alive, well, and in good hands; the kin of Nguyen Hai.

Ba had claimed he was the reincarnation of Tran Hung Dao, and the slab of jade was given to him, but maybe he was descended from Troung Van Ba instead. Who knows, after all, they shared the same first name, Ba. She laughed at her own humor. Ba was a name for Number Three Son. The story of the two lovers really touched her heart. The hardships and then living the wonderful life they earned, and in a way it paralleled her and Tolbane's lives because of the Jade Cross. Both Couples had an arduous journey and lived a happy life thereafter. After drying her eyes, at the way they passed away she couldn't help but, to cry a little more, she could hardly wait for Travis to get home so she could relate the story to him. Of course now she also had another big story for him and he'd be floored. She was pregnant with their third child. She wondered why people thought old men couldn't produce.

Tolbane, on the return from Vietnam, was pretty emotional about the way it turned out and what it had done to Mai. He really wanted to go back to Vietnam and beat that son-of-a-bitch Ba to death. It wasn't so much that he had been duped and attacked by his thugs, but to covet his own step-sister and murder so many to satisfy his perversions, and reach his idiotic goal was the lowest of the low. After all of the years he thought Ba was his friend and the grief caused over his phony death was mind boggling. Now Parnell, Carly and he kept an eye on Mai as best they could. No one wanted her to lose the baby. He stayed calm, cool and collected at home but it was dragging him down. He threw himself deeper into his job at the mall and began working longer hours. He found himself, sometimes, being cruel to shoplifters and other law breakers, not physically, but much sterner and handling them almost too firmly. He really felt he was at the end of his rope when Mai began to get better. As her mood swings lessoned so did the pressure he felt. Finally, he was able to reduce the extra hours he worked each week. It was soon a pleasure to go home after work to the woman of his dreams and what's more, their love making blossomed anew.

Mai Rose brought joy to the house hold. The two thought she was the most beautiful baby ever and she had a head of black hair like her mother. Neither one, Mai nor him, could hold the baby or play with her long enough at a time. Mai knew they were going to have a spoiled one. Rant and Rave, as dogs are prone to do, became protective of her when neither parent was in the room. Tolbane was doubly happy because he had a beautiful daughter and his beautiful Mai was really back to her old, wonderful self and was becoming quite the cooing and attentive mother. He did though have one problem though. It was changing a certain type of soiled diaper; at times he felt he needed a gasmask or something. Another year of good living had him and her feeling a lot younger than they were. Having a very boring day at the mall he gave up and came home early one after noon and they were sitting around talking about the news in the Nashville paper when Mai shocked him silly.

"Hey big guy, I have a very serious question to ask you and I really do need an answer sometime today." He nodded his ascent. "What are we going to name it if it's a boy? Or if it's a girl."

"Are you joking?"

"Not this time!"

"WOW! Damn woman, that's great!" He walked over to her, put his arms around her, picked her up and swung her around and round, and knocked over the stand and lamp beside her chair. They ended up falling onto the couch. She didn't bother to tell him that if it was a boy he would be Travis Jr. Wives just have a penchant for making these decisions for their husbands. Of course the wise acre he was he just had to quip, "I know! We'll call him 'Ho Chi Minh!" Mai, always quick with her retorts, came back at him when he nibbled on her neck, and got her own two cents in. "Maybe Dracula's wife will call him, 'Vlad, The Impaler' because his mother had been impaled by his horny father on, many, many occasions."

Their lives were ideal and they lived the quintessential life style many would die for. Mai had to remind him often though that their son might not want to play football or learn to shoot a gun when he's seven years old. From time to time he would comment that their daughter would never be an exotic dancer. They really didn't want to force the kids into anything they didn't want to do and would support them in any endeavor. The college funds they set up for the kids would be theirs when they graduated from High School. So, If the kids didn't want to go to college that was ok too. The only steadfast condition was for them to graduate high school. Secretly, Tolbane hoped that someday Travis Jr. would play for the Washington Redskins and beating the Cowboys time and time again unmercifully. Then he dreamed he'd spend the off seasons camping and hunting with him. Mai had her own dream. She secretly hoped that Mai Rose would be a tough Criminal Prosecutor and get the death penalty for dumb ass bastards like Ba.

Ba's group was only charged with threatening the Americans with a weapon at first, killing Houng and Lam, and they were sentence to prison for forty years, but could be out in thirty years. They still had other charges of rape and murder and other crimes to face that were committed before joining the Masked Man and would be in trial for them about a year after starting their forty years, so they would probably be locked up for quite a few more years unless sentenced to death.

The light charge of threatening the Americans, conspiring to kill Hung and Lam was to hold Ba temporarily because Kowloon, Hong Kong, Hawaii, and the State of Tennessee had all filed for extradition on Capital Murder charges and other sordid crimes. He was later found guilty of the murders of young girls, but not sentenced until the other countries had their shot at him, and he was under house arrest with a 24/7 guard while waiting on the court's extradition verdict. He would be tried and sentenced after he was finally returned to Vietnam, if ever. He was not liked by the guards for they remembered the victims. If he screwed up they would not hesitate to giving him a knock on the head with a rifle or a club to the knees. To make things worse he only had two light meals a day, at mid-morning and one in the early evening. He was going stir crazy. All of his dreams and aspirations of reuniting Viet Nam under his Cause were down the drain. His loss of the Jade Cross, wherever it was, and his Cause weren't the worst part. The loosing of Mai to that American scum and her willingness to lie in his bed was most devastating. No one deserved her but him. His predominate thoughts were if he ever got free they would both die by his own hand and by the best knife and scalpel he could purchase. He could never forgive or forget how he had been betrayed and attacked by his one true love.

Parnell was promoted to Lt. while he was in Viet Nam and had retired from the NMPD around the same time Tolbane retired. He and Carly were now dating and seemed to have a serious relationship developing between them. Maybe wedding bells would be in their future. He and Tolbane had developed two hobbies. One was fishing, which they did on Percy Priest Lake twice a week. The other was collecting hand guns and rifles and they would go target shooting once or twice a week depending on other activities. Both became die hard 2nd Amendment supporters and NRA life members. Sometimes they would bring Rant and Rave along when fishing in Percy Priest Lake and let them romp around their fishing spots till their hearts were content. At least once a week the two couples would meet at O'Charlies restaurant in Hermitage for a good steak dinner and a couple of brews. On occasions they would go to 'Zanies' Comedy Club in Nashville, depending upon which Stand Up Comic was performing, for a good time, and for Tolbane a bowl of their Zanies' chili.

Five years after the Vietnam experience they got a phone call from the MNPD. The Desk Sgt. that called was a Rookie when the crap started with Ba and the faux No Name. He began with a cordial introduction to himself then he asked Tolbane if he and Mai would be willing to meet with someone who was familiar with some of Ba's crimes in Kowloon, Hong Kong. Tolbane gave him an okay and agreed that he and Mai would be happy to meet whoever it was at the Mount Juliet Waffle House at eleven o'clock AM, lunch on him. He inquired how he and Mai would know the person who would meet them there. The Desk Sgt. laughed a little bit and offered that, "The person you'll meet knows what you and Mai look like. Yep, she knows all about you two!"

Mai contacted the lady who baby sat for them on occasion and she agreed to be at the house by ten thirty. She was five minutes early and the pair left immediately for the Waffle House. The lunch crowd hadn't begun to arrive so they were able to get a booth by the front window and where they could watch the door. They ordered coffee and let the waitress know they were waiting for a guest before ordering. At eleven O'clock on the nose, a very beautiful Asian Lady entered the restaurant. She was well endowed, was wearing a very expensive baby blue business suit with matching pumps, handbag and long black hair. She moved from the door striding confidently as the waitresses called out, "Welcome and Good Morning". She strode straight to their booth, sat down across from them and announced in a straight forward manner, "Hi Travis and Mai. My name is Sue and I'm from Kowloon, Hong Kong. I know your step-brother Ba intimately, I'm sad to say Mai, but only by the different name he gave me."

Surprised by her introduction to them, Mai and Tolbane exchanged a curious look between themselves. Then they turned their eyes back to her and greeted her, explaining that they were expecting to talk with another stuffed shirt person making another excuse for Ba not being extradited yet. They questioned her about her trip to America and how she liked this Country so far. She gave good responsible answers to their inquiries and asked about their city, Mount Juliet as it seemed somewhat rural, but quite peaceful to her.

Finally the woman turned the conversation to why she was meeting with them. "I know your curiosity is getting the better of you two so I will begin." She explained how she had owned, inherited it from her father, and operated the house of ill repute in Kowloon and her work at the Chek Lap Kok international Airport. That was where she had met Ba. He had introduced himself as Bao, a distant relative of Bao Dai the former Puppet Emperor of Vietnam. He was handsome and seemed a nice guy so she offered him information on transportation into Kowloon, a hotel to stay at, a means to get to her house of business, and the best of women, herself included although he didn't know that at the time. She went on to tell them his surprise meeting her at her establishment, of the single night spent with her, then the next night with her and Xing and then the trio event with him on the third night. Mai was awed at how candidly she related her story to them.

"On the fourth night Xing and the bar Girl, Le Wong, a young beautiful young prostitute in training, did not show up for work. Both of them were always very dependable. Never missed any day or night duties. I was concerned because they were both absent at the same time. I called many places I knew of to see if I could locate them, but I had no luck. I even tried Ba's hotel, but he had checked out and I figured he was on his way to Vietnam. As the next few days went by I was really worried. Xing and I had known each other a long time and were very close friends and I was climbing up the wall with worry about her. I didn't know the bar Girl very well, but I was concerned about her too. It was so strange. The last time they were seen was the morning and late afternoon the day after the threesome. Several days later somebody complained to owner of the apartment where what was left of their bodies was found. The complainer said that every time he walked past the doorway on the street he could smell the evil from a dragon coming from it. The owner investigated the complaint, found the remains and notified the police. It was three days after that that they were finally identified."

She continued with a faraway look in her eyes, "The Coroner notified me right away when he had an ID on them. He was a valued client of my establishment, as were many men in law enforcement, and felt he owed me an answer. I was heartbroken at their horrendous murders. What really bothered me the most was how they had met their fate. How mutilated their' bodies were. I couldn't bring myself to understand what kind of evil being could actually do something like that to those two lovely persons." Sue's eyes were beginning to tear up and one ran down her cheek, causing a slight run from her mascara. She took a tissue Mai handed her and wiped it dry.

He began to ask a question, but Mai jumped in ahead of Tolbane and offered her sympathy for this woman's friends, and asked her, "How did they ever link that horrific crime to Ba?"

"The Detectives found that the apartment was void of clues and out of curiosity one of the detectives happened to ask the owner if the murderer had signed a contract for it. He had and they were able to get his finger prints from it. Of course at that time they had no idea who the prints belonged to. The area we call Hong Kong receives newspapers from a lot of major cities around the world. The Detectives on the case were well aware of the crimes being committed in Nashville. They had also received information on two horrific murders by knife in Honolulu, and then the bigger story forwarded from Nashville's MNPD about a Vietnamese's murder and one from guy in Missouri by knife also. He got a picture of Ba from Airport cameras taken the day he arrived. It took a little over a week to receive them. They showed me a picture of him talking to me at the Information counter, although it was not a full face shot. There was no doubt about who it was to me. It was the man I knew as Bao and is your step-brother, Ba."

"That must have been a very terrible time in your life. Ba had fooled Mai, me and our friends Parnell and Carly too!" Tolbane conceded. "Ba and I had been through a lot together in war and peace, and I thought we were the best of friends forever. I remember when he brought Mai to meet with me at the Mall. He betrayed every one that befriended him as well as Mai," he stated. "You and Mai were more deeply hurt and as bad as I was affected I can't even begin to imagine what it did to you two. It's too horrible for words."

Sue continued, "The reason I came to you is because I think I need to have what you in this country call, some closure. I feel a lot of guilt because I brought him into my house. I kind of liked the guy at the time and because of me, Xing and the Girl met a fate unlike any civilized person should ever endure or deserve. As a witness in the case I learned about you two and what you must have felt towards this man. When I was asked to come to Nashville to relate my experience with him to the prosecuting Attorney here I thought I'd like to meet you and tell you what happened in Kowloon. I rather liked him. Looking back at the time I first saw him at the airport he was always a gentleman, seemed to be very kind and the people at the house thought he was very well behaved. I know that Xing and I liked being with him. That ordeal made me wonder if I could ever put trust in any man again. I always believed I could sense the good from the bad in men, now I don't really know. I struggled for two years, after the murders with my conscience and it got the better of me and I hid out and let my manager take over. I sold the business to her within a short amount of time, made a small fortune from it as she had a really rich backer she was having sex with. Now I don't party that way anymore. I donate my services to a couple of different battered women organizations that I organized."

"I'd like to know what you two felt about him and what kind of person you felt he was, and was I right in trusting him right off the mark. This, I think, knowing the Ba you knew once will help me to clear my mind and move on. Maybe still my guilt. I need to know that I wasn't wrong in trusting him initially as I did. Can you help me?"

Feeling Sue's pain Mai's tears began to flow down her cheeks. Mai knew she only was fooled by her step-brother' fake death, but this woman had lost her friends in the cruelest of ways and it troubled her soul very deeply. "I will do my best, so will my tag-a-long here, to help you in any way we can. How long will you stay here in Tennessee before you must return?"

"I'm done with the witness business in Nashville for now, I've given a deposition, and I can stay at the Downtown Sheridan as long as I want. I can leave here any time before the Chinese trail happens for Ba in absentia. I'll stay there, I guess, until I need to return to Kowloon to testify or in Hawaii to show his proclivity, I believe they said. This is what I know from varied authorities, but the stories vary and might not be accurate. In Vietnam Ba will be tried and convicted of the brutal rapes and the murders of the children, the men, and your' kidnapping when everyone else is done with him, and is he's now more or less in in house arrest in Vietnam, but it's like solitary with guards, and he has not been sentenced for any of the matters yet, and won't be until China and the US are finished with him. It seems that Ba will be tried in Kowloon first and after sentencing, most likely the death penalty there, he'll be sent to Honolulu for trial then he'll be sent here to Nashville. The powers to be of China and the US are all seeking the death penalty for him. After his Chinese trial I may think about moving here and starting my life anew after testifying. My testimony here is only to identify and show the vile murderous path he traveled. I still carry a lot of baggage in Kowloon. Many there still blame me for the deaths of those two wonderful women because I had brought him into our lives enabling him to destroy us. Also, this seems like a good area to live in and find something new to dedicate my time to. I am rather wealthy and I understand there are a lot of great charities here"

"Yes there are!" Mai responded. I have a wonderful idea. Why don't you come to diner at our house this evening? We'll have a cook out and we can tell you a lot about what happened here in the local area and in Viet Nam. I can get retired Detective Lt. Parnell who was in on all of this with us from the beginning, and my very good friend Carly, who was brutally beaten and raped by Ba, to come also. They can add so much more to the story. The story of Ba is so convoluted and difficult to fathom. It started with Travis. He, Ba and Parnell were on a patrol in Vietnam in the summer of 1966, found a Jade Cross buried, and then reburied it and that started the evil path Ba took for what he called his Cause. Later on, Ba was with Travis when he saved me from being raped in Sai Gon at age ten, now Ho Chi Min City, plus, we had no idea that he had been doing his vile things to girls earlier in his life. It's quite a sad story from start to finish the way he deceived everyone and the horrors he committed. You deserve to know the whole story and I believe when you do you won't feel so terrible about having trusted him initially. He was also a great con artist, easily gained people's trust, and as close as I believed we were I never knew him at all."

"Mai," Sue responded, "I want to know about everything that happened here, Hawaii, and in Vietnam. The story is that you took him down single handedly. I know what happened in Kowloon, but I couldn't put you out like that. I'm a stranger here that you know nothing about, a little shy anymore, and I hate to intrude on people, especially good people like you two."

Tolbane now took the chance to speak up! "Don't let that worry your very pretty head. We never feel intruded upon; our door is always open. We're always inviting people over for one reason or another. We're party central in Mount Juliet. The more people that come to party means the more the merrier we become. Besides, Mai, and Carly too, really like to make new friends, and maybe they could get themselves a new pen pal from Kowloon. Besides, your sparkling beauty might even spruce up the place a bit." He got elbowed hard in the ribs, nearly taking his breath away, and Sue's face turned a light shade of pink.

"Don't let him and his verbiage worry you any," Mai retorted. "He's been trained to the max with my whips and chains and what he calls my magnificent body. I allow him to look at good looking gals, but with his eyes tightly closed, but not to touch the merchandise or I will demonstrate my castration skills on my pet rock's most cherished part of his anatomy. I have his K-Bar knife and it's very, very sharp, is not that so my unworthy one?"

Tolbane, who had panted from the elbow in the ribs, caught his breath and replied to Sue in a matter of fact manner, began, "Well, Sue, as you can see with your own eyes I'm one hen pecked lowly, unworthy, verbally abused and beaten male servant and a sex slave to a Beautiful Vietnamese Goddess of Sex. I must bow down to her every sexual wish each night and in the mornings submit to her every Sex Goddess needs that her magnificent body desires of me. Seriously though, I hope I didn't offend you. It's kind of an American custom for a guy to offer compliments to lovely ladies who take good care of themselves. You are a lovely lady and you're in great shape, a real Hot Babe with a smoking hot body in my estimation. You deserve to be complimented on your beauty and the way you've taken care of yourself over the years."

"I'm really not offended. Your comment just caught me by surprise. I loved it! I haven't been so complimented for a few years; not since I sold the house and left the business for good. Many of my customers over the years practically swooned over me all the time and I enjoyed it immensely.

All the customers thought I was, as you Americans say, Hot to Trot and they would be willing to pay a fortune for me! However I only plied my trade with a very few men that appeared to be worthy of me as I was not a regular working girl. I am pleased that the compliment comes from one as honorable as you, Travis." The police and the States Attorney's people I've been around in Nashville have many good things to say about you. You're a very respected individual they say. Mai, If I may say so I am happy to see you have him well trained. Did it take you long?"

"Not long at all. I set my sights on him when I was ten years old. He kept me from being raped by a Vietnamese soldier. He kicked the rapist's ass good and proper, and I fell in love with him forever and a day, right then and there. When I walked into his office many years later, I was dressed my sluttiest. With what I was wearing, the stupid look on his face, and his being speechless, he jumped up and almost broke his knee on his desk. I knew right then that I not only had him hooked, but I had hooked really him good for life! He took a big bite on my hook, line, and sinker like the guppy he was then. He's my faithful little puppy dog now. Speak puppy! Speak for Ma Ma!" Mai's tears had dried up and she beamingly looked at her guy and blew him a kiss from the palm of her hand, squeezing his thigh with the other, temped to squeeze a little higher up.

Tolbane responded with, "Arf! Arf! Arf, and Bow Wow! Wow! I bite too don't I dear!" Thinking about it he added, "but, only Mai's thighs. Damn, I'm a poet and don't know it!" That deserved another elbow.

Sue was laughing at him! "Sue, in all deference to you I won't tell him to, 'Bite Me!' Knowing him he just might do it in an embarrassing spot; in this booth, right here and now." Mai quipped and Tolbane grinned. He definitely wasn't against the idea. In fact he savored it.

Sue giggled and knew she had done the right thing for herself by contacting the Tolbane family through the MNPD. It had been too long since she felt so at ease around people and she felt like she was having fun for a change. She was very close to feeling as though she belonged here. "I'm hungry. I haven't eaten yet this morning," she said and picked up the menu, looked over the breakfast fare and couldn't help but ask, "What the hell is scattered, covered, smothered, chunked, and this other friggen stuff?" Mr. and Mrs. Tolbane couldn't help but laugh.

They were both laughing and before Mai could answer her, Tolbane giggled and said to Sue, "Let me officially welcome you to the big, wide wonderful world of the best in American Cuisine, Waffle House style. Nothing like it any place in the world." Then Mai had fun enlightening Sue about Waffle House hash browns and the great waffles her sex slave consumes, along with tons of bacon, sucking it up like a vacuum cleaner whenever he gets a chance. She also told her about Carly, her friend and one of Ba's victims working at the Waffle House in hermitage and now being the Manager there.

That evening it was quite a blast for the five adults, two kids, Carly's son, now 13 years old, was absent as he was staying with his dad for the month, and four dogs Bar-B-Quing on the patio. After the kids were put to bed the adults began their versions of the events leading to Sue being there as a witness, and then as the guest of honor for the evening. All learned a lot more about Ba's actions, both sane and insane. The only answer for Ba's evil personality change was still elusive to them. Mai wasn't sure even a psychiatrist or phycologist could understand him and his motives. She damn sure couldn't. Sue was amazed at the series of events that was endured and how these people had coped with the horrors and how they handled things. Now she understood that the guilt she felt was misplaced. She hadn't been alone in her trust of Ba. She felt much better about herself now. Being able to talk freely about the events was comforting. Maybe she could lose her guilt now. These people were the medicine for her psyche that she needed more than anything a doctor could prescribe.

When all decided to call it a night Sue could not thank them enough for opening up their ome to her, their stories and feelings to her about Ba and for listening to hers. She told them she felt as though she belonged there with them, almost like being at home, a feeling she hadn't felt since losing her parents, and then the mutilation of Xing and the Girl, Le Wong. Shyly and softly she asked if they could be friends of which the other two women thought was a no brainer, and of course, she agreed to be Mai's and Carly's pen pal when she returned to Kowloon.

Before she left Tolbane was curious and asked her what she would be doing during the next few days. She replied she'd not yet made any firm plans, maybe she'd do some shopping and some sightseeing. "Well," He pled, "since you haven't any firm plans for the near future, why don't you let Mai and I take you and the kids to Pigeon Forge, show you around Dollywood, go to Gatlinburg, breakfast at the 'Burning Tree restaurant,' then have a cruise on the General Jackson in Nashville, or maybe even tour Jack Daniel's Whisky plant, get a good lemonade there, no Jack samples because it's a dry county, and maybe even visit few other places in Music City USA during the next week? I know Mai and the kids would love to go and would want your companionship too. I know I would. Plus I think the kids really like you. Parnell and Carly may want to come along to some of the places too." Mai and Carly agreed with Tolbane for a change.

"I like the kids too. They are the sweetest and a lot of fun." She felt a thrill go through whole body that she might be wanted by anyone just for friendship instead of for her body. "I think that would be so wonderful. I have read so much about these places and heard tales from Chinese tourists, returning from here, about them and how much they had enjoyed the places. We have nothing in Hong Kong like them, probably not even in all of China. I would love to go with you and see them for myself. During my life I never had a big sister or big brother to teach me or show me around. Working in a brothel during child hood was not the most educational experience. Can I think of you two as my big Brother and Sister? I would love to call you two that! Can I wear the American short shorts you call Daisy Dukes and a halter when we go?"

Tolbane and Parnell got big grins on their faces and both got a slap on the back of their heads for it from Mai and Carly. Tolbane, as might be expected, had visions of wonderful double back flips on the bed he remembered from her old suite in Kowloon.